GEORGIE AND THE VISCOUNT

They were in sight of the stone bridge when she finally spied the perfect place. A massive weeping willow with branches so thick she could barely see the bench built around one side of the tree. "Oh, look. That is enchanting!"

She dropped her hand from his arm and turned them off the path toward the tree with Turley following closely behind. "It certainly looks old."

Georgie stopped herself from rolling her eyes. Did the man not have any romance in him? "Of course it is, to be so large. I would simply like to stop and sit under it."

"If you wish." He took her arm again and helped her, carefully guiding her over any possible dips in the earth or rocks.

In another mood, she would have wondered how he thought she got around in the country, but now she enjoyed how considerate he was being. He held the branches aside for her to enter the bower made by the tree.

It was as if someone had made a place for a lovers' tryst. She dropped her hand and slowly twirled around taking in the arbor, then Georgie turned back to him and he was staring at her with a strange look in his eyes. "Is something wrong?"

"No." His voice was rough as if it had not been used in a very long time. "There is nothing at all wrong."

She stood completely still as he slowly moved toward her. Her heart began beating so hard she was sure he could hear it. This was really going to happen. He was going to kiss her. . . .

D0043306

Books by Ella Quinn

The Marriage Game
THE SEDUCTION OF LADY PHOEBE
THE SECRET LIFE OF MISS ANNA MARSH
THE TEMPTATION OF LADY SERENA
DESIRING LADY CARO
ENTICING MISS EUGENIE VILLARET
A KISS FOR LADY MARY
LADY BERESFORD'S LOVER
MISS FEATHERTON'S CHRISTMAS PRINCE
THE MARQUIS SHE'S BEEN WAITING FOR

The Worthingtons
THREE WEEKS TO WED
WHEN A MARQUIS CHOOSES A BRIDE
IT STARTED WITH A KISS
THE MARQUIS AND I
YOU NEVER FORGET YOUR FIRST EARL
BELIEVE IN ME

The Lords of London
THE MOST ELIGIBLE LORD IN LONDON
THE MOST ELIGIBLE VISCOUNT IN LONDON

Novellas
MADELEINE'S CHRISTMAS WISH
THE SECOND TIME AROUND
I'LL ALWAYS LOVE YOU

Published by Kensington Publishing Corp.

The MOST ELIGIBLE VISCOUNT In LONDON

ELLA QUINN

ZEBRA BOOKS
KENSINGTON PUBLISHING CORP.
www.kensingtonbooks.com

ZEBRA BOOKS are published by

Kensington Publishing Corp.
119 West 40th Street
New York, NY 10018

All Kensington titles, imprints, and distributed lines are available at special
quantity discounts for bulk purchases for sales promotion, premiums,
fund-raising, educational, or institutional use.

Special book excerpts or customized printings can also be created to fit
specific needs. For details, write or phone the office of the Kensington
Sales Manager: Attn.: Sales Department. Kensington Publishing Corp.,
119 West 40th Street, New York, NY 10018. Phone: 1-800-221-2647.

Zebra and the Z logo Reg. U.S. Pat. & TM Off.

First Printing: April 2021
ISBN-13: 978-1-4201-4969-2
ISBN-10: 1-4201-4969-5

ISBN-13: 978-1-4201-4970-8 (eBook)
ISBN-10: 1-4201-4970-9 (eBook)

10 9 8 7 6 5 4 3 2 1

Printed in the United States of America

Chapter One

Featherton House, Mayfair, London, October 1818

Miss Georgiana Featherton—or more properly Miss Featherton since her elder sister had wed—remained standing as Gavin, Viscount Turley, possessed himself of one of her hands and knelt on one knee. He looked so solemn she repressed the smile that fought to appear. For months, since last Season, he had courted her. And ever since the beginning of the autumn Season, she had been expecting to receive a proposal of marriage from him. Now. Finally. It was happening.

As he gazed up at her with his light blue eyes, her heart fluttered as if butterflies had taken residence. His fingers on the hand he held sent tingles up her arm. As far as Georgie was concerned, Lord Turley with his golden curls and broad shoulders was the handsomest gentleman in all of London and soon they would be married. Then they would belong to each other for the rest of their lives. Just the thought of it made her want to hurry him along. She knew some ladies liked grand proposals, but as long as two people loved each other, what did it matter how one proposed? The purpose was to wed. To create a new family. A new life together.

He swallowed and still did not speak. Why was this taking him so long? All he had to say was that he loved her and wanted her as his wife. As she had stopped the smile, she stopped the frown wanting to form. Perhaps he had memorized a speech and had forgotten it. That could throw anyone off.

Finally, he opened his wonderfully sculpted lips then closed them again.

Just when she thought she would go mad with impatience, he cleared his throat. "Miss Featherton, as you probably are aware, I admire you greatly. We get on exceedingly well. You are the only lady I have met who possesses every quality that a gentleman, a peer like myself, could wish for in a wife." Georgie almost interrupted him to tell him she would love to marry him. But that would be rude. Lord Turley had obviously spent time preparing his proposal, and, despite her impatience, she must allow him to complete it. "I am not the wealthiest man in England, nor am I the poorest. I am fortunate to have several estates all of which are in good repair. I also have other holdings, and I will be able to provide you and any children we have with the elegancies of life." He cleared his throat. Perhaps she should have had tea brought. "The Turley lineage dates back to King William I. We were barons at first, but the viscountcy dates back to King Henry III. Therefore, you have nothing to be embarrassed about there." Why did he feel as if he needed to tell her any of this? His lineage was in *Debrett's* for anyone to read. "As my wife you would have complete control over all the houses and domestic staff at all my estates. When I spoke with your father I assured him you will have a generous allowance." The thrill

Georgie had initially felt was fading rapidly and being replaced by dread. This was not going at all the way she expected it would. "I assure you that I am a responsible landlord, and, from our conversations and letters over the summer, I know that you will be interested in not only the estates and the dependents, but will enjoy an involvement in politics that being my viscountess will allow you." He swallowed. Tea would have been a good idea. "Would you do me the honor of being my viscountess and wife?"

That was it? It sounded more like he was presenting his qualifications for a position than a marriage proposal. Georgie stared at Turley for several long moments. Other than the actual asking for her hand, there was only one thing she had wanted to hear from him, and he had not said it.

She bit the inside of her bottom lip, afraid now of the answer to the question she was about to ask. "Do you love me?"

His eyes widened and he stilled like a deer ready to run for its life. The lips she had so looked forward to kissing moved but emitted no words. She closed her eyes and did the hardest thing she had ever had to do. "Thank you for your kind offer, my lord. However, I am unable to accept the honor of being your wife. Benson will show you out."

Georgie forced herself to stroll calmly out of the front parlor and up the main staircase. Once she reached the second floor, she increased her pace until she was running, straight to her room. Tears pricked her eyes, and she blinked hard to keep them from falling. But as she stepped into the corridor leading to her bedchamber they defied her attempts to halt the blasted things.

Drat, drat, drat!

After months and months of waiting, Turley had finally

proposed and the one thing—the only thing—she had needed to hear from him had not been uttered. She should not even have had to ask if he loved her. His lack . . . That he hadn't mentioned it at all despite the fact he had stated every other reason she would be happy married to him should have given her a hint.

But noo. She'd had to ask if he loved her, and he couldn't even answer. The look on his face seemed to be burned into her mind. He had acted as if it was the last thing he expected to hear. At the end he could not even meet her gaze. She reached her bedroom and collapsed onto the bed. At least he had been honest. Even if he couldn't bring himself to answer he had not lied. A lie would have been worse. That he did not love her was bound to have come out at the worst possible time and probably not until after they had wed when it would be too late for her to do anything about it.

Trying to stem her tears, she gulped huge breaths of air but it didn't help. At first tears just rolled down her cheeks, but then her nose began to run. Turning to her side, she pulled out a handkerchief and blew her nose. Then her chest began to ache. Why did this hurt so much? Georgie had heard about hearts breaking, but she never thought it was physically possible for it to happen. Apparently, she was wrong. Despite all the attention he had paid to her, deep inside of her she must have known he did not love her, otherwise she would not have asked. Therefore, his lack should not affect her this much. Unfortunately, this eminently commonsensical thought did nothing to help.

The combination of tears and a running nose caused her to hiccup, and then she began to sob.

Great huge sobs so hard she could barely breathe.

Perhaps she just should have accepted his offer. Then she

would have years to make him love her, and she wouldn't be so miserable. Yet now that she knew for certain he did not love her, she could not agree to wed him. She tried to draw a deep breath and could not. She felt as if part of her had been ripped asunder.

Georgie didn't know how long she remained in bed before she stirred. The curtains were still open, but her room was darker than when she had entered. If only she could pretend nothing had happened. That Lord Turley had not come to propose marriage. That it was a day like any other.

She rolled onto her side as the door opened.

"My darling Georgie." Grandmamma Featherton hurried to the bed and perched on the side next to Georgie, then took her hands, rubbing them between her fine, strong hands. "What has happened to cause you to cry so? We wanted to give you time, but, my dear, it has been over an hour. We need to know what we can do to help you."

We. Meaning her mother, grandmother, and her grandmother's closest friend, the Duchess of Bridgewater. Naturally, they would all be there to congratulate her.

"Darling, how could a proposal go so very wrong?" Her grandmamma's normally good-humored face took on the look of a warrior's. "He did not insult you, did he? I will see him destroyed if he did."

"No." Georgie struggled to hold back another bout of tears. "He does not love me."

Grandmamma lifted one pale brow. "Are you certain?"

"Yes." A sob burst forth, and Grandmamma gathered Georgie into arms that had always been much stronger than they looked. "I asked, and he could not answer."

Grandmamma soothingly stroked Georgie's back as if she was a child again. "That is very bad. But not, perhaps, irredeemable. Men can be complete fools about love. In fact, they seem to make a habit of it," she seemed to muse that last part. "You must understand that it complicates their lives, and they want things in their lives to be easy. They are simple creatures and love confuses many of them. They much prefer passion to a declaration of the heart."

Georgie had never thought of it in that way. Perhaps she should attempt to view it from a male perspective. "Truly?"

"Absolutely. I would never lie to you about something this important." Her grandmother nodded decisively. "That is not to say that you should settle for anything less than love. In my time, even in your mother's day, our matches were arranged, but many of us found love with our spouses. Although, there *were* those who did not. I believe there was a trick to making successful matches. Your grandfather told his father he was interested in me"—her grandmother blushed adorably—"and a match was arranged. Your father did the same with your mother. It is my belief that matches where there is no attraction are not as likely to succeed. Not all, mind you, but it was more of a risk."

Georgie blew her nose again. "I love him."

"Of course you do." Grandmamma hugged Georgie harder. "That is the reason you are so unhappy." Her grandmother took out her own handkerchief and wiped Georgie's eyes. "Let us see what we can do about this problem. I have a feeling the young man is no more happy about this than are you."

Her maid, Smith, entered the room and Grandmamma rose. "Allow your maid to bathe your face in some cool water, then join me in the morning room. I have assembled a council of war."

Despite herself, Georgie smiled. "Is the duchess here?"

"Naturally." Her grandmother grinned conspiratorially. "We cannot make plans without her."

"And Mama?"

"Ah, well, you know how your mother feels about what she considers to be undue interference." Grandmamma wiggled her fingers as she left the room.

So it was true. Georgie had heard Mama would not engage in the schemes her grandmother and the duchess formed for Meg, Georgie's older sister, or for Kit, her older brother. Georgie did not understand the reason her mother found it distasteful. Both times her grandmother had become involved in matchmaking had resulted in successful marriages. She had never seen her brother and sister happier, and Meg was well on her way to being as canny as Grandmamma in arranging matches. Still, Georgie could think of nothing that the two older ladies could do to make Lord Turley love her. It wasn't as if he could be tricked into it.

She lay back down and her maid covered her eyes with a cool cloth that smelled like cucumbers.

Or *could* he be fooled into loving her? If so, how on earth would that work? And was it the best way forward? Georgie did not like the idea of deceiving him. She frowned to herself. She actually did not have anything to deceive him about.

Several minutes later she entered the morning room. The cheery parlor was everyone's favorite place in the house. The walls were covered with cream-colored silk paper, and large, bright floral patterns gave one the feeling of a garden in full bloom. Some of the flowers on the furniture and hangings were the same as those planted right outside the windows and in pots on the terrace. When the windows were open, the sweet scent of roses infused the room. The parlor even managed to cheer her a little.

Her grandmother poured a cup of tea and set it on the table next to the empty space on the small sofa. "I remember that you liked two sugars and milk."

"Yes, thank you." Georgie picked up the cup and sipped, letting the warmth of the tea sink into her. "It is perfect and just what I needed." Her mother always said that tea inevitably helped one feel better.

Her grandmother and the duchess sipped their tea as well. Finally, Grandmamma put her cup down. "I believe you should leave Town for a short holiday."

The duchess gave the same sort of decisive nod Grandmamma had done earlier.

Georgie almost dropped her cup. That was the last thing she had expected to hear. "But why? Where would I go? It is in the middle of the autumn Season. What excuse would I have?"

The duchess tilted her head to one side, her sharp dark blue eyes fixed on Georgie. "The alternative is flirting with other eligible gentlemen—"

"Or ineligible gentlemen." Her grandmother grinned wickedly.

"But," the duchess continued, "out of sight is not always out of mind."

"Very true." Grandmamma nodded sagely. "There are many times when it is wise to make a gentleman search you out."

But would he? Would Lord Turley search for her in the middle of the Season? Then again, if he did not, she had her answer. He did not love her and never would. "How do you plan on accomplishing it so that I do not appear as if I am running away?"

"Good girl." The duchess's dark eyes sparkled over her cup.

"As it happens"—Grandmamma took another sip of tea—"Your father mentioned that he must leave Town because of a problem with one of their properties to which Kit cannot attend because of his and Mary's new baby. I am certain that he will insist your mother accompany him." In other words, Grandmamma would convince Papa that Mama should go with him. "And the duchess and I cannot chaperone you as we have a prior engagement in the country with friends."

Georgie did not understand how that would help her. "Where shall I go?"

"Why I believe you have received an invitation to visit your friend Lady Littleton." Grandmamma's countenance showed nothing but the total innocence that made people believe she was nothing more than a sweet older lady.

The duchess gave a sly smile. No one would ever describe her as anything but shrewd. "And Lord Littleton is bound to mention that you are visiting his wife to certain of his friends."

"After a little time, of course," Grandmamma added.

Georgie glanced from her grandmother to the duchess. "You knew this was going to occur."

"Well, one cannot always *know* certain things for a fact." Grandmamma lifted one shoulder in a very Gallic fashion. "However, I have known the Turley family for a very long time. I will only say that there was a distinct possibility."

That was as clear as mud. But, the ladies had helped

others find their true loves. Georgie would have to trust them. "Very well. When do I leave?"

"You must first inform Lady Littleton that you are accepting her kind offer," Grandmamma said.

"I will arrange to have it delivered by messenger," the duchess added.

"I shall have to cancel any invitations Mama has accepted for me." Georgie would consult her mother about those.

"Yes, indeed." Grandmamma nodded. "All must appear to be unexpected, but not too very odd."

Georgie turned to the duchess. "When do you think you will have a response from Lady Littleton?"

"If you write the note immediately, I shall send my groom to Surrey. He can probably be back this evening. I have horses posted along the road for changes if necessary."

"In that event"—Grandmamma placed her cup on the table next to the teapot—"you will be able to depart tomorrow after luncheon." She tilted her head and regarded Georgie. "If you can be ready that soon."

As far as Georgie was concerned, she could leave today and let her maid follow her. "Yes. I will be more than ready to leave by then."

"In that case"—the duchess rose—"we will leave you to write your friend and cancel your appointments. Send your letter to me."

"Thank you, I shall." Georgie bussed the duchess's cheek and hugged her grandmother. "Thank you both. I do not know what I would do without you."

"Let us pray it will be a long time before you need to worry about that." Grandmamma took Georgie's hands. "Remember, we are always happy to assist you."

"Indeed we are, my child," the duchess said. "Whatever occurs I firmly believe that all will end as it should."

Georgie hoped the older woman was right. Still they were her best chance for happiness, and she had complete faith in them. "I am certain you are correct, ma'am."

Chapter Two

After Georgie had accompanied her grandmother and the duchess to the front door, she went to look for her mother, whom she found in her parlor.

Mama glanced up from her curved cherry writing desk when Georgie knocked and entered the room. "I am glad you are here, my dear. I was coming to find you after I finished writing to cancel our engagements. We have a slight dilemma. Your father is insisting I accompany him to York-shire. I had hoped your grandmother could take you, but it appears as if you must come with your father and me."

She took a seat on one of the woven-backed chairs in front of her mother's desk. "Adeline Littleton has invited me to visit her whenever I wish. I would rather go there."

After regarding Georgie for a moment, Mama leaned back in her delicate French leather chair, a considering look on her face. "Perhaps you should tell me exactly what happened with Lord Turley. I would not wish you to visit Adeline only to have him show up there when you do not want to see him. As I recall, he and Littleton are par-ticular friends."

Georgie explained to her mother that Lord Turley had not been able to tell her that he loved her. "If he could bring himself to love me, I would marry him."

"I see." A frown marred her mother's smooth forehead, and Georgie thought she saw a bit of silver in Mama's dark tresses. "In that case, you may ask if she is able to have you visit."

Georgie let out the breath she had been holding. "Thank you." If her mother had insisted she travel all the way to Yorkshire, that might have thrown a spoke in her grandmother's plans. Whatever they were. Come to think of it, she actually had no idea what the two ladies were planning. Perhaps she should have asked. "I shall write to her now."

"Do you have any events you have not told me about?"

"Not that I can think of. I should apprise Henrietta and Dorie I will be out of Town."

Mama nodded. "Very well."

Georgie hurried to her parlor and went to her desk. She mended the nub of her pen and pulled out a sheet of pressed paper, then crossed her fingers for luck before she began to write.

My dear Adeline,

I hope this letter finds you well. I would write a longer letter, but I am hoping to be able to tell you all the news I have when I see you.

Georgie stopped and tried to think of the best way to put her request. Her friend liked directness. She would just make the request.

May I visit you for the time my parents are
traveling to one of their northern estates? I can be
with you as soon as tomorrow if you agree.

> *Yr. devoted friend,*
> *Georgie*

She sanded and sealed the letter, then rang for a foot-man. As soon as he arrived, she handed him the missive. "Please take this to my grandmother immediately. She is waiting for it."

The servant bowed. "I'll go straight away, Miss Featherton."

She wrung her hands. Now, how to spend the next several hours? They were bound to be agonizing. She went to her dressing room where she found her maid. "Smith, we are leaving for several weeks"—no matter if she went to Adeline's or north, the trip would take at least that long—"I anticipate we will leave tomorrow afternoon."

"Yes, Miss Georgie. Her ladyship's maid is packing as we speak."

"We might not be traveling with my parents. It is possible we will visit Lady Littleton."

Smith was silent for a second. "Then I'll wait to pack your warmer clothing until we know which way we're going."

"Thank you." Yorkshire was always much colder than Surrey, where there would be no need to take heavy woolens. "I am going to Merton House to see Miss Stern and then to Exeter House."

"I'll have most of the packing done by the time you return. I take it that you will not attend the ball this evening?"

Lord Turley was certain to be there, and because of that

Georgie did not wish to attend. "I'd forgotten all about it. You had better ask my mother's maid. She will know better than I."

"Very well, miss. I'll do that."

Smith handed Georgie her gloves. After she donned them, her maid helped her into her mantel and put her hat on her head, affixing it with a large hatpin.

A knock came on her door, and the footman she had sent with the letter said, "It's done, Miss Featherton."

"Thank you. Do you have any other duties or are you free to accompany me on some errands?"

The servant straightened his shoulders. "Mr. Benson assigned me to assist you today."

Thank Heaven for their butler's perspicacity. "What is your name?"

"It's Henley, miss."

"Well then, Henley, let us be off."

He held the door open, and she went through feeling like a ship under full sail. "We shall visit Merton House first." It was likely she would find Henrietta and Dorie together. "If necessary we shall go to Exeter House afterward."

The black cloud that had hovered over Georgie lifted and hope that she and Turley would eventually be together rose. After all, Grandmamma and the duchess had taken matters in hand.

She rejected me!

It had never occurred to him that was even a possibility.

Gavin stared at the open door of the small drawing room. He should have told Georgie what she wanted to hear. In fact a lie had risen to his lips, but there it froze. It had taken several seconds before he was able to open his mouth. Even then, he could not utter a word. The look in her lapis eyes as she had waited for him to answer made him feel like the veriest cad. She had been happy to have him propose. He saw it in her face when she'd entered the room. Then he'd gone and spoilt everything.

Blast it all.

Why the devil had he knelt? If he'd been standing, he could have pulled her into his arms and distracted her from her concerns.

A hole had opened in his stomach. And before he had been able to form an argument, Georgie had turned on her heel and strode gracefully out of the parlor. If he forgot about her eyes, the only sign she was under distress was the invisible iron rod that appeared to be holding her spine erect.

Bloody hellhounds!

He'd practiced his proposal until he'd got all the words right. He'd even gone down on one knee—that had been anything but helpful. Reminded of his position, he rose. Not an hour before he'd received permission from her father to address her. He had carefully set forth to her all the advantages of being Viscountess Turley and reminded her how much they had in common and that they enjoyed each other's company.

Gavin raked his fingers through his perfectly brushed hair. A motion he'd seen other men make, but for which he had never understood the reason. Until now. His valet was going to be "very disappointed." Although the man would never say the words.

Why the devil did love matter so much? His sister had insisted on it before she'd married. Well actually—now that Gavin thought of it—she hadn't demanded to hear the words and had, subsequently, made poor Harrington's life hell until he'd uttered them. Even Dorie Exeter, a vastly sensible lady, had wanted a love match. Last Season, Gavin had pitied Exeter having to go through working out how he felt. A trickle of dread crept up Gavin's neck. No man should have to expose his inner self so. He straightened his jacket and sleeves.

Still, he should have known. The fact that Viscount Featherton had refused Gavin's request to arrange a match with his daughter ought to have given him a clue that something more than mere social compatibility was required. After all, Georgie was a viscount's daughter. With their lineage her family could look higher than another viscount. But he had been so pleased with his lordship's acceptance of his suit he had considered the war won.

That had been another miscalculation.

Yet, love was an emotion in which Gavin could not afford to indulge. His parents had been a love match and look how that had turned out. After his mother's death his father had recused himself from the world. Papa had left Gavin to run around after him trying to stop the depredations to the viscounty his father's lack of care threatened to cause. Then he'd had to listen as his father criticized everything he did. His sister—not even out of the schoolroom—had been expected to run the household and care for their dependents. Eventually, his father's sense of loss had led to an early death.

For the sake of all those who depended on him Gavin could not allow that to happen to him. Love was too dangerous an emotion. Even when it went well—there was no doubting his parents had loved each other—it caused destruction. He could not permit himself to love a woman so deeply that he lost himself when she died. He could not, and would not allow Rivercrest, his main estate, or indeed any of the properties to go to wrack and ruin because of love. Or rob his children of an opportunity to grow into their roles rather than being thrust into them with little knowledge or experience.

Gavin made his way out of the parlor and into the hall where he collected his hat and cane from the Featherton butler. He was glad the older man's countenance did not display even a hint that the servant knew what had occurred. Although, obviously, the man was well aware that all had not gone well.

He strode through the door as if nothing was amiss, walked down the shallow stairs, and stopped at the pavement. Now what was he to do? This year's crop of young ladies just came out, and some who had been out for a while had been picked over. It had been a busy Season at St. George's on Hanover Square. Not to mention that no lady other than Georgie had captured his attention either last spring or this autumn.

Now that he considered it, from the first moment he'd seen her he had been so intent on courting Georgie, he had not even truly considered another lady. He blew out a frustrated breath. And now she wouldn't have him because of this ridiculous idea of love matches. Damn that lady author and all the other novel writers who put ideas into the heads of perfectly sensible ladies. Or rather ladies who would be perfectly sensible if only they hadn't decided to make fiction a reality.

Gavin heaved a sigh. It didn't help that his best friends had fallen in love. He wondered what would happen when their marriages fell apart. He supposed he'd be expected to help them pick up the pieces. He turned right toward

Curzon Street and headed to Brooks's. His closest friend, Littleton, wouldn't be there. Now that he had married Adeline, who didn't like Town any more than he did, he'd probably never come to London again unless he had to. But Exeter might be found. A brandy was definitely in order, but Gavin didn't like to drink alone.

He climbed the steps to Brooks's and the door opened.

"Good day, my lord." One of the footmen bowed.

"Good day, Johns. Have you seen Lord Exeter?"

"Aye, my lord. He's in the reading room. Just got back from Paris from what I heard and wanted to find out what has been going on here during his absence." The servant took Gavin's hat and cane. "Told he me had an excellent time."

Well he would, wouldn't he? He'd been on his honeymoon. "Thank you."

"Pleasure, my lord."

Gavin walked through the hall and down to the reading room where he found Exeter with a stack of newspapers next to him. "Finally back, I see."

"Turley!" The man stood, knocking over some of the newssheets. "Well met." Exeter looked happier than Gavin had ever seen him. His friend grabbed his hand and shook it.

Eying the newssheets, Gavin said, "I see you are making sure you didn't miss anything that happened when you were gone."

"Dorie"—his friend's face took on a happily distracted look at the mention of his wife—"and I ventured away from Paris where there was no news from England to be found. When it was time to depart, rather than returning to Paris we headed straight to Calais and back home."

Exeter grinned. "She had ordered all the newspapers to be delivered to the house and is no doubt going through them as we speak. But I thought I might discover additional information here." He stared at Gavin for a moment, and his brows drew down. "Is everything all right?"

"I need a brandy." Or the whole bottle.

"That bad." Exeter put down the paper he'd been holding. "Let's go to the dining room. It must be almost time for luncheon." They went to the corner table their little group had claimed as their own last Season. "What has occurred? Your sister and her family are still well? Nothing has ensued since we saw them last month, has it?"

"There is no need for concern on that front. Elizabeth, Harrington, and their daughter thrive. I received a letter from her that she is expecting their next addition in the spring." Gavin debated telling his friend what was troubling him and decided he needed advice as well as someone with whom to share a drink. He took a breath. "I offered for Miss Featherton, and she refused me."

"Really?" Exeter's eyes widened as if in shock, and his jaw dropped for a second before he recovered himself. "I mean that is unexpected."

Why was he so astonished? Or perhaps the question should be what had Gavin missed? "I feel as if you know something I do not."

The man glanced to the side and seemed to focus on something on the far wall. "Yes, er, well. You see. Dorie was certain." Exeter frowned as if unsure how to continue. "And I too was under the impression Miss Featherton was expecting an offer from you and would be, er, happy to receive it."

Blast it all. Gavin wanted to kick himself. If only he could have brought himself to lie. Yet that was not an ideal basis upon which to begin a marriage. "That might very well have been the case, but she requires something I am unable to offer."

One of his friend's dark brows rose in a question.

Damn this was too embarrassing, but he still wanted to marry her, and he needed help. "She asked if I loved her, and I was unable to answer."

Exeter took a sip of wine the waiter had brought instead of the brandy Gavin sought. He'd forgotten that his friend was averse to brandy during the day. "Not wise. Not wise of you at all."

"I worked that out on my own." Gavin couldn't keep the sarcasm out of his voice. "You know I will not follow in my father's footsteps. Love matches are all well and good for those who can manage them—although I'm not at all sure they last—but after seeing what Father went through when my mother died . . . Well, I refuse to put any family I have or my dependents through that. It's not fair to them."

"I understand your concern," Exeter said before taking another sip of wine. "Obviously, my parents were not in love—at least not for many years—and the expectation of it from my mother destroyed their marriage. But Dorie's parents were and are still in love. As you are aware, I had my doubts about a love match. We have only been married a few months, but I predict a long future for us." He shrugged. "Then again, she has seen how to go about it. If you still want her, perhaps Miss Featherton can help you. I have heard that not only her parents but her elder brother and sister married for love."

Gavin couldn't believe what he was hearing. "How do you even know about her brother and sister?"

"I heard them talking about it. Dorie and Miss Featherton." His friend flushed. "Not that I go about eavesdropping, you understand, but Dorie said my name as I passed the morning room door—"

"Don't." Gavin held up a hand. "I do not need an explanation."

"They mentioned you as well."

Hell!

Still, he couldn't stop himself from asking. "What did they say?"

"That she was expecting an offer from you, and she was looking forward to being married." Exeter frowned again. "She must have thought you loved her. I wonder what made her doubt you and ask."

That was a very good question. "I have no idea." His lack of an answer to that inquiry had troubled him during the walk to Brooks's. Why *had* she posed the query? "I practiced the speech before I went to speak with her father. To her I detailed all the reasons I believed we could make a good life together, and set the question of marriage before her. That was when she asked if I loved her."

"Hmm," Exeter uttered thoughtfully, and took another sip of wine. "That might have been the reason."

Gavin downed his glass of wine and poured another. "*What* might have been the reason?"

"Oh, that you were not romantic." His friend's brows drew together, then he nodded to himself. "Yes. I believe that's it. If you would have simply taken her hands, proclaimed that you needed her in your life as your wife and the mother of your children, then kissed her, she would not have thought to have asked you."

Cobwebs seemed to have taken up residence in Gavin's head, and he shook it trying to make sense of Exeter's words. It didn't help. "I do not understand."

Exeter leaned back in his chair, steepled his fingers in front of him, and tapped them together. "You approached her in the same way I imagine you approached her father. Using logic and good sense. But, when it comes to marriage, ladies like my wife and Miss Featherton have previously ascertained those things are part of a marriage. And they have already decided that the gentleman they want can meet those requirements. Your job was to convince her that you are passionate about her." His brows lowered as he pierced Gavin with a look. "You are passionate about her, are you not?"

Considering that he'd been dreaming of having Georgie in his bed for months . . . "Yes. Extremely passionate."

Exeter nodded. "As I thought." He sat up and took another small drink of wine, then slowly shook his head. "I'm afraid now that you've made a mull of it, I cannot think of any advice for you except to tell her you love her."

Gavin tossed off his wine and poured another. He really had created a pickle. If he had followed his instincts instead of his head he'd be betrothed, and the dreaded issue of love would not have arisen. "Your analysis is not at all helpful."

"I suppose it isn't," his friend acknowledged amiably. "I shall give it some more thought, shall I? There might be another way for you to come about."

"That would be helpful." Although what Exeter could do Gavin had no idea. Still, he had been able to help Exeter and Littleton with their problems obtaining wives. Well, they had helped each other. Ergo, maybe Exeter could assist Gavin. "Thank you." A thought occurred to him that his friend might ask his wife for help. "I would appreciate it if you could keep this conversation between the two of us." He took a breath. "In other words, please do not ask your lady for help. It might get back to Miss Featherton."

Exeter's expressions had gone from confused, to insulted, to understanding. "Ah, I see. I am certain that if I ask my wife for her discretion, she will give it. However, it is your difficulty, and you have every right to request my prudence. It is, after all, your story to tell, not mine."

It was a story Gavin did not wish to have anyone else know about. Truth be told, he felt like a fool. What man did not know that showing a lady how much he wanted her was better than attempting to convince her of the rightness of his cause? "Thank you."

"If you wish to discuss your strategy before approaching her again, I am happy to listen." Exeter flushed. "I might be of some use."

Gavin almost chuckled. When his friend first suggested marriage—because it was just that—to the lady who was now his wife, she had soundly rejected him. "Well, you worked out the way forward, which is more than I can say."

"That is only because I fell in love with my wife." Exeter grimaced. "I wish it hadn't taken me so long."

That was something Gavin could not do. "Thank you. If I need to bandy about ideas, I will come to you." He emptied the rest of his glass. "As soon as I have any new thoughts, you will be the first to know."

Gavin saluted his friend and left the club. Now that he'd made a complete mess of his proposal, how was he to go about convincing her to marry him? If only someone could give him the answer he'd be a happy man.

Chapter Three

Luck had clearly decided to smile upon her. When Georgie arrived at Merton House both of her friends were there. Henley was sent to the kitchen for refreshments while Georgie joined her friends in Henrietta's parlor. It was a large room facing the square and furnished more for comfort than for style.

Henrietta glanced expectedly at Georgie. "I was told that Lord Turley was at your house earlier."

How Henrietta was able to discover information so quickly never ceased to amaze Georgie. "He was." Even as the tears tried to gather in her eyes, she was determined not to let them fall. Unfortunately, she could not keep the hitch from her voice. "He proposed, but when I asked him if he loved me, he could not answer, so I refused him."

"Idiot," Henrietta growled.

Georgie could not believe one of her best friends had just called her an idiot.

"Not you, him," Henrietta said hurriedly, putting her arm around Georgie and leading her to the sofa.

"I am not at all surprised he made a mess of it," Dorie said as she poured Georgie a cup of tea and handed it to her. "Nor am I shocked that he doesn't know his own heart. But I've seen the way he looks at you."

"I have as well." Henrietta joined them. "We shall simply have to find a way to bring him around."

"I hope to go to Adeline." Georgie's friends looked shocked. "My parents have to see to some problems on one of their estates, and I would rather visit her than go to Yorkshire."

Henrietta's eyes flew wide. "In the middle of the Season?"

"I could have chaperoned you." Dorie sounded a bit disgruntled.

Georgie smiled at her friends. "I know, but I need some time to think." And find out what her grandmother and the duchess had planned. She debated telling her friends about her conversation with her grandmother. They might be able to help as well. "Also, my grandmother and her friend are looking at ways to . . . help."

"We"—Dorie glanced at Henrietta—"shall do what we can to assist you as well."

"Indeed we will." Henrietta narrowed her eyes. "When he comes looking for you we will torture him by not telling him where you are."

"If he even notices I am gone." Georgie sighed. "He might decide he would rather have an arranged match with a lady who has no interest in loving him."

"I do not believe that for a second," Dorie said. "He has focused on no one but you since last Season." She tapped her chin with a finger. "I will wager that he'll speak with Exeter. When he does, I shall be able to find out what Lord Turley is thinking."

"Yes," Henrietta agreed. "I would be surprised if he gave up so easily. He is not that type of gentleman."

Georgie hoped her friends were right. "I do not want

him to know where I am until I am ready to see him again."
Her friends nodded their agreement. "First I must decide
what I'll do if he does come to Littlewood."

"When are you departing?" Dorie asked.

"If Adeline agrees, I shall leave tomorrow in the early
afternoon."

"That is an excellent idea." Henrietta took a sip of her
now-cold tea, then leaned over and tugged the bellpull. "It
will take him a day or two to rally for the next attack."

Georgie gave her head a shake. "This is not a battle."

"No, my dear friend, it is a war." Henrietta raised her
chin. "One which you, with a bit of help from your friends
and family, will win."

Georgie had never thought of waging a war against
Lord Turley, but the analogy was apt. There were times
when one had to fight for what one wanted in life. And she
did want his love and a chance to be his wife.

On the third day after he'd proposed, Gavin stared at the
empty red door to Featherton House. The knocker was
gone. That meant the family was gone.

That means Georgie is gone!

Where the devil had she and her family got to in the
middle of a Season?

And when the devil had that happened, and why?

A footman came from the side of the house to the pavement, glanced at him, and said, "They left Town."

Closing his eyes, he suppressed the curse that sprang to
his lips. "Do you happen to know if they have returned to
Lord Featherton's estate?"

"Well"—the footman rubbed his chin and looked as if
he'd like to chat—"Lord and Lady Featherton went to one

of their properties in the north, but we all think they wanted to see their grandchild. Got a letter from Master Kit just before they left, they did. The dowager was supposed to be looking after Miss Georgie, but then she and the duchess had somethin' they had to do, and they sent a message that they were leaving this morning."

Gavin's tempter was hanging by a thread. Where the hell was she? He bit his inner cheek and spoke as calmly as he could, "And Miss Featherton?"

The man grinned. "She's off visiting friends in the country." He frowned for a moment. "I think that's what I heard."

Gavin's hands curled into fists. He needed to hit something or someone. Why couldn't people just give him all the information he wanted at once? "Do you happen to know where she went?"

"Na." The footman shook his head. "Ain't no one said."

Gavin closed his eyes and breathed. Damn it all. She was gone. How could he have let this happen? Focusing on the servant once more, he asked, "Do you know how long they plan to be away?"

"Couldn't say, my lord." A voice sounded from the back of the house. "I have to go. Mr. Benson don't believe in being idle."

Gavin considered asking the butler where everyone had gone, but the man probably wouldn't tell him. Butlers were not known for divulging information. "Thank you."

The footman raced to the back of the house, leaving him to try to find out how to find Georgie.

For a while he walked aimlessly, not caring which direction he was going. When he finally glanced up, he was in front of Exeter House. Lady Exeter must know where Georgie had gone. If not, then surely Miss Stern, Georgie's other friend who was in Town and lived on the same square, would know. But would they tell him? Gavin shrugged. There was only one way to find out. He knocked on the door.

"My lord." The butler bowed. "His lordship is not in at the moment. Would you like to leave your card?"

"Actually, I have a question to ask her ladyship if she is receiving."

"I am certain she would be if she were here. Would you like to leave your card for her?"

He drew out his card case, removed one of his gold-embossed cards, and handed it to the butler. "Please give it to whoever returns first."

"I shall, my lord." The man bowed before closing the door.

Well, so much for that. Turning, Gavin stared down the square and across at the portion of Merton House visible through the trees. As long as he was here he might as well ask if Miss Stern knew where Georgie was.

Several minutes later, he was escorted to the Merton House garden and announced. Miss Stern, sitting on a stool facing a semicircle of children, closed a book and rose. "You may run around and play until you are called to eat." She stood where she was until the last child left before facing him. "My lord, to what do I owe this visit?"

From the corner of his eye, he saw a maid slip out of the house onto the terrace and take up a position next to the French windows. "I have come to ask if you know where Miss Featherton has gone."

One of Miss Stern's black brows rose, reminding him sharply that she would not be on his side. "Why do you care?"

Hell and damnation!

He didn't even know the answer to that question. "I wish to speak with her." The second brow rose, joining the first. Damn. "I feel as if we left things"—left things what?—"Er. Unfinished."

Closing her eyes for a moment, she shook her head, then addressed him as if he was an imbecile. "It is my understanding that you were perfectly clear."

Gavin gritted his teeth as his normally steady temper began to fray for the second time today. "Will you please simply tell me what I wish to know?"

That was obviously not the right tack to take. Miss Stern's chin rose and her eyes narrowed. "I am not sure that I would. Fortunately, I do not know. She is going to write to me once she arrives."

Gavin didn't believe that for a moment. The ladies were as thick as two thieves. This was how men went mad. "Can or will you tell me when she left?"

"It might have been yesterday or it could have been the day before that." Miss Stern glanced at the maid. "Can you get the stool for me, please?"

"Yes, miss." The servant, no older than a schoolgirl, hurried to where Miss Stern stood and picked up the stool.

"Thank you." She curtsied to him. "Good luck on your hunt, my lord." The tone of her words told him that she most certainly did not wish him luck, and that he'd need a lot of that particular commodity. "The butler will show you out." A slight smile tilted her lips. "But you already knew that."

Gavin bit down on the inside of his lip, willing himself not to respond with more than a bow. At least he knew now that Lady Exeter was unlikely to help him. He wondered if Exeter would.

"Ah, Turley." The Marquis of Merton strolled out to the terrace. "My sister-in-law said she had left you out here."

Literally left him. "I came to ask her if she knew where Miss Featherton had gone, but she was unable to tell me."

"Indeed." The man sounded unconvinced of the truthfulness of his sister-in-law's assertion. "If so, that will not be the case for long. I was sent to tell her a letter from Miss Featherton had arrived." Merton motioned for Gavin to follow him into the house. "Would you like to wait until she has had an opportunity to read it?"

He was tempted to ask Merton if he could compel his sister-in-law to reveal Georgie's location, but thought better of it. Gavin knew enough of the lady to know she could not be made to do anything she did not wish to do, and Lady Merton would support her. "It won't do any good."

Merton gave Gavin a sympathetic look. "I take it there is some difficulty between you and Miss Featherton and the ladies have closed ranks as it were."

"That sums it up neatly." Georgie couldn't be that far if a letter had already arrived. Unless it was sent by a messenger. In that event, she would only be less than a day's travel from Town. Littlewood was only a few hours away. But if she was there, why wouldn't Littleton have written him? "Is it possible to discover if the letter was franked and by whom?"

"I believe I am able to do that." Merton stepped to a bellpull and tugged.

As if waiting to be called, a footman entered the parlor and bowed. "My lord?"

"Ask Parkin to attend me in my study."

"Yes, my lord." The servant hurried out.

"It is better for us to leave this room," Merton said. "My

wife might decide to join us, and as much as I enjoy her company, I do not believe she will be particularly helpful concerning this matter."

Anything but, if Miss Stern's behavior was an indication. "Thank you."

"Indeed you should. It is only my duty to my fellow gentleman that compels me to assist you. If my wife discovered what she would deem as my perfidious involvement, I'd be in her black book." Merton grimaced. "Not a very comfortable place to be."

Gavin fought the grin attempting to form. "I don't doubt that at all."

They reached the study and had just settled down with glasses of claret when the butler arrived.

"My lord, you wished to speak with me?"

"I did." Merton set his glass down. "A letter arrived for Miss Henrietta today. Can you tell me if it was franked?"

"Yes, my lord. Lord Littleton franked it. I thought it might be from Lady Littleton and had it sent to her ladyship immediately. Is something amiss?"

"Not at all. I was merely curious. Thank you." He waited until the door closed before saying, "You have your answer. What do you intend to do with the information?"

Gavin knew what he wanted to do. "Go to Littlewood?"

Merton picked up his glass of wine and drank. "Once there, what will you do?"

Convince her to marry me.

"As I thought."

Gavin panicked for a second, thinking he'd spoken the words out loud, then Merton continued, "As I thought. You don't know. It does not take a soothsayer to tell you that whatever caused Miss Featherton to leave Town must be repaired before she will accept you."

But the problem was that he couldn't fix it. Not and remain sane. "Thank you. I shall take your advice."

"I would not wait too long if I were you," Merton added as Gavin stood. "She might be upset now, but once she calms down you will have a better chance to convince her of your suit."

If only his friend knew the truth. He bowed. "Thank you, again."

"I'll see you out." Merton rose. "And, Turley, I do wish you good luck."

Not long later, Gavin was once again on the pavement, and he began to walk. He was starting to feel rootless. He'd been so sure Georgie would accept him. He had even imagined her in his house, managing everything and everyone. Children would follow and his empty abode would be filled with the sound of the laughter that had been missing since his mother's death. But what was the chance that she would marry him if he refused to love her?

Not very good.

Was she in love with him? The thought stopped him, causing a man behind him to mutter a curse and brush past him. She must love him if she wanted him to love her. Could a marriage work if only one of the parties was in love? Gavin started forward again. He wanted her friendship and her affection. He even wanted the inevitable arguments so they would have an excuse to make up. Damn. What he wanted was her in his bed as well as his life. Were not lust and deep friendship enough to mimic love without the dangerous elements of the emotion? Could he convince her that they were? Or perhaps the question was how would he convince her friendship and passion were enough?

Despite Merton's advice, Gavin could not repair the

damage he'd done without seeing her. What he required was a new way of approaching her. A way to make her believe she would have everything she wanted, just not in the way she thought she wanted it.

Yet, first he must determine if she would give him a second chance, and the only way to do that was to write to Littleton and ask him for the information. If Littleton would assist him. He had his wife to deal with as well. Gavin turned up the short path to his house. If Georgie was at Littlewood then why had Gaven not heard from his friend by now?

All this was making Gavin's head ache.

Upon entering his house, he strode straight to his study and wrote to Littleton, asking if Georgie was visiting. Gavin affixed his seal and sent it off by messenger. If he received a return letter stating she was at Littlewood, he'd go down and . . . and find a way to get her to say yes to him.

Why couldn't procuring a wife be simple?

Chapter Four

Georgie arrived at Littlewood and was immediately embraced by Adeline Littleton, who obviously already knew about Turley's proposal.

"Come with me to the morning room." She turned her head. "Creswell, please bring tea." She linked her arm with Georgie's. "I am so very glad you decided to come to me."

"I am too." When she had visited for Adeline's wedding, Georgie did not remember being in the morning room. As at Featherton House, the room seemed to invite the garden indoors. Although here the walls reminded her of green apples. The trim on the windows and doors was painted in soft yellow, and the curtains added even more color in the form of a flowered pattern. The furniture, however, had been chosen more for comfort than for style. That, though, was not a surprise, considering how large Littleton was. Two small sofas faced each other across a low walnut table. Adeline sat on one of them and Georgie took the other.

The butler carried in a large tea tray complete with biscuits, cake, and small sandwiches.

Adeline poured. "Littleton expects to hear from Lord Turley as soon as he discovers you left Town."

Georgie gratefully took the cup and sipped enjoying the warm comfort the tea offered. "Who wrote to you, Henrietta or Dorie?"

"Both of them." Adeline grinned. "The letters came by the same messenger."

"That would have been Henrietta's idea. I suppose they could not agree on what to say."

"The letters are different," Adeline agreed. "Shall I let you read them?"

Georgie shook her head. "Allow me to guess. Henrietta was angry that Turley had been such an idiot and thought he deserved to suffer for his disastrous proposal, and Dorie agreed that he handled the whole matter badly, but she stated that he might not understand what he is feeling."

"That sums it up nicely." Adeline's hand settled on her slightly rounded stomach, and Georgie felt a pang that she would not soon be in the same condition. "I am not sure that Henrietta has ever doubted herself, and she does not understand why anyone else would doubt themselves."

"Whereas Dorie and Exeter went through a fairly long process of working out how they each felt," Georgie added.

Adeline's curious eyes held Georgie's gaze. "What do you intend to do about it?"

"I do not know." She shrugged. "I do not know if it is I who should do something."

Silence surrounded them as they sipped their tea, then Adeline said, "If he wants you as badly as I think he does, you will see him shortly."

"That is the only point upon which everyone seems to agree." Georgie just had no idea what would happen after that. "But if he does not want love in a marriage, why would he want me? He is not unintelligent. Surely he has realized that I love him. Otherwise, why would I have asked him if he loved me?"

"You have a good point." Adeline selected a butter biscuit and stared at it. "Perhaps we all believe that he will come to love you."

"I do wish he would." The real question was what if he did not.

What would she do then? Could one fall in love more than once, or would she be destined to live life as a spinster? That thought did not appeal to her at all.

Two days later she was again sitting in the morning room at Littlewood with Adeline and Adeline's mother-in-law, the dowager Lady Littleton. At Adeline's feet was a sleeping eight-week-old Great Dane puppy, Jeremy, and at her side was Maximus, a three-year-old Dane. Georgie and the other two ladies were embroidering new chair cushions for the breakfast room, which even Georgie had to agree needed to be replaced.

By the end of the previous day, Lord Turley had still not arrived, nor had Frits Littleton received a missive from him. That Lord Turley had done neither thing broke her heart all over again. She'd had to face the fact that he obviously did not care about her enough to find her.

She had fought tears and for a while had lost the battle. Today she tried not to think about him at all. After all, there was no point in pining over a gentleman who did not care about one. She was glad the activity helped quiet her mind. There was something peaceful about following a pattern and placing well-practiced stitches. Still, her thoughts kept going back to Turley, and they should not. If he had cared about her even a little he would have come to see her the next day at her family's house and he had not. Clearly she had been nothing more than a lady he thought would accept him because of his title and wealth.

Stop it. You are not to think about him again.

"I must say, Adeline." The dowager's words broke the silence. "I think this new design and the colors are just the thing to refresh the room."

Adeline's cheeks grew pink under the praise. "I am glad you like it."

"Oh, my dear." The dowager smiled. "It is not for me to like it. I had my turn to make the house my own, now it is your time."

A knock sounded on the door, and the butler entered holding a silver salver. "My lady, a message came for Miss Featherton."

Georgie held out her hand. "I wonder who it's from."

"It is franked by Lord Exeter, miss."

"Thank you." She popped the seal, shook out Dorie's letter, and perused it. Georgie's heart beat so hard she thought it would fly out of her chest. Her hand shook as she handed it to Adeline. He must care. "Turley is searching for me."

"I told you he would." Adeline took the letter. "He probably went by your house shortly after you left."

The dowager cleared her throat. "I have no wish to intrude, but I have known Gavin Turley all his life. His mother and I were the best of friends. Perhaps I might be able to be of assistance with whatever it is that has happened."

Georgie supposed anything was worth a try. Still, she was reluctant to bare her heart to a lady, however kind, she did not know well. She glanced at her friend, who nodded.

"I am not sure anyone can help. He proposed, and when I asked him if he loved me he was silent."

The dowager's brows drew together as if she was thinking about what Georgie had said.

Adeline handed the letter back to Georgie. "Well, I think he *is* in love with her, but cannot admit it or does not know what love is. Look how long it took Exeter and Dorie to realize that they were in love with each other."

"You make an excellent point, my dear." The dowager tied off her thread. "Another one completed." She placed the cover on top of the others they had finished. "Now you must excuse me. I have the vicar's mother joining me for tea."

"I did not know she was visiting," Adeline said. "We must have them to dinner."

"Yes, indeed." The dowager gave Adeline a peck on her cheek. "Be sure to invite the eldest daughter as well. She is making her come out in the spring and needs to be out locally if she is to gain some experience."

"I'll do that."

The older lady turned and smiled. "Georgie, I shall give the matter some thought. I'm sure there is a solution."

"Thank you, my lady." Although, what the dowager could do Georgie had no idea. Lord Turley might be looking for her, but despite what her friend thought and what she wished, that did not mean he had suddenly fallen in love with her. And that put them in the exact same place as before.

"It is my pleasure." The dowager patted Georgie's cheek. "All things work out as they should in the end."

That is what her grandmother always said. She prayed it was true. The lady left via the open terrace doors and skirted around the side of the house.

"Where is the dower house?" Georgie asked.

"It is in the opposite direction about a half a mile away." Adeline grinned. "My grandmother-in-law resides there. Mama-in-law lives in a house Frits's father bought for her in the event he predeceased his mother."

"That showed excellent forethought." As much as they liked each other, Georgie could not imagine her mother and grandmother living in the same house. Then again, her grandmother had solved the problem by purchasing a house with the duchess.

"I have come to understand how thoughtful Littleton men are." A soft smile grew on Adeline's face.

One by one Georgie's friends were finding love and marriage. She had even received a letter from Augusta announcing her marriage to Lord Phineas. If only Georgie hadn't fallen in love with a gentleman who did not return her feelings. She sighed. Then again, her sister Meg had been betrothed twice before finding true love with the Marquis of Hawksworth, and her brother Kit had been on the Town for so long that their father had finally made him promise to find a lady and wed before he'd fallen in love with Lady Mary Tolliver. Perhaps that was what Georgie would have to go through as well.

"She is right." Adeline leaned over and placed her hand over Georgie's. "It will all work out."

"I know." Now if only she could make herself believe it.

There was a knock at the door and the Littleton butler bowed. "My lady, Lady Turner and Mrs. Fitzwalter have come to see you. I put them in the blue parlor and told them I would ascertain if you were receiving."

"Yes, I shall see them shortly," Adeline said. "Have you already arranged tea and biscuits?"

"Yes, my lady."

As the butler left, Adeline glanced at Georgie. "You do remember that Miss Tice married Mr. Fitzwalter and Miss Martindale wed Lord Turner, do you not?"

"I do, but why are they not in Town for the Season?" Just about everyone was, and Lord Turner was active in the Lords.

Adeline's lips formed a thin line of disapproval. "As to that, I am not the only lady expecting a blessed event. Once old Lord Fitzwalter discovered her condition, he refused to fund a Season for her and her husband. He insists the air is better for her here."

"Well, he is absolutely correct about that. But still, she cannot be very far along at all. Attending the Season would not have harmed her." It seemed as if the old man was intent on causing problems, as he had with the weddings. Thankfully, Mr. Fitzwalter had thought of a way around his father's demands.

"The real truth is that he is an old skinflint and thinks it's a waste of money."

"And, of course, Miss Martindale—I should say Lady Turner—would not go without her dearest friend."

"Naturally." Adeline tucked her needle in the cover. "Poor Turner has been bolting to Town every time there is a meeting he must attend."

"Fortunately, it is not far." Georgie set her cover down and rose. "Do they visit often?"

"Not too terribly often." Adeline set aside her cover as well and stood. "When they have business in Littleton. They have a very nice market town near them, but we have an excellent milliner and finer fabrics. I must say that marriage has improved them both."

That was saying a great deal. Last Season Miss Tice

had attempted to compromise Frits into marrying her. Fortunately, Georgie and Adeline had overheard the scheme.

They entered the parlor and greeted the ladies. What Adeline had said was immediately apparent. Neither lady giggled or simpered as they had when they'd been single. In fact, both presented a mature and elegant countenance.

"Adeline." Lady Turner held out her hands. "I am so pleased to find you at home."

"Mary, good day to you." Adeline turned to Georgie. "You remember Miss Featherton?"

Mary Turner smiled brightly. "Yes, of course. It is good to see you again."

Georgie returned the smile and could truthfully say, "It is good to see you too."

Amanda Fitzwalter greeted her and Adeline as well. "The Season must be very dull if you have come to our little area of the world in the middle of it."

Now what was Georgie to say to that?

Fortunately, Mary responded, "We have heard that it is not as exciting as usual."

"Yes, indeed." Amanda exchanged a smile with Mary. "That is the reason we decided to have a house party."

"It will be at my house," Mary said. "And we hope you will both be able to attend some of our entertainments."

"Lord Littleton as well," Amanda added.

Adeline glanced at Georgie. A house party would provide a diversion. She inclined her head slightly.

"Yes," Adeline said as she poured the tea. "We would love to attend some of the events. What do you have planned?"

"There will be a garden party with rowing on the lake," Mary said. "As well as a ball at the end of the week. There will also be a dinner we would like you to attend, as well as some other events."

"We are still putting it all together," Amanda added. "We would dearly like to do something different."

"It sounds like a great deal of fun." Georgie took the cup of tea and three ginger biscuits. She had not eaten very much during the past few days, and suddenly she was famished. Perhaps it was time to forget Lord Turley. He might be looking for her, but that probably only meant he wanted to try to talk her around. And that she would not allow to happen. Not only that, but he had taken months to come up to scratch. Georgie would not permit him to break her heart again. She would have love or nothing. Now that she considered it, it would not surprise her to discover he simply thought he should marry, not that he actually *wanted* to wed *her*. She would have to harden her heart. Perhaps she would meet a gentleman at the house party who interested her more than Turley.

"An excellent idea," Adeline said approvingly. "When do you plan to have it?"

"In a week's time," Amanda answered. "We shall send the invitations and a schedule in the event you would like to join us for our other activities."

"We have invited other local families as well," Mary added.

"I am looking forward to it. I'm sure it will be delightful." Georgie had finished the last of her biscuits and set her cup down.

Amanda and Mary rose. "We should be off," Mary said. "We shall see you again soon."

Once the ladies left, Adeline rubbed her stomach. "I am famished."

"I am as well." Georgie's stomach made its agreement known. It was good to feel hungry again.

"After we eat, let's take a walk to town." Adeline tugged the bellpull. "I am in need of a new bonnet."

That sounded like a good idea. A new bonnet, a party, and possibly a new gentleman. "An excellent idea."

Gavin dragged a hand down his face. He'd spent the last two hours in a committee meeting and was on his way to the next one. Normally, the discussions would have held his interest, but today all he could think of was Georgie. He should stop sulking over her and do something. The problem was that he had no idea what to do.

"You look like hell." The new Earl of Bolingbroke slapped Gavin on the back.

He felt like hell. If he'd known being rejected would cause this much agony, he never would have proposed. Drinking certainly had not helped. "I haven't had a good couple of days."

"It will get better," Bolingbroke said loudly—although that might be the fault of the brandy Gavin had consumed last night—and much too cheerfully. "They always do. My grandfather always told me that, and he was right."

"So I have heard." Gavin wished the man would go away. Bolingbroke hadn't even formally taken his seat in the Lords yet. "What are you doing here?"

"Seeing how things work. My grandfather told me a great deal, but I needed to see it for myself. I've been invited to a house party though. That will be a pleasant diversion until my ceremony."

Who the devil would give a house party during the Season? Not that this autumn had been much fun. "A house party?"

"Indeed. Lady Turner and Mrs. Fitzwalter are hosting it," Bolingbroke said. "I've known their husbands for years."

Gavin felt his brows lowering without his consent. Blast it all, he couldn't even control his own features. But something was nagging at him. "Aren't their estates in Surrey?"

"They are. It's not far from Town."

And not far from Littlewood. Or from Georgie.

Bloody hellhounds!

How could he have forgotten? Turner's and Fitzwalter's estates bordered Littlewood.

The one thing he did not want was for other gentlemen to be sniffing around Georgie. "Do you happen to know who else has been invited?"

"Not really." The man frowned. "I do know St. Albans is going."

The Earl of St. Albans was a courtesy title and, from what Gavin had seen, the man had little to keep him occupied. "I'm surprised that he would consider a house party very interesting."

"It depends which ladies are there." A smirk briefly appeared on Bolingbroke's face. "Then again, I've heard both Lady Turner and Mrs. Fitzwalter are pretty high sticklers. He might need a repairing lease."

That sounded more likely, but it also meant that his lordship would be more than willing to entertain the ladies. "I wish you a good time."

"Thank you. I hope you feel better." Bolingbroke sauntered off. He was only a year or so younger than Gavin, but the man made him feel ancient.

Exeter came up as his lordship left. "Have you decided what you're going to do?"

Gavin did not need to ask what his friend was talking about. It was Georgie. All of his thoughts, all of his difficulties revolved around her. "No. I was going to ride to Littlewood, but then I thought it would make me appear desperate."

"You are desperate." Exeter's tone was as dry as sand.

"Yes, well, I don't wish to *look* like I am, do I?" The more Gavin had thought about his plan to convince Georgie to marry him, the more it seemed like an idea that was bound to fail.

"I suppose it depends what you want," his friend said unhelpfully.

What he wanted right now was to take a swing at someone. "You do realize that you are not being at all helpful?"

Exeter just shrugged. "Dorie heard from Georgie. According to what my wife told me, she is having a wonderful time visiting Littlewood. They are even going to attend some of the events at a house party."

That was the last straw. "I'm going to Jackson's. You're welcome to join me if you wish."

"Now?" Exeter sounded shocked. "But we have another meeting."

"I need to hit someone, and it's better I do it there than here." Gavin was having trouble being polite to anyone at the moment.

"I shall tell you if anything of significance occurs." Exeter placed his hand on Gavin's shoulder. "I wish I could tell you what to do."

"So do I." He wished someone, anyone, could tell him what to do.

Chapter Five

Lucinda, the dowager Viscountess Featherton, was in the morning room of the house she shared with her oldest and dearest friend Constance, the dowager Duchess of Bridgewater. After searching for several months, they had been lucky to find the property on Mount Street that pleased both of them. Lucinda looked up from the letter she had received by messenger from the dowager Lady Littleton—what a pity that they all had dowager as part of their titles. There must be a better way to address widowed peeresses—in response to a letter Lucinda had written to her longtime friend. She was determined to find out whether Viscount Turley was indeed the right gentleman for Georgie. If not, she and Constance would simply have to find another prospect for the poor girl. "According to Cristabel, it appears that Viscount Turley's father lost his beloved wife and proceeded to promptly lose his mind, leaving the boy to keep everything together at a young age. Ergo—"

"The stupid boy has decided that, despite all the evidence to the contrary, he might do the same." Constance scowled. "Men are such fools."

"Well, they *can* be," Lucinda said slowly. "But you must admit that not all of them are."

"No, no, you did a wonderful job raising yours. And if Turley's mother had not died when the children were young, he would not be having this particular problem. But what are we going to do about it?"

"She—Cristabel has a plan."

"I am glad someone does," Constance grumbled.

Lucinda grinned. They had been going round and round and had still not come up with a suitable scheme. "She will arrive in Town late today. She might even be here now." She did not even bother to give her friend the letter to read. Constance preferred to be told the information.

"Does she wish to stay with us?" Constance asked. "We can easily have rooms made up for her."

"No, she has sent orders to open up Littleton House. Once she explained the matter to her son, Littleton agreed that she should become involved. I do hope she comes by soon after she arrives." Lucinda found the passage she wanted in the letter. "She writes that Frits is convinced that Turley is in love with Georgie, but that he is too afraid of putting the viscounty at risk if he allows his heart to rule him."

Constance grunted. "Perhaps I was a bit harsh when I said Turley was a fool."

"He also opined that his friend was deluded for thinking that anyone can tell their heart what to do." Lucinda had to agree. Although it was amazing how many people tried to do just that with horrible results.

"He has a point there." Constance frowned. "If only more people, young and old, realized the heart has a mind of its own." She reached over and tugged the bellpull. "What role are we to play?"

"That will remain to be seen. However, I shall tell my maid to have my traveling bag packed. There is no telling when we might have to dash off somewhere."

"I shall do the same," Constance responded.

Lucinda was about to rise when a thought occurred to her. "It will behoove us to find a way to convince Turley to visit Littlewood."

"Perhaps that is the reason Cristabel is coming to Town." Constance laid her book in her lap. "For all we know he has no idea where she is."

"Hmm." Lucinda perched her elbow on the arm of her chair and placed her chin on her hand. "Or he does know but either has no interest in following her, or he has been given to understand that she does not wish to see him, or has been told not to follow her."

"I think that describes all of our options, but how shall we discover which one it is?" her friend asked.

"I believe we must rely on Cristabel to find the answer." Lucinda heaved a sigh. "It might be tomorrow before we see her."

"You might not have to wait for long." Constance pointed toward the door. "It appears we have company."

No sooner than she had finished the sentence than their butler announced their friend. "Cristabel, my dear." Lucinda rose to greet the younger woman. "We are very glad to see you."

"I did hope that you would not mind me simply coming by." Cristabel embraced Lucinda and held her hand out to Constance. "What a pickle that young man has made of the whole thing."

The tea tray arrived and Lucinda poured. "So we gathered. He definitely made a mess of it with poor Georgie."

Cristabel withdrew the pin from her bonnet and removed

it. "What a lovely room. I adore how you have combined the richer colors with lighter ones."

As much as Lucinda wanted to get on to her granddaughter, this was one of her favorite rooms in the house, and it was the result of a great deal of compromise. "Constance selected the wall coverings"—a rich red—"and I found the hangings to lighten the room." Lucinda had been fortunate to find a lovely print on a white background with splashes of the same color as the walls. "We are very pleased with the results."

"As you should be." Cristabel took a cup of tea from Lucinda. "You will want to know that I spent some time with Georgie at Littlewood. She is putting on a good face, but she is clearly blue-deviled."

Constance leaned forward to accept her cup of tea before saying, "We need to discover what Turley's feelings are."

Cristabel's finely arched brows drew together. "Is there an entertainment such as a soirée or musical evening being held within the next day or so? That would be much better than a ball where he would be sure to be asked to stand up with young ladies."

Lucinda mentally reviewed their schedule. "Lady Matthews is having a musical evening tomorrow."

"In that event, I shall write a note to Turley asking him to escort me," Cristabel said. "He has been in the way of thinking of me as an aunt and might confide in me without my having to ask."

"That is an excellent idea." Constance nodded approvingly.

"It is indeed." To Lucinda's mind, having Cristabel ferret out what Turley was thinking and feeling about Georgie was the best possible idea. Soon the three of them would be able to plan their campaign to either see Georgie and Turley married or find another gentleman for her.

Gavin sat on the side of his bed, cradling his face in his palms. After going to Jackson's, he couldn't rid himself of the image of Georgie carrying on as if she did not care about him at all. So much for thinking she might love him.

Damn. There was a reason he didn't make a habit of getting jug-bitten. He felt like hell. At least he remembered everything. But that thought made him cringe. Including the ladybird who'd tried to interest him in going upstairs with her. Why the devil had he ever gone to a brothel? She'd not been at all happy when despite her efforts he couldn't seem to form an erection. She'd had some choice words about men drinking too much, but he knew it wasn't the brandy that had done it. *She* had not interested him. In fact, none of the light-skirts had stirred his blood even a little. It was after that realization that he'd really begun to drink.

"Drink this down, my lord, and you'll feel better directly." Ardley, his valet, handed him a mug.

Gavin didn't dare even smell it for fear he'd toss his accounts. Ready or not—holding his breath, he gulped it down in one long draw. "That wasn't as bad as I thought it would be."

"I added a bit of honey," his valet admitted, speaking softly. "The recipe doesn't call for it, but you don't make a habit of overindulging."

So Gavin wasn't to be punished for dipping too deep. "Thank you. I have remembered exactly why I don't drink to excess."

"Last evening you received a letter from Lady Littleton. Would you like it now or after you dress?"

Why the devil would Adeline Littleton write him? Gavin hoped there was nothing wrong with Georgie. Then again, would Lady Littleton write to him about Georgie? Perhaps something was the matter with Littleton. Gavin tried to concentrate on the missive, but his eyes were having trouble focusing and his head felt like horses had trampled upon it. "I'll read it after I've had a strong cup of coffee."

"Coffee, my lord?" Ardley's tone was definitely one of shock.

The only time Gavin drank coffee was in a coffee shop. His mother, then his sister complained that it made the house smell. "If we do not have any, then strong tea."

"Yes, my lord. I believe that can be arranged." The door opened, water splashed, and the door clicked shut. "If you would like to wash, I shall shave you, if you wish."

He usually liked to shave himself. It had started as a small defiance against his father, but this morning he had better let his valet do it. He had no doubt that his hands wouldn't be any steadier than his eyes. "Thank you. I do wish it."

By the time he began to tie his cravat, Gavin was feeling immeasurably better. His eyesight was not fuzzy any longer and his headache had receded to a faint throbbing. When he arrived in the breakfast room, Lady Littleton's letter was next to his plate and Broadwell, his butler, placed the teapot and a rack of hot buttered toast on the table.

"How would you like your eggs this morning, my lord?"

Good Lord. The whole household must know Gavin had been in his altitudes. He took stock of his stomach. "Soft-boiled as always."

"Yes, my lord."

He poured tea that was as dark as any coffee he'd drunk and added three lumps of sugar to it, then pulled the toast to him, before he remembered the letter. Gavin broke the seal and read.

My dear Turley,

I have come to town for a few days to do some shopping, but there is a musical evening tomorrow, and I would appreciate it if you would act as my escort.

Your friend,
C. Littleton

Gavin caught himself letting out his breath. He'd forgotten there were now two Lady Littletons. He hadn't planned on attending Mrs. Matthews's entertainment, but for the dowager Lady Littleton—Good God, he'd better not call her dowager when he was around her—there was little he would not do. Accompanying her ladyship would also give him an opportunity to discover how long Georgie planned to remain at Littlewood. Straight after breakfast he'd write to Lady Littleton agreeing to accompany her.

By now everyone in the *ton* would know Georgie and her family had left Town and that might not bode well for him. Not that he thought he would be the cynosure of every unmarried lady's attention, but he would feel as if he'd been thrown to the proverbial wolves. This would be the first time since last Season he would be without Georgie for protection. Although, he doubted she saw it that way. He knew that as long as he was with her, the other ladies and their mothers considered him lost to their wiles.

After consuming two more pots of tea, a nice cut of rare

beef, another rack of toast, and two eggs, Gavin felt much more the thing. His head no longer hurt, his eyesight had returned to normal, and his hands weren't shaking. He wrote the message and had it sent to her ladyship, then decided to apply himself to correspondence and other business he'd left unattended since Georgie had turned him down. No matter what happened, he was not going to think about her today.

Several minutes later he perused a letter from the steward of one of his estates asking for advice in dealing with a dispute between two tenants who had never liked each other. For the past several months, Georgie had given him advice. Even during the summer, he'd written to her father and asked him to relay a message to her. He just wasn't good at making decisions when it involved the emotional side of things. Give him a boundary dispute, or a matter of right or wrong, and he was perfectly capable. That was one of the reasons he needed her as his wife. She always knew exactly the right thing to do. He set the note aside. Perhaps Lady Littleton would be able to help him.

Gavin worked through luncheon and by the time he was finally called to dress for dinner and the evening, he had managed to reduce the amount of paper on his desk. Leaning back, he wondered what he'd do if he could not convince Georgie to marry him. He glanced around the room and imagined that as his wife she would enter, chiding him about working too late. He would stand and go to her, pulling her into his arms. His member began to stiffen as if his thoughts were real, and Gavin looked at the decanter of brandy on the sideboard.

No.

He was not going to do that again. It hadn't helped at all. He would also be careful how much wine he consumed this evening. He damn sure wasn't going to indulge as his father had done.

Two hours later Gavin arrived to collect Lady Littleton from Littleton House.

A butler he didn't know answered the door and bowed. "Her ladyship is waiting in the drawing room. If you would follow me?"

As if he hadn't run tame in this house for years. But this new butler had no way of knowing that. He inclined his head. "Of course."

Once he was announced, her ladyship came to him holding out her hands and searching his face. "Gavin, how are you?"

Suddenly he felt as if he was a small child who just wanted to be comforted. "I've been better."

She led him to the sofa and indicated the chair next to where she sat. "I imagine so. Would you like to tell me about it? You know how discreet I am."

"There is not much to tell. I proposed to Miss Featherton and she rejected me." He had been dancing around the word "rejected," but that was how he felt. She had not simply refused to marry him. She had run away from him. "I don't know what to do."

Her ladyship handed him a glass of claret and sipped her own before saying, "I already knew that you proposed, and that she refused you."

He set his glass down untouched. "I have heard she is at Littlewood. Have you seen her? Is she well?" *Bloody hellhounds.* He sounded like a veritable popinjay. "I mean—"

"I believe I know what you mean." Reaching out, Lady Littleton patted his hand. "Would it make you feel better if I told you that she is no happier than you are?"

Yes! Thank the Lord Lady Exeter had lied to her husband. That had to be it. Georgie would have no reason to fib to her friend. "I suppose not. I should not wish her to be miserable." Except that he did.

Her ladyship gave him a pitying look. "And are you miserable?"

If ever there was a time to lie, it was now. His reputation as a rational man was at risk. Then again, he'd never in his life been good at lying to this woman. "I am not sure I would call it *miserable*, but I have not been sleeping well, and last night I-I got foxed."

"Oh, my dear boy. You have not done that since you and Frits first came on the Town." She took another sip of wine. "What do you intend to do about it?"

"I don't know." Gavin sipped his wine, resisting the urge to take a large gulp. "I have a feeling that she wants a love match, and I dare not . . . I cannot take the risk."

"Hmm." Her ladyship gazed in his direction but not at him. "That is a bit of a problem." She glanced at the clock. "Look at the time. We must go if we are to be there before the music begins."

He jumped to his feet when she rose, and held out his arm. "Please do not leave me alone to the young ladies tonight."

Her smile was kind, motherly, and he knew he'd be safe with her. "I would not think of it. Naturally, you require time to sort out your thoughts."

The butler was at the door with her cloak and his hat, and Gavin led her to his town coach. One of his footmen opened the door. "Who is the butler? I've never seen him before."

"His name is Crothers. He was the under-butler at Littlewood, and I decided to filch him when I set up my own household. He was inadequately employed there, and I had need of a butler." The coach lights were lit and Gavin could see her roll her eyes. He almost let out a whoop. She would have punished him if he'd done that. "I would not have dared take Creswell. Littleton would have objected to that."

Lips twitching, Gavin could barely contain his laughter. "I'm sure you're right."

"Also, it would not have been fair to Adeline. Having an excellent butler in the country is even more important than having one in Town. So many of our neighbors truly believe they have an absolute right to visit one when they wish whether one wants them to or not."

That had not been his experience, but, then again, he was a bachelor. What would happen when he brought a wife home? Georgie would know how to handle it, he was sure. Damn. There he went again. Should he at least see if there was an unmarried lady who did not want a love match? Yet, the thought of not waking to Georgie next to him every morning soured his stomach. "I can imagine."

The coach pulled up and, before he thought about it, Gavin jumped down to help her ladyship descend. When he had visited Littlewood or been with Littleton in Town, it had always been a competition between Gavin and Littleton who could do it first. Gavin supposed if it had been his friend's mother who had died, the shoe would be on the other foot. Lady Littleton's presence had been the one thing that had saved him. She had stepped in after his mother's death to provide a steady hand. His sister, Elizabeth, had had help from their aunt, but he'd always had her ladyship. But could Lady Littleton help him now? Could she help explain to Georgie that he could give her everything she wanted but love?

Chapter Six

That evening, Gavin escorted Lady Littleton into Lady Matthews's house and immediately regretted coming. They had not gone two steps beyond the receiving line when the first matron with a daughter to marry off approached them, daughter in tow. The lady could not have been older than forty as her dark blond hair showed not a glint of silver. The girl next to her was pretty enough, but somehow seemed not quite up to snuff. Nothing like Georgie, who could not be more than a year the young lady's senior.

"Lady Littleton, I vow I have not seen you in years," the woman simpered.

Her ladyship raised one eyebrow. "Are you certain, Mrs. Barton? I am positive that I saw you last Season with"—she tapped her cheek with her fan—"oh, I remember now. Your third daughter." Lady Littleton smiled politely. "You were in anticipation of an offer for her hand. Did you receive it?"

Interestingly, the other lady seemed to forget the girl at her side as she beamed at her ladyship. "How good of you to remember, my lady. We did indeed receive a very eligible offer for her, and she is now happily married. I trust your son is doing well?"

"Indeed he is." Lady Littleton's smile widened. "I shall be made a grandmother again this winter." She inclined her head. "I am dreadfully sorry, but you must excuse us. Lady Bellamny wishes to speak to me."

"Oh, of course, my lady." The other woman gave a slight curtsey. "Come along, Tabitha. We must find our seats."

Gavin stared after the woman and her daughter. "I believe I have been taken down a peg. I would have sworn she was attempting to have me introduced to her."

"I have no doubt she was." Lady Littleton's eyes twinkled with mirth. "But mentioning her success with her other daughter distracted her sufficiently for her to forget her purpose in approaching us."

"Very well done." Gavin glanced around. "Did you really see Lady Bellamny? I never look forward to meeting her."

"Naturally, you would not. No unmarried gentleman does." Lady Littleton began to steer him farther into the room. "But to answer your question, I did. She is speaking with two of my friends." She gave him a chiding look. "If you wish, I can leave you to your own devices—"

"No." He placed his hand over hers to keep it there. "I do not have your talent to distract."

"Very well. Stay by my side. I see Lady Matthews has left her post in the receiving line. She would be pleased to make you known to several young ladies."

Gavin couldn't suppress a shudder. "I'll stick to you like a leech."

Her ladyship frowned at him. "What a singularly disgusting analogy."

"It was, rather." He found himself grinning. "You must bring out my younger self."

"In that event, do try to control yourself. Behaving like a schoolboy will not help you at all."

"I wish I'd appreciated how simple my life was then." Before his mother had died. Before his father had lost his mind. "After you greet the other ladies might we discuss what I am going to do about Miss Featherton?"

"Of course." She patted his hand that was still covering hers. "I have a few ideas of what you could do to return to her good graces."

They reached the older ladies in question, and Lady Bellamny was the first to speak. "Cristabel, I'm glad to see you in Town."

"It is a short stay, but it has given me time to visit a few shops. As well stocked as Littleton is, it cannot compare with London."

"Lord Turley." Gavin felt his spine stiffening as if he was about to be scolded. "I would have thought you would be seeking to be presented to the young ladies instead of hiding behind Lady Littleton's skirts."

At least his instincts were correct. He bowed stiffly. "Good evening, my lady. I have already found the lady I wish to marry."

Lady Bellamny's black eyes narrowed at him. "Then why are you not with her?"

"She is out of Town at the moment," Lady Littleton said. "Really, Almeria, you are being too hard on the boy."

The tallest of the older ladies snorted.

"Duchess"—Lady Littleton brought Gavin forward a step—"allow me to present Lord Turley. Turley, this is the Duchess of Bridgewater."

Bowing, he took the hand she'd held out. "A pleasure, your grace."

"We'll see about that," the duchess retorted, giving him a hard look.

As he rose, the other lady, who reminded him of Georgie, raised both brows as if challenging him somehow.

"My lady, allow me to present Lord Turley." Lady Littleton glanced at him. "I do not believe you have mentioned meeting Miss Featherton's grandmother, Lady Featherton."

He swallowed before bowing. "My lady, it is a great pleasure to make your acquaintance. Your granddaughter resembles you."

"In more than mere appearances." Her blue eyes narrowed. "You would do well to remember that."

"Yes, ma'am." He was being judged and judged harshly. Obviously, the duchess and Lady Featherton cared a great deal for Georgie and were clearly hostile toward him. The worst of it was he couldn't think of a thing to say to change whatever opinion she had formed about him. Gavin wished he could leave, but Lady Littleton was still speaking with the duchess. When Lady Featherton gave him one last glare and joined the conversation her friends were having, he almost groaned with relief.

Finally, the party was called to take their seats, and Lady Littleton led him to two chairs set in a bow window. "We cannot leave the room, but we will not bother anyone if we speak softly. There are four things I believe you should do." She held up one finger. "Write Littleton with a letter for Miss Featherton asking for her forgiveness." Gavin opened his mouth to object, but her ladyship shook her head and held up a second finger. "Ask Littleton if you can go to Littlewood. Although, Adeline might convince him you should not be allowed to visit. Three, admit that you need not be afraid of loving the woman you wish to wed." He shook his head, and Lady Littleton sighed. "Four, go to Littlewood and try to convince Miss Featherton that you are worth her risking her heart."

He shook his head again. "I need a plan before I see her."

Her ladyship let out an exasperated sound. "And exactly how long do you intend to wait before you come up with this elusive plan?" He winced at the acidity in her ladyship's tone. "How long has it been since you saw her?"

Too long. "Not that long. It has only been a week."

For a moment he thought her ladyship had not heard him. Then her lips formed a moue. "Delude yourself if you wish, my boy, but you cannot fool me." Shrugging lightly, she focused her attention on the stage that had been built. "I have no more advice to give you."

Bloody hellhounds.

There had to be another way to convince Georgie to marry him. The problem was that her ladyship was right, as usual. He had no plan and wasn't even close to forming one.

Frits Littleton ambled into the morning room where Georgie and Adeline were finishing the last two cushion covers. "I say, a horse arrived last night by the name of Lilly. Do either of you—"

"Lilly?" Georgie couldn't believe what he'd just said. She jumped up before he could finish, knocking over the tambour frame holding her needlework. "She's here?"

He inclined his head as if he was being serious, but his eyes danced and his lips twitched as if he would burst out laughing at any moment. "She is, and it appears to my stable master that she is looking for someone."

"Give me a moment to change." Georgie dashed out of the room, not even apologizing to Adeline. And, forgetting all the years of decorum she had learned, shouted for Smith to attend her immediately. Georgie had not thought her mare would arrive at all.

Smith arrived in Georgie's dressing room at the same time she did. "I must change into my riding habit."

"The nankeen or the velvet?"

"The nankeen." Georgie unmoored the buttons on her day dress. "I want to put Lilly through her paces."

Smith frowned. "Try not to fall off this time."

Not again. Georgie almost groaned at her maid's lack of understanding. "I keep telling you that the falling off is important. One must always be ready, and Hawksworth taught me how to fall. It is something that must be practiced."

"You're going to break your neck," Smith warned unrepentantly.

"The point of practicing is so that I do not break my neck or any other part of me." Georgie pushed the day gown down, stepped out of it, and held her arms up to receive the skirt of her riding habit.

"Harrumph." Smith dropped the garment over Georgie's head. "I pray to the Lord you're right."

Georgie kept her grin to herself. "Trust me, or rather Hawksworth, I am." She shoved her feet into her riding boots, and stood still as her maid affixed her hat, a bit of straw with a feather that curled under her chin. She pulled on her gloves, opened a box, and took a handful of dried apple pieces. "I shall see you later."

"Do not forget you will need time to bathe before tea," Smith called as Georgie strode out of the room.

"I will be back in time." She descended the stairs in a rush as a footman held the door open.

"Have a good ride, miss."

"I shall," she threw over her shoulder. The whole house must know her horse had arrived. Her maid had not even been surprised by her demand.

When she reached the stable, Lilly was already saddled and standing next to the mounting block. "Lilly!"

Spinning around, the mare yanked her reins out of the stable boy's hands. She stepped forward and waited.

"Down." Georgie clapped as her horse kneeled down low enough for her to mount without help. "Good girl. Rise." Lilly stood as Georgie straightened her skirts.

The stable boy's jaw dropped. "I ain't never seen nothin' like that."

Outside of Astley's, neither had she until her brother-in-law had taught her horse to perform, and had taught Georgie how to train the mare to do other tricks as well. "She is a very intelligent horse."

One of the older grooms rode up beside her. "I'm Johnson. His lordship said as I was to go with ye until ye know the place."

Although she would have liked to be alone, she knew that was not a possibility. It would also have been unwise for her to go off on her own. "I shall be happy for the company." Georgie glanced around. "Which direction shall we head?"

"If ye be wantin' a good gallop, off to the left there's a long straight path and a field."

"Lead the way." The groom trotted forward, and she

held Lilly back until they had reached the path, then gave the horse her head.

They flew past the groom, who grinned as if he'd expected it, and continued for about a mile before reaching a field of late summer blooms mingling with autumn flowers, and tall grass. Georgie brought the mare around. "This looks like a good place to practice. Are you ready?"

The horse vibrated with excitement and Lilly's large head nodded as if she knew exactly what Georgie had said. "Kick." She held on as the mare kicked out with her back legs. "Still." Immediately, Lilly stopped. "Prance left." She sidled to the left, and Georgie gave the command to stop. "Prance right." Lilly performed the same maneuver to the right. Georgie stroked the mare's neck. "Rise and kick." She held on as the horse rose onto her back legs and hit out at an invisible foe. "Still." Once again she stroked the horse's neck. "Excellent. Now off." As Lilly rose, Georgie jumped off her back.

"Miss!" The groom raced to her, fear infusing his words. "Dear God! Are ye hurt? His lordship will be right angry with me if anything happened to you."

Georgie stood and shook out her skirts. "I am perfectly fine. We are just practicing. My brother-in-law is a former army officer, and he taught us to be ready for anything." Georgie took in the worried look on the man's face. "I apologize. I should have warned you what to expect." She gave Lilly a bit of apple. "Shall we ride for a while? I will tell you when we are ready to repeat the maneuvers."

The groom glanced from the horse to Georgie. "As long as I know what ye're doin'."

"We won't surprise you again. I promise." She gave another piece of apple to the horse. "Lilly, down." The mare kneeled and Georgie scrambled onto her back. "Rise."

"I have to say that horse is a marvel," the groom said, shaking his head.

"She is very special." The horse nodded, and they followed the groom across the meadow alternating between a trot and a gallop. This was what she had missed in London. The freedom to ride her horse without being hemmed in by *tonish* rules.

Johnson led them to the end of the meadow then around through the woods where the leaves were turning into brilliant reds and golden browns, and back to the house as a church bell in the distance struck the hour. "That was excellent timing, Johnson."

The older man smiled. "I've had plenty of practice getting folks back for tea."

"It shows." She smiled then spoke to Lilly, "Down."

As Georgie dismounted, clapping started. Frits stood to one side. "That was impressive."

Georgie's face heated under the praise. Everyone at home was used to Lilly's skills and paid no attention. "Thank you."

Frits strolled over to Lilly. "I'll have to ask if you can teach Adeline's mare to do that."

"I would be happy to try." Georgie wondered if she actually could teach another horse. "Though, I have to admit Hawksworth taught Lilly and me."

"I won't expect miracles. But I would like to see how it is done." Frits watched as the horse stood calmly munching.

"Very well." Georgie slowly fed Lilly the rest of the apple bits. "Perhaps tomorrow morning would be a good time. Before breakfast," she suggested, then frowned. "Adeline will only be able to mount and dismount. Surely she is not still riding."

"Ah, no." Frits rubbed his chin. "Getting on and off will

have to suffice for now. She has missed riding a great deal. I'm hoping just being able to do that will make her feel better." He held out his arm. "What else can Lilly do?"

"She can sidestep and kick out at anyone who might be up to no good." Georgie hoped that she was never in a situation where someone wished to cause her harm, but she had agreed with her brother-in-law that she should be prepared. "I was also taught how to fall and not injure myself."

"Once Adeline finds out, she is going to be even more upset by her limitations." Frits pulled a face. "Fortunately, it's not for that long in the grand scheme of things."

"I suppose not." He seemed as if he was feeling Adeline's constraints himself. When she finally found the man she would wed, Georgie wanted him to feel the same about her as Frits felt for Adeline.

A belated sorrow for her friend made Georgie bite her lip. "I was extremely rude to run out the way I did."

"Don't feel badly. She started laughing before you were out of the room." Frits smiled. "It reminded me of her when her horse arrived here."

They had been friends for months now, but they had never spoken of horses. "I did not even know she liked riding."

"She doesn't in Town. But get her in the country and she rides like she was part of the horse."

"That is how I feel. I know that Dorie and some other ladies rise early to take their horses out. When I first went to Town I did not realize I could even do that. Then my mother told me she did not approve of galloping in the Park no matter the hour." Georgie sighed. "Next Season I shall bring Lilly even if I can go at no more than a trot."

She gave herself a shake. "Will you and Adeline ever come up to Town?"

"Perhaps." Frits shrugged. "After the baby is born we shall. We have discussed it and agreed that what we did not like was being on the Marriage Mart."

"I completely understand." Through much of the spring and early autumn, Georgie had thought she was off the Marriage Mart only to discover she was not. "I am not at all looking forward to next Season."

Frits glanced at her and raised one brow. "Things might change between now and then."

Only if Turley met her need for a love match, or if she met another gentleman at the house party whom she could like more than him. Perhaps she would remain in the country. "They might."

Chapter Seven

Marc, Earl of Lytton, strolled into Boodles after a particularly trying hour with his solicitor. His grandfather's will could not be broken. He had two months to marry a lady of whom his aunt—a high stickler if there was one—would approve. If he did not, much of the money he was counting on receiving to help the estates his father had plundered would go to a cousin. A female cousin he would happily wed if only for the inheritance. Unfortunately, she was already married with three children. Thus far, Marc had been singularly unlucky when it came to finding a lady who met his aunt's requirements and who would accept him. He was getting damned tired of proposing marriage and being turned down.

As he strolled into the dining room he noticed Lord Turner and Viscount Bottomley across the room and headed in their direction.

"But, Jonathan, you must attend," Turner said beseechingly. "I have been given the task of finding two more gentlemen to round out the numbers for my wife's house party. And I can't fail."

Bottomley had a rather mulish look on his face. "It is only for a week?"

Turner nodded enthusiastically.

"And I can stay at my own home and attend the entertainments from there?"

"Yes. I said you could. We don't actually have the room to accommodate you. Littleton and his lady and Miss Featherton are going to do the same."

Bottomley's eyes widened. "Miss Featherton, you say? I'd heard she'd left Town with her parents."

"She will indeed be there. I don't know about her parents, but she is visiting Littleton and his wife." Turner seemed to warm to his topic. "We also have several other very eligible ladies attending."

"Who?" Bottomley questioned as if not quite believing Turner.

"I can't remember their names, but my wife assures me they are from good families."

Bottomley appeared to be chewing the inside of his mouth much like a cow chewed her cud, before saying, "Well, if Miss Featherton is attending, I imagine the other ladies must be eligible."

Marc didn't believe that for a minute. Lady Turner was well born, but not of the *haut ton*. However, procuring the attendance of the Littletons and Miss Featherton was a coup for the lady. It might be worth his while to attend this house party. He cleared his throat. "A good decision, Bottomley."

The man stared at Marc with large brown eyes that reminded one again of a bovine. "In that case, you can finish rounding out Lady Turner's numbers and attend as well." Bottomley must have suddenly remembered it was not his invitation to give and swung his head to Turner. "If you have no objection."

"Not at all." Turner grinned. "You have made my life easier." He rose. "I must be going. I have to return home this evening." He executed a short bow. "I shall see you gentlemen on the day after tomorrow."

Bottomley unhappily inclined his head, but Marc was delighted. "I look forward to it." He pulled out a chair and sat. "Is there a particular reason you do not wish to attend the house party?"

"Nothing in general. I simply dislike having my schedule disrupted." The man stared at his brandy. "You may stay with me if you like. It must be a very large party if Turner's house can't accommodate everyone."

It was more likely that Turner knew he'd never get Bottomley there if he couldn't stay at his house. "Thank you. I am happy to accept your offer. How far is your estate from Turner's?"

"Only about two miles. It's one of my lesser estates, but I spend time there every summer, and I keep it staffed to provide employment for the area."

Marc never kept everyone on at his properties, only the caretakers. There was no point in having servants who had nothing to do. Even if he could have afforded to do so. "When will you depart?"

"Tomorrow early in the afternoon at the latest. Turner told me his lady wants to gather everyone for tea in the afternoon." Bottomley looked at Marc. "You can travel with me if you do not wish to take your own carriage."

The idea of being stuck in a coach with a man who had no conversation did not appeal to Marc at all. "I would prefer to ride in my own carriage. However, I shall follow you down."

"As you wish. Meet me at one o'clock tomorrow and we shall depart from my house on Green Street."

"Very well. Thank you for the invitation." Rising, Marc smirked to himself. He'd heard a rumor that Turley was no longer interested in Miss Featherton. If he was here in Town and not at Littlewood with her, the rumor was most likely true. That would give Marc an opportunity to court the lady. After all, an earl was better than a viscount.

Gavin plied the knocker of Littleton House and was admitted by the new butler. "Good morning, my lord."

"Good morning, Crothers. Is her ladyship in?"

"She is." He took Gavin's hat and cane. "If you will follow me?"

Nothing had been resolved the previous evening mostly due to his rejecting every piece of advice Lady Littleton had given to him. But after a long, sleepless night, he now knew there was nothing to do but follow at least one of her suggestions. What did they say about pride going before a fall? He'd fallen lower than he'd ever been and could not even figure out how it had happened.

She rose when he was announced. "Gavin, I was not certain I would see you again."

He took a breath. "I have been giving what you said last evening a great deal of thought. May I escort you to Little-wood?"

The corner of her lips twitched as if she was stifling a smile. "You may indeed. I shall leave within the hour."

"I thought as much and had my staff ready my traveling carriage. It will follow behind yours if that suits you."

"Yes. It will give us an opportunity to discuss more ideas as to how you should approach Miss Featherton."

He knew exactly how he wanted to greet Georgie. Take her into his arms and kiss her senseless until she agreed to marry him. "I had planned to ride."

"Of course you did." Lady Littleton gave an exasperated sigh. "What young man does not?"

Gavin felt guilty but not guilty enough to ride in the coach. "I shall be back before an hour is up."

Lady Littleton shook her head. "I shall see you then."

Now that that was accomplished, Gavin only hoped Adeline Littleton did not refuse to allow him to stay at Littlewood.

Lucinda Featherton opened the note their butler Habersham handed to her. "We have been invited to join Cristabel at her home near Littlewood."

Constance leaned forward the slightest bit. "Has she come up with a plan? God knows *we* have not been successful."

"She has convinced Lord Turley to travel with her." Lucinda was not sure how she felt about that. "She must be certain that he has feelings for Georgie beyond what he believes he does."

"I think we ought to accept her offer," Constance said slowly. "One must remember that she considers Turley to be a son, and one never knows when Georgie will require our assistance."

"Of course we must go." Lucinda could not get over the sensation that there was more to all of this than met the eye. "I shall write to her accepting her offer and give the order that we will depart in the morning."

Her friend leaned over and patted her hand. "Do not

worry. We have successively arranged Meg's, and Kit's and Mary's marriages. We shall do the same for Georgie."

"I know." Lucinda placed her hand over her friend's. "I just have that feeling in my neck. The one I used to get when Meg was in danger."

"In that case, the sooner we arrive the better. Tell Cristabel we shall be there before noon."

"I am so glad you understand." Lucinda went to the writing table. "I shall feel much better when we are there." She picked up her quill and pulled out a piece of paper. "Should we inform Georgie we will be close?"

"Yes, do write to her."

Lucinda penned a short missive to Georgie.

My dearest Georgie,

The duchess and I have been invited to spend some time with the dowager Lady Littleton.

We will arrive tomorrow. I hope we will be able to spend some time together while we are all in the same area.

> *Your loving grandmother,*
> *L*

That afternoon, Georgie and Adeline had just finished the chair cushions when Frits entered the morning room. "Do you have time to take a carriage ride? I thought Georgie would like to see some of our follies."

Her friend glanced at her, and she nodded. "After hearing so much about them, I would love to be able to see them."

"And I can use the fresh air. It is too bad I cannot ride at the moment." Adeline made a neat stack of the cushion covers. "But you may if you like."

Georgie was torn. She would rather ride, but if Adeline had to go in a carriage . . . "If you are sure you do not mind."

"Not at all. Frits will be with me." She smiled at her husband.

"Indeed." He grinned at her and waggled his eyebrows. "We'll take the landau. It will give me a good reason to cuddle with my wife."

A spear of something akin to envy pierced Georgie. They were so happy and so well matched. It was as if all the difficulties they'd had coming together had never occurred. Perhaps it would work out for her and Turley. Except that he was still not here, and he must have discovered where she was by now. He had probably decided to arrange a match with another lady. It was a good thing she had decided to look at other men.

"Georgie?" Adeline's voice was sharper than usual.

"What is it?"

"You were woolgathering. Frits asked if you would like to dine at one of the follies."

"Oh." Georgie really need to pay better attention. "Yes. That would be lovely."

Adeline linked her arm with Georgie's. "In that case, Frits, my love, will you tell Cook and order the carriage and Georgie's horse while we change?"

"It would be my pleasure." He bowed to them and left the room.

"You truly like being married to him," Georgie mused more to herself.

"I do." Adeline led them out of the room. "Just as you will enjoy being married when you find the right gentleman."

"I thought I had." In fact, Georgie had been certain Turley was the one for her—until the proposal.

"Mary Turner wrote to me and related that there would be several eligible gentlemen at her house party. If Lord Turley does come here, he will find he has some competition for your hand. And there is nothing wrong with that."

Georgie murmured her agreement. After all, she had been thinking much the same thing. They reached the door to her chamber. "I shall meet you outside."

Less than an hour later, she was showing Adeline and Frits the tricks Lilly knew.

When the horse bowed to let Georgie on, Adeline began to clap. "I think that is very handy. It is much better than having to find a stump or log in order to mount."

"But then you wouldn't need me to lift you," Frits objected in a rather heated tone.

A blush covered Adeline's cheeks. "I do not need you for that now, but I do enjoy it."

She and Frits gazed besottedly at each other, and Georgie was tempted to roll her eyes. Perhaps visiting happily married newlyweds was not the best idea for a lady suffering from a broken heart. The coachman stared ahead as if ignoring the couple.

Georgie gathered Lilly's reins in her hands and glanced at the landau. "Where is the picnic basket?"

"It will be delivered to the cottage," Frits said as he lifted Adeline into the carriage. "It is in the middle of the follies."

On Georgie's father's main estate there were two, but she had been told there were many more here. "Exactly how many follies are there?"

"Seven. The oldest is the Norman tower." Frits started using his fingers to tick them off. "We have a cottage built by my great-grandfather for his wife. A Dutch farmhouse that my grandfather built for my grandmother because she was homesick. A French farmhouse."

She wondered what it was about farmhouses that made those in the aristocracy feel at home. "Was it based on Marie Antoinette's Hameau de la Reine?"

"No." He shook his head. "It was built in the late seventeenth century. We also have a Grecian temple, Roman ruins, a Turkish tent, and a gloriette."

Georgie was about to ask about the Turkish tent, but she had never heard of a gloriette. "What is a gloriette?"

"It is a room built up off the ground with a balcony." Adeline settled herself on the carriage bench. "It looks like something out of the play *Romeo and Juliet*."

"Except the couple who had it built lived a long and fruitful life," Frits added. "We shall begin with the tent."

Georgie kept pace with the carriage and chatted with Adeline as they rode toward the northeast corner of the estate. The day was sunny and warm for October. The trees here were more red than golden. Soon she saw a structure that looked very much like a huge tent but was made from marble. "I have never seen anything like it."

"I doubt anyone else has either," Frits said as he helped Adeline down from the carriage. "Never having seen a real Turkish tent, I cannot vouch for its authenticity."

"What is in it?" The entrance to the tent had been painted to resemble a canvas flap but was a wooden door that slid back.

"Not much more than a bed and a stove for warmth and tea," Adeline said.

Georgie wandered inside and looked around. Large carpets covered the floor, and chests of various sizes stood along the walls along with cushions and a stove. A large bed hung with blue velvet curtains was in the center of the room. "This is incredible." She pointed to a low round table atop legs that looked as if they could fold in the middle of several brightly colored silk cushions. "Is that gold?"

"Brass, but gold would be easier to clean," Frits answered. "I know because my housekeeper complains about the work it takes to keep it shining." He pointed to the back of the tent. "There are several other tables back there, but the tops have been taken off and stored and the supports folded."

Georgie strolled over to the tables and noticed how well maintained everything was. And it was clean. There was not a speck of dust anywhere. She wondered if it was due to frequent use and had to fight the heat rising to her cheeks. "She does a very good job of keeping everything clean and polished."

Frits offered his arm. "We should go or we'll never get to all of them."

The gloriette was next and it really did look as if it belonged in a scene from *Romeo and Juliet*. It, as well as the tent, was clean, stocked with tea, and the beds were made up with fresh sheets. How large was their staff? It must be huge. It was strange she had not realized it before.

When they arrived at the cottage, she was surprised to find footmen putting the finishing touches on a table set with porcelain dishes, silver, and serviettes. She pulled her friend aside. "Adeline, how many servants do you have on staff?"

"Only about one hundred full-time staff. However, we train local girls and boys and help them find positions. It is better than the alternatives, them not finding work that pays well or leaving for the Americas."

Their friend Henrietta had told them about girls and some boys who went to London to try to find jobs and were preyed upon by unscrupulous persons. Henrietta's sister had formed a charity to help people like that. "Who started the scheme?"

"Frits's mother began it after one of the local girls departed for Town. When her family did not hear from her they told his father, who eventually found her locked in a brothel." Adeline shivered. "She was never the same afterward."

Georgie found herself curling her hands into fists. She could not imagine the horror the girl went through. She hoped someone paid for their treachery.

"Well," Adeline said in an overly cheery tone. "We are doing what we can to stop others from finding themselves in the same position."

They dined on cold meats, fruit, and their local cheese, which was excellent, then finished the meal with a plum tart. The cottage had doors leading out to a small terrace over the river.

"This is my favorite folly." Adeline got a misty smile on her face, and Georgie got a strong feeling she did not need to know the reason for it. "Frits offered to build me one of my own, but this cottage suits me perfectly."

They strolled the small curtilage then finished their tour of the follies.

When they arrived back to the house, two coaches were standing in the curved drive.

"One of them is my mother's," Frits said as he went to the other side of the carriage to help Adeline down. "And the other belongs to—"

Georgie's throat closed painfully as she recognized the crest on the second coach. She forced out the words "Lord Turley."

"Oh, dear." Adeline touched Georgie's arm. "Are you all right?"

Georgie swallowed and for a moment could not speak. She had wanted him to find her, but had begun to think he would not. Despite the fact that she had been considering other unknown men now that he was here, she did not know what to think or feel. She was almost numb from indecision as to how to greet him. It was not at all helpful that her heart was beating so fast she felt breathless. "I shall be fine."

Chapter Eight

The day was warm, especially for October, but this *was* Surrey. Gavin and Lady Littleton had arrived to discover Frits, his wife, and Georgie were out looking at the follies. A tea tray appeared and Lady Littleton suggested they drink it on the terrace. They had been there for about twenty minutes when he heard the sounds of a carriage and a horse approaching the front of the house. "They have returned."

"Are you ready?" her ladyship asked.

"Yes." Or rather he thought he was. If he saw any indication that Georgie did not wish him to remain at Littlewood, Gavin would stay with her ladyship. That, however, would put him at a disadvantage as he would have to wait for an invitation to visit Littlewood or be forced to wait and accompany Lady Littleton when she visited. "I shall go out to meet them."

Her ladyship gave him a doubtful look, but he did not want Georgie to walk out here and see him. She should have some warning. "Good luck."

"I have a feeling I might need it." Gavin had not simply

shown up at Littlewood without sending word in a very long time. Even Littleton hadn't known he'd come.

Gavin reached the front door in time to see Georgie's reaction to his coach. Her finely arched brows had drawn together slightly, and her lovely lips were flattened. When Frits's wife place a hand on Georgie's arm, she did not react. She did not appear particularly happy. Then again, she did not look angry. In fact, she seemed a little stunned. The younger Lady Littleton said something to Georgie, and she answered before donning a polite smile. That wasn't promising at all. He hadn't expected her to show joy at his presence, but he'd hoped she might be a little happy.

Gavin pasted a smile on his own face and strolled out onto the stoop. "I hope the timing of my visit is not problematic."

Littleton—the only one who did not appear surprised to see Gavin—exchanged what looked like meaningful glances with his wife before coming forward. "Not at all. Welcome. It's always good to see friends. Let's go to my study while the ladies change."

Gavin inclined his head. There was nothing in his friend's face to betray how he would really be received. He'd know soon what he was up against. He followed Littleton through the hall to his comfortable study and took a seat by the lit fireplace while Littleton poured two glasses of claret.

After handing a goblet to Gavin, Littleton lowered himself into the opposite chair. "Adeline and I discussed what should be done if you came." He took a drink of wine. When he lowered it, his countenance reminded Gavin strongly of the old Lord Littleton just before he began a lecture. "Until such time as you and Georgie work out what you are going to do, you cannot stay at Little-wood."

Gavin was tempted to drain the glass, but contented himself with twisting the goblet around. "Your mother offered to give me a room at her house."

Littleton nodded. "You will be allowed free run. As long as you are not residing here, Georgie will be able to see you or not as she wishes."

That might work. Gavin sipped his claret. "How much freedom will I have?"

"You may take your meals here, if you like." His friend stared at him consideringly. "I suggest strongly that you begin anew with Georgie. I cannot agree with your stand that you will not fall in love. If you continue in that vein, you might never convince her to marry you. But Adeline and I agreed to allow you a second chance to make Georgie want to spend her life with you." Frits finished his wine and set it on a sturdy walnut side table. "There are three rules you must follow. You may not under any circumstances compromise her." Gavin nodded. He hoped he would not have considered that option. But when a man becomes desperate . . . "And you may not follow her around like a puppy. If she does not wish to see you, you are to take yourself off."

He inclined his head in assent. He doubted his pride would allow him to behave in that manner, but one never knew. "You will address any written invitations or other correspondence you wish to send Miss Georgie to me." Gavin had thought—had hoped—there might be a little relaxing of propriety, but apparently not. When he didn't answer, Frits continued, "For the time she is here, Adeline and I are responsible for her. We intend to do our duty.

Neither of us will be put in the position of having to explain to her parents any sort of misfortune she may experience."

He had a point. If it was Gavin's daughter, he would expect the same. Suddenly he had a vision of a little girl with dark chestnut curls and blue eyes. "I understand you. For the purposes of this courtship, I shall treat you as her guardian."

"In that case, we will not have any problems." Littleton's tone was solemn. Still, Gavin was a bit surprised that the man's ready smile was nowhere to be seen. He really was taking his responsibilities seriously. "Lady Turner and Mrs. Fitzwalter are hosting a house party. We will obtain invitations for you to the events which we are attending."

"Thank you." And thank the Lord for good friends.

"I wish you luck." Littleton finally grinned. "I have a feeling you might need it."

"I have a feeling you might be correct." Georgie had acted as if Gavin was not present when he walked out to greet them. He finished his wine. "Time to beard the lioness."

"I would make that plural," Littleton said as he rose. "Adeline is very fierce when it comes to her friends. Much as she will be with our children."

Thinking about his conversation with Miss Stern, Gavin grimaced. "They all are."

Frits and Gavin made their way back to the hall and to the morning room on the other side of the house. They arrived to find the doors to the terrace open and light female laughter floating in from outside. He stood in the doorway and watched as Georgie laughed at something Lady Littleton—the dowager—said. The woman he hoped to make his wife was dressed in a light yellow muslin gown that appeared to float around her as she sat in a chair. She had never looked more beautiful or more desirable.

Frits walked past him. "I hope there is something more than fruit tarts and biscuits."

"Of course, my love." His wife smiled up at him. "We have sandwiches as well." Adeline Littleton glanced at Gavin. "You may join us, my lord."

He made himself put one foot in front of the other. Why was he so hesitant? This was what he wanted. "Thank you." He bowed to Lady Littleton the younger. "Thank you." He winced at the repetition. He must be more nervous than he'd thought. Then he turned to Georgie and bowed again. "Miss Featherton, I am glad to see you."

Her smile tightened as she inclined her head. "Indeed?"

This was not going well. Perhaps it was a good thing he'd be at The Lilacs with Lady Littleton. That said, if he wanted to marry Georgie, he had to do something to set things on the right path again. He smiled down at her and saw uncertainty in her deep blue eyes. Gavin had not been the only one wounded by his bungled proposal. Was she dreading that he'd stay at Littlewood? If so, it was time to ease her mind. "Yes, I am. I shall be residing at The Lilacs for the nonce."

She let out a shallow breath. If he had not been so focused on her, he wouldn't have noticed it. "I am sure her ladyship will be happy for the company."

"I must say that I am." Lady Littleton smiled beatifically at all of them. "It will be quite like old times having Gavin around." Then she spoke to him, "Gavin, stop looming over Miss Featherton and take a seat. You and Littleton still do not seem to realize how tall you have grown." She indicated a platter of sandwiches. "You might as well eat.

There will most likely be nothing at my house until dinner."

"Yes, ma'am." Gavin dutifully sat on the other side of her ladyship, and accepted a cup of tea from the younger Lady Littleton. "Thank you, my lady." From the corner of his eye, he saw a small grin on Georgie's lips.

"Oh dear." Adeline Littleton's lips formed a moue. "You should probably call me Adeline. I imagine you will always think of Mama-in-law as Lady Littleton."

"It has been getting a bit jumbled in my head." Although why that should be, he didn't know. He knew more than enough dowagers.

"I should have thought of it when you visited before." She reached for a lemon biscuit then sighed. "I should not."

"Of course you should," Lady Littleton said. "If one cannot indulge a bit when one is in a delicate condition, then I do not know when one may."

Adeline bit into the sweet and sighed. "They are delicious."

"I would not wish to deprive Frits and Adeline of their cook," Gavin said. "But I do wish she had gone with you."

"Bite your tongue." Littleton glowered at Gavin. "That sort of poaching would have caused a family rift."

Everyone laughed, but it seemed a little forced. Had he made a mistake coming here? Clearly, Georgie was no longer comfortable in his company. The problem was that he had no idea what to do.

She covered her mouth and yawned. "If you will excuse me, I am going to rest for a bit."

"Yes, of course," Adeline said, and he and Littleton got to their feet. "We shall see you at dinner."

They took their seats when she disappeared through the

door. Once Gavin was certain she was gone, he glanced at Littleton. "Perhaps this was a bad idea."

"No!" Lady Littleton and Adeline pronounced at the same time.

"She was merely not expecting you," Adeline said. "In fact, she had convinced herself you no longer cared. If you did in the first place." This last bit was said in a harder tone.

"Of course I care about her." For some reason, he sat up a little straighter. It had been a long time since he'd had to answer to anyone. Yet convincing Adeline that he truly wanted Georgie was essential to getting her to marry him. "She is the only lady with whom I wish to spend the rest of my life." He wondered how far he should go . . . Well, she was a married lady. "She is the only one I can imagine waking up to. To having my children with."

She tilted her head as if she could see him better from a different angle. "But you do not love her."

"If there was any woman I could love, it would be her." Gavin had to make her understand. "I can't put my—"

She held up her hand, silencing him. "Frits told me about your father." She rose, causing Littleton and Gavin to stand. "I cannot say that I understand you. On the other hand, I shall not stand in your way . . . Yet." Adeline narrowed her eyes. "If I see you harm her in any way, you will no longer be welcome at Littlewood."

"That is more than fair." And a good deal more than he expected from a friend of Georgie's.

As Adeline left the terrace, Lady Littleton waved her hand toward the tray. "Finish your sandwich. I have a great deal to do before tomorrow."

He'd taken a rather large bite and had to swallow it before asking, "What is going on tomorrow?"

She gave him a wide, innocent look. That usually meant she was scheming. "Did I not tell you?"

He shook his head as she expected him to. "The dowager Viscountess Featherton and the dowager Duchess of Bridgewater are joining us."

Littleton barked a laugh and slapped Gavin on his back when he choked. "Georgie's grandmother?"

"Indeed. My daughter-in-law is not the only one who is concerned about Georgie's future."

Gavin ran his finger between his collar and his neck. He didn't even want to think about what the three older ladies would get up to while he was trying to court Georgie. Maybe he should prostrate himself at their feet and ask for their help. Then again, that might not be a bad idea. He obviously needed all the assistance he could get.

Georgie had been pacing the parlor in the rooms she had been given since she'd reached their sanctuary. Although the sun was sinking, light still filtered through the mullioned lacework that decorated the top of the long casement windows, making patterns on the large Turkish rug. If only she'd had some notice that Turley was arriving, she could have been more prepared. As it was, she'd made a fool of herself, exhibiting no conversation and acting like a frightened child. She could absolutely not continue in this manner. If only she knew how to respond to his presence. Perhaps she would have to be blunt and explain that she could not marry a man who did not love her?

A light tap sounded on the door to Georgie's parlor. Smith opened it and stood aside as Adeline swept into the room.

"I did not think you would be resting." She sounded pleased to have been right. "How are you doing?"

Georgie shrugged. "I wish I knew."

"I can tell you that he does want very much to marry you." Georgie pulled a face. "Yet he is still haunted by his father."

In an attempt to help, Littleton had told Adeline who in turn told Georgie about the mess the former Lord Turley had made of everything after his wife had died. "I understand why he thinks he should not love his wife, but I do not understand how one can stop oneself from falling in love." And that was the essence of the matter. Georgie firmly believed that love was the thing that held two people together during difficult times. She began pacing the room again, changing directions so as not to wear a path in the rug. "Do I give him another chance? Or would I be wasting my time? If he is so certain he will not love his wife, I do not see what I can do to change his mind."

Adeline's forehead creased in thought. "Allowing him until the end of the month to convince you would still give you time to go back to Town before the Season ends, and it would answer your questions."

"I suppose you are correct." Georgie stopped pacing. Why was this so hard? She closed her eyes and reached deep into her heart. There was a chance that there might be another gentleman out there who was even more perfect for her than Lord Turley only because this unknown gentleman loved her. But until she knew for certain that Turley would never love her, she would give him an opportunity to prove himself. "I shall give him one more chance."

"I need to tell you one more bit of information." This time her friend had a wicked grin on her face. "Your grandmother and her friend the duchess arrive tomorrow. They are staying with Mama-in-law."

"And Turley." Georgie felt her eyes widen. "Oh my. That will be interesting. What I would not give to hear what they have to say to him."

"That is exactly what I thought," her friend agreed. "Frits has suggested that he be allowed to come here as often as he wishes in order to court you. Do you have any objections?"

Georgie began pacing again. For some reason, she could not remain still. Littlewood really was the perfect place for a courtship. Other than the house party entertainments, they could spend time out of the eyes of the *ton*. It would give her—them—both the opportunity to attempt to resolve the differences in what they each wanted in a marriage. "No." She wondered what role her grandmother and the duchess would play. "No. I have no objections." Having a course of action would, at the very least, help her shake off the malaise she had been experiencing. "In fact, I believe I am looking forward to seeing how he intends to convince me I should enter into a loveless marriage."

"That is a very interesting way to put it." Adeline tapped a finger against her chin. "Somehow I do not think Lord Turley would describe what he wishes for in a marriage in exactly that fashion."

Georgie studied her friend, and wondered what Turley had said that Adeline was not sharing. "What else would one call a marriage not based upon love?"

"And that is an extremely good question." Adeline's eyes sparkled with mischief. "One you should pose to him when the time is right."

"And one he will have to answer if he wishes to make

me his wife." And his response was what Georgie would insist on hearing.

Adeline wiggled her fingers as she left the parlor, and Georgie went to the window seat. She had thought she'd known Turley, but did she truly? He had written to her—via her father, of course—over the summer asking for help with his tenants. And she had responded—via her father's secretary—giving him the advice he needed. Those letters had led her to believe that she knew him. Yet, obviously, she did not. Georgie had not, for example, known what he wanted in a marriage. How deep did his fear that he would turn out like his father go? If he did find himself in love with her, would he turn that against her?

She blew out a puff of breath. There were too many questions and not enough answers. And the only way to find out what she wanted to know was to spend more time with him. But that took her right back where she began. The only thing to do was to be prepared for anything.

Chapter Nine

Gavin rode alongside Lady Littleton's coach as they traveled the short distance to The Lilacs. From what she'd said, he'd got the impression that it was a small manor house and was surprised when they entered a drive lined with linden trees. At the end of the drive was a house built in the same Elizabethan manner as Littlewood, and not nearly as small as he'd thought it would be. Mullioned windows on all three floors reflected the sun, and in the middle of the circular drive was a flowerbed of seasonal blooms surrounded by boxwood edging.

He dismounted from his horse as a footman hurried out to help her ladyship out of the carriage. "This is a beautiful house."

"It is, isn't it?" Her eyes lit up as she looked up at the building. "I think I like it all the better because it belongs to me."

Her remark took him by surprise. He'd never thought about the fact that ladies frequently did not own the property in which they resided. No matter the changes and improvements a female made to a house, it belonged to her husband. And in most cases, the lady had to depart the main house when he died or her son married.

"Come along. Cook might be able to provide some refreshment."

"Give Lord Turley the large apartments in the front," her ladyship said to Crothers as she strode through the door and handed him her gloves and bonnet.

"Yes, my lady. Where would you like tea served?"

"In the morning room. It is becoming a little chilly for the terrace."

When the butler left, Gavin decided it was time to ask the one question that had been on his mind. "Why are Miss Featherton's grandmother and friend visiting as well?"

"My dear boy, if you require assistance in bringing her up to scratch, you will have need of them. First, though, you will have to convince them you are serious about Georgie." He followed as she entered the still bright morning room. But as he looked around it was clear that the brightness seemed to come more from the color of the walls, that resembled a newly ripened peach, than the windows. "I've never seen a color like this."

Her ladyship gave a satisfied smile. "It was not easy to achieve. I had a painter mix the color I wanted. We had several misses before he got the desired result. Then he had to work with the house painter to create a paint suitable for the walls. I am glad you like it."

Gavin took in the cream-colored trim on the windows and French doors, both of which had curtains decorated with a fruit and flower motif on a cream background. He wondered if Georgie would like something in the same vein at Rivercrest. "I do like it. Very much."

Crothers brought in the tea tray and set it on the low

table between two couches then left. "How am I supposed to persuade the ladies that my feelings for Georgie are honest?"

Her ladyship lifted a brow. "By being forthright. Neither of them are fools."

"I did not think they would be," he grumbled to himself. His luck wasn't running in that direction.

"I have already taken the liberty of informing them about your father and your fear you will do as he did."

"Of course you did." Gavin breathed the words more than said them. At the rate this was going, the whole world would know of his fears.

"What did you say?"

"Nothing." He took a seat on the sofa opposite the one Lady Littleton occupied. "Er, thank you for relieving me of that responsibility."

"I thought it would be helpful." She handed him a cup and pushed the plate of biscuits toward him.

There was entirely too much thinking going on. If he'd only not let Georgie think of that question, he'd be betrothed and looking forward to soon having a wife. "When tomorrow do you expect them to arrive?"

"Sometime before noon. The duchess does not travel well. You might want to find something to occupy yourself until later in the day."

Or the day after that. "Frits said I could spend my days at Littlewood."

"Just remember to break your fast before you depart. I seem to remember your being rather surly in the mornings before you had eaten."

Leave it to her to recall something from his childhood. And what was sauce for the gander was sauce for the goose.

Or something like that. *She* never even came down to breakfast. "That was when I was twelve!"

The cup hovered in front of her face, hiding her expression. "You were not twelve this past August."

He crunched into a ginger biscuit, chewed, and swallowed. "My valet usually brings me toast and tea when I awaken."

The eyebrow rose again. "I am aware. However, that reminds me to instruct my cook to have it prepared."

There was no point in attempting to get anything past her ladyship. Now that he thought about it, it was while he was visiting Frits that toast and tea began to appear in the mornings. Gavin mustered all the dignity he could after being treated like a little boy again. "Thank you." Setting down his cup, he stood. "I shall see you at dinner."

"I would send a note to Littlewood advising them of when in the morning you will arrive. You do not wish to get there and find Georgie is elsewhere."

"That is what I was going to do." Or he was now. Her ladyship was correct. If Georgie wished to lead Gavin a dance, she'd be up and gone before he arrived at Littlewood. He only wished he knew how she planned to handle his being around much of the time.

When he reached his chamber that turned out to be a set of three rooms, he found an already trimmed pen, paper, and everything else he required. Bearing in mind his instructions, he dashed off a note to his friend stating that he would arrive after breakfast and asking that a message be passed on to Georgie asking her if she would like to ride with him if she did not have any other plans. Frits had an excellent stable and could easily find a horse for her.

* * *

That evening Georgie and Adeline were enjoying an excellent claret when Frits strolled into the Littlewood drawing room holding a piece of paper. "Georgie, Turley would like to know if you have the time to ride with him after we break our fast in the morning."

He certainly was not wasting any time. "I do wish to go for a ride." She glanced at Adeline. "There is no reason I can think of that I cannot respond to the note myself."

"Nor I." Adeline gave her husband an approving smile. "Although, I think he was quite proper in addressing his letter to Frits. Do you not agree?"

"Yes." It was odd having Adeline, who was a month younger than Georgie, and Frits, who had had the reputation of a rake, in charge of her and performing the duty so diligently. Addressing an invitation to him was the right thing to do. Then again, Turley was always proper. Georgie had thought it charming, but now she wondered if it was because he did not love her and felt no real urgency to marry her. Yes, she knew that he wanted to wed her, but there had to be more than simply wanting to make a lady a wife. Neither Kit nor Hawksworth, Meg's husband, had been exactly proper when they'd been courting Mary and Meg. Georgie glanced at Frits hovering over Adeline. In fact, Frits had not been proper when he had courted her. Perhaps observing the proprieties was what one did when one did not wish to become too close to another person. After all, formality did not breed intimacy.

Georgie sighed to herself. The only thing she could do was see how their ride went in the morning.

The first clear rays of the October sun had yet to reach the windows when Georgie awakened the next morning and pulled back the bed curtains. The only sign that it would make an appearance at all was a gentle lightening of the bedchamber. It seemed as if the sun was rising later each day, but Georgie's mind refused to change the time it decided to awaken.

A maid quietly opened the door and started the fire.

Georgie leaned over. "Do you happen to know the time?"

The maid jumped, probably startled by being addressed at this hour. "Not quite six thirty, miss." The maid picked up her bucket. "Do you wish me to call your dresser?"

Not late at all. She collapsed back against her pillows. "No, thank you."

She tried to go back to sleep but Morpheus refused to cooperate. Flinging back the covers, she threw her legs over the side of the bed and tugged the bell-pull. If she could not sleep, she might as well get ready for the day. Padding over to the window, she opened it and stuck her head out. Birds sang and a soft breeze caressed her cheeks. Hmmm. Even this early the weather boded well for a relatively warm day. She hoped it would last.

She had finished her ablutions when Smith entered from the dressing room. "I thought you might want to dress in your riding habit instead of changing after breakfast." She held up an emerald green nankeen riding habit—one a bit nicer than the one Georgie usually used—and a red velvet riding habit. "It seems like a nice day. I recommend the green."

"I think that will be perfect for today." Even though her thoughts warred between wanting Turley to fall in love with her and wanting not to care what he thought, she did wish to look her best. Georgie noticed a small tray with a pot of tea, a small pitcher of milk, sugar, and one piece of toast. "Thank you."

Smith draped the green habit across a chair. "I thought you might be a bit peckish if you had to wait another hour to break your fast. Let me put this other one away, and we'll get you dressed. You can eat while I'm putting your hair up."

An hour later, Georgie met Adeline going to the stair. "Good morning."

Adeline grimaced. "I should have stayed in bed longer."

That did not sound good, or like her. Georgie saw her friend's hand go to her stomach. "What is wrong?"

"Not wrong. It is only that the baby has recently begun to move. He feels like a small fish swimming around. Unfortunately, I kept waking up when he moved. It is so light, poor Frits cannot feel him."

She felt sorry for her friend's interrupted sleep. "Have something to eat and take a nap. That, I have been told, is one of the benefits of carrying a child."

Adeline looked unconvinced. "I have a great deal to do, but I suppose an hour would not hurt." She looped her arm through Georgie's. "It is quite likely that Lord Turley will join us for breakfast."

Georgie's breath rushed out of her body leaving her a bit dizzy, and she was grateful she had already eaten something. "Oh . . . Well, I do not suppose it matters. I would have seen him soon in any event."

They reached the hall and stepped off the bottom tread in unison. "Georgie, you do not have to see him if you do not wish. I am perfectly capable of telling Frits that he must go back to Town."

That was tempting. Tempting but cowardly. "No. I want to know if we have a chance of a future together, and now is the time to do it. When we are not around dozens of other people."

Adeline's brows furrowed. "It will not be for long." Then she grinned. "This evening is the 'grand dinner.'"

"Oh my, yes." Georgie chuckled. "I wonder just who exactly Mary and Amanda have invited. Neither of us thought to ask."

"We should ask if Lord Turley knows." They turned down the corridor to the breakfast room. "After all, he has just come from Town and must have all recent goings-on."

As if they were not kept au courant by their friends. "I suppose what he hears will be different from what either Henrietta or Dorie write to us about."

Adeline patted Georgie's hand. "Here we are."

She straightened her already straight shoulders and stepped into the room. As her friend had said, Turley was present and in the process of sitting when he saw them. "Good morning, my lady, Miss Featherton." Frits pulled the chair out next to him for Adeline, then proceeded to make a plate for her. Turley held a chair out. "Please." His expression was contrite and his tone—oh, "pleading" was not the word, but it was clear he wished her to sit next to him.

This was all a little awkward, but it could have been worse. "Thank you, I wish to get my breakfast first."

"Yes, of course." He stood back and waited while she picked up her plate and added coddled eggs and a slice of beef to it. As soon as she walked the three steps back to the table, he took her plate and set it on the table then waited to seat her.

"Thank you." Before she could reach for the rack of toast, he placed it in front of her. "How did you know that was what I wanted?"

"It was the way you looked at it." He grinned. "It was either tea or toast."

"Indeed." She found herself grinning in response. "If I did not get to the toast before my brothers, I would have to wait until the next rack was ready." She cut her toast into three pieces as was her custom. "Would you like me to pour?"

"If you would please." He slid his cup and saucer to her.

She was well aware that he liked his tea with no sugar and was surprised when she saw him add two lumps. Turley slid a shy glance to her. "I drink my morning tea sweet."

Georgie fought down a blush. This was the first time they had taken breakfast together. Yet, it was something they had in common. "I do as well."

"I must beg your pardon for showing up without an invitation but when I went down to the breakfast room at The Lilacs, I was informed breakfast would not be for at least another hour."

Adeline waved one hand in front of her face and covered her mouth with the other as she yawned. "I had a feeling you might join us."

"That is it, my love," Frits said. "Directly after we eat, you are going back to bed. Our daughter needs to learn not to keep her mother up."

Adeline raised her chin. "And how do you know it is not a son?"

Frits appeared offended on behalf of the entire male species. "If it is, I'll be sure to teach him the proper way to treat his mother."

Georgie brought her hand up to hide her laughter, and Turley caught her eyes, his pale blue ones dancing with mirth. "You do realize that this little one is not due to make an appearance until March?"

"It's going to be a very long five months at this rate," Turley added.

"I am sure he or she will calm down or you will learn to sleep through the movement," Georgie said. "My sister did. She said the only reason it kept her awake at first was because the feeling was new and strange."

"It is that." Adeline took a sip of tea. "At first it felt as if fish were swimming around, now it feels more substantial."

Frits leaned down and spoke firmly to her stomach. "You must allow your mother to rest."

Georgie could hold her laughter in no longer, nor could Adeline and Turley as they all went into whoops.

Fanning her face with her hand, Georgie tried to get herself under control. "I am s-s-sure that will have the desired effect."

Between bouts of laughter, they finally finished eating, and Frits carried Adeline up the stairs.

"We had better be going." Turley stood and helped Georgie rise. "At some point they will remember that they left us alone."

"I suppose you are correct. Give me a moment to don my hat and fetch my gloves. I shall meet you in the hall."

Turley walked with her to the main staircase. "I'll be here waiting."

She made herself ascend the stairs calmly as if she had all the composure in the world when her heart was racing, urging her to hurry back to him. Drat it all! She had not wanted that reaction. When she turned into the corridor, she raced to her chambers. "Smith—"

"Here you are, Miss Georgie." Her maid pinned the small cap with a long feather that curled on her cheek to her hair and handed her the heavier gloves she used for riding. "Have a good time, and be careful."

Georgie returned to the hall with as much grace as she could. She would not allow herself to betray her feelings for him. That would not do at all. "My lord." She placed her hand in his palm. "Shall we?"

Turley tucked her hand in the crook of his arm. "Do you know we have never ridden together?"

"I am aware of that. There was no reason to bring Lilly to Town. She would have been miserable having to keep to a sedate walk, and my mother would not allow early morning rides."

"A pity, that." He angled them toward the stables. "You must have missed riding."

"More than you know." Turley probably had not even known she liked to ride. "Lilly is a very special horse. I was there when she was born."

"You saw the birth?" His head snapped back as if he was aghast as well he should be. Even Georgie did not know any gently born young ladies who attended a horse birth.

"Not that, but I saw her shortly after the event." She recalled how amazed they all were at the little white filly with matching black socks, ears, and nose. "I knew immediately she would be mine."

"I look forward to seeing her," Turley said. "And riding with you."

Now that she thought of it, she had never seen him ride either. Unlike Frits, he had always taken his carriage. "And I with you."

When they reached the stable, a large bay stood next to Lilly. Both horses were saddled and Johnson was waiting for them. Georgie felt like giggling. She was not sure she had been this well chaperoned at home.

Chapter Ten

Gavin had been admiring the way the green habit fit over Georgie's upper curves and regretted that the fashions didn't allow him to see her other curves as well. When the older groom led out his horse, he stifled the curse rising to his lips. For whatever reason, he'd got it into his head that he and Georgie would be alone this morning. But naturally, Frits would have a groom, and Johnson of all people, accompany them. He'd been the same groom who had accompanied Littleton and Gavin when they were children. The man never missed a thing. Not that Gavin planned on trying anything inappropriate with Georgie. He simply did not like having his every movement watched. He blew out a breath. They might have a chaperone, but he would still be able to help her onto the mare. His hands tingled in anticipation of circling her waist and tossing her up onto the saddle. Gavin moved closer to Georgie's mare. When she came around the horse, he stepped forward, but before he could act, the mare knelt, enabling her to mount without his assistance.

Hell and damnation!

This ride was not going at all how he'd expected it to, and they had not even started yet.

Gavin's frustration rose with the mare, but he managed to maintain an outward calm. "I've never seen a horse do that before." Outside of Astley's Amphitheatre, that was. "Who taught her?"

"I did with help from my brother-in-law." Georgie straightened her skirt. "Shall we go?"

"Er, yes." He went back to his horse, Lochinvar, and swung up onto the saddle. "Where do you want to ride?"

With a mere shift in her legs, Georgie coaxed her mare to walking. Gavin had had no idea she was such an experienced rider.

She glanced around as if trying to decide, then shrugged. "You know the area better than I do. I shall follow your lead."

Knowing women, that was probably the first and only time he'd hear her say that. "Would you like to have a good gallop?"

The smile that lit her face combined the sun and all the stars. If he had known how happy being on a horse made her, he'd have insured she had a chance to ride in Town. "That would be lovely."

Johnson followed them out of the stable yard. "Mind now, miss, none of your tricks unless you let me know."

Tricks? What the devil did the groom mean by tricks?

When Gavin slid his eyes to her, she had a guilty look on her face. "I shall be sure you have prior warning."

The groom grunted, but fell silent as they quickened to a trot.

Still, she must have done something she should not have. "What was he talking about?"

Georgie's deep blue eyes opened wide. "Nothing very

much. Lilly and I practice certain things I have trained her to do. Johnson was just a little uneasy when he saw them the first time." She pulled a face. "I have promised to warn him when we do them again."

Things? "Such as?"

"Hawksworth, my brother-in-law, wanted to teach me how to make myself safer when I was riding." Her evasiveness did not ease Gavin's mind.

"Perhaps you can show me." He'd like to see what sorts of contrivances she was talking about.

"Perhaps I shall." Her lips tilted up slightly, convincing him that she had definitely not told him nearly what he wanted to know. "However, now I would like to gallop."

He was leading them over a meadow of tall grass that was still resplendent with wildflowers. "There is a path that goes through the wood and thence to the town that has a nice straight piece that is long enough to race without worrying about one's horse stepping into a rabbit hole."

The day was rapidly growing warmer and they took their time crossing fields of newly harvested crops until they reached the path. Georgie and her mare rode as if they were one. Gavin had never seen a lady with a better seat and very few men. A stream ran along one side of the road and they stopped to water their horses.

Jumping off Lochinvar, Gavin ran to Georgie before she could make Lilly kneel again. "Allow me to help you."

Her sharp and wary blue eyes searched his face before she inclined her head. "Very well."

As soon as she unhooked her leg from the pommel, he clasped his hands around her waist, making sure her foot was not caught in the stirrup. Gavin felt her breath quicken as he slowly lowered her feet to the ground. That was what he'd wanted, to feel her response to him. Georgie might not want him as much as he desired her, but she would if he had anything to say about it. The lacy scarf tucked into the habit's bodice didn't hide the rapid pulse in her throat. She tilted her head up to look at him, and he began to lean forward. Their lips were only inches away from each other's. He could almost feel the softness of her mouth—

"Good day for a ride," Johnson said in his laconic tone.

Blast it all!

Gavin had completely forgotten the groom was with them. With the spell broken, she stepped back. "Yes, it is." The mare swung her head around to look at him as if accusing him of doing something he should not. "Are you done, girl?"

Georgie backed up again and waited while Gavin got his horse. "Shall we race?"

He was relieved to see her smile again. "I would love to race. Adeline may no longer ride and Frits is always busy."

That was the best piece of news Gavin had had since he arrived. But, once again, before he could reach her, Lilly kneeled and Georgie mounted the mare. He'd need to be much faster if he hoped to get to her before she mounted by herself.

Georgie was not going to let Turley hold her again. At least not until they had worked out what was going on between the two of them. The feel of his palms still burned into her waist, and if Johnson had not been there Turley would have kissed her and, drat her, she would have allowed him. It was definitely not safe to be alone with him. She did not think he would attempt to compromise her. She could not have fallen in love with him if he was a rogue. Still, it was better not to allow herself to be put in a position where she might be tempted to do something she ought not do. On the other hand, he had never before attempted to kiss her. And part of her, well, a great deal of her hoped he'd try again. Her sister had once said that a marriage needed passion, and she wondered if she would enjoy his kiss.

She led Lilly back to the path, trying not to look at him, but good Lord, he was a handsome man. She bit down on her lip before turning to face him. "I take it this is where you wish to race?"

"Yes. It's nice and straight here until the bend." He pointed to a place far down the road.

Georgie gazed in the direction he indicated. "I can barely see it from here." She glanced around, pleased to find no hedgerows. There was a sparse planting of trees to one side and a meadow beyond. On the other side was the river. Neither would prove dangerous if one fell from a horse. "It is almost perfect."

Turley flashed her a boyish grin. "We used to think so. Isn't that right, Johnson?"

The groom was sitting on the grass with his back against a tree. "Aye, it is, Master Gavin."

Georgie could not stop the laughter that came bubbling out. "I see he is used to you and Frits and your antics."

"When we were boys." Turley narrowed his gaze at the groom. "But that was a long time ago."

"Not that long ago. Remember it like it was yesterday, I do." Johnson tapped his nose. "And that's a good thing too. Won't be long afore I have another young'un to train to a pony."

Now, that was interesting. "I had no idea you and Frits learned to ride together."

Turley swung onto his horse in one fluid movement, and her heartbeat quickened. "My mother and his mother were great friends. We used to spend a lot of time together as boys."

"That must have been wonderful." Georgie's best friends were her sisters—when they were not squabbling. "I would have loved to have had a good friend when I was growing up."

His brow furrowed. "Why didn't you?"

"There were no girls around my age, and I did not attend school." Then she smiled. "I had my sisters, and I do have good friends now, and that is what matters."

Turley gazed at her with a considering look. "I had not thought of it before, but my sister was in the same position of not having friends when she was growing up. Unfortunately, we had no other brothers or sisters. It was just the two of us." He gave himself a shake. "Are you ready to race?"

That was more than he had ever told her about himself. What more could she learn while they were here? "Yes. Let's race. On the count of three?"

"Johnson?" Gavin called.

"Aye, Master Gavin." A smile cracked the groom's weathered face. "One, two, three."

Lilly threw her heart into the race and they ran neck and neck until the end. Georgie brought her mare to a walk. "That was fun!"

"She's a lot faster than I thought she would be." Turley gave Lilly a long appraisal. "What is her lineage?"

"She is a descendant of Eclipse. Her mother is descended from the Byerley Turk." Georgie leaned over and stroked Lilly's neck. "I had the opportunity to have her trained to race, but I decided I would rather she remain my riding horse."

"I can almost understand that." Turley gave Georgie a rueful grin. What gentleman would not want such a horse to race? Fortunately, neither her father nor brother were interested in the sport. "Yet, you two appear to have a strong bond. I doubt she would have been a happy race-horse."

She could not but agree. "I think you are right. She much prefers to be a pampered hack." They turned by mutual consent and walked the horses back to the start of the path. His horse, although much larger, was a good match with Lilly. "Would you like to have one more race?"

"I'd like that." He glanced at Lilly and sighed. "What I could have done with a horse like her."

Georgie chuckled. "I will eventually breed her. Perhaps you would like one of her offspring."

He took several moments before he responded. "Per-haps."

When they returned Johnson seemed to be asleep. "We will have to count for ourselves."

Turley glanced at the sleeping groom. "Don't be so sure about that. Let's start back down the lane and see what he does."

They had not got the length of a horse when the older man said, "If you're goin' back, you'll have to wait for me."

Once again, Georgie started to chuckle. She had not laughed so much in a long time, and it felt good. "I think Lord Turley was teaching me a lesson. You see, I thought you were sleeping. We have decided to race one more time."

"Well then." The groom gave Turley an approving look. "Get ready, and I'll count."

On the count of three Georgie gave Lilly her head. The mare dashed down the track but Lochinvar stayed right with her until just before the bend in the road when he drew ahead. The mare gave a neigh and tossed her head. "She doesn't seem happy that your horse won."

But Turley wasn't paying attention to her. "What is it?"

"I don't know." He shook his head slowly. "There is a coach attempting to turn around."

Riding forward so she could see the vehicle better, Georgie glanced from him to the carriage. "Should we ask if they require assistance?"

For a brief moment he stilled, and his jaw tightened. "No. We shall wait here and make sure they do not require help."

There was something he was not telling her. "What is it?"

One of the footmen looked behind him and gave a salute before he jumped down, turned the horses around so they were facing in the right direction, then returned to the back of the vehicle. For a moment the crest on the side was visible, but the only thing Georgie could make out was a serpent.

"Nothing." Turley gave her a smile meant to reassure, but it did not. "Nothing at all. We should go back to the house. It will soon be time for luncheon."

Mostly due to Frits's appetite and Adeline's need for nourishment in the middle of the day, luncheon was always served. "Yes, I suppose we must."

"We can use the roads," Turley said as he watched the vehicle make its way slowly away from them and toward the town. "It's longer, but the horses don't have the energy they did earlier."

This was ridiculous. He was obviously not happy about

the coach, and if it was a danger of some sort, she had a right to know. "What about the carriage is bothering you?"

He pressed his lips together in a thin line. "The owner. I do not particularly like him."

She made a *come on* motion with her hand. "And why is that?"

Turley started his horse back down the lane. "I can't tell you exactly what it is as it is not my story to tell, but I do not trust the man."

Well, that was all well and good, but she was still in the dark about the identity of the gentleman. Georgie almost rolled her eyes. "What about him do you not like? Is he a ravisher of young ladies? Does he have a gambling habit?" Turley smiled at that which just made Georgie more determined to ferret out the story. "Is he a fortune hunter?"

"As far as I know he is none of the things you have mentioned." He stopped as if wrestling with his words. "Let us simply say that he did something a long time ago that hurt a friend of a friend, and a lady was involved. She was also harmed."

"That is clear as mud." Well, possibly a bit clearer. Still it did not tell her what she wished to know. "If he is in the neighborhood, is he someone to whom I should give the cut direct?"

"Not unless you wish to create talk." His tone was as dry as the sand at Brighton.

If Georgie had not been riding she would have thrown up her hands. Why did gentlemen always think they needed to take care of ladies by not giving them information? Although, deep inside she knew there were several reasons they did so. "Very well. I shall not cut him. Not that I could as I do not know who he is. Unless, of course, I see his carriage again."

Turley grinned again. "I really cannot tell you his name. Not that I think you would gossip, I do not. But unless he misbehaves in some way, which he has not for a very long time, I would not want to defame him." He captured her eyes with his gaze. "Unless something changes, can you live with that?"

"I suppose I have no choice." Until she had an opportunity to look for the crest. There were most likely not many that had a serpent on them.

By the time they returned to their starting point, Johnson was on his horse. "Ye ready to go back, are ye?"

Turley nodded. "I cannot miss luncheon."

The groom smirked. "No, I don't suppose ye can, and Miss Georgie don't be needing to miss a meal."

Miss Georgie? "Have you been speaking with my maid?"

"Ye're coachman," the groom answered unabashed.

She thought he had gone back to Town, not that she had inquired. "He is still here?"

"Yes, miss. Has quarters over the coach house. His orders were to stay here in case ye wanted to leave."

"Oh." That had been nice of her father or whoever it had been. "Thank you for telling me."

"I take it that you didn't know," Turley said.

"I had not even thought about it." Although, now that she had it made sense. The coachman would have gone back to Town and waited to be summoned. "And I have had no reason to visit the coach house. But now that I do know, I will not have to bother asking Adeline if she wishes to go to the market town with me. I can simply take my maid and go by myself." That reminded her of something. "I suppose my footman remained as well."

"Not that I know of, miss. I ain't seen any footmen in strange livery."

"That is too bad. If they left me the coach, they should have left me a footman. Now I shall still be required to request one from Adeline." A smiled played at the corners of Turley's lips. "What?"

"It just occurred to me that if you had both a coachman and a footman, you would be able to come and go as you please. I doubt that under the circumstances that would make Littleton or Adeline very comfortable."

He was probably right about that. Both her friends had been taking their positions as de facto guardians seriously. "I shall have you know that I am not subject to piques of fits that would cause me to go rushing off without consulting them."

He looked at her as if he could see right through her. "But what if they had disagreed with you?"

"I will have you know that I am very even tempered." Most of the time. In general, it took a great deal to upset her. Although, Turley seemed successful at it.

"I do not doubt the truth of that, but at times anyone can be pushed beyond their limits."

She glanced at him. He was much more perceptive than she had given him credit. "Very true. We all have our limits."

Georgie wondered if she would discover what hers were or, perhaps more importantly, what Turley's limits were.

Chapter Eleven

Marc Lytton glanced out the window of his coach and was surprised to see Miss Featherton mounted on a gray horse staring at him. She spoke to someone he was unable to see before his coachman had the carriage turned. He turned to his valet. "Where are we?"

"I shall inquire, my lord." The servant stood, opened the roof-hatch, and spoke with the driver. "We turned onto the wrong road, my lord. Lord Bottomley's estate is in the direction we are now heading."

Marc bit back the scathing remarks that sprang to his tongue. "In other words, he has no idea."

"That is what I gathered, my lord. The person from whom he received directions apparently mentioned so many times not to turn this way that turning down this lane stuck in the coachman's head." His valet appeared to consider that for a moment. "I can ask again, my lord."

"No. We'll soon be at our destination. I would like you to make inquiries after we arrive."

"As you wish." The servant reclaimed his seat on the backward-facing bench.

His coachman's family had served his family for multiple generations. Unfortunately, the man was good-natured and loyal, but not very quick-witted.

A few minutes later, Marc noticed that the road broadened and soon they passed a gate. His thoughts turned back to Miss Featherton. Then it occurred to him that Turner had said she was visiting Lady Littleton. As the lane was clearly not the main road to Littleton's estate, it had to be a back entrance. Marc wondered if she often rode in that area. If so, it might behoove him to make a point of discovering if she had a schedule. He could easily borrow a hack from Bottomley and pretend to run into her. Not only that, but she would be at the house party. That was, after all, the main reason Marc had left Town for the week.

His coach drew up in front of a substantial red-brick manor house that had been added onto by virtue of a one-story addition to one side of the house. The addition was well built with many long windows, but it gave the rest of the structure a lopsided appearance.

Large, wooden double doors opened and several footmen clamored down the steps. Standing in front of the door was a tall silver-haired man dressed in a black suit. Obviously, the butler. By the time the coach door was opened and the steps let down, the butler was at the carriage.

Once Marc had reached the ground, the man bowed. "My lord, welcome to Bottomswood. His lordship was afraid he would miss your arrival and bid me to tell you that you will be dining with Lord and Lady Turner this evening. I have arranged for a bath to be set up in your apartment, and a cold collation to be sent up. If there is anything else you require, please advise me."

"Thank you. I shall send my valet, Ridgeon, if I require anything else."

The man bowed again. "Allow me to escort you to your rooms."

Marc inclined his head and followed the servant into the house and up the stairs. He made a point to notice the good repair of the house and furnishings. He'd need to marry well in order to keep his house in such good order. Thus far, his aunt had not selected a wife, but if he did not find one soon he had no doubt the old besom would be happy to involve herself. And that was the last thing he wanted.

From what he'd gathered, the only lady of excellent breeding and a fat dowry attending the house party was Miss Featherton. Marc would simply have to find a way to attach her affections or her attention before the week was over. The idea of a wife being selected for him left a sour feeling in his stomach.

When Gavin and Georgie reached the stables, he was surprised to discover that she insisted on rubbing down and brushing her horse.

She took the currycomb from a stable boy. "Thank you, Jamie." Then she turned back to Gavin as he was wondering how she had remembered one stable boy from another. Littleton must have dozens of them. "My old groom—he is our stable master now—told me that I should get in the habit of grooming her myself. By doing so it would make her feel closer to me."

Picking up another brush, he started to rub down his horse. "That sounds like good advice. Did he teach you to saddle her yourself?"

"Yes," she said from the other side of her horse. "And, if the horse is already saddled, to look at the girth and make sure it is tight enough but not too tight."

"More good advice." He moved to Lochinvar's other side. "I had a pony that would puff out her stomach when she was being saddled."

"That could be dangerous." Georgie placed the comb on a nearby shelf and led the mare into a stall.

"She eventually came to trust me. I think someone had cinched her too tightly at one time." Gavin finished grooming his horse and put him in the stall next to Lilly.

He watched with appreciation as Georgie ran her palms over her mare's legs and stomach before lifting her hoofs and looking at the bottoms. "I knew something was off." She glanced at him. "Can you bring me the pick? There is a small stone I must remove before it causes her harm."

Gavin handed it to her. She made him feel like a shirker, but he knew one of the Littlewood grooms would be in to perform the duty. He waited until she was finished with the mare. "Are you ready?"

"I am." Georgie gave the horse an apple from a barrel kept in the stables. "I am hungry as well."

That was one of the many things he liked about her. He knew from what his sister had said that ladies were encouraged to eat sparingly when out. But even in Town, Georgie had not been afraid to eat. He winged his arm out and she took it. If he accomplished nothing else today, she had got over her initial reticence about being with him. Unfortunately, he still had a long way to go. He'd have to think about what he could do to make her wish to marry him. Perhaps it was time to show her a different side of himself. One that was not as formal.

Gavin and Georgie joined Frits and Adeline for a

substantial luncheon. After which, Adeline requested that Georgie help her with some plan for the nursery. That made Gavin wish Georgie was at his house redecorating that nursery.

Before she could rise, he pulled out her chair. "Would you like to go riding again tomorrow morning?"

Her blue gaze searched his eyes. He wished he knew what she was looking for. "Yes. I would like that."

"Thank you." He watched Georgie's graceful glide as she left the room. There was no point in staying here hoping he'd be able to spend more time with her today. "I shall see you this evening."

"As you wish." Frits walked with Gavin to the hall. "Do you want to accompany us to Lady Turner's dinner?"

He stared at his friend. "Lady Turner's dinner?"

"Yes." Frits nodded. "It is the first event of her house party. I am positive it is this evening. Come with me."

They entered a small office next to his friend's study, and spoke to a bespectacled older man sitting at the desk. "The dinner at Lady Turner's house is this evening, is it not?"

"Yes, my lord." The secretary picked up a card. "Yes, this evening." The man glanced at Gavin. "She added a note that Lord Turley is also invited."

His friend grinned. "I thought I was right." They strolled back to the corridor. "Will you ride with us?"

"Yes, thank you." Gavin would be stupid not to. Arriving with the Littletons and Georgie would give him more standing with her in the eyes of the other gentlemen present. He damn sure wasn't going to give anyone a chance to think she was free while he worked on a way to make her his wife. "What time should I arrive?"

"About six thirty. That will give us an opportunity to have a glass of wine before we depart."

"I shall see you then." They ambled back to Littleton's study before taking his leave. "Do you happen to know who the other gentlemen attending are?"

Littleton gave an irritating smirk. "Trying to find out who the competition is?"

Gavin knew there was no way his friend wouldn't know exactly what he was up to. "Wouldn't you do the same?"

"Of course. Unfortunately, I'm unable to help you. Adeline mentioned some of the ladies, but I don't remember meeting any of them. I believe Turner was responsible for inviting the gentlemen."

Turner? There was nothing wrong with the man but . . . "I do know that Bolingbroke is attending. Other than that, I imagine they will all be on the younger side."

Littleton nodded. "We're going to feel ancient."

"If they are all younger, then I won't have much to worry about. They'll flirt with Georgie, but none of them will likely be in the market for a wife."

"We will have to take their measure when we arrive." Littleton sat behind his desk. "If you do not mind, I have some work I must finish before this evening."

"I don't mind at all. I'll see you later." Gavin strode out of the door toward the stables, and saddled his horse again. He arrived at The Lilacs in time to see a traveling coach being led to the coach house. It looked as if Lady Featherton and her friend had arrived. He took his time going into the house and washed up before going down to see Lady Littleton and Georgie's grandmother. By the time he entered the room, they were having tea. "My lady."

"Ah, here you are." Her ladyship held out her hand as she greeted him. "Did you have a pleasant ride?"

"I did, indeed, and we are going again tomorrow morning. Frits asked if I wished to accompany them this evening. Apparently, Lady Turner is having a dinner to begin her house party." It occurred to Gavin again that he wished he knew who would be present at the house party. He hoped that Lytton had not been invited, but couldn't think of another reason for him to be in the area.

"Gavin." Lady Littleton glanced at the two other women. "You remember the Duchess of Bridgewater and Lady Featherton."

He pasted a smile on his face and bowed. "Your grace, my lady, it is a pleasure to see you again."

The smaller of the two women had sparkling lapis eyes that reminded him of Georgie's. But instead of dark hair, Lady Featherton's looked as if it had been blond. "I am happy that we will have the time to know you better."

The duchess harrumphed. "You are a good deal too forgiving, Lucinda. It remains to be seen if we are happy to know him." She fixed her sharp eyes on him, and he didn't dare move a muscle. "As far as I am concerned you have a great deal for which to answer."

That put him in his place. Fortunately, Lady Littleton waved him to a chair between the two couches the ladies occupied. "You will have time to interrogate him to your heart's content, Constance, but I shall give him a cup of tea first."

Brandy might be a better idea, but tea would do. "Thank you, my lady. I am rather parched."

He was in the process of taking his first sip of tea when Lady Featherton said, "Lady Littleton told us you had been riding with Georgie this morning."

"Yes." He balanced his cup on his leg, not at all certain he would be allowed to finish it. "After we returned we had luncheon with Frits and Adeline." He snatched another sip. "We have made plans to ride tomorrow morning as well." The duchess opened her mouth, but thinking he knew what she was going to say, he forestalled her. "Frits has ordered a groom to accompany us." The duchess nodded as if satisfied. It was rather odd that she took him in greater dislike than Georgie's grandmother. Although, that had not appeared to be the case at the musical evening. "May I ask what I did to incur your ire?"

The duchess glanced at Lady Featherton, who shrugged lightly. "You broke our Georgie's heart."

Broke her heart?

Gavin drained his cup and really wished it was brandy. Even after her question to him, it had not occurred to Gavin that *she* might be in love with *him*. Well, it had *occurred* to him, but he hadn't *known* she was. Good Lord. Now it all made sense. The way her friends had behaved toward him. Frits making sure they were chaperoned and the promises he had extracted from Gavin. Her hesitancy to see him. Apparently, her feelings toward him made her less likely to marry him unless he returned her sentiments. But even if he could not allow himself to love her he could—he *would* make her happy. He knew they were meant to be together. He glanced at the duchess and Lady Featherton.

"God save me from tedious young men," the duchess muttered.

"Not tedious, my dear." Lady Featherton patted the duchess's hand. "Merely featherbrained."

"And concerned," Lady Littleton added. "The question is what do we wish to do about it."

Three pairs of eyes focused on him. If there was a time to enlist their help, it was now. He merely had to convince them that marriage to him would be the best thing for Georgie. Her ladyship filled his cup again. "I have never before cared to whom or when I wed. But the more I got to know Miss Featherton the more I knew she was the one lady I wanted to be my wife and the mother of my children. We are . . . friends." He wasn't sure that was precisely correct. "Or rather we get on well and could be great friends." His throat closed as he thought about what else he wanted from her, and he took another drink of his tea. "I cannot imagine living with another lady." The women were still staring at him, seemingly unconvinced. "I"—he glanced at Lady Littleton, and she nodded encouragingly—"I feel great passion for her. If I could love anyone it would be her."

Her ladyship gave him an approving smile. "It is as I said."

He wished he knew exactly what she meant by that.

"I believe you are correct," Lady Featherton commented.

"I agree." The duchess set her cup down. "We shall see how this story will play out."

As if as one the ladies rose and walked out of the morning room. When the last slip of skirt had disappeared around the corner, he put his cup on the low table between the sofas, went over to the sideboard, and poured a brandy. He had a feeling they knew something he did not.

But what was it?

Chapter Twelve

Cristabel herded her friends up the lovely old split walnut staircase with carvings of woodland animals and birds on the newel posts and balusters. It was the staircase that had captured her the first time she saw the house. Once they were seated in her parlor, she poured them each a glass of claret. "Well?"

"I do agree that he is in love with her," Lucinda said as she strolled around the room looking out the windows. "It is a problem that he cannot see it himself."

"I do not know that that knowledge would be helpful at the moment," Constance added as she took a place on a wide French caned-back chair. "He's got it into his head that he cannot afford to love his wife." She drank some of the wine. "Yet, I believe that in time he will come to admit it."

"Then what happens?" This was the problem about which Cristabel had been concerned. "Will he run away from it and her?"

"Running away would be exceedingly awkward after they wed." Lucinda's tone was not usually so dry. She turned from a side window. "How lovely that you have windows on two sides of your parlor and a small balcony."

"It makes the room extremely pleasant in warm weather."

"Back to the matter at hand." Lucinda twirled the glass in her hands. "It appears as if we must find a way or bring about circumstances that will make him recognize his feelings for Georgie before he proposes again."

Constance rose to gaze out the windows as well. "Now that he knows she loves him, you do not think he will use it against her, do you?"

"In what way?" Having already seen the view out the windows over the gardens to a small lake in the distance many times, Cristabel made herself comfortable on a large chair covered in yellow velvet and put her feet up on the light brown leather ottoman.

Constance turned and leaned back against the wall. "By compromising her."

"I know for a fact he will not do any such thing." Cristabel was glad she'd had a frank conversation with her son about his duties toward Georgie. "Frits has made him promise he will not."

"Very well then." Lucinda sat on the chair Constance had abandoned. "We must engage in a concerted effort to bring about a marriage between the two of them. What do we know about this house party?"

"What are you thinking?" Constance moved to the sofa on Cristabel's other side.

"I think it would not be a bad thing for Lord Turley to have a little competition for her hand." A smile hovered around Lucinda's mouth. "If we knew who was going to be there we might be able to arrange—oh, some little machinations such as happened with Kit to bring him to the point with Mary."

Cristabel remembered the story about Georgie's older brother when he and his eventual wife were in Scotland.

The friends with whom they were residing decided to find a gentleman to make Kit jealous. He and Mary wed shortly thereafter. Cristabel was glad for her foresight. "I did have a conversation with the dowager Lady Turner, and she sent me a list of the guests. The gentlemen who will be staying at the house are the Earl of Bolingbroke, the Earl of St. Albans, the Marquis of Montagu, and Viscount Barfleur. The Earl of Lytton and Viscount Bottomley will be going over for the entertainments."

Constance leaned forward. "Lytton. I know his aunt."

Lucinda's brows came together. "Is she not the sour woman with gray hair who is always complaining about everything and everyone?"

"Yes. Lady Witten." Constance nodded. "I remember a story—it must be five years ago or more now—Lytton had contracted a marriage, but before the wedding could take place the lady's father died. Lady Witten told him if he married the young lady she would withhold his inheritance."

"He must have obeyed her." Cristabel did not think much of a gentleman who would jilt a lady. Still . . . "Why is she in such a powerful position?"

"The earldom has never been wealthy," Constance explained. "Lytton's mother was a considerable heiress, but her grandfather had made his money in trade. His father was apparently not good with finances, and the estate is still in need of funds. The marriage to the lady had been arranged by Lytton's mother, who was a good friend of the lady's mother. She was in Bath for her health when Lady Witten intervened. Apparently, Lady Witten's father left a great deal of money to his grandson if he married a lady of whom his aunt approved. You see, he had not approved of his son's marriage."

"And her ladyship did not approve of the young lady her nephew was to have wed?" Cristabel asked. This all sounded a bit Machiavellian.

Constance raised her brows. "She did not approve of the means of the father's death."

"Ah. Now I understand." There must have been a rumor that the gentleman had committed suicide. Cristabel shook her head. It was disgusting how some people played with the lives of others.

"You are saying," Lucinda said, "that Lytton will be looking for a wife. I must admit that after hearing he jilted a lady, I do not want him around Georgie."

"Neither will Lord Turley." Constance smiled smugly. "It might be just the thing to inform Lady Turner that Georgie is still looking for a husband."

Lucinda appeared thoughtful for a moment. "A hint in Lytton's ear?"

"What more do you know about what Lady Witten wants?" It seemed to Cristabel that there must be something else going on. "One would think that a woman as controlling as her ladyship would have already selected a wife for her nephew."

"Indeed." Constance nodded. "She has grown tired of Lytton's inability to find a wife and has decided upon a lady."

"And will the lady be at the house party?" Lucinda asked.

Constance turned to Cristabel. "Which ladies will be there?"

"I have no idea. I was only interested in the gentlemen. And as the party will begin this evening, does it really matter? I have arranged for us to visit the dowager Lady Turner. We will be able to discover who is there after we arrive."

"Excellent." Constance inclined her head. "I shall look forward to it."

Cristabel was as looking forward to it as well.

Georgie looked at herself in the mirror and made a face. "I shall be happy when I can wear colors other than white, yellow, and light green." The only exception was her red riding habit and only because she did not ride in Town. "I wonder if my mother will make an exception for next Season."

"You will have to ask her," came her maid's noncommittal reply.

Or if she married.

Georgie had never been happier that she had trained her mare to kneel than she had been today. The feel of Turley's hands around her waist sent her senses scurrying. It was too thrilling and tempting, and made her want to throw herself into his arms. She would like to think that she had enough love for both of them, but that was a poor way to enter into a marriage. And the time she had spent with him today made her wonder just how well she actually knew him. He seemed different. Lighter. As if he was not being weighed down by responsibilities. Was it the difference between his Town persona and the way he was in the country? Or had he put a distance between them because he had already decided he did not love her? Or would not allow himself to love her. Yet if that was the case why the difference in his behavior now? She stifled a sigh. If only she knew what to do. When she had first heard about the house party, Georgie had decided to forget Turley and get on with her life. But now that he was here she could not stop herself from hoping he would change his mind about loving her. Fortunately, her grandmother and the duchess were either already here or would be soon. She had received a short note informing her of their pending arrival.

"Miss, I'm done."

Smith's voice brought Georgie out of her reverie as the ornate marble and gold clock on the fireplace mantel struck the half hour. She rose. Smith placed a light pashmina wool shawl covered with images of colorful birds and flowers over Georgie's shoulders and handed her a pale yellow reticule. "There you are, Miss Georgie. Your gloves are in the reticule with your pins, fan, and handkerchief."

"Thank you." The shawl made her happier. "I do not think we will be too late."

"Not with as tired as her ladyship's been recently." Smith began straightening the toilet table.

Georgie really should have been in the drawing room before now, and she hurried down the stairs. Turley would be here soon, and she would rather be with Adeline when he arrived. As it was, just as Frits handed Georgie a glass of claret, the front door opened, and Turley could be heard greeting the butler.

"You look nervous." Adeline's tone was evidence of her concern.

"I shall be fine." Or Georgie would if she could stop thinking about how his hands had seemed to burn through the cotton of her habit and her petticoats. Perhaps she should start wearing long stays. But wearing long stays while riding would not be comfortable. She took a long drink of wine and almost choked when Turley entered without being announced.

He greeted Frits and Adeline before making his way to

Georgie, then took her ungloved hand and bowed, touching his lips to her fingers. "Miss Featherton, good evening."

The warmth of his lips caused her fingers to tingle and she almost forgot to curtsey. "Good evening to you, my lord."

He glanced at Frits. "Thank you for sending the coach."

"You're welcome." Frits looked at Adeline. "It was my wife's idea. She decided that walking would not do your dress pumps any good, and you'd probably not think to ask for the use of my mother's carriage."

Turley pulled a face. "And you were correct, my lady. I was about to set out on foot when the coach arrived. Thank you."

"Better that than riding a horse." Her nose wrinkled. "My mother once told me about an American who rode to a dinner party. She said he smelled of horse the whole evening."

"That must have been unpleasant." Georgie could not imagine such behavior.

Frits pressed a glass into Turley's hand. "I have attempted to find out, but I still have no idea what or who we'll find at Turner's house."

That reminded Georgie about the coach she and Turley had seen earlier. "Is there anyone who lives close enough that a visitor might get turned around on the back lane to Littleton?"

"Bottomley has a house in the area. I suppose that if he had a visitor they could have missed the turn to his estate and landed up on our road." Frits cast a look at Adeline. "Bottomley isn't usually here during the Season."

"Perhaps he has come for the house party and invited a friend," she suggested.

"Hmm. I suppose that might be the case." Frits groaned. "Do you have any idea who it could have been?"

"I know exactly who it is." Even earlier, Turley's tone had not been so forbidding. "Lytton."

Georgie almost rolled her eyes. Why couldn't he have simply told her earlier instead of acting as if it was a great secret?

"Oh, dear." Adeline set her empty glass of wine down. "I know that neither of you nor Exeter like him, but do you know anything that would make the man ineligible?"

Frits and Turley shook their heads.

Turley drained his glass and set it down. "Only that Lytton is said to have been involved in hurting a friend of Exeter's and a lady."

"That sounds rather ominous. Still, we cannot cut him if we do not have a reason." Adeline picked up her reticule. "Shall we depart?"

"I'll write to Exeter tomorrow," Frits said. "I'd rather know what we are dealing with."

Adeline smiled warmly at him. "That is exactly the proper thing to do."

Georgie thought they were making too much of it. After all, the reason Exeter had helped a young lady last Season stay away from Lord Lytton was because she was waiting for the gentleman to whom she had been secretly betrothed to return. Now that she gave it some consideration, Georgie remembered dancing with Lytton a time or two, possibly more. If her memory served her, she had not been impressed by his conversation. He was too concerned with his own self-importance. She much preferred gentlemen— actually people in general—who did not take themselves too seriously. Or were secure in their place in the world. Still, she wondered what was meant by "hurting a lady." That did not sound good at all. Perhaps he was one of those men who hid a dark side.

She turned toward the door only to find Turley waiting to escort her, and the instant she placed her hand on his arm, the sensations started. Even donning her gloves had not helped. "It will be interesting to see who the other guests are."

"Hmmm," he answered noncommittally.

They arrived in the hall just as the front doors opened. "What does that mean?"

"Only that I am not very interested in who else is in attendance." His shoulders rose in a light shrug. "I would be perfectly happy spending time with you"—he stopped as if waiting for her to respond, but she could not think of anything to say—"and Frits and Adeline."

Did Turley think mentioning their friends at the end of the sentence, almost as if they were added on at the last minute, would make his statement more acceptable? Or was "acceptable" the right word? Perhaps "singular" was a better word. Because he had clearly singled Georgie out. As they descended the shallow stone steps to the coach, she raised her chin. "You have only been here one day. Surely you must know by now that forming good relations with one's neighbors by attending their entertainments is one key to being comfortable in the country."

As he handed her into the coach, he murmured, "That doesn't mean I would not rather spend the time with you."

Even as Georgie fought the blush, she could not but acknowledge how she delighted in his words. "You are impossible."

A crooked smile appeared on his face, and he raised her fingers to his lips. "Not entirely."

"What are you two whispering about?" Frits asked.

She snatched her hand back and stepped into the coach, leaving Turley to answer, "The other dinner guests."

Frits's brow creased. "We don't know who they are."

"Exactly what we were discussing." Turley entered the coach, sat facing her, and assumed a look of total innocence.

"You lied." Holding her hand to the side of her lips so Adeline couldn't see, Georgie mouthed the words, and he just smiled.

Warmth infused her and she hoped she was not blushing. She did not want his smile to affect her this way, or his hands, or lips. She had to find some method of holding him at arm's length until he fell in love with her. Did that even make sense? If she was more aloof toward him, and did not allow him to become closer, then did it not make more sense that he would probably not fall in love with her? All this was too confusing, and she was beginning to wish she had gone with her parents.

"I do believe this is the first time since I came out that I have no idea who the other guests will be," Adeline commented.

"That is true." Since Turley had arrived, Georgie had not thought much about it. "In Town one generally knew who would be at the entertainments. It is strange to think that we might not know any of them."

Adeline adjusted her shawl. "I have not received correspondence from any of our friends saying they were attending."

Neither had Georgie. "It will be an adventure."

The inside lights had been lit and she could see her friend shake her head.

Turley, who was sitting on the backward-facing bench, exchanged a look with Frits and groaned. "We have come to the conclusion that Turner would have invited younger gentlemen of his acquaintance."

That was something Georgie had not considered. It might very well be that the gentlemen were too young to be interested in marriage.

"Unless Bottomley has a guest and they attend," Adeline mentioned.

"In that event, we will know at least two people other than the Turners and Fitzwalters." Georgie knew her friend did not like being around a number of people she did not know. She wished she had remembered that before. She patted Adeline's hand. "It will be fine."

"I know. I expect we shall have a wonderful evening." If only her words sounded convincing.

"My love." Frits's eyes searched his wife's face. "You have nothing to worry about. If you should become uncomfortable or tired simply tell me you wish to leave. After all, you are carrying our child."

"There, you see?" It was interesting to see how well he took care of Adeline. "There is nothing to concern you."

"How nice to have such a convenient excuse." She relaxed back against the soft leather swabs.

Now all Georgie had to do was work out what she should do about Turley.

Chapter Thirteen

When Gavin had first seen Georgie this evening, he knew there was no more beautiful lady in England and possibly the world. On the way to Littlewood, he had decided to spend this evening attending to her. Then the other gentlemen at the house party had been mentioned, ruining his plan, and reminding him that he'd rather dine at Littlewood than at the Turners' house.

Ever since seeing Lytton's coach and being reminded that Bottomley lived in the area, Gavin could not be happy about the dinner. He wondered how formally the guests would be seated for dinner. Even though he did not know who'd be there, there was a more than even chance that he and Georgie would be paired together. After all, he was a viscount and she was a viscount's daughter. Unless none of the other ladies were the daughters of peers. In that event, Turley could very well escort her to dinner. But if she was the only daughter of a peer, Lytton outranked him, and she might have to go in with his lordship. If only Littleton could have demanded the guest list, none of them would be having this conversation.

They passed the open gate. There was nothing he could do about it now, and he'd know soon. None of this would be an issue if he'd had a little more confidence in the ladies planning this party. But the last he'd seen them they both had more hair than wit.

The coach pulled to a stop. They waited until a footman opened the door and let down the steps. "Good evening, my lords and my ladies."

For some reason Gavin couldn't guess, Georgie grinned at Adeline. What would be amusing about a greeting?

Littleton climbed down and Gavin followed. Then they each claimed their lady's hand as they stepped out of the carriage. Simply having Georgie on his arm improved Gavin's mood.

They were escorted to a large drawing room, and he was pleased to see that he knew most of the gentlemen, and they were indeed younger. However, he could not place any of the ladies. Then again, the moment he'd seen Georgie, she had become his lodestone, and he'd failed to make a point of meeting other ladies. In fact, the only reason he knew the former Miss Tice and Miss Martindale was that he had been made to dance with one of them.

The ladies and their husbands came forward. "Good evening. We are only waiting for Lord Bottomley and Lord Lytton," Lady Turner said. "Let us introduce you to the others."

Gavin took in the bevy of ladies and gentlemen and realized, as he hadn't upon first glance, that his chances of escorting Georgie to dinner had decreased dramatically. If he included Lytton and Bottomley, there were one marquis, three earls, and another viscount. Then he glanced at the ladies. He did not recognize any of them and was never going to remember all their names. Not that it mattered. He would do his best to stay out of their way and with Georgie.

He placed his hand over her fingers. "Do you know any of them?"

"Only Lady Aurelia Tapton," Georgie whispered. "Do you know them?"

"Most of the gentlemen. A few of them are in the Lords, but I rarely socialize with them."

Lady Turner took charge of Georgie and Turley while Mrs. Fitzwalter began to shepherd Frits and Adeline around the room. Soon they'd met everyone. Gavin took the opportunity to whisper to Georgie something about each of the gentlemen he knew, so that she would have an easier time remembering them. Although, he really needn't have bothered. She was adept at asking each guest a question or two about themselves. Soon the ladies were tracing their family lines to determine if there was any relationships or friends of friends or families.

Lytton and Bottomley arrived several minutes later, and they went into dinner. Although Littleton escorted his wife, Gavin was pleased to see that the young Earl of St. Albans escorted Georgie. St. Albans was definitely not in the market for a wife. In fact, Gavin wondered how Turner had got the man to the party in the first place. On the other hand, Gavin's dinner partner, Miss Lydia Codell, the youngest daughter of a viscount, had nothing on her mind but marriage.

"My sister has just got betrothed," she said as she fluttered her lashes at him. "It took her three Seasons. I trust it will not take me so long to meet the gentleman I wish to wed." The last part gave him the impression that the lady thought her sister was lacking in some way.

He'd definitely have to enlist Georgie's help in keeping him safe from the young ladies. "Indeed. Who is the fortunate gentleman?"

Miss Lydia pushed some peas onto her fork. "The Marquis of Nuneaton," she practically mumbled.

Miss Lydia's sister had done very well for herself even if it had taken three Seasons. Gavin knew exactly who Nuneaton was but he still asked, "The Duke of Leicestershire's eldest?"

"Yes." This time Miss Lydia's tone was softer and, he thought, a bit embarrassed.

It was one thing for an older sister to have been out three years and not have much to show for it. It was entirely another thing to be marrying a duke's heir. She began applying herself to eating, leaving Gavin to allow his gaze to stray to Georgie just as she chuckled lightly. What the devil was St. Albans saying to her? He'd better be behaving himself or Gavin would have to speak to him.

As Miss Lydia had become quiet, he turned to the lady on his left, Miss Blomefield. "Are you taking a holiday from the Season as well?"

The lady's large brown eyes regarded him seriously. "I find London is not to my taste. Once this week has ended I shall return home."

Her voice had a determined tenor to it. "Why do I have the feeling that you did not wish for a Season at all?"

"You are very perceptive, my lord." Her lips tipped up at the corners. "I did not. My father is a diplomat in Holland, and I have met the gentleman I wish to marry. However, my mother insisted I have at least one Season."

"Ah." He wondered how often that happened. He didn't think he'd ever heard of a young lady not wishing for a Season. He wondered if in some way or another the gentleman had not found favor with the lady's mother. However, to ask would be impertinent. "I wish you good luck."

"Thank you. Although, I am certain I shall succeed." Her smile broadened. "My aunt is quite unable to—to, oh how shall I say it—"

Gavin chuckled. "Stop an immovable force?"

"Something like that." She glanced across the table. "I take it that you are interested in Miss Featherton."

"Something like that." He would not say more. No one else needed to know that he had a long road ahead of him when it came to courting Georgie.

"In that case, I wish you luck." Bottomley, on the other side of Miss Blomefield, addressed her and Gavin went back to his food.

Georgie glanced at Turley, sitting directly across the table from her, as he grinned at Miss Blomefield and jealousy almost flooded her.

"She's not interested in him," Lord St. Albans said. "She has a beau in Holland."

Part of Georgie wanted to deny she was looking at Turley, but her curiosity got the better of her. "How do you know?"

"Her aunt is a friend of my mother's, and my mother always has an eye out for likely brides for me." He chuckled. "She knows I'm not ready for the parson's noose, but I suppose she wants to keep in practice."

"Until you are ready?" Georgie had to grin at him.

"Indeed." He nodded. "I can't put the inevitable off

forever. Nor do I wish to. I will have to marry at some point."

She looked at the lady on Turley's other side, who seemed to be studiously eating. She had a recollection of Miss Lydia Codell from Town, and in Georgie's opinion the girl was much too green to be out. Yet she had been speaking with Turley earlier. What had he said to make her so quiet?

"Miss Lydia is not a threat." St. Alban's tone was a bored drawl. "She is barely out of the schoolroom. In fact, I believe she escaped from it and should be immediately returned."

That was blunt speaking. Georgie tried to remember who the lady's sister was and could not. "She has an older sister who is out?"

"Yes. She is to be married soon. I think her father thought he could get his second daughter off his hands as well."

"Your mother again?" It seemed as if everyone but her had a mother who knew things about the unmarried members of the *ton*.

He gave Georgie a rueful look and she laughed. "I have been told that part of finding a daughter-in-law is knowing who would not suit."

"Where are the mothers?" She knew that some were attending the house party, but she had not seen any of them.

"They are in dowager Lady Turner's wing. My understanding is that they are leaving the new Lady Turner and Mrs. Fitzwalter to handle the guests but will step in if needed."

"That is an interesting idea." It would certainly force Mary and Amanda to remain alert. Neither of them would wish to be embarrassed by an older lady being called to manage the events.

"That is not precisely how I would put it. I find young ladies to be far too interested in getting to the church and not for the Sunday sermon."

"If you think that, why did you agree to come?" She tasted the fish and found it to be extremely fresh.

He shrugged. "I couldn't say no to Turner. He's been a friend for a long time. Why are you here?"

"I am visiting Lady Littleton. Lady Turner and Mrs. Fitzwalter are neighbors. Ergo, we agreed to come to the major entertainments." Georgie smiled to herself. "I suppose we will assist with the younger ladies."

"The good thing is that there are no truly older gentlemen. Or no one over five and thirty. Most of the rest of them are like me and not interested in marriage. I expect it will be entertaining for a week."

Georgie recalled how at least two ladies had attempted to trap Frits into marriage last Season. "I would suggest that you gentlemen could be more at risk than the ladies. You might want to make sure you do not stroll around alone."

Suddenly alert, Lord St. Albans straightened. "That is an excellent idea. I shall tell the others."

Deciding she had done her civic duty, Georgie applied herself to the third course that had been set out, and chatted with the gentleman on her other side for a few minutes.

She had just finished an excellent piece of an apple dish when Mary Turner rose. "I believe it is time to leave the gentlemen to their port. Ladies?"

Once the ladies had repaired to the drawing room, and glasses of wine and lemonade had been handed out, the talk turned to the single gentlemen.

Adeline came to stand by Georgie just as Miss Lydia

said, "I think Lord Turley is very handsome, even if he is too old."

Georgie was just about to take a sip of claret and was very glad she had not. What *had* he said to the girl? In fact she might not be able to drink it at all because the next thing she knew Adeline retorted, "He is not older than my husband who is one and thirty."

Miss Lydia glanced at Adeline. "That is what my sister says about her betrothed, but she is older than I am. That is most likely the difference."

"Said with the certainty of the very young," Georgie whispered, and tried not to laugh. "She sounds almost exactly like my younger sister. I would wager she is not above sixteen."

"I think you are probably right." Adeline took a sip of claret. "When I have a daughter, remind me that she may not be presented to Polite Society until she is at least eighteen."

"I don't think Frits would let her come out until then." Georgie was finally able to control her urge to laugh, and finally got to taste the wine which turned out to be very good.

Adeline grinned. "He might not want her to come out at all."

"Who is coming out?" Frits asked as he came to stand next to his wife.

"Our potential daughter." She smiled at him. "We were discussing one of the ladies who we believe is much too young to be in Polite Society."

Turley took his place at Georgie's side and appropriated her hand, placing it on his arm. The thought that she should really put some distance between them came to her again, but it felt so right having him next to her. If only he'd fall in love with her everything would be perfect.

"Let me take a guess," he said. "Miss Lydia."

Georgie was finally going to find out what he had said. "Do you have any idea why she became so quiet at dinner?"

"I might." The devil placed his fingers over her hand, warming it in a way that a fire never could. "After telling me it would not take *her* as long to wed as it had her older sister, I asked who she was marrying." He stopped and looked at each of them.

"Well?" Frits asked.

"She is betrothed to the Duke of Leicestershire's heir."

Georgie almost rolled her eyes. "I think any mother or father would forgive a daughter being out for three years if at the end of it she had made such a good match."

"Indeed." Turley raised a brow. "I believe it was that realization that made her understand how foolish she sounded."

"I can guarantee you," Frits said, "that when my daughter comes out she will be far beyond making a cake of herself."

They all nodded in agreement.

Adeline yawned, and Frits glanced around the room. "Do you see either Lady Turner or Mrs. Fitzwalter? We must go home before Adeline becomes too tired."

"Lady Turner is next to the piano." Turley motioned with his chin. "We will all go. That way no one can delay us."

Georgie was ready to depart as well. She did not wish to be caught in any musical performances that usually occurred after dinner. It had been fun to attend the dinner, but it was time to return to Littlewood.

Frits signaled to one of the footmen. "Please call the Littleton coach."

Once the servant left, they made their way to the piano where Mary Turner was arranging piano performances by the young ladies.

"We do apologize," Adeline said. "I am growing tired and my husband insists on taking me home."

"Yes, of course." Mary moved them away from the group that had surrounded the piano. "I suspected that would happen."

Several minutes later they drove through the gate and onto the road. Adeline slumped against the side of the coach. "All of a sudden I have lost all my energy."

Georgie knew that her friend would be much happier with her head on Frits's shoulder. "Frits, change places with me. That way you can take care of Adeline."

Once they resettled and Adeline was comfortable, Georgie wished she could lean against Turley. Instead, she peered out the window. It was past ten and had been dark since six. "It seems so light."

"It's due to the combination of the road materials and the moon," Turley remarked. "Littleton's father found a Scottish engineer by the name of Telford who had a new way to build the roads. He convinced the neighboring landlords to rebuild all the roads to the villages and estates. After I saw how much better the roads were, I did the same thing at Rivercrest."

Frits snugged Adeline closer to him. "It makes a great deal of difference when we have a lot of rain. The roads don't become muddy bogs."

Georgie gazed out the window again. "It's almost as if the roads are glowing under the moonlight."

"It does," Turley agreed. "It will make traveling back and forth this week easier." He put his fingers over the hand she had on the cushions. "Did you have an interesting conversation with St. Albans?"

Georgie grinned, but he probably couldn't see it. They had not lit the inner lights. "I discovered that his mother is very much like Frits's mother. She knows everything about everybody. And that he came to the house party as a favor to Lord Turner. He has no interest in marrying any time soon."

"I had wondered why he was here." She wanted to turn the hand Turley covered and clasp his fingers.

"Remembering what Frits went through last Season, I warned him to always keep a friend with him."

Both men barked laughs.

"That was helpful." Turley squeezed her hand.

"I thought so. You might want to follow my advice as well."

"I plan to stay close to you for the rest of the week."

Georgie almost responded, but decided she wanted to consider what he had said. She knew he still wanted to marry her. Did that mean he might fall in love with her as well?

Chapter Fourteen

Thanks to Bottomley's apparent inability to arrive anywhere on time, Marc missed his opportunity to speak with Miss Featherton before they were called into dinner at Lady Turner's house. Afterward, the Earl of Bolingbroke, one of the other guests, held Marc back to discuss a canal venture, thus making him one of the last gentlemen to enter the drawing room. By the time he was able to rejoin the ladies, Turley was planted firmly at Miss Featherton's side. Marc didn't want to waste any more time on a lady who did not wish to wed him—he'd already done that more than once to his detriment—and he tried to make out from her expression if she was pleased Turley was there or not. Unfortunately—at least for his purpose at the moment—she was much too well-bred to allow by either her mannerisms or her expression how she felt about the situation. Before he could even greet her, the Littleton party left. Marc would clearly have to think of another way to speak with Miss Featherton.

"My lord." Lady Turner came up to him. "I do hope you are having a pleasant time." She glanced around as if afraid that someone would hear her. "I was not aware of Lord

Bottomley's tendency to dawdle. If you would like us to send a carriage for you, you have only to say the word."

Marc hadn't thought much of the lady when she had been Miss Martindale, but she had certainly improved since last Season. And, although he had his traveling coach with him, it was really not the type of vehicle one wished to take on a short visit to a neighboring house. "Thank you, my lady. I appreciate your very kind offer. Now that I know of his propensity, I shall see what I can do to counter it."

"Nevertheless, the offer stands." She placed her hand on his arm. "Many of the ladies here are of the younger set, but I think you might enjoy meeting Lady Aurelia. She is known for her lack of missishness."

He was primarily interested in Miss Featherton, and still intended to pursue her, but meeting another lady of rank was not a bad idea. "Yes, of course. I would be delighted."

Lady Turner led him to a lady with reddish-brown hair who seemed to be in a rather intent discussion with the new Marquis of Montagu.

As they came closer he heard her say, "Yes, yes, John. That is all well and good, but England must lead the way in this matter."

Marc didn't get to hear what Montagu might have answered because Lady Aurelia, having seen them approaching, greeted Lady Turner. "You have assembled an interesting party. I commend you."

"Thank you." Her ladyship blushed slightly. "Lady Aurelia, I would like to present Lord Lytton."

When she glanced up at him, he noticed how petite she actually was. Her head only came to his shoulder. As she held out her hand, her smile reached her enchanting blue-green eyes. "Good evening, my lord. It is nice to make your acquaintance." She indicated the marquis. "I suppose you have already met my scapegrace brother?"

Montagu rolled his eyes, and Marc covered his laugh with a cough. "I have indeed."

The younger man gave his sister a beseeching look as he stepped back. "May we please not discuss politics this week?"

She heaved a frustrated sigh. "Very well. You may have a respite. But this subject is not over."

"Of that I am well aware." Her brother looked around like a fox intent on making his escape. "I shall see you later."

"You must excuse me as well," Lady Turner said. "I should go help Mrs. Fitzwalter with the tea." Her ladyship did not wait for an answer before heading to her friend.

"Well, my lord," Lady Aurelia said. "Would you like to engage in polite small talk, or would you rather have a more substantive conversation?"

For the first time in a long while, he chuckled. "We have just met. Do we even know one another well enough to speak of matters beyond the weather?"

She gave him a wry smile. "I must warn you that I can only tolerate small talk for a short period of time. My failing vastly distresses my family."

Marc felt his smile broadening. "Such as your brother?"

"You noticed?" Her dark pink lips twitched. "You would never know that we are twins. One need only to look at the two of us to realize how much truth there is to the idea that females mature faster than males."

"Twins?" He would never have guessed. They really did not look that much alike. And as to their personalities, she did, in fact, seem much more mature than her brother. Marc wondered how old she was. At least one and twenty for her brother to have taken his seat in the Lords. "You're correct. I would have never known if you had not told me."

This time her smile broadened. "I am known as the sensible one."

He could see why. "I find sensible ladies to be highly underrated creatures."

She glanced in the direction of the tea tray. "Shall we fetch our cups of tea, my lord?"

"If you wish." He held out his arm, and she placed her fingers on it.

All the ladies he had been interested in last Season and this Season had been rational. He would enjoy coming to know Lady Aurelia. Still, he wondered why she was not already wed. Was there some secret or circumstance that made her ineligible? His aunt would never stand for the possibility of a scandal. And how would he find out? Or should he even bother given he was interested in Miss Featherton? Then again, Marc had thought Turley had given up on her, but apparently the rumors had been false. He gave himself an inner shrug. He'd simply have to allow the circumstances to play out as they would. At least now he had an alternative to his aunt's ultimatum that he find a suitable lady to marry before the year was out. He had managed to if not ignore, then not keep his dilemma at the front of his mind, but lately he had not been able to forget about it. Marc didn't care if he had one of those love matches that were all the rage, but he would like to know he could get on well with the lady he'd wed.

"How do you like your tea?" Lady Aurelia's question broke into his musings.

"Two lumps of sugar and more than a splash of milk." She procured his cup of tea before getting her own. "Shall we retreat to the chairs by the fireplace before anyone else notices them?"

Her question conjured a vision of him sitting next to a fireplace with a lady, but he could not quite picture who the female was. He was about to answer in the affirmative, when he noticed she had taken his arm and was leading him in the direction she wished to go. She was definitely a determined female. But would he like being managed? He supposed it depended on who it was and how it was done. They found the chairs were close enough together for a comfortable coze. He could become used to this.

Lucinda, Constance, and Cristabel had been waiting all evening in the well-appointed private parlor of Catherine, the dowager Lady Turner, to see if the first step of their new plan had gone well. Lucinda had never seen such an arrangement for a dowager made in the same house as the rest of the family. Everything from the private entrance to the kitchen and other facilities in her wing of the house had been well designed to allow her complete autonomy.

Catherine nodded as her maid whispered in her ear.

"Did it happen?" Lucinda asked.

"Yes." Catherine grinned. "My daughter-in-law introduced Lady Aurelia and Lytton. They are having tea together by the fireplace."

"I do hope they prove to be well suited," Constance said. "It would solve all the problems that currently plague him, and her. I would dearly like to see my niece settled."

"I am simply pleased that her mother convinced her to come and meet him." Lucinda took a small sip of wine. They had not known until they had arrived this evening that Aurelia was attending the house party and for what purpose. "From what I know of your niece, she would not agree to wed him if she did not like him."

"From what I understand, she has been a bit hard to please," Catherine added.

Constance snorted. "The girl has turned down two dukes as well as other assorted gentlemen."

Lucinda noticed that Catherine had dropped her jaw for a moment, and stared pointedly at Constance. "I do not suppose that would have anything to do with her great-aunt offering to take her in if her father attempted to force her to marry against her wishes."

At least Constance had the grace to blush a little. Although she tried to hide it by taking a drink. "You know very well that after the debacle of a marriage my dear departed husband made for our son, I vowed no one else in my family would suffer the same thing. I firmly believe that if not for that marriage, my boy would be alive today."

Well, at least she had stopped blaming her husband's nephew who had inherited the title. "I have no doubt you are correct, my dear." Rare tears blurred Constance's eyes, and Lucinda patted her friend's hand.

"At least we know why many of the gentlemen don't like poor Lytton," Catherine said.

Apparently his behavior had been compared to a Cit, always attempting to ingratiate himself. "I have no doubt it is because his aunt could find no good in the boy." The thought of the insults that he must have endured because his great-grandfather was in trade angered Lucinda. "His aunt never made any secret that she disapproved of his mother's breeding. And it is my opinion that after his parents died and he was left with his father's family he was starved for affection and did not truly understand his place in the world."

"If you'd been treated as if you were always lacking, you might have done the same." Constance shook her head. "The right wife can bring him around. But I will not have Aurelia marrying him if she doesn't want him."

"We have all agreed on that." Catherine poured more wine in their glasses. "I must say, even though it is only the first day, I never believed this house party would be so well organized. I was certain I'd be called down for any number of problems."

Lucinda nodded. "It is also fortunate that the mothers who did accompany their daughters are pleased to have their own parlor."

Constance heaved a sigh. "Thank you, Catherine, for thinking of that. I can think of little more tedious than having to listen to mothers of young ladies."

Catherine chuckled. "Neither can I. Thankfully, I was only given one daughter, and she knew exactly who she was going to marry."

"I do not think it was so difficult when my daughters were ready to wed," Lucinda mused. "Now, Featherton almost gave me fits until he met his wife." Her daughter-in-law frequently did not see eye to eye with her, but she never allowed that to stand in her way of doing what was necessary to ensure her granddaughters married the right men. "If only we knew how Georgie and Gavin got along this evening."

"I shall ask my maid to find out the next time they are here," Catherine offered.

"Thank you. I would have so liked to be able to see what was going on." Lucinda glanced at Catherine. "I do not suppose you have any secret passageways and holes placed in the eyes of paintings."

"Unfortunately, no." Her friend laughed. "I am told the old house had them, but this one is too new."

"Ah, well. I shall have to wait to hear about it." Despite his ridiculous fears, Lucinda had formed a very good opinion of Gavin Turley, and she hoped Georgie would eventually accept him. Time would tell. And while they waited, there was another match to make.

In the carriage, Georgie yawned, and Gavin wanted to cuddle her next to him like Littleton was doing with his wife. Conversation had died down, and Littleton's head was resting on Adeline's. Gavin would wager they were both asleep. The steady pace of the horses lulled him. As it was, the only thing keeping Gavin awake was Georgie.

He glanced at her. It was worth a try. "Would you like to lean your head against my shoulder and snooze for a while?"

"No, thank you." She turned from gazing out the window. "It's not much farther. I shall be fine."

She sounded tired. He wished he could see her face. If she started to slump down, he'd hold her. Just then they turned into the Littlewood gates. He'd lost his chance this time. "Littleton, you're home."

He sat up abruptly and rubbed his face. "Sorry about that. I didn't mean to fall asleep on the two of you."

"It was no problem at all." Georgie yawned again. "The silence was peaceful."

Gavin had to think about what she'd said. He had been so engrossed in wanting to cuddle her he'd not considered it. But she was right. The silence had been . . . comfortable. That was another thing he appreciated about her—although he hadn't realized it until tonight—she did not feel the need to fill the air with mindless chatter.

The coach came to a stop, and he jumped out and let the steps down. Littleton came out next then turned to gather Adeline in his arms. Gavin helped Georgie down. "Do you still want to ride in the morning?"

"Yes." She opened her eyes wider. "Goodness, I am so tired, and it cannot be midnight yet. How do we go on in Town?"

He brushed the back of his knuckles across her cheek. "I think it's the country air and the slower pace."

He thought for a moment she would lean into his caress, but she did not. "I shall see you in the morning. If I'm not down when you arrive, have them send for me."

"Why don't we plan to go after breakfast?"

"That might be a good idea." She removed her hand from his arm. "Until then."

When he arrived at The Lilacs, he was informed that the ladies were still out. "Where did they go?"

"To visit a friend, I believe," the butler said. "Would you like anything to eat or some tea before you retire?"

"No, thank you. I am for my couch."

"Very good, my lord. Have a good night."

His valet was in the dressing room when he strolled into his apartments and started removing his cravat. The second it hit the back of a chair, Ardley came out. How he could hear that, Gavin had no idea.

"I trust you had a pleasant evening, my lord." The valet removed his jacket, frowned at the way he toed his shoes off, and began picking up the items of clothing Gavin tossed to him.

"It was pleasant." But that was about all it was. He'd have to find a way to sit next to Georgie at dinner. When was the next dinner? Damn. He had no idea of the events they were scheduled to attend. "Don't wake me in the morning. I feel as if I've attended an event in Town."

"Very well." Ardley took the discarded clothing to the dressing room.

Gavin stretched before walking over to the bed. He knew he'd dream about Georgie tonight and did not want any of it interrupted. Throwing back the sheets, he climbed into bed and shivered for a moment. One day, he'd learn to wait until his valet had run the warming pan between the sheets. On the other hand, it was just as well they were cold. He'd walked around half the evening with the beginnings of an erection. How much more time did he have to give her before he could start showing her that how he felt was as good as being in love? It was even better. He'd seen couples fall out of love and that created major problems. If a man and woman were already friends, and they had passion, then they had everything they needed, and wouldn't have to worry about falling out of love.

I am an idiot.

That was exactly the argument to use with her. The only problem was how soon he could make it. Perhaps the ladies would know. They had seemed receptive to his decision not to fall in love. Surely they'd help him.

The cold sheets had not worked after all. He dreamed she was in his bed, under him, over him, kissing him everywhere, and awoke with a massive erection. He'd have to do something soon.

Chapter Fifteen

Georgie trudged up the steps to her rooms. It had been all she could do not to lean against Turley as Adeline had done with Frits. Yet that would not have helped her cause. If Turley wanted to marry her, he had to love her or admit he loved her. Georgie really could not accept anything else.

She entered her chamber and stood as Smith undressed her and put Georgie into her nightgown.

It was all very confusing. He was doing everything she had seen her brother and his friends do with their wives. He'd kept glancing at her during dinner. Of course she had sneaked looks at him, but she made sure that he hadn't seen her. He had come and stood next to her as soon as the gentlemen entered the drawing room, acting as if he dared any other man to approach—none of them did. And at the end of the evening, he had handed her into and out of the coach.

She sat and could have moaned with pleasure when her maid released her hair from its elaborate design and began to brush it. She had been so excited when she was first allowed to put it up. Now she wished she could wear it down at times. Ah, well. People often sought what they could not have. Children wished to grow up. Older people wished for youth. The poor wanted wealth, and the wealthy . . . She frowned. They still wanted wealth, but many of them did not want the responsibility and duties that came with it. If only she could be happy with a gentleman who would care for her and give her the life she wanted. But she could not. She wanted more, and one way or another she'd have it. Georgie felt as if she was going in circles.

One of the house party entertainments was to visit a local village fair. Perhaps a fortune-teller would be there, and she could have that woman tell her what her future held.

"Come along, Miss Georgie." Smith stepped back. "I've just finished running the bed warmer between the sheets and it's time for you to go to sleep."

Georgie glanced at the clock as she covered her mouth and yawned, again. It was not even eleven o'clock. "It's been a long day."

"And tomorrow won't be any better." Her maid started putting away hairpins, ribbons, and the combs that had held her hair. "I understand there is to be a gypsy hunt, whatever that is, you will be attending."

That almost woke her up. "A gypsy hunt? Why would we do that?"

"I'm sure I don't know." Smith plucked up Georgie's gown from the back of a chair. "All I was told is to have you ready by ten so that you can make the drive over to Lady Turner's house."

But Georgie was supposed to ride with Turley in the morning. Had he even been informed about the entertainment? There was nothing she could do about it now, but when she saw Frits at breakfast, she'd ask him to send a note to Turley.

"In that event, I'd better go to sleep." She climbed into bed and her maid drew the covers up over her. "Good night, Smith."

"Good night, Miss Georgie."

In her dreams, Turley held her close to him, and she snuggled into his warmth. She lifted her head and stared at his well-formed lips.

She woke to something landing on the bed, and loud purring. "Sebastian." The ginger and cream cat nudged her hand to be stroked.

What would it be like to feel Turley's lips on hers? Yet, as she tried to imagine the kiss, it occurred to her that he had only once attempted to kiss her. At least that's what she thought he was doing. She turned onto her back. Not for the first time, she remembered that he had never been anything but perfectly polite. Yes, his touch burned through the layers of clothing to her skin, sending pleasurable shivers through her body, but other than that—and she truly hoped he did not know how he affected her— he'd done nothing to show her he wanted her. Was that because he did not love her? But surely passion was important in a marriage, even one without love.

Sebastian settled next to her, and she turned her pillow over and rolled onto her side. She would give Turley this week. If he had not managed to at least attempt—again?— to kiss her, she'd give him up as a forlorn hope. She had almost slipped into sleep when another thought occurred to her. Had Mary and Amanda already paired their guests for the gypsy hunt or would she be able to be with Turley? If Adeline were not already asleep, Georgie would be strongly tempted to go ask her friend. Instead, she rolled over again. Answers, one way or the other, would come in the morning. But why wait for someone else's answer?

If they arrived early, Adeline could ask either Mary or Amanda if Georgie could be paired with Turley. It would be seen as an attempt at matchmaking. With her mind now settled, she closed her eyes again. Tomorrow could prove to be interesting.

The next morning, she came upon Adeline in the corridor. "May I speak with you for a moment?"

Adeline's stomach growled as she glanced longingly at the door to the breakfast room, but nodded. "Will this take much time?"

"It will not take long at all." Georgie pulled her friend into a rarely used parlor and closed the door. "If this game is not actually hunting gypsies—in which case I hope you will join with me to stop it—and it has teams, will you ask either Mary or Amanda to put me on the same team as Turley?"

Adeline nodded again. "Of course." Then she pinned Georgie with a look. "What is this about?"

There was no reason not to relate what she had been thinking. "You remember when Frits first kissed you?"

"Yes," Adeline said slowly.

"And how after that you became much more interested in him?" Georgie wondered if she was going to have to walk her friend through everything she had considered.

"I take it Turley has not kissed you at all."

She could not keep from sounding as disgusted as she felt. "He has not even acted like he wanted to. Well, only once, but I might be wrong about that."

"Ergo, you wish to give him a chance," Adeline concluded.

Georgie bit down on her lip. "I thought that if he did

not kiss me, even when I gave him an opportunity, then I should forget about finding a way that he could fall in love with me."

"If only we could ask Frits's advice," Adeline mused. "But I am afraid that would put him in a difficult situation and not only because of his duty to you. He and Turley have been the best of friends for most of their lives. He might feel as if he was somehow betraying Turley."

Georgie had not even thought about asking Frits. He of all people would be able to tell her what to do. Still, her friend had a point. "I suppose you're right."

Adeline's stomach growled again. "I am famished."

"You will ask about—"

"Yes." She opened the door. "But now I must eat."

Chuckling to herself, Georgie followed her friend into the breakfast room. As she filled her plate, she thought about what Adeline had said about approaching Frits. It would be a last resort, but Georgie might just do it.

The next day dawned with a chill in the air reminding Gavin that it was getting later in the month. And every time he'd thought about marrying Georgie, he had imagined her at his home during Christmas. It had been so many years since the house had been filled with love and warmth. He might even invite his sister and her family to join them. It would be fun to have children running around. Mayhap, Georgie would be pregnant by then. He threw back the covers. If he wanted his wishes to come true, he had to get busy.

"My lord." His valet entered the room carrying a letter. "This came for you after you had retired."

"Thank you." He took the missive and opened it and read it twice.

Gypsy hunt? Why the devil would they want to hunt gypsies? Granted, many people didn't like the Romany, but that was no reason to hunt them. And why would the ladies be involved? They barely went fox hunting. He'd better go in the event they actually planned to hunt gypsies and put a stop to such foolishness.

Gavin refolded the note his valet had given him. There would be no time to go riding with Georgie this morning. Unless, of course, Adeline had decided not to attend the entertainment.

He went behind the screen to wash and shave. What possessed Lady Turner and Mrs. Fitzwalter to hold any entertainment so early in the morning? Or at all? He shook his head. He had no control over what his hostesses did. What he might have some influence over was being paired with Georgie. Provided it was an actual game. That would be the only good thing about playing silly games. After all, considering the intellect of the two ladies in charge, how hard could it be? They would not play to win, which would give him more time with her. And the more time he spent with her the better his chances at convincing her to marry him. The question was should he leave early and attempt to persuade the ladies that they should allow him and Georgie to be a team or write to them. Surely this was a team sport? No, writing was probably not a good idea. He didn't want his desire to fall into anyone else's hand. Not because he would be embarrassed, but she might. As soon as he was dressed and had a morsel to eat, he'd go over early to Littlewood and attempt to convince Frits to arrive at the Turners' house beforetime. That would give Gavin an opportunity to speak with Turner and have him speak with his wife about putting Gavin and Georgie on the same team. Although, he hoped that the teams turned out to be coupled. After all, it was not that large of a party. In fact, he had better write a missive for Littleton now and have it delivered so that he received it the first thing this morning.

Gavin went to the cherry desk that held not only space for writing, but a bookshelf as well, and pulled out a piece of foolscap that had already been cut.

My dear Littleton,

I wish to depart early for the Turners' house if possible.

> *Yr. friend,*
> *G.T.*

After sanding the letter and sealing it, he called for his valet. "Please have this delivered to Littlewood. Littleton must have it before breakfast."

"As you wish, my lord."

Perhaps this gypsy hunt would not be so bad after all. As long as they weren't hunting real gypsies. His home was just far enough north that the Romany would have left by now. Were they still in this area?

It was early, but no one would care when he arrived at Littlewood. "Ardley."

"My lord?" He appeared from the dressing room carrying Gavin's clothing.

"Please have a carriage ready to take me to Littlewood." He reached over and grabbed his shirt.

"You do know it is only shortly after seven o'clock?"

"Thank you. I am aware of the time. It is better that I be there as soon as possible."

"As you wish. Would you like a cup of tea?"

"Please and some toast. Breakfast won't be ready there until eight." It only took a half hour to drive to Turner's during the day.

The valet left the room, and Gavin donned everything but his cravat and jacket. Several minutes later, Ardley returned with a pot of tea and several pieces of toast. That should keep him until breakfast. By the time Gavin was fully dressed and downstairs, the coach was waiting.

"Good morning, my lord." The coachman doffed his hat.

"Good morning to you. I hope I didn't get you up." Not expecting an answer, he climbed into the carriage.

When he arrived at Littlewood, he didn't bother to knock, but strode through to the breakfast room where the food was just being set out.

"My lord," Creswell said. "I shall inform his lordship you have arrived."

"I'll wait in his study." That was the place where Gavin was least likely to be overheard making his request.

"That is for the best," the butler said cryptically.

While Littleton was fetched, Gavin made his way down the corridor to the study. He'd always liked the contrast of the light oak paneling with the darker brown leather chairs and sofa.

He'd no sooner lowered himself into a chair when his friend entered. "Good morning. I was about to send for a coach. What is this all about?"

It was still not quite eight o'clock. "Are you departing early then?"

"We are." Frits remained standing as if he was in a hurry. "Adeline wishes to speak with either Lady Turner or Mrs. Fitzwalter before the event begins."

Gavin rose. "I wished to speak with Turner before the

event, as well. I'm hoping he can arrange for me to be on the same team as Miss Featherton."

"Ah. I wonder if . . . Never mind. Come and break your fast. At least we will not have to gulp down our food, but we cannot tarry."

Despite what his friend had said, Gavin was surprised to find both the ladies already at the breakfast table when they reached the breakfast room.

Georgie's gown had long sleeves and a higher bodice than usual. That must be due to the weather. Still, she was lovely. "Good morning."

"Good morning." She smiled at him and his chest felt as if a small bird had taken up residence.

"I wish to depart no later than nine," Adeline said. "Earlier if possible."

"Of course." He tucked into the baked eggs and ham he'd taken from the sideboard. "I hope today will prove to be interesting."

Littleton made a choking sound and quickly carried his napkin to his mouth.

"Are you all right, my love?" His wife began to rise.

He held up a hand, forestalling her. "I'm fine."

Georgie waved her fork in the air. "I do wonder what a gypsy hunt could be."

"As long as we are not hunting real gypsies, I have no idea." He took a piece of toast from the rack that had been set next to him.

Other than glancing at Gavin, his friend did nothing to give away his dislike of games.

"Oh." Georgie's eyes widened. "You don't think they could . . ."

"I cannot think either Mary or Amanda would consider

such a thing." Adeline shook her head. "Surely not. It must be some sort of game."

Georgie set her fork down and picked up her cup. "I suppose we will not know until we arrive."

He hoped she would like being with him. Ever since his failed proposal, he'd been having trouble reading her. "I wish I knew as well."

Adeline looked at the clock. "Georgie, if you are finished, we should fetch our gloves and bonnets."

"Yes, I'm done." Gavin leapt up to pull out her chair. She gave him a small smile. "Thank you."

"It was my pleasure." He watched as she left the room, before turning to Littleton. "I believe I still have a toothbrush and powder here."

"If you do they will be in the room you normally have." Littleton swallowed the last of his food. "I'll come with you. I'll never hear the end of it if my wife doesn't leave when she wants to because of me."

The journey over seemed to go more swiftly than it had last night. Georgie and Adeline kept up a stream of talk regarding what other surprises might be in store for them during the course of the week.

"I certainly never expected to have a missive waiting for me when I arrived in my rooms," Georgie declared.

"Nor did I," Adeline agreed. "I am very glad we are keeping country hours."

"Yes, indeed." Georgie's eyes sparkled as if she was looking forward to an adventure. "We would not be up and about at this time of day."

One of Littleton's brows rose. "If I recall correctly, my love, you were up and about very early in the morning even in Town."

"I was." Adeline blushed lightly. "However now that I have the baby and you I am finding it more difficult."

"I daresay," he drawled, "that one has something to do with the other."

This time Georgie's cheeks turned a deep shade of pink. Gavin wondered if he and Georgie would feel comfortable enough to engage in this type of banter when they married, or if it was reserved for people who fell in love. Once again she was gazing out the window as if she was studiously avoiding looking at him. Or perhaps, she was attempting to ignore their friends' conversation. He considered saying something but decided to let well enough alone. So far they had been getting on well. He did not wish to go backward.

They passed the gateposts to the Turner estate. "Here we are."

Gavin hoped he'd have luck convincing Turner to talk his wife into putting Georgie in his group or with him if they were in pairs. Gavin had seen games done both ways. Acting as couples would be the best for him. He had been on his best behavior this Season and last Season. That had, apparently, caused Georgie to doubt him. It was time to show her how he felt.

Chapter Sixteen

As the tall and intricately carved walnut case clock began to chime the hour, Mary Turner and Amanda Fitzwalter gathered their guests in the hall.

"I'll wager that clock wasn't made here," Turley whispered to Georgie.

His breath was like a soft warm breeze caressing her cheek, and she had to stifle the urge to step closer to him. The timepiece was covered with depictions of creatures both mundane and fantastical. Flanking the clock face on each side stood a man and a woman garbed in practically nothing. "I certainly have never seen anything like it."

"Now," Mary said smiling. "From your questions this morning, I take it that no one knows what a gypsy hunt is. It is *not* hunting for gypsies I assure you." Next to her, Turley let go of the breath he'd apparently been holding. "It is a searching game that our families played. I have the list of teams and the instructions. Each team will search for different objects. After I read out the names please find your partner, and Mrs. Fitzwalter will hand you your tasks."

She read the first few names then announced, "Miss

Featherton and Lord Turley. Lady Aurelia and Lord Lytton . . ." When Mary had finished, she stepped back as people glanced around for their partner.

"How fortunate that we do not have to search for someone." Turley's voice was low and clearly meant just for her.

"Fortunate indeed." Georgie must remember to thank her friend for successfully pleading her case. She made the mistake of looking up at him at the same time he glanced down at her. His light blue eyes twinkled with something close to merriment, but not quite that. Satisfaction? He must have hoped they would be together as well. After all, he had made it clear that he still wished to wed her.

"Lord Turley." Amanda's impatient voice caused them both to look at her. "Here is your task. Good luck. The first person to complete all the requirements wins the game."

He took the folded and sealed paper. "What, may I ask, is the final prize?"

"That, my lord, depends upon who wins." She turned away and went to the next pair.

A line formed between his brows. "I never knew she was so devious."

"Yes, you did." Georgie took his arm and strolled away from the rest of the group. "Do you not remember that she plotted to trap Frits into marriage last Season?"

"You're right. I had forgotten." He glanced back at the lady who was now with her husband. "Thankfully, he managed to drag Fitzwalter to a ball to meet her."

"Only after Frits promised him Gertrude." At first Georgie couldn't believe he had given a heifer away, but he was determined to marry Adeline.

"That actually worked out to his benefit." And to Gertrude's. She was expecting her first calf.

"Yes. It did." Georgie took the paper from his hand and cracked the seal. "Let us see what we have."

I am made of chalk and the egg white of a goose.
Gold surrounds me.

"What the dev—deuce does that mean?" Frowning, Turley took the bit of foolscap and read it out loud. "Chalk and egg white of a goose? They must keep geese here." He handed her back the clue. "I'll have your bonnet and cloak fetched."

She tightened her grip on his arm, stopping him from leaving. "I believe we should visit the portrait gallery first."

"Why there?" He appeared so adorably confused she wanted to kiss him.

"I shall explain." She started leading him in the direction of the gallery. "Chalk and egg white are elements of paint. I cannot imagine either of the ladies wanting us to search out all the paintings in the house. Therefore, the portrait gallery is where the painting is most likely to be located."

"Goose eggs are used in paint?" He sounded incredulous, but kept pace with her.

"Not necessarily goose eggs. Egg whites in general." Georgie steered him up two flights of the main staircase and toward the right corridor. "It would not surprise me to see a painting with a goose in it."

"I can't imagine a lady would pose with geese," he scoffed.

"We shall see." She used her most superior tone. The one her mother used when she knew she was right.

They entered the gallery through massive double wooden doors. A long Turkish rug covered a highly polished oak parquet floor that ran down the center of the corridor. Brightly colored ornamental tiles in the same blues and reds as the rug lined the floor along the walls. Long windows with red curtains filled half of the room with light, leaving the delicate paintings on the opposite side shaded, but easily seen. Other paintings were hung between the windows above tables holding colorful vases and miniatures.

"Goodness." Georgie had seen many portrait galleries, but none this colorful. "What an interesting place."

Turley tugged on her arm. "If we are to have any hope of winning this contest, we need to get to work. If you will begin here, I'll start at the other end."

He did have a point. It would be nice to win. "Yes, I must suppose that finding the painting is only the first of our tasks."

"I have no doubt you are correct."

Not knowing if the painting was large or small, Georgie quickly glanced at all of them as she strolled through. Finally, about halfway down the room, she saw a large painting of a woman dressed from early in the last century, holding a gaggle of goslings in a basket on her lap.

"My lord, come here. I think I've found what we are looking for."

His long strides brought him quickly to her side. "What's this?" He plucked a piece of paper she had not even seen from her angle that was behind the painting and opened it. "I knew it."

Georgie leaned over his arm to read the list.

You have passed the first test. Now you must find:
   A basket
   A red ribbon
   A special feather
   A lady's cap
And bring them to the hall.

"I knew it." Turley sounded disgusted. "We're going to have to brave the geese. I like my own, but they're not friendly to strangers."

Georgie studied the painting. Everything they needed to locate was in the painting. "Look." She pointed. "I do not think we need to disturb the geese. The lady is holding a gold feather."

"Who keeps a gold feather around for people to find, and where are we supposed to discover all these things?" He squinted at the painting. "I haven't seen a cap like that since my great-grandmother wore one."

It was lovely. The lady's face was framed by a pleated sheer linen trimmed in white work with a red ribbon woven through the edge of the main part of the cap. "I have only seen one in paintings." But where to look for everything on the list? There could only be one place where all of these things could be found. "The attic."

Turley glanced at her, surprise writ on his lean face. "You're right. I wonder how many attics there are in this house."

"We're not going to find out by standing here." Georgie took his arm again and started leading him toward the far end of the gallery.

"Why are you so sure it's this way?" Although he sounded as if he was objecting, he remained beside her.

"Because one never accesses the attics via the main

staircase. Aside from that, we have a better chance of finding a servant who can direct us to the right attic going this way."

Georgie had a point. It had always amazed Gavin how women could think of things men never would have. Then again, he'd never had the urge to go rummaging around an attic. But his sister had. Aside from that, he rather liked the way Georgie was managing him. "Excellent idea."

"Thank you." She granted him a wide smile, and that batting feeling returned to his chest. He hoped he wasn't having heart problems like his father had died of.

They went through the doors at the other end of the gallery and found themselves in an older part of the house. "From the way the lady in the painting dressed, we might find what we're looking for above us."

She looked around. "I believe you might be correct. Let's find some stairs."

They found one pair of stairs, but they only led to rooms filled with old furniture and no trunks. On the way to another door, one of the maids carrying a mop and pail almost bumped into them.

She bobbed a curtsey. "Oh, miss, sir, I'm that sorry, I am."

"It was no bother at all," Georgie said warmly. "Would you by any chance happen to know where we could find the attics with trunks from last century?"

Gavin wasn't at all sure the maid could give them that much information.

"Hmm." The maid's lips pressed together as if in thought. "There was a masquerade party a few years ago, and her ladyship was looking in one of the attics." The woman stopped again. "Let me take ye there, it's a little hard to find. This house isn't as old as some, but I wouldn't want ye to get lost." She started forward then stopped.

They almost bumped into her, and she started walking again.

Finally she opened the door to an attic filled with trunks, and Gavin groaned. "It will take us all day to find what we're looking for."

"It's not that bad." But Georgie's voice held a good deal of doubt. "Is there any order to the trunks?"

The maid shrugged. "Couldn't say, miss."

Georgie gave a soft sigh, and Gavin wanted to hear her sigh for him when he kissed her. "At least it's all clean."

"Oh, yes, miss. Mrs. Hopper, the housekeeper, keeps the whole house clean."

"Well, thank you . . ." Georgie's words trailed off.

"Cooper, miss," the servant said.

"Thank you, Cooper." Georgie gave her a coin. "We will simply have to search."

"It would have been too easy otherwise." Although, after they'd found the maid, Gavin had hoped she'd be able to lead them right to the things.

"Yes, indeed." She turned to the servant. "Thank you again for your help. Now we must look for the items on our list."

"Is it a game for the house party?" the woman asked.

"Yes. We found the painting of the woman with the baby geese." Georgie handed her the list. "Now we have to find the items in the painting."

"Well, if it helps. I was told she was the old Lord Turner's mother who liked to dress up."

"That helps a great deal," Georgie said with a conviction Gavin did not share. "We had better not keep you from your work."

"Yes, miss. Good luck." The maid bobbed another curtsey.

He raked his fingers through his hair. "Where do you suggest we start?"

She studied the room for several seconds. "It makes sense to me that the older trunks would be in the back of the room. From what I understand, when this house was finished they were all moved over here. I do expect that they are rather a jumble." She turned in a slow circle. "But, I think the ones that were filled here will be in some sort of order."

He walked to the closest ones. "Shall we begin with these?"

She stared at the trunks before which he was standing, and strolled past the first row. "Many times fabric is reused for new gowns. However, the clothes the lady in the painting was wearing were not particularly rich. I would not be surprised to discover that she had an affection for geese and visited them."

He tried to follow her reasoning. "So you are saying that she would have kept clothing that she did not worry about ruining?"

"Something like that." Georgie stopped in front of a large dark wooden trunk banded with decorative metal, also dark with age. "Let's try this one first."

Fortunately, the key was in the lock. That was odd. He looked at the other trunks. "Miss Featherton, I believe you are to be commended." Gavin turned the lock and opened the lid. On top lay the cap with the red ribbon nestled in a basket. Also in the basket was a feather that looked to be made of gold. "I say." He lifted the feather. "I wonder if this is our prize."

She pulled her bottom lip between her small white teeth. "That would be hard to share."

Not if they were married. "You're right. But, at least we

found what was on our list." He started looking to see if there was another piece of paper. "I can't believe it was this easy."

"Considering we are to go into the town today for the market, she could not have made it too difficult." Georgie opened her pin-watch then glanced at him. "Aside from that, it was sheer luck that you took one end of the gallery and saw the paper. We might not have known to look for it if you hadn't found it."

"And we found the maid." That had been a stroke of luck.

"Indeed." She nodded. "Can you imagine how long it might have taken us to discover this room if we had not?"

"At least an hour, I would imagine." He picked up the basket. "Let us trace our way back down."

She gave him a chagrined look. "I am glad you remember the way back."

Gavin tucked her hand in his arm. "Never fear, my lady fair. I shall find the way out of the maze."

"Lead on then, sir."

Even though there were several doors and two corridors that could have tripped them up, it was not too difficult to trace their way to the portrait gallery. He was surprised that she trusted him to lead. Generally, she was the one who was so certain. Then again, she admitted she did not know the way. Still, it gave him a sense of accomplishment to know she trusted him. At least this much. But he needed her to trust him much more.

As they approached the hall, Gavin heard the front door open and grabbed Georgie's hand. "Someone else is coming in."

They sprinted into the hall and stopped in front of their hostesses just before Lytton and Lady Aurelia arrived. Her ladyship gasped and burst into laughter, causing Georgie to do the same.

"I had no idea we would be so competitive," she exclaimed. "But it seems that we are." Taking the basket from Gavin, she handed it to Mrs. Fitzwalter. "That was a great deal of fun."

"It was indeed." Lady Aurelia gave Lady Turner a wooden bucket.

Despite the ladies having a good time, Gavin could have sworn Lytton glared at him for a brief second.

"We are so glad you enjoyed it," Lady Turner said. "We have arranged for a light luncheon before we go to town for the market."

"It is set up in the dining room," Mrs. Fitzwalter added.

"But before you go, we must give you your prize." She glanced at Gavin and Georgie, and his muscles seemed to tighten. "You each receive a prize. One is to go into meals with the person of your choice, and the other is the feather."

"Ladies first." Gavin held his breath. He wanted to be able to sit next to Georgie at every meal they had here, but it was up to her to decide.

"How could I not take the feather?" She grinned. "But are you certain you wish to give it up?"

"Oh, yes," Lady Turner said. "We would not have offered it otherwise."

"In that case." He looked down at Georgie. "I wish to escort Miss Featherton to dinner for the rest of the week." And the rest of her life.

Her cheeks turned a pretty pink, and he was happy she was pleased.

"Very well, my lord." Mrs. Fitzwalter and Lady Turner exchanged a conspiratorial look.

Now, what was that about? "I do have a question. Where did the name 'gypsy hunt' come from?"

Lady Turner grinned. "When we were children the gypsies that camped near us had the most interesting items for sale. At some point, our mothers decided that instead of simply purchasing the items and giving them to us, they would hide them and make us search for our gifts."

That sounded innocuous enough. Although he still could not like the name. Gavin held his arm out to Georgie. "I'm famished."

"I am becoming peckish as well." She looked at their hostesses. "Do you know where Lord and Lady Littleton are?"

"In the dining room," Lady Turner said. "She has been a bit tired." The lady touched her stomach. "I suppose I shall experience that in a few months."

"Oh, Mary!" Georgie hugged the other woman. "I am so pleased for you." Then she looked at Mrs. Fitzwalter. "It looks as if there will be several births close together."

He hadn't known the other lady was with child as well. An image of Georgie round with his child came into his mind. With any luck at all, she would not be far behind the rest of the ladies. "Congratulations. Your husbands and families must be delighted."

"Thank you, my lord," the ladies said as one.

As they strolled to the dining room it suddenly occurred to him that whoever had put Georgie and him by themselves in an attic might have been doing some matchmaking. Even though the door had remained open, they had been completely alone. Part of him wished they had been found, but a larger part of him knew that would not have helped his cause to convince her to marry him because she wanted to.

Chapter Seventeen

Over the next hour or so the rest of the group straggled into the dining room having had various degrees of success. What really interested Georgie was the last arrivals. The Earl of St. Albans and Miss Blomefield—who had asked the ladies to call her Delia. Although she was making her first come out, it had been delayed by two years. Therefore, she was older than most of the other single ladies, including Georgie. Both of them appeared a little worse for wear.

"Please excuse me." Delia brushed at her skirts. "I must change." She left the room rather abruptly.

St. Albans's cravat was creased and haphazardly tied, and his usually elegant jacket was covered with straw and grass, making it appear as if he'd been doing something he ought not to have been.

Lips twitching, Adeline slid Georgie an amused look. They were not the only ones to have noticed. Mr. Barfleur, one of the younger gentlemen, opened his mouth to speak and got elbowed in the side by his companion.

Lord Turner entered the dining room, took one glance

at St. Albans, and said, "What the devil, er, deuce happened to you?"

"Geese." His lordship closed his eyes and shuddered. "I hope never to have to obtain anything from those creatures again."

Next to Georgie, Turley dropped his head into one hand and his shoulders started to shake. Mary Turner's eyes widened and she covered her mouth with her hand, and Amanda Fitzwalter groaned.

"What?" the earl demanded.

"You were supposed to have found a painting . . ." Amanda's words trailed off. "Never mind. Please go change, and I shall send up luncheon for you and Miss Blomefield."

"Thank you. I shall. What time are we due to depart for the market town?"

"In an hour. That should give you sufficient time to eat and change." Amanda glanced at her husband, who gave a nearly imperceptible shake of his head. "Off you go then."

"I shall see you shortly." St. Albans gave a stiff bow and left the room.

Turley let loose the laughter he'd been hiding and that started the rest of the gentlemen. After a few moments, Georgie punched him in his side.

"What?" He gave her an injured look. "It's deuced funny, if you ask me. If I hadn't listened to you we would not have found the . . . Good Lord!"

So he had realized that they had been left alone for a considerable period of time in a remote room, and they were not meant to be left alone. She wondered if the possible ramifications had dawned on him. Unfortunately, all they could do was trust that neither Mary nor Amanda said anything.

Lips pressed into a line and brows raised, she gave him one of her mother's looks. "Indeed."

Across the table, Adeline's brows drew together. That was a conversation that Georgie would not be able to avoid. She and Turley had already told their friends about how they found the gypsy hunt items. What she wanted to know now was where the other painting of a lady with geese was and how it differed from theirs.

"Geor . . . Miss Featherton"—Turley hastily corrected himself. Had he been calling her by her first name in his mind?—"I—um."

"Not here." If they discussed it at all it would definitely not be here. "Everything is fine." Except that six other people now knew they had been together, without benefit of a chaperone and for a considerable amount of time. If he proposed in order to save her reputation, she would . . . she would . . . well, she would do something more drastic than hit him in the side. She wanted to tell him she did not ever wish to discuss it, but he would never agree to that.

"Yes, of course." He finally seemed to realize that other ears were turned their way. "Not here." A smile appeared slowly on his lips. "Geese are interesting animals," he said to no one in particular. "Did you know they even began the theme of a seventeenth-century protest song against aristocrats who rob from the common man?" Only Frits's lips tipped up as if he knew what was coming.

Without waiting for anyone to answer Turley began to sing.

The law locks up the man or woman
Who steals the goose from off the common,
But turns the bigger robber loose

Who steals the common from off the goose.
The law condemns the man or woman
Who steals the goose from off the common,
But leave the greater villain loose
Who steals the common from off the goose.

Whose is the Kingdom, the power and the glory?
For ever and ever, will it be the same old story?

The law demands that we atone
When we take things we do not own,
But leaves the lords and ladies fine
Who take things that are yours and mine?

Whose is the Kingdom, the power and the glory?
For ever and ever, will it be the same old story?

The law demands that we atone
When we take things we do not own,
But leaves the lords and ladies fine
Who take things that are yours and mine?

Whose is the Kingdom, the power and the glory?
For ever and ever, will it be the same old story?

The law locks up the man or woman
Who steals the goose from off the common,
But turns the bigger robber loose
Who steals the common from off the goose.

Whose is the Kingdom, the power and the glory?
For ever and ever, will it be the same old story?

The poor and wretched don't escape
If they conspire the law to break.

This must be so, but they endure
Those who conspire to make the law.
Whose is the Kingdom, the power and the glory?
For ever and ever, will it be the same old story?

The poor and wretched don't escape
If they conspire the law to break.
That must be so, but they endure
Those who conspire to make the law.

The law locks up the man or woman
Who steals the goose from off the common,
But turns the bigger robber loose
Who steals the common from off the goose.

Turley surprised Georgie by having a lovely melodic baritone that she could have listened to for hours. He was joined by Frits, with a slightly lower voice, singing harmony during the first chorus. They had both raised their glasses of wine which the butler was happy to refill. By the second chorus, most of the other guests had had their glasses refilled and joined in. In fact, the only one who had not sung was Lord Lytton. Although Georgie had not given it any thought, he might very well be a Tory. In that case, he would not have enjoyed the song at all.

"Bravo!" Mary Turner started to clap and the others quickly joined in. "I do not think I have ever heard such magnificent singing from gentlemen."

"We must definitely add a singing evening to our events," Amanda added.

"Or perhaps to augment the evening the ladies were to show their talents," Mary said.

Low moans were heard from some of the men, but others

grinned and raised their glasses again. Georgie would wager that most of them had a great deal of experience singing songs that were not fit for a lady's ears.

"The question is," Lord Bottomley said, "do you have the proper sheet music?"

Mary's eyes widened. "I have no idea. We shall have to sort through it all. But if we are in need of it we have an excellent circulating library."

Turley barked a laugh. "If not, Littleton and I can write down the words of songs we remember." Turley pulled a face. "I don't know about the music, though."

"That is not a problem." Georgie had blurted out the words before thinking about them. "If you sing the song to me I can probably pick out the tune. I do not need sheet music."

"Do you not?" He gave her a considering glance. "That's amazing."

Before she could demure, Lord St. Albans came back into the room looking much better than he had when he'd left and very much on his dignity. "Miss Blomefield's maid said she would be down shortly." He held up a finger that had a plaster on it, and focused on their hosts. "Before you send your guests to visit the geese, I would suggest you train them not to attack."

"A very good idea, my lord. I do not know why that was not taken care of before." Mary's face flushed, but Georgie did not think it was from embarrassment as her voice shook with what sounded like suppressed laughter.

While the rest of the table stifled their laughter, Littleton caught Gavin's eye. His friend must have realized that Gavin and Georgie had been accidentally left alone. Damn the man, Littleton was going to subject him to "a talk." It was not as if he and Georgie had planned to be in the attic alone. If St. Albans had had the sense to listen to Miss Blomefield and look for another painting—it wasn't possible they were meant to find the same one—they would have been with them. Now that Gavin thought about it, finding the maid had been extremely fortunate. Had the maid left because she was supposed to find the other couple? Somehow, he'd find time to ask St. Albans exactly what had happened, but in a way as to not arouse suspicion. As to Georgie, he had promised he would not compromise her, and if anything happened to cause anyone to think she had been compromised, he would stand by her decision.

Miss Blomefield finally arrived and the Turners and Fitzwalters shooed everyone out to the hall. Fortunately, Fritz had the forethought to call for his coach. Gavin had no idea how far the town was, but he knew Adeline might not be up to the walk back here before going home. Or were they going home? No, they must be. None of them had brought evening kit.

They had reached the hall when Frits said, "I'd like to speak with you."

Then Gavin heard Georgie say, "I think we should all go outside. I gather we are taking the carriage."

Frits inclined his head. "Very well. We'll let the others get sorted."

The four of them continued out the front door, down the steps, and off to the side of the drive where they could not be overheard.

Littleton's mouth flattened in a good imitation of a displeased father. "From what just occurred, I assume that another couple was to have been in the attic with you. Exactly how long were you alone?"

Georgie crossed her arms under her breasts, plumping them and making Gavin want to groan.

"Not long at all." She went on to explain how they'd found the maid and that she had led them to the attic. "She was present while we asked questions. After that, we found the trunk in just a few minutes, gathered the items, and left."

He nodded his concurrence with what she'd said. "It occurred to me after I saw St. Albans that the maid had probably been waiting for us and went to search for St. Albans and Miss Blomefield."

"Who were fighting real geese." Adeline leaned against her husband and started to laugh. "I—I haven't heard anything that funny in a long time."

"It was humorous." Georgie began to chuckle.

He glanced at Littleton and shook his head. "We'd better not start. With four of us we'll never stop."

Other conveyances drew up in front of the house and the guests began climbing in. Gavin held his arm out to Georgie, who was wiping her eyes. "We had better go. Have you ever been to this town?"

"I have not." Her voice still shook a bit. "But it is the one where both the Turners and the Fitzwalters married."

She went on to relate the story of the ladies wishing to marry on the same day if not in the same ceremony, and Lord Fitzwalter refusing to have a wedding at St. George's, and Mr. Fitzwalter saving the day by remembering about the church in Croseton, a town owned by both families.

"I daresay it holds fond memories for both of them," Georgie concluded.

"I imagine it does." Where would she like to have their ceremony? But Gavin was getting ahead of himself. First he had to convince her to marry him.

They reached their coach and he handed Georgie up then climbed in. "Knowing some of the history makes me more interested in seeing the town."

"Speaking of history," Georgie said. "I had no idea you sang so well."

"Do not forget my Frits," Adeline added. "He has an excellent voice." She gave her husband a hard look. "One I have never heard before."

Littleton flushed slightly and scratched his ear. "I haven't had much of an opportunity. I do plan to sing to our daughter."

"Or our son."

This was a continuing theme between them. "I don't think either of you care which it is."

"Nor do I." Georgie's dark-blue eyes were sparkling with merriment. "I think they just like debating the sex of the baby."

"If only there *were* a way to know." Adeline rubbed her growing stomach.

"Visit a gypsy at a fair," Gavin suggested. "Other than that, I don't think there will ever be a way to know."

"It is just so frustrating having to wait." She pouted for a second then smiled again. "I shall simply pray for a healthy baby."

One of Littleton's hands had formed a fist and the knuckles were turning white. "The only thing I want is a safe delivery for you and our child."

Gavin resisted the urge to glance at Georgie. He did not love her and never would, but the thought of her dying in childbirth caused a sharp pain in his chest. He would do everything in his power to stop that from happening. Better yet, he absolutely would not allow it to occur. How he didn't know. He just knew that her not being a part of his life forever was not an option.

Chapter Eighteen

Marc clinched his jaw as Miss Featherton left with the Littletons and Turley. At this rate, Marc was never going to have a chance with her. Not only that, but he was certain that Littleton and his wife were helping Turley. Marc had planned to visit the area where he'd seen Miss Featherton riding, but the gypsy hunt had put paid to that idea. At least for today. Well, there was always tomorrow. Then again, Lady Aurelia was proving to be a very pleasant companion. Still, he felt as if he had to make a final push in the direction of Miss Featherton.

He surveyed the rest of the guests as they assembled in front of the house. Standing on the top step, Lady Turner called out names and footmen escorted ladies and gentlemen to the various conveyances waiting to take them into the market town.

She looked over at Lady Aurelia then glanced at him. "Lord Lytton, you and Lady Aurelia will ride with my husband and me."

He didn't even have to paste a polite smile on his face as he strolled over to Lady Aurelia. Thus far, he'd been happy to spend time with her. "It would be my pleasure."

Lady Turner went back to her list.

And Lady Aurelia's smile was genuine. "I am glad we shall be riding together. I had a great deal of fun with you during the gypsy hunt."

He didn't understand her. "But we didn't win."

"Winning is not everything." She raised one dark blond brow. "Sometimes playing the game is enough."

To him winning had always been what mattered because his aunt cared so much. Or he thought she did. Then again, he had never been able to please her. Even when he had backed out of a pending betrothal with a lady on his aunt's orders because of the death of her father, she still had not been happy with him for long. But soon he'd be free. Once he married, he wouldn't have to care about what his aunt thought anymore.

"My lord?" Lady Aurelia's eyes captured his gaze when he glanced up.

"I am sorry. I was remembering something else. You might be correct that winning is not everything. I must give it further thought."

The corners of her lips twitched, but instead of responding she placed her hand on his arm. "Shall we find our carriage?"

They approached one of the footmen and were escorted to the coach at the front of the line. "It's this one, my lord."

Turley handed the servant a coin. "Thank you."

The steps were already down, so he handed Lady Aurelia into the carriage and waited for Lord and Lady Turner to arrive. Even under these circumstances, it would not help him at all to be caught in a closed coach with a lady.

She sat on the forward-facing bench next to the door. "Have you spent much time in this area?"

"No." Marc had been looking for Turner and now faced Lady Aurelia. "This is my first time here."

"Mine as well." She graced him with another smile. "I do think the countryside is lovely, and it is not nearly as chilly as it is at home."

Had she not been in Town? "Were you not taking part in the Season before coming here?"

"No." She shook her head as if to emphasize the point. "I do not like to be looked over as if I were a mare to be purchased. And as you know, I am not fond of small talk."

He understood her point. He wouldn't like it either, but how was she to find a suitable husband? Or was her mother arranging a match for her? Marc had been surprised by her depth of knowledge regarding politics. He had no doubt she was conversant on a number of other subjects as well.

Suddenly she let out a peal of light laughter. "Oh dear. If you could see the consternation on your face. You wish to ask me how I am going to find a husband, do you not?"

Heat crept up Marc's neck and he was grateful for his collar and cravat. She really was the most straightforward lady he had ever met. He cleared his throat. "It had crossed my mind."

"The answer is quite simple. I have not yet met the gentleman I wish to wed."

"Are you waiting for a love match?"

"Dear me, no." She fluttered her hand as if to ward off such silliness. "I am much too rational for that. Although, if it did occur I suppose I would accept it. I am looking for a gentleman with whom I shall find it easy to live. After all, marriage is for life."

Marc couldn't deny that. "So it is."

He wondered if he had been going about courting the

wrong way. He liked Lady Aurelia, but was still drawn to Miss Featherton. He gave himself a mental shrug. There was only one way to find out.

It was no surprise that Georgie and the others had arrived in Croseton before the rest of the group. They *had* left first. "Do you know where the Cross and Crown is located?"

"My coachman does," Frits replied. "One of his sisters married a man from here, and he comes to visit her."

They stopped in front of a well-kept Tudor inn built of wattle and daub. The lower front windows were made of colored glass with windows so clean they sparkled in the early afternoon sun. Turley handed her down and she could see that the building had two floors and attics. "It is lovely."

He placed her hand on his arm as they strolled toward the entrance. "I agree. The whole town seems to be in excellent condition."

Georgie surveyed the other buildings. There was no faded or peeling paint on any of them. Each shop's sign was in good repair. The pavements were clean as was the street. "I wonder how much of this is due to the fact that two families own it."

"Quite a bit I'd say." He turned as Frits and Adeline came up. "This is impressive."

"That is just what I said," Adeline commented. "I feel the need to help Littleton look as well maintained as Croseton obviously is."

"It is almost like stepping back into time." Georgie had seen many buildings that were centuries old. They even had some in her family. But she had never seen a whole town that appeared as if it had been suspended in time. "I almost expect to see men walking around in long coats and stockings."

Adeline grinned. "And ladies in gowns with low waists."

"And even lower necklines," Frits said in a deep voice.

"Where is the market?" Turley quickly asked as if trying to change the subject.

"Mary said there is a field at the end of town." Georgie stepped toward the street and found stands beyond the last building. "There it is."

The others peered in the same direction.

"It is quite large," Adeline said. "I would love to go down there now, but we did promise we would remain here until the others arrived."

"In that event—" Turley started to the inn's main entrance with Georgie in tow. "I'm for tasting the inn's ale."

"Excellent idea." Frits smiled. "Would you ladies like tea?"

"I would like to try a sip of ale." Despite having two brothers, or perhaps because of them, Georgie had never sampled ale.

"I would like tea." Adeline tugged on her husband's arm.

A large private parlor on the first floor had been reserved for the party. The landlord himself led them up a short flight of stairs, and Georgie now understood why the windows on one side of the building were taller. They had just finished their refreshments when the first carriage stopped at the inn.

She rose from her chair, causing Frits and Turley to jump up. "Shall we meet them in the yard?"

"Yes." Turley took her hand and tucked it into the crook of his arm. "I am looking forward to the market, and if we let them in here the gentlemen will wish to have at least one drink."

Once the other vehicles had deposited their passengers, Mary and Amanda with their husbands led the way to the market. When they arrived at the last building, Amanda announced, "We will meet back up at the inn in three hours. Although, if anyone becomes fatigued the landlord will be able to accommodate you."

The party dispersed into the market. Georgie and Turley, by unspoken consent, went to the stands on the far side.

"Is there anything in particular you wish to purchase?" he asked.

"I think I shall buy some ribbons for my younger sister and something for Kit and Mary's new baby."

They passed a stand selling meat pies, and she was sorry she'd had so much to eat earlier.

Turley glanced at the pies as well and sighed. "Don't you have a younger brother as well?"

"He is actually older than I am, but younger in that he is not yet on the Town." She stopped at a stand carrying lace being sold by an older woman. "He is at Oxford preparing for a diplomatic career."

Georgie picked up a length of the lace. "This looks as if it was made in Belgium."

"You have a good eye, madam." The seller brought out a piece of lace so exquisite that Georgie almost dropped her jaw.

Ferns and chrysanthemums seemed to dangle on vines. "This is a work of art." She had done it now. Everyone knew never to let a vendor know how much you liked the wares. "How much is it?"

The woman named a price that was surprisingly on the

reasonable side of expensive. "I try to keep my prices fair. It would cost much more in London."

It was a good price. Still, it would take most of the money she had brought with her to buy it. Then again, even in Town one would be hard-pressed to find such beautiful lace. She would simply have to buy the rest of her presents later. "I shall take it."

"A good decision, madam." The seller carefully rolled the length and placed it in a small white cotton sack.

Georgie took the coins from her reticule, which was suddenly a great deal lighter. But what did that matter when she had enough of the lace for herself, her older sister, mother, and grandmother? "Thank you, madam."

The only problem was that it would not fit in her reticule. She should have brought a maid or a footman.

"Allow me." Turley took the bundle now wrapped in brown paper from the seller. "I could see from the look on your face that the lace was worth the price. I would be happy to give you—"

"I could not ask it of you," Georgie knew she had cut him off, but there was nothing else she could have done. Her mother would be appalled if she accepted money from a gentleman to whom she was not betrothed. "It would not be appropriate."

Even though Turley murmured his assent, he did not seem to be convinced. But there was nothing she could do about that either.

"Will you use all of the lace?" The package looked heavy, but he carried it as if it weighed nothing at all.

"No. I bought enough for my mother, older sister, and grandmother as well."

"That was generous of you. My offer still stands." His tone was hopeful.

But her ability to accept his offer had not changed. A different subject was in order. "Look, there is Lady Aurelia and Lord Lytton. Shall we join them?"

"No." Turley started heading down one of the alleys made by the stalls and away from the couple.

Georgie knew he and Frits did not like the man because of the story they had heard. Still, it must have been several years ago, and the wrong had not been done to them. "He has always been pleasant to me."

"He acts like a Cit." His mumbled answer made no sense at all.

"I do not know what you mean by that." Determined to discover the truth, she halted their progress. "I have met several Cits and they were all very pleasant men."

"You mean obsequious?"

Was that what she meant? Georgie thought about Mr. Taylor, a merchant with whom her father did business. He actually did not seem to be in awe of her father's title. "Not at all. Naturally they are polite. Everyone should be. I do not know why he should be fawning. He is an earl and before that he was the son of an earl."

Turley's frown wrinkled his forehead. "It always felt as if he wanted to become friends with other fellows because of who they are." He started them ambling around the stalls again. "Naturally, he did not have much use for either Littleton or me. Exeter still calls him Loathsome Lytton."

It was sad that a little boy could be so derided, and his behavior years ago still held against him. "He certainly was not very wise. Many times one's rank has little to do with one's standing in Polite Society."

"Precisely." Turley stopped in front of a stand with children's toys. "I should find something for my niece. She is only just over two years old. My sister is expecting another child in the spring."

There were several brightly colored wooden toys. "Do you think she would like the horse on wheels or a doll?"

He studied the selection as if the decision was of great importance. "I think she would find both of them fascinating. She has a doll, but not a wooden one."

There were other animals on wheels as well. "Either a toy on wheels or a doll would work. Children tend to be easy to please."

"I can get her one of each." He flashed her a smile as he selected the horse and a doll.

"I think I will take that rattle for my young nephew. He was born a few months ago." She picked up a plain wooden rattle and paid for it before slipping it in her reticule.

The vendor handed Turley his purchases wrapped up in paper, and he balanced the first package on top of the second. "What I need is someone who can take these to the inn."

"Sir," the seller said. "My son will be here directly. He can take them if you tell me which inn you want them taken to."

"Thank you." Turley took out two coins and handed them to the man. "The Cross and Crown."

"I'll see they get there."

They strolled past the other booths, and even though there were several things Georgie would have liked to purchase, she was aware that she did not have the funds.

"Do you like that shade of ribbon?"

She looked at the red ribbon at which he was pointing. "It is beautiful."

"I think so as well." When she married or got old enough, it was one of the shades she wanted to wear.

He ordered a length of the glib, and stuck it into the pocket on the tails of his jacket.

"I have always thought that was an interesting place to put pockets." Georgie wished gowns still had pockets. Especially now when the skirts were wider. Perhaps she should speak with the modiste about fashioning them.

"They can be extremely useful." He held his arm out to her again and she tucked her hand into its crook. The church bell struck the hour, and they turned back toward the inn. Georgie was happy that they had got to spend time together and actually spoke of subjects other than what was merely polite. She'd had no idea that he had a young niece or that he was careful about the types of gifts he purchased. Perhaps this week should be used simply to get to know each other better, and deciding to marry.

Chapter Nineteen

Gavin glanced at Georgie as she walked beside him. She obviously had no idea he'd bought the ribbon for her. It would look perfect in her rich, dark brown tresses. He'd like to give her rubies and emeralds, but the gewgaw would have to do for now. The question was when to give it to her. He did not want to do it with the entire house party around. Perhaps on the way back to Littlewood would be the best time. Littleton and Adeline would be with them, and it would all be aboveboard, and Georgie wouldn't be able to refuse the gift. It struck him that he'd sent her flowers but had never bought her anything else. He could tell from the way she had perused the fabrics and other items that she wanted to make more purchases. If only she would have accepted a loan. But he hadn't offered a loan. He'd offered a gift.

Damn me for a fool. Well, I'll know better the next time.

He'd been impressed that she bought lace for members of her family. Despite the months he'd spent with her he had not known how generous she was. It struck him that he liked that about her. It was an excellent quality to have in a wife and helpmate.

He still wanted to find a way to give her the ability to purchase some of the other things she had seen. The town of Littleton had a market. Would they have the same wares? If it was not mentioned on the way back, he'd have to ask Littleton. Or would Georgie know? "It's been a long time since I've been to a market with so many different items for sale."

"I know what you mean. I always seem to miss the one at home. I wonder what the Littleton market is like."

Gavin was glad he'd been thinking about the same thing. Otherwise he'd probably not have said what he should have. Shopping had never before mattered to him. Well, shopping that didn't include plows, cattle, seed, horses, or what he needed to buy for the Season. "We should ask."

"That is a good idea." They approached the inn and several of the other guests were mingling in front of the building. "I do not know which market is superior and do not wish to make either Lady Turner or Mrs. Fitzwalter feel badly if theirs is not."

"Of course, you are right." Georgie grinned at Gavin, and his chest seemed to puff out. All sorts of strange things were happening to his chest when he was around her. The puffing out he understood, but not the birds.

Still, courting her here was infinitely superior to doing it in Town. On the other hand, they might be getting to know each other better, but he didn't feel as though he was coming closer to convincing her to marry him. He'd not wanted to, but he was going to have to ask Lady Littleton and the other ladies for suggestions to make Georgie want to be his wife.

"Here we are." The others were showing off items they had found at the market, and there was a great deal of giggling. The other ladies might be the same age as Adeline and Georgie, but they did not have the same level of maturity. He felt as if he was in the midst of a bunch of schoolroom girls. "Do you wish to find Littleton and Adeline?"

"In a moment." She led him toward Lytton and Lady Aurelia. "Did you find anything worth taking home with you?"

Lady Aurelia smiled and pointed to several packages Lytton was holding. "I did indeed. Did you see the lace at the one booth? It was all from Belgium."

"I bought several lengths to share with my mother and sister. After that, the only other present I could afford was a rattle for my nephew."

"Oh, you poor thing!" Lady Aurelia gave Georgie a rueful smile. "We were told after tea last night to be prepared to spend more than we might normally do in a country market town."

"I am sorry I missed the advice," she said, her tone wistful. "Then again, I am very pleased with my purchase."

She turned to Lytton. "And you, my lord. Did anything catch your fancy?"

"It made me wish I had family to buy things for." He shifted the packages. "We should go in."

"Yes, of course." Lady Aurelia turned toward the door. "Those must be getting heavy."

As they entered the inn, Georgie held Gavin back. "I think his statement about not having anyone to give presents to was sad."

It was, actually. Still, he had trouble separating his animosity for his lordship and feeling sorry for the man. Maybe Georgie was right, and he had not had much sense when he was younger. Nevertheless, he would say what she wanted to hear, and give it more thought later. "I agree."

She walked through the door he held open for her. "I think he and Lady Aurelia make a good pair."

"Yes, indeed." If his lordship was concentrating on her ladyship, Gavin would not have to worry about Lytton attempting to capture Georgie's attention. "Are you planning to matchmake?"

"Me? No. I was making an observation." She waited for him to close the door. "I leave matchmaking to my sister and grandmother. They have become very good at it."

He hoped that meant that Lady Featherton would take an active part in matching Georgie and him. "My aunt used to like matchmaking. But now her daughters and my sister are all married, and the children are too young."

They reached the parlor that had been reserved for the house party. "Do you see your cousins much?"

"Hardly at all. They are all a fair distance from me and never come to Town. I suppose I would see them more if my sister were not in Paris. I seem to spend a great deal of time sailing to France and back."

Georgie heaved a sigh. "If my sister was in Paris I would do the same thing."

He wished he could tell her he'd take her there. "Perhaps you'll visit someday. Didn't Lady Augusta go to Paris?"

"Yes." Georgie nodded. "They traveled on from there. Did you know that she and Lord Phineas married?"

"No." But Gavin hadn't known the man well enough to keep up a correspondence. "In Paris?"

She worried her lip. "No, at a castle in Slovenia. They are in Padua at the moment. Augusta was told she would be accepted for a course of study at the university."

They were now in the parlor and it was all he could do

to maintain a calm countenance. Ladies did not attend university. Then again, the lady's family was extremely forward thinking. Still, he did not think they would like that getting around. Then again . . . Damn, he was babbling to himself. "I suppose they will not return for a while."

"Yes," she said slowly. "I should be receiving a letter from her soon. She writes often."

Once he'd got over his shock, he could actually say something that made more sense. "I will be interested to hear how she is doing. Padua is considered one of the best universities there is."

"So my brother told me." Georgie removed her hand from his arm, and he felt as if he'd lost part of himself.

He quickly held out a chair for her and sat in the one next to her. "I would appreciate hearing what she thinks of it."

That earned him a grateful smile. "Thank you for not thinking she is some sort of anomaly."

"She must be an extraordinarily intelligent lady." As he'd hoped, her smile widened.

"She is." Georgie chuckled lightly. "But she is also interested in most of the things we all are. I do wonder how Lord Phineas changed her mind about marrying. She was determined not to until she had finished her studies."

Gavin would like to know that too. "Maybe you should ask her."

"I think I shall. It should make for an interesting story." She took bread and cheese from a tray that was being pushed along the table.

He wondered how long it took for a letter and the response to get to Padua and back to England again. Probably much too long. Gavin helped himself to some ham and bread from the platter. He needed advice, and the sooner he could get back to The Lilacs, the sooner he could ask for it. Fortunately, Adeline looked to be fading. Littleton caught Gavin's eye and he nodded. "Adeline is ready to go home."

Georgie immediately took out a handkerchief and wrapped her sandwich in it. "I am ready."

Gavin finished his sandwich on the way to the coach. By the time they arrived at Littlewood it was time for tea. He took Littleton aside. "I shall leave you and return to your mother's if you don't mind."

He frowned. "Are you sure you don't want to spend more time with Georgie?"

"I need to ask the ladies for help. Am I invited to dinner?"

Littleton gave a knowing nod. "Naturally. I'll see you then."

Gavin attempted to use the time to formulate a series of questions to pose, but it all came down to one: How did he get her to agree to marry him?

Fortunately, he arrived as tea was being served. He bowed to the ladies, and Lady Littleton ordered something more substantial to be brought.

He'd no sooner taken a sip of tea when the duchess asked, "Have you kissed her yet?"

Gavin swallowed in a hurry. "No. I mean, of course not. We aren't betrothed."

"Slow top," her grace mumbled into her cup.

That wasn't at all fair, and he had almost kissed her. "But what if she doesn't want to kiss me?"

"In that case, my boy," Lady Featherton said, "you had better look elsewhere for a wife."

Good Lord. Nothing he'd done was right. "You think she wants to kiss me?" Three pairs of eyes, brows raised, stared at him. "I—I did not think she would kiss me if we were not betrothed."

"Gavin, my dear boy," Lady Littleton said. "I shall tell you about the first time Adeline considered that Littleton might want to marry her. Naturally, this is between the four of us." Gavin nodded encouragingly. "They were at some garden party and somehow she and my son were alone. He brushed his lips against hers. She told him that he should not kiss her, and he said he knew."

Why hadn't he heard that story? Not that a gentleman should tell anyone about kissing a lady. "You think I should kiss her lightly?"

Her ladyship gave him an exasperated look. "I think that you should begin the kiss, and see where it leads."

He glanced at her grace and Lady Featherton. Both of them nodded.

"I'm dining there tonight." He offered the information hoping they would give him more of an idea when he should kiss Georgie.

"No, not in the house." Lady Featherton held her cup out for more tea. "Pick a place where it does not look as if you have to hide."

"We will most likely go riding tomorrow."

"Without a groom?" the duchess asked.

"No. Johnson is always with us." And there was no way that Littleton would let Gavin go off with Georgie without a groom.

"Is there not a garden party at the Turners'?" Lady Littleton asked.

He raked his fingers through his hair. "I have no idea."

"Lord help me," the duchess groaned. "Cristabel, do you not have the schedule?"

"I do." She went over to a desk tucked in the corner of

the room. "And I made a copy in the event we required it." She took out a piece of foolscap and handed it to him. "It is always a good thing to know what is being planned."

Much to his chagrin, he felt like a child again. "Thank you, my lady."

"It is my pleasure. Once I see you settled I can look forward to even more grandchildren. Even if yours are not of my blood."

He held the list out to her. "No, take that and make note of any opportunities you can contrive to kiss my granddaughter."

Somehow he got the feeling that this wasn't the first time she had done something like this. "I shall follow your advice."

"It's about time," her grace muttered.

Gavin finished his tea and suppressed the need to dash from the room. With any luck, his valet would have brandy in his chambers. He was grateful for their advice, but it was a bit overwhelming. Especially the part about kissing Georgie. Not that kissing her wasn't exactly what he'd been wanting to do for months, but that her grandmother and the duchess were so adamant that he do so soon.

He strode into his parlor and his valet handed him a glass of brandy. "How the devil did you know I'd need this?"

Ardley cleared his throat. "A footman stands at the door of any room her ladyship is occupying in the event she might want something. He overheard what the duchess said, and sent up the brandy with a message."

Gavin downed half the goblet. "Good God, don't tell me the servants gossip."

"Not outside of the house, my lord." His valet straightened up a desk that did not need straightening. "Lady Littleton is particularly kind and pays very well. They would never betray her." Ardley finished and straightened. "Shall I order a bath?"

"Yes, please. I am dining at Littlewood."

"Very good, my lord." He helped Gavin rid himself of his jacket.

Drat, he'd forgotten all about the frippery. "There is a length of red ribbon in the tail. Please put it in the jacket I'll wear this evening."

"As you wish. If you need anything else, I shall be in the dressing room."

"Thank you, Ardley."

"You are quite welcome, my lord."

The door closed and Gavin paced the room. He'd not even spent enough time here to notice it more than in passing. It was a large parlor that had windows on two sides. He wandered over to one set of windows near the corner of the room and looked out. In the distance he could see one of the top towers of Littlewood peeking through the trees. Georgie was there, and he wished he was with her. That wanting brought him back to his conversation with the ladies. Why had he not kissed her? Just a brush across the lips. Lord knew he'd been wanting to do it for months. But he'd convinced himself that he should not kiss her until they were betrothed. But Littleton had kissed Adeline and, according to the ladies, it had aided his case. Gavin perused the paper he still held in one hand.

Garden party
Informal dance
A ride to ruins
Ball

He knew from catching snatches of conversation that there was an extensive wood on the estate. Some of it was planned with benches, ornamental sculptures, and a path to a lake. Perhaps he and Georgie should take a stroll. He should be able to find a place to steal a kiss. On the other hand, part of him was afraid she would reject him. Then it might be as Lady Featherton had said. She was not for him, and he should look elsewhere for a wife.

He didn't like that idea at all. He tossed off the rest of the brandy. Well, he wouldn't know until he tried.

Chapter Twenty

Georgie paced the parlor she had been given. She'd been happy and satisfied with the day until just a little while ago. Turley had seemed more at ease, and she certainly had been easier around him at the market. But now she wondered why she and Turley had not spoken more in Town. Did no one have normal conversations there? She shook her head. It wasn't that. Frits and Adeline had fallen in love there. As had Dorie and Exeter. What was wrong with Georgie that she and Turley had not done so? Was it the whole bit about him not wishing to love his future wife? But if that was the case, then why were they more open now? Was he falling in love with her? How would she know? After all, she had thought he loved her before his disastrous proposal.

Georgie poured a glass of wine from the cut-crystal decanter that had been left on a small table, took a sip, and stopped. She had never before been given wine in her room to drink. Naturally, her mother and grandmother had wine in their parlors, but she was apparently too young and unmarried. Just having it in her room made her feel older and more mature. She would have to remember to thank her maid or whoever had brought it.

On the walnut desk standing between two sets of windows was the schedule for the house party. They would not attend all of the events. Neither she nor her friend had any interest in archery contests. But tomorrow afternoon was a garden party. Frits had first kissed Adeline at a garden party. Georgie wondered if Turley would take the opportunity to kiss her when Johnson wasn't around. She heaved a sigh. If only ladies were allowed to make the first move when it came to kissing. But they were not. It would be seen as horribly forward and even a gentleman who thought he was in love with a lady would be appalled at such forwardness. What she could do was suggest a walk in the woods. Although she had not had an opportunity to explore them, Mary Turner had been effusive about all the interesting sights they held. What would it be like to be able to learn about one's future home before one was married? Both Adeline and Mary had been able to do just that. Come to think of it, Georgie did not even know where Turley's main estate was. He never mentioned it. Now that she thought about it, she wondered what the reason could be. Most gentlemen were happy to describe their holdings in detail. Rivercrest was the name of his main estate, and she wondered if it actually had a river. Or it might be that he did not like his main estate and preferred to live on another one. She tried to recall what he had said during his proposal, but could not. Perhaps she would ask him about at least his main property. If he *had* told her and she had forgotten then it served him right for not being in love with her.

"My lady." Smith came out of the dressing room. "Your bath is ready."

"Thank you." Georgie put down the glass. "And thank you for the wine. I appreciate it."

For the first time since the maid had come to work for her, Smith blushed. "Thank you, miss."

Georgie took her time bathing and then selecting a gown for the evening.

By the time she entered the drawing room, Frits and Turley were already there. "Where is Adeline? She is not overtired, is she?"

Turley handed Georgie a glass of claret. "No. There was a problem she had to see to. I expect—ah, here she is." He bowed. "I hope everything is now in order."

"It is." Adeline smiled as she accepted a goblet of wine from her husband. "A question arose with one of the maids in training."

"In training?" He appeared confused.

"Yes." Georgie took pleasure in knowing something about Littlewood that he did not. "You are aware of all the follies?"

His blond brows drew together making his expression serious, and she could imagine him giving that look to a child with the same light blue eyes and blond curls. "I am."

"They are being used to train maids and footmen." She did not even try to hold in her grin as his brows shot up to his hair.

"How interesting. How often do they have to attend to the follies?"

"Every day from what I have seen." Georgie raised a brow as if to challenge any complaint he might make.

"That is an excellent idea." He turned from her to their friends. "I assume you help to place them after their training is completed."

"We do," Frits said. "We work closely with an employment agency that my family has used for years now."

"Considering how difficult it is for young men and women in the country to find reliable and appropriate employment, I might just have to find a way to institute a program at Rivercrest."

So Rivercrest was where Turley lived when not in Town. "You have never told me about your estates. Other than to say there were several of them."

"Have I not?" He studied Georgie for a moment. "I suppose it's because my sister told me how gentlemen drone on and on about them. What would you like to know?"

Well, that gave her a carte blanche.

"My ladies, my lords." Creswell bowed. "Dinner is served."

Turley held his arm out to her. "You may ask anything you like."

She placed her hand on his arm, and in an attempt not to focus on the feelings touching him gave her actually paid attention to its strength. "Do you do some of the physical work? My father and brother do."

"Yes, when I'm needed." He started to amble in the direction of the small dining room. "All my tenants know they can call on me."

"Did your father do the same?" Suddenly his face shuttered. What had happened? Was it her mention of his father? Oh, drat! It was. How could she have forgotten what his father had done when his mother had died?

Thankfully, he seemed to force the memory or reaction away. "When I was younger he did. However, in his later years he was not himself."

She had to keep in mind his family problems as she delved into what she wished to know. After all, she did not want him to refuse to answer her questions. "But you followed the example and do the same."

"I do." His arm, which had become as hard as steel, relaxed. "It gives me a great deal of pleasure and a sense of accomplishment to work with my tenants."

"I understand that." She gave his arm a squeeze, and he smiled at her. "When we are home or on another of my family's estates, my mother and I always make baskets and visit the tenants. It is good to know how they are doing and be able to help if we are can."

"Who takes care of them when you are not there?"

"All my father's stewards are married." She reviewed what she knew about them. "I believe it is a requirement."

"The steward's wife makes the visits when your mother is not present."

"Yes," she said, confirming his statement. "Then when my mother visits, the steward's wife goes over the list with her." It had not occurred to her before how important that was to the estate and how it ran.

The corners of his lips twitched as he gazed down at her, making her heart flutter. "I'm learning a great deal this evening."

Her heartbeat increased to a tattoo, and Georgie glanced away quickly at the door to the dining room, but then forced herself to meet his eyes. "I suspect there is always more to be learnt no matter the subject."

Gavin searched her lapis blue eyes. "I have to believe you are right." He helped Georgie take her seat and, as always sat next to her. "I look forward to having someone give me other opinions and challenging my thinking."

"Are you?" A hint of doubt entered her eyes, and he knew that although they had spent time together, they had not spent the right time together.

"I am absolutely serious about it. One will become averse to change without it." They were interrupted by a footman pouring wine and then by dishes being passed around. Dinner with the four of them was extremely informal. "Would you care for Brussels sprouts?"

"Yes, thank you. I adore the way Cook does them with bits of ham."

He almost groaned, knowing that his friend would launch into the quality of his ham, but surprisingly, Littleton did not. Which made Gavin say perversely, "It is the way the pigs are raised."

"So I have heard." Her lips quivered as if she would burst into laughter at any moment.

How he would like to see that. He would especially like to see it at Rivercrest. Merriment had not filled the house in many years. And he was more certain than ever that he would like to see Georgie as its mistress.

She speared a piece of Brussels sprout with a bit of ham and ate it. "I would like to have ham like this. Of course, one must have chestnut trees."

He was very close to saying, *Marry me and you may have what you want.*

In fact, he had a grove of chestnut trees. For the first time, Gavin had to ask himself why he had not done as they had at Littlewood and fed the pigs on the chestnuts. "This is excellent."

"What do you wish to do after dinner?" Adeline was sitting at the end of the very small table next to him.

Georgie glanced up. "Shall we sing? Or rather, the rest of you can sing and I shall play the piano."

He was surprised that she had not offered to join them. "Do you not like to sing?"

She pulled a face. "My skill on the piano is better than my voice."

Somehow he doubted that. He wouldn't push her tonight, but someday, he'd find out just how well she held a tune. He could not be the only one singing to their children.

The talk turned to the house party and the entertainments they would attend and those which they would avoid at all costs.

"Mary and Amanda mentioned a musical evening," Littleton said. "I enjoy my lovely wife's voice and yours, of course"—he glanced at Gavin—"but I am not going to be trapped into hearing a bunch of young ladies either sing, play piano, or play the harp."

"I agree with you, my dear," Adeline said. "You will have enough of that when our daughters come out."

Littleton's face turned to one of shock, and Gavin and Georgie exchanged looks as they stifled their mirth.

"My daughters will not make their come out until they are at least five and twenty."

Georgie cut a look at Gavin before saying sweetly, "In that case, they will have the right to marry as they choose."

"Drat. I hadn't thought about that." Littleton drank a healthy portion of his wine. "I shall have to spend the first eighteen years of their lives teaching them how to know when a gentleman is dangerous to them and how to defend themselves."

"That should be interesting," Adeline murmured. "Considering I thought you were a rake."

Georgie held her serviette to her lips as her shoulders shook.

"As did some other ladies." Gavin took a sip of wine and forced himself not to spew it over the table at the look on his friend's face. "As Shakespeare says, all's well that ends well."

"At least I'll have years to find a way to deal with all of this," Littleton grumbled.

He looked so put out that they all went into whoops.

"Wait until you have a daughter," he groused at Gavin.

"Ah, but you forget that I had my sister to partially raise." It was a good retort, but he knew that a daughter would be different somehow.

"I knew you had a sister," Georgie said. "But I did not know you helped raise her."

Damn, he really didn't want to go into this. Still, if she was to know him better, if she was to be made to understand he could not fall in love with his wife, he had to tell her. "I already mentioned that my father was not himself in his later years. The fact of the matter is that after my mother died, he became another person. He let the estates go, he insisted my sister act as the mistress of the house when she was still in the schoolroom, and he became very difficult. I decided there was nothing to do but to take over the role of master and father, but he fought me. He did not want the responsibility, but would not allow anyone else to have it."

Her eyes seemed to be riveted to him. Strangely, there was no pity, which he could not have borne. "But you did what you had to do to care for your sister and for your lands."

"Yes." They were the hardest years of his life. And he still regretted his estrangement from his father. "I kept the estates going, and protected my sister from some truly horrible matches he had in mind for her. I had to enlist my aunt—my mother's sister—to help."

"But she would have needed to have been sponsored by

a lady in any event." Her voice was soft and firm at the same time. "No gentleman can sponsor a lady no matter his rank."

And thank God for that strange rule of the *ton*. "Yes. That made it easier for my aunt to take my sister under her wing and difficult for our father to disagree."

"In that case, I'd say that you did an excellent job of caring for her and your estates." How she could be so certain, he didn't know. "Almost everyone knows Lady Harrington and admires her. You did what you had to do and succeeded."

Intellectually, he supposed he knew that, but deep inside, he was terrified that presented with the same tragedy as his father had suffered, he would behave in the same manner. "Thank you for your confidence."

"You are welcome." Her words were spoken quietly, but firmly. As if she might have the faith in him that he did not.

The table fell silent as the second course was set out. Even though it was the four of them for dinner, each course still had five removes. He supposed that was to reward the servants. Littleton carved the roast and the footmen brought it around. "I don't know if this is beef or lamb?"

"Beef." Georgie smiled softly at him. "I saw the menu."

"It amazes me how much a lady must learn before she comes out." It had shocked him how much his sister had known when their mother died.

Georgie closed her eyes for a moment. "If only all gentlemen understood how much instruction we are required to take. Granted, we do not learn Greek and Latin"— she paused and frowned—"but we must master a number of other subjects including estate management. After all, someone must know what to do when a peer is attending sessions of Parliament."

"I do not think that that has changed very much," Adeline added. "Back when we had all those wars, the ladies always had to manage and even defend the castles."

"You have got them started now," Littleton said with a grin. "The only politics in which my wife is interested is when it comes to women and children."

"And why not?" Georgie challenged him. "Who else is going to be vocal on that subject if not for ladies?"

Littleton rolled his eyes, but couldn't keep the smile from his face. "You have a point. Obviously we gentlemen have not been sufficiently involved."

"Or in the right way," Georgie said.

Gavin wondered if he agreed with her. That was another thing he'd have to consider.

"I must say that I agree with Henrietta Stern," Adeline said. "Ladies should be able to vote if they meet the same qualifications as men."

"As peeresses in their own names they should be able to have a seat in the Lords," Georgie pronounced.

Gavin had no idea he'd landed into such a hotbed of radicalism, and addressed his friend, "Did you know this about your wife before you married her?"

"Well, I did know that her friends had radical tendencies." Littleton took a piece of fish. "Therefore, I was not surprised. I am simply happy that she handles it the same way I do."

"Don't tell me." Gavin took one slice of lamb and one of fish. "She asks to have the bill or whatever it is sent so that she can make notes."

"Exactly." Adeline looked very pleased with herself. "Georgie, however, would rather be in the thick of it."

Georgie's blue eyes sparkled with excitement. "I would indeed."

And that was another thing he wanted in a wife. Not simply a woman who would support him, but one who would make a great political hostess. With her as his wife, life would never be dull.

Chapter Twenty-One

Georgie had gone to bed more hopeful about Turley and the prospect of marriage to him than she had been in a long time. Instead of singing, they had remained up discussing the most pressing issues of the day, as they saw them. She had known that he was interested in politics but not to what extent. She had also felt free to express all of her opinions. That was the first time she had done that with any gentleman other than the ones in her family and Frits. And the other thing she discovered was that she was more interested than she had been before in marrying Turley. During the course of the evening he showed himself to be open about the role ladies should play, and she had fallen more deeply in love with him. Georgie could only pray she was not setting herself up for a long, hard fall. She still wanted a love match, and he had yet to give her any indication that he was falling in love with her. But they had made plans to meet after breakfast for a ride, and riding was always fun.

The next morning she woke and immediately dashed to the window, and opened the curtains and the window. It was colder than it had been, but the air was crisp, and the sun shone brightly on the horizon. If the weather remained like this, it would be an excellent day for not only riding but the garden party as well. She was about to tug on the bell-pull when Smith entered the room from the dressing room.

"You're up earlier." She placed a day dress over one of the chairs.

"It might be better if I wear my riding habit. I am going out straight after breakfast."

"As you wish." Her maid picked up the gown and went back into the dressing room.

Georgie performed her ablutions, donned her stockings and riding boots. By the time she was finished her maid was ready to dress her and put her hair up in the simple knot she usually wore when riding. "It is a beautiful day. You should take some time and enjoy it."

"Thank you. I shall. The gardens here are delightful."

They were. But she had not spent much time exploring them. "You must tell me which areas you like best."

"I will. Have a good ride." Smith began straightening up the table as Georgie picked up her gloves and bonnet.

"I shall see you before luncheon." But probably not much before then. The only other time she had been riding with Turley, they had been out for several hours.

When Georgie arrived in the breakfast room, the staff was just setting out the chafing dishes under Creswell's watchful eye. "Good morning, miss." He nodded at one of the footmen who rushed out. "Lord Turley asked that he be informed when you came down to break your fast."

"Thank you for telling me." She was glad he had made a point of knowing when she was ready for breakfast. That meant he would be here soon, and she wouldn't have to wait for him. After all, *she* couldn't send a message to *him*.

Just as she had finished her first baked egg, he strode

in bringing the cold fresh air with him. "Good morning." He grinned and went straight to the side table. "Are you ready to be trounced?"

She narrowed her eyes at his broad back covered in a dark blue hacking jacket. If he won today, she would make a point of practicing her starts. Lilly didn't like to lose any more than Georgie did. "We shall see what happens."

He set his plate next her hers as he usually did and lowered himself into the chair. "Have you been outside yet? The air is invigorating."

She finished chewing a piece of toast and swallowed. "I stuck my head out of my window. It is perfect weather."

He dug into his plate of kippers and eggs. "We've been lucky it hasn't rained."

"Do not jinx us." They had been fortunate. October could be a very wet month. "I hope this weather lasts for a few more weeks."

He gave her a dubious look. "At least until the end of this week."

"Yes." Neither Frits nor Adeline would want to travel to the house party in the rain. "You never said where Rivercrest was located."

"It's not far from Gloucester on the River Severn. The climate is a bit cooler than it is here, but the countryside is still beautiful. I would argue even more so than here"—his eyes lit with merriment—"but never within Littleton's hearing."

"No. Never that." He was convinced that Littlewood was Heaven on earth. "Nor in Adeline's. She has quite come to love it here." She finished her toast and pulled over her other small dish of baked egg. "What about your other properties?"

"All over the country. I have five of them." He picked

up his cup of tea, drank the last of it, and handed the cup out to be refilled. "I even have one with a small section that borders Littlewood."

It was a good thing Georgie had already poured the tea or she would have spilt it all over him and the table. "If you have a house so close, why are you staying at The Lilacs?"

"I didn't say it was a large estate." He was prevaricating and she did not like it.

"What is it then?" She could not believe he would take advantage of Lady Littleton's generosity if he had a perfectly good abode close by.

"It houses my uncle and his family. The property still belongs to the viscountcy, but it is in the manner of a dower property and usually given to the second son for his lifetime if he requires it. In this case, my uncle was seriously wounded in the Navy and had need of it."

That made sense. "I see. Do you visit him often?"

Unable to answer with food in his mouth, Turley shook his head. When he was finished, he said, "No. He doesn't like to be reminded that it doesn't belong to him." Turley grimaced. "He's also not that fond of my side of the family." He put his fork on the plate. "He was always Army mad, but in our family, the second son went into the Navy. After he was injured, he convinced himself that had he been able to go into the Army, he would not have become so debilitated."

"What happened?"

"He got caught in a battle and lost his leg and arm on one side. It could have occurred in the Army as well, but it's not worth arguing over."

Again a sensible answer as far as it went. "That does not explain why he doesn't like you."

"His first son went into the Army, but his second son wanted to go to sea. When my uncle would not recommend him for a position as a ship's boy, my cousin asked my father to do it, and he did."

Now everything made sense. "And how is your cousin faring?"

"Excellently." Turley smiled. "He is now a commander."

Before he had told her the whole story, she had wanted to see the property. Now she was happy to leave well enough alone. She finished her fourth cup of tea. "Are you ready to go?"

"I am." He rose and held her chair for her. "I'm surprised that neither Littleton nor Adeline are down yet."

"It was a late night, and he usually waits for her to rise." Georgie thought that was sweet, but Turley was sniggering.

Their horses were being saddled when they reached the stables, and the groom was waiting.

When Lilly nickered Georgie took a carrot out of a bucket and gave it to the mare. "Good morning."

She and Turley led their horses out, but before Lilly could kneel, Turley's hands clasped Georgie's waist, sending tremors of pleasure through her body. Fortunately, she was not facing him, for she was certain he'd be able to see how his touch affected her. When she finally landed on her saddle, she took a breath and managed what she hoped was a serene expression.

"Ye two ready?" the older man asked.

In one graceful movement, Turley was on Lochinvar. "We are." He glanced at her. "The racing spot?"

"Of course." She bit off a remark about beating him, and instead patted Lilly's neck and whispered, "Do your best today."

After trotting out of the yard, they gave their horses their heads for several minutes, before slowing them to a walk. It would not do any good to wear them out on the way. The day was bright and the grass was frosted in some areas.

When they arrived at the lane, Johnson moved off to the side. "Let me know when ye want to start."

She glanced at Turley. "Are you ready?"

"Yes." He nodded.

"Anytime," she called to the groom.

"Right then. On three. One. Two. Three."

Lilly started a little ahead of Lochinvar and managed to stay ahead of him until just before they reached the finish when the other horse caught up with her. Still, a tie was not what Georgie wanted. They raced thrice more, and at the end they had tied twice, and each of them had won once.

They turned to walk the horses back when Lord Lytton came out of the woods. "Good morning."

Georgie thought Turley scowled, but when he greeted the other man there was no sign of it in his face. "Good day to you."

"Good morning," she said. "What brings you here?"

It was a good thing Marc expected that he'd be asked that question and had formulated an answer. "I must have turned the wrong way. I was out riding and meant to go back to Bottomley's house."

Turley stared steadily at Marc letting him know that he was intruding. "It's an easy mistake to make. You just need to turn around and go the other way. Did you not remark the direction when your coach made the same mistake?"

"Er. It appears not. However, I frequently work when I'm traveling and don't pay attention to the road." He gave them an apologetic look. "I'll know the next time." He glanced around him, hoping Miss Featherton would ask him to join them. "It's a good straight path here. Is this where you usually ride?"

"We race," the lady said. "But it is time for us to return." She and Turley exchanged glances and Marc knew that he was decidedly de trop. Turley and Miss Featherton had the look of a settled couple, and Marc would not be surprised to hear of a betrothal in the near future. "Have a pleasant day, my lord." She gave him a polite smile. "If you attend the garden party, we shall see you there."

"Yes, of course."

Turley waved as he turned his horse. "You shouldn't have any problems finding the way back."

"No. I don't suppose I will." This was disappointing, but not a complete waste of time. He knew without a doubt that Miss Featherton had no interest in anyone but Turley. He retraced his way back to Bottomley's. Marc had spent the last two Seasons looking for a wife, and had yet to find one. The only other lady in which he could be interested and who met his aunt's qualifications was Lady Aurelia. But was she interested in him? He supposed it was time to start looking at her in a new way.

He rode slowly, enjoying the day and not wanting to spend more time than necessary with Bottomley, who was already missing Town and making noises about returning. Thus far, Marc had ignored the man's hints, and would continue to do so. Once he was in Town and then back at his estate, he'd have no further chances to meet eligible ladies.

When he finally entered the stable yard, his coachman, groom, and the other man he'd hired in Town as a guard were milling around his coach. "Is there anything wrong?"

"No, my lord," Stratton, his coachman said. "I'm just doin' some work on it. Don't do us any good if a pin or somethin' comes out when we're travelin'."

"How'd your meeting with the lady go?" his groom asked, with a hopeful look on his face.

That was one thing about old retainers, they wanted to know everything and didn't hesitate to inquire. Then again, his whole household knew about his aunt's requirements, and his inability to find a suitable lady. She had not used any discretion at all when informing him about them. Now much of his staff was as concerned about him marrying as he was. "Not as well as I hoped it would. It appears as if I shall have to find another lady."

His groom's and coachman's faces had fallen at the news. "I'm sure someone will come along." He didn't dare raise their hopes about Lady Aurelia until he was sure of her. In a misguided attempt to calm his servants, he'd made that mistake before. Marc shouldn't have mentioned Miss Featherton at all. "I shall be attending a garden party this afternoon at about one. If you could help ensure that Lord Bottomley's carriage is ready, I would appreciate it."

"Yes, my lord." Marc's coachman's tone was glum.

Marc dismounted and handed his horse to the groom. "Don't worry. It will all come right."

"Yes, my lord."

Confound his aunt. If only she'd kept her demands between them.

* * *

Despite attempting to like Lytton more, or at least not be outwardly unpleasant to him, Gavin had not appreciated his time with Georgie being interrupted. Not only that, but he didn't believe for a moment that Lytton had come upon them by accident. It was almost exactly the same time as when his coach really had gone the wrong way that the man appeared today.

Fortunately, Georgie didn't seem to be interested in him at all. After last evening, Gavin finally felt as if they were getting closer. That he was making some progress. He supposed he could have been more open with her about his family before now. He should have also told her that he could not allow himself to love his wife, but if he could, he would . . . what? Love her? He wasn't in love. He had vowed not to be in love. Yes, he enjoyed spending time with her. It was actually more than that. He liked listening to her thoughts and hearing her laugh. He wanted to be with her all the time and share his thoughts with her. His desire to bed her was a constant physical ache. Every time he even thought of her breasts and what they'd look like he got an erection. For that matter, almost any part of her gave him the same reaction from her dark chestnut hair to her dainty feet. Not to mention the surge of irritation he experienced when he thought another gentleman might be interested in her. Perhaps it was more than mere irritation, but whatever it was, he didn't like it.

"Do many people become lost going to Lord Bottomley's estate?" Georgie asked.

They were almost halfway back to the house and both of them had been quieter than usual. "I don't know. He's rarely here. It's not his main estate."

"Hmm." She became quiet again for several seconds.

"Perhaps I shall suggest that Frits put up a sign. I cannot think it would be comfortable to—to know that anyone could mistake their way."

Especially if someone such as Adeline, Georgie, or a future child could be harmed. "I think that is an excellent idea."

A small smile tugged at her lips, but she was clearly concerned about the matter. "Perhaps you could mention it as well."

"I'll be happy to do so." After that unexpected meeting, Gavin trusted that Lytton understood in no uncertain terms that Georgie was not for him. Soon Gavin would have to have the conversation with her that he'd hoped to avoid. Telling her that he could not marry for love. But he would wait until after the ball.

"It might be a good idea to put up a gate across that road," Johnson said. "Doesn't happen often as far as I know, but I agree with Miss Georgie. Twice is too many times. It ain't safe."

"A gate would be the perfect solution," she agreed. "Thank you for the suggestion."

"Don't you worry none. Ain't nothing going to happen to you when I'm around." The groom nodded emphatically as if to make his point. "I kept their lordships from coming to harm, and they were a lot more trouble."

At that, Georgie started to chuckle. "I imagine they were."

Gavin found himself grinning as well. "We were adventurous."

Johnson's eyes widened. "Is that what ye called it?"

Georgie's laughter became louder and deeper. "I wish I could have seen the two of you."

"Ah, but would you have tried to join in, or were you the little girl who kept clean and sewed her samplers?"

She cast him a coy look as she and Lilly moved as if one into a gallop. "Wouldn't you like to know," she called back over her shoulder.

"Minx," he shouted at her, urging his horse to catch up.

Chapter Twenty-Two

Georgie slowed Lilly to a walk before they reached the stable yard. Turley and the groom were close behind. She had been having so much fun with him over the past few days, and it still amazed her that she had known so little about him before now. After they took care of their horses, he went back to The Lilacs, and she ascended the stairs to her apartments aware that she smelled as if she was bringing Lilly into the house with her. A bath was definitely in order. Fortunately, her maid had everything but the hot water prepared, and with the pump that brought the water to this floor that was easily obtained.

"You are very organized," Georgie praised her maid as she stood to be undressed.

"I knew you had to return soon for luncheon before departing for the entertainment."

Was she that late? She turned her head and looked at the clock. Good Lord! She'd had no idea how long they had been out. It certainly hadn't seemed that long. Well, there was no point in drawing attention to Turley's and her failure to note the time.

Soon she lowered herself into the tub and wished she

had time to linger. After a quick scrub, she stood for water to be poured over her shoulders, and took the warmed towel from her maid. The sound of running in the corridor could be heard in the room. "What is that?"

"Maximus and the puppy have been playing." Smith sounded unconcerned. "If I may say so, they are very sweet together. Maximus takes great care not to harm little Jeremy."

Aside from hunting dogs, the only dogs in the Featherton household had been much smaller than a Great Dane. Since coming to know the breed, Georgie had been entertaining the idea of getting one as well. "I hope they will still be running around when I am ready to go down for luncheon."

"I predict"—Smith's lips tilted up—"that this will be a fairly common occurrence. All the breakables have been removed from this area of the house."

Georgie had quickly dried herself and handed the towel to her maid. "That will be fun. I have hardly seen the dogs lately."

"Mr. Creswell said that there was a new calf that has interested Maximus."

She did not want to even imagine how foul the Dane had smelled if he'd spent most of his time with the cows. "I see. Or I think I do."

"I understand that he takes great delight in . . . acquiring a suitable scent for the calf."

"He probably thinks he is related somehow." Frits had told her about the dog actually pretending to graze on grass in order to interest the cows in him. "They are interesting animals."

"That they are, miss." Smith held up Georgie's chemise, and she lifted her arms.

In less time than she had thought possible she was ready to go down to eat. Although why they were dining, when they had been told there would be food at the garden party, she had no idea. Then again, her friends did as they wished. Which, all things considered, was not a bad way to live one's life. Perhaps that was the reason they did not enjoy being in Town that much with all the rules of Polite Society.

Unfortunately, by the time she strolled into the corridor the dogs were gone. That was a shame. When she reached the breakfast room Turley was already in conversation with Frits and Adeline. But the footmen were still setting out the meal. At least she was not *too* terribly late.

When Georgie entered, he smiled brightly at her and rose, holding out the chair next to his. "Thank you."

His eyes warmed as he seated her. "I was just asking why, if we are being provided with delicacies at the Turners', we are eating now."

"And I was about to explain," Frits said, "that I require more than delicacies. Not only that, but my beloved must have nourishing meals before she can gorge on cakes and biscuits, or whatever is there."

Adeline wrinkled her nose at him. "I had much rather not be hungry than eat things that will make me feel ill. I am just now beginning to enjoy food again." Her hand went to her stomach and she grinned at Frits. "He is moving much more vigorously." She glanced at Georgie. "This morning was the first time Frits could feel him."

"How exciting for you." Even though Georgie was genuinely happy for her friends, she could not but wish that she too would have a child soon.

She followed Frits's stare to Turley and the wistful look on his face. It had never occurred to her that a man could want a child as much or in the same way a woman did. Had her father and brother been like that? It warmed her heart that Turley was. Could he love a child and not the mother? She almost wished that she had not been told about his fear he would be like his father. On the other hand, what would her lack of knowledge change?

Creswell served the soup, a broth with chicken with large pieces of vegetables, as well as bread she had never seen before. Cut into slices, it was brown with large holes as if it had not been kneaded enough and a thick crust. "What is this?"

"It is a recipe from Frits's great-grandmother," Adeline said. "In German, the soup is called an *Eintopf* and the bread is *Bauernbrot*. It is really just a soup with large pieces of chicken and vegetables and farmer's bread."

Georgie dipped her spoon in and sipped the broth. "This is very tasty."

"I think so," her friend agreed. "Try the bread with the butter. We add a bit more salt when we make it."

She took a slice of bread and broke off a piece of it, spread the butter, and tasted it. "Oh. That is wonderful. Will you give me the recipes?"

"Of course." Adeline nodded. "I find it the perfect meal for a cold or rainy day."

Next to Georgie, Turley had been applying himself to the soup and bread with such relish that she knew he'd had them before. "I had better eat mine before there is nothing left."

He glanced at her and got a sheepish look. "It is one of my favorites. However, I shall make sure not to finish the tureen."

She tried to maintain a serious mien, but her lips were quivering. "I am certain there is more in the kitchen."

He appeared surprised. "I never thought of that. Littleton and I used to rush to be the first one to empty the bowl." He glanced at Frits. "I don't remember anyone ever offering to refill it for us."

Frits's brows came together, and he frowned. "I don't either. Yet, that must be the case. Cook would never have sent all of it up. There had to have been a goodly amount in the kitchen."

Adeline clapped her hand to her forehead, and Georgie laughed. "I can only imagine that it was to keep the two of you from gorging yourselves and being sick. You are both eating like you had a cake instead of soup."

"Cake is not nearly as good." Gavin picked up a slice of bread. "And this is as good as the best biscuit."

It was excellent and different. She was glad she could have the recipe. However, in the end, the bowls, which were smaller versions of the tureen, were so large that she could not finish all of it. Though, to be fair, she had her share of bread as well. "I do not think I will be able to eat anything at the garden party."

Adeline held her nose in the air. "We shall sample small bites of what looks good and be thought to be very refined ladies."

Georgie cast her eyes to the ceiling. "We *are* refined ladies."

"Yes, but with healthy appetites," her friend retorted.

"I, for one, like females who are not afraid to eat," Turley said.

"Here, here." Frits set his spoon down. "That was one of the things I noticed about my darling wife, she enjoyed food. One cannot live here without that sort of appreciation."

"You do have a point, my love." Adeline included Georgie

and Turley in her look. "We have so many receipts from other countries, I am lucky I have not gone to fat."

One thing Georgie resolved to do was to gather as many recipes as she could before she left Littlewood. Yet, once again, she had learned more about the gentleman she wished to wed than she had before. She wondered if being around their friends who were so obviously in love would make him change his mind about love.

"My lord, my lady." Creswell bowed. "The carriage will be brought around shortly."

Turley's mouth turned down. "No dessert?"

Even she had understood that would not be served. "The garden party."

"Ah. Yes." He sighed. "I suppose I shall find something there."

When she went up to her chamber to fetch her gloves and other accoutrements, she took the time to brush her teeth. If she could get Turley alone, she was going to give him an opportunity to kiss her. This week would not last forever.

After the ladies left the breakfast room, Gavin rushed upstairs to the room he usually occupied. There he found what he'd been expecting. Tooth powder and a toothbrush. He quickly brushed his teeth. If he could organize an opportunity, he would kiss Georgie. He'd been wanting to do it for months, and now that he had her grandmother's permission, there was nothing holding him back.

When he arrived in the hall, only Littleton was there. "I shall give you fair notice that I intend to take Miss Featherton for a walk on the forest path." Littleton's jaw tightened. "I have her grandmother's permission."

That surprised him. "I take it you asked for advice?"

"I did." Gavin was damned if he'd tell his friend every-thing, but that he had been given leave to be alone with Georgie should be enough.

His friend's look changed from stern to considering. "I can't say I disagree with the plan. After all, I first kissed Adeline in the woods."

"You weren't supposed to have worked that out," he said to himself.

"It did not take enormous deductive powers," Littleton said drily.

"No, I suppose not." Gavin glanced up the stairs. "It is only that I have never courted her before. Or courted her properly. I thought I had, but I'm discovering so many new aspects of her, that I could not have been doing it or doing it right when we were in Town."

"Not surprising. I was fortunate with Adeline, but I had Maximus to assist me. One can learn a great deal about a lady when walking a dog."

"I seem to recall that you had other moments alone with her." Gavin had not thought to arrange the same situations. Was it because he did not wish to become that close to her? No. He did wish to be close to her, as a friend. But that didn't make sense if he wanted to bed her. Before he could give the issue due consideration, the ladies were rounding the upper corridor.

"You're right. I did." His friend held out his hand to his wife, and her whole face lit with love.

Gavin gave himself a shake and held his arm out to Georgie, and she gave him a light smile. It wasn't what he wanted, but somehow he would make this work.

On the way to the entertainment, the four of them chatted about the change in the landscape as summer turned to autumn, and winter. Georgie asked about other dishes from the different ancestors that they enjoyed. It turned out that many of them were considered peasant food, but were enjoyed as part of a larger meal.

Addressing Littleton, Georgie said, "I find it very interesting that many of your ancestors married ladies from other countries."

"They weren't from that far away," he responded. "Dutch, French, and German. We don't have anyone as exotic as Spanish or Portuguese."

She widened her eyes for a moment. "I do not think we have anyone other than English."

"I don't think we do either," Gavin replied.

"I can tell you that we are Saxon through and through." Adeline frowned. "There might be a Norman in there somewhere, but I doubt it."

His title was so old no one in his family had considered it for years, but . . . "You and I are probably in the same position."

"It would not surprise me at all," Georgie said, "to discover that you can both trace your lines back to Harold, and whatever Norman married into the line."

"I have no doubt you are right." He wanted to take her hand and raise it to his lips, but he did not yet have the right.

"Here we are," Adeline pointed out. "I cannot remember the journey over here going by so quickly."

Littleton chuckled. "But the trip home is always fast."

She punched him in the arm, and he clasped his hand around her fist and kissed it. "It is not my fault that by evening I am tired. Blame your son."

"I think as contrary as that babe is, it will be a daughter." Before she could make a retort he laughed and kissed her.

Gavin was glad they had arrived. He didn't know how much more he could take of a couple in love. When the coach came to a stop, he hopped out, and held his hand out for Georgie. Still, he would like to have moments with her that their friends did. Just because he could not love her didn't mean he couldn't desire her, and be her friend, and be happy and playful when she was carrying their children. Of course he could. He wasn't a cold man. He simply needed to maintain control over his emotions and not fall in love. The only problem was that he was beginning to doubt what that meant.

She placed her hand in his as if it belonged there. To him. "Do you have any idea of what is scheduled?"

"Not at all. I do know the gardens and wood are large and planned out. I am only surprised they do not have a maze."

That was the one thing they didn't need. One either quickly found the key to a maze or got lost. "Do not suggest it. I have no doubt Lady Turner would be happy to have one designed and planted."

Georgie smiled suddenly and it took his breath away. "I have no doubt you are correct."

They were ushered into the hall and back to a morning room before they were announced.

After they greeted the Turners and the Fitzwalters, and were handed glasses of champagne, they were bid to explore as they pleased.

"You will find tables filled with delicacies all over the gardens," Lady Turner assured them.

And indeed she was correct. He and Georgie strolled through the various areas of the formal gardens that appeared to date to at least Queen Elizabeth's time and at every turn there were tables set with cakes, biscuits, fresh and dried fruits, nuts, cheeses, and everything else one could want, even forced strawberries.

"I must admit I am impressed," he said, taking a small handful of nuts.

"I am as well." Georgie plucked a biscuit from a platter. "I like how there is something different on each table."

She bit into the confection and closed her eyes. "Lemon, but unlike one I have ever had before. It is spicy."

"You will have to ask for recipes." He guided her toward the wood.

"I do not think I will be successful. Adeline asked for the recipe for a seed cake from Amanda Fitzwalter, and she had been sworn to secrecy by her mother."

"Shall we take samples home and ask if the Littleton cook can work out what is in them?"

She chuckled as she finished the biscuit. "That is actually an inspired idea."

He tucked her hand more securely into the crook of his arm. "Do you know anything about the wood path?"

"Only that there are seasonal plantings, benches, and other items of interest." Her eyes were wide with innocence when she looked up at him. "Would you like to explore it?"

"Yes." God yes! And only with her.

Chapter Twenty-Three

Thank the Lord that he agreed to her suggestion.

As Georgie and Turley started meandering along the woodland path, she kept an eye out for likely places to encourage a kiss from him. She could not believe her wait was almost over.

They passed by several interestingly carved wooden benches that seemed to reach out and beg one to make a pause in one's ramblings. Marble statues were tucked amid bushes of cotoneaster and sea starwort, as well as other autumn-blooming plants. The path—she had been told—led around the lake and over the stream that fed the lake.

They were in sight of the stone bridge when she finally spied the perfect place. A massive weeping willow with branches so thick she could barely see the bench built around one side of the tree. "Oh, look. That is enchanting!"

She dropped her hand from his arm and turned them off the path toward the tree with Turley following closely behind. "It certainly looks old."

Georgie stopped herself from rolling her eyes. Did the man not have any romance in him? "Of course it is, to be so large. I would simply like to stop and sit under it."

"If you wish." He took her arm again and helped her, carefully guiding her over any possible dips in the earth or rocks.

In another mood, she would have wondered how he thought she got around in the country, but now she enjoyed how considerate he was being. He held the branches aside for her to enter the bower made by the tree.

It was as if someone had made a place for a lovers' tryst. She dropped her hand and slowly twirled around taking in the arbor, then Georgie turned back to him and he was staring at her with a strange look in his eyes. "Is something wrong?"

"No." His voice was rough as if it had not been used in a very long time. "There is nothing at all wrong."

She stood completely still as he slowly moved toward her. Her heart began beating so hard she was sure he could hear it. This was really going to happen. He was going to kiss her.

Turley took her hands, placing them between his much larger ones, and she wished they were not wearing gloves. Slowly, he brought her hands to his lips and placed feather-light kisses on each knuckle. Still keeping his blue gaze on her, he bent his head. Georgie allowed her eyes to flutter shut as she waited for his lips to touch hers.

"What'd you think your doin'?" someone shouted.

Oh, God. We've been caught!

She and Turley jumped apart as if they'd been burnt and looked around them. But there was no one there.

"Gimme back my fish. I caught 'em!" The person was much angrier now.

Putting one finger to his lips, Turley pulled back the branches on the river side of the tree just enough to look out. On the opposite bank of the small river was a youth, probably about ten or eleven. His chin jutted out and his eyes narrowed contemptuously. Across from him was one of the gentleman guests—Mr. Barfleur if she was not mistaken—holding a fishing rod. "I'll pay you for them." Reaching into his waistcoat pocket he drew out a few coins and handed them out. "You can take this."

The boy spit, narrowly missing his highly polished boots. "Ye think I'm stupid? I can get more for 'em than that."

Mr. Barfleur's lips curled into a sneer. "Not if you're caught poaching."

Yet the obvious threat did not appear to upset the youth at all. "It ain't poaching unless I'm getting them from the lake."

"I am taking the fish. You may have the coins or not." Mr. Barfleur lifted the keepnet and hadn't even turned around before the boy jumped on him.

"Ye gimme back my fish!"

Turley looked at her and heaved a sigh. "I suppose I'd better stop this before someone gets hurt."

"I'll go with you. My presence might not stop the lad, but it should make Mr. Barfleur think a bit." She sighed to herself. The promise of a kiss was clearly at an end. For now.

"Good idea." Turley held out his arm, but she clasped his much larger hand instead. At first he looked shocked, then he grinned. "Let's go." The second they came out from under the tree, he shouted, "Barfleur, give the boy back his fish."

The man's jaw dropped, but he recovered more quickly than she'd thought possible. "This is not your business, my lord. Aside from that, they're mine."

242   *Ella Quinn*

"That is not what the child said." Georgie glared at him, daring him to deny what they had heard.

"That's right." The youth slid off Barfleur's back, grabbing the keepnet as he did. "Didn't think ye'd get caught, did ye?" The lad took a deep breath and looked like he was about to air his grievances when Turley gave his head a slight shake and motioned for the boy to go. Surprisingly, the youth took his unspoken advice and dashed toward the meadow.

He crossed his arms over his chest. "I cannot believe you would attempt to steal fish from a local child. What the devil were you thinking?"

Barfleur said several mumbled words, but the only one Georgie heard was "wager." She bit down on her lip and counted to ten, but it didn't help. She fisted her hands on her hips and didn't care what she looked like. "You were going to *rob* that poor boy who was probably trying to keep his family from starving for a wager? Do you know what would happen to him if *he* had stolen from *you*?" The man dropped his head and shrugged. "He would have gone to prison where he could have been hanged or transported."

"Miss Featherton is correct," Turley said. "If your positions were reversed, the penalties for the lad would have been severe. If he calls for the magistrate I shall be forced to stand as witness against you."

Barfleur's head snapped up so fast, she thought she heard it. "His attention is finally engaged." She had kept her voice low enough that only Turley could hear her. Now she raised it. "You might wish to find a way to forestall him from getting the magistrate involved. We do not know his name, but I could give a good description of him and we can discover where he lives. Whereupon, you may send over an offering sufficient to calm his ire."

"I agree with Miss Featherton. The lad didn't look like the type to keep this quiet. If word gets around that one of Lady Turner's guests attempted to rob a local child, it would harm her reputation."

For the first time the gentleman looked nervous. "Yes. I shall—I shall do that. If you can assist me in finding him I shall make amends."

She and Turley followed Mr. Barfleur back to the house. Once there, she would set about trying to identify the child.

But when she excused herself, Turley said, "I'll go with you."

"I thought you might guard Mr. Barfleur."

"There is no need. He won't want his hostess to gain a reputation for hosting unsavory fellows at her house." Turley grinned. "Aside from that, Turner would thrash him."

"Very well." She removed her bonnet. "I thought I would start in the kitchen."

Turley's brows slanted together. "Why the cook?"

Apparently, he'd missed the lad saying that he could get more money for them. "He had a lot of fish. I would wager my pearls that he sells them." She raised one brow. "And who do you think in this area would require that large of a catch?"

Gavin would never have thought of that. He'd always known Georgie was extremely intelligent, now he had proof. "Of course. That also explains why he refused to accept Barfleur's miserly offer."

He followed her as she went through the green baize door and down to the kitchens. The sight was astonishing. Kitchen maids were chopping, cracking eggs, and doing all manner of other things, while small boys ran around fetching and carrying. Everyone was shouting orders. It was amazing that they knew who wanted what. One of the tallest women he'd ever seen stood at the stove tasting and adding seasonings to pots while casting a gimlet eye on the meats roasting in the fireplace. The other thing he noticed was how clean the kitchen was kept. Whenever anything fell to the floor it was immediately cleaned up.

Georgie poked him in the arm and motioned to a basket set far away from the heat where a young maid was cleaning fish.

It wasn't until one of the boys almost ran into them that anyone knew they were there. Then, suddenly, the kitchen went quiet and the cook glanced around.

"Can I help you?"

Georgie smiled and stepped forward. "We are looking for a youth who saved one of the guests from making a very bad decision. He had a large catch of fish, and I thought that you might know who he is."

"If he's got wheat-colored hair and looks like someone's starving him to death, that'd be Jem."

"Thank you." Gavin couldn't believe she'd got the information that easily. "Where can we find Jem?"

The cook glanced at a clock on top of a large cabinet. "I'd try The Running Dog in the village."

"Croseton?" That would be a long way to go.

"No. Hillborough. The one outside the gate and about a mile east." She glanced at the spit. "If you don't mind, I've got work to do."

Georgie smiled at the woman. "Thank you very much for your help."

"For all he's young," the cook added, "Jem's a good worker and fisherman."

Gavin inclined his head. "Thank you."

He and Georgie headed out of the kitchen and back to the hall. "I've never been in a kitchen at this time of day before."

"Many gentlemen have never been in a kitchen at all," came her dry answer. "Shall we find Barfleur?"

Gavin would rather take care of the business without the younger man, but Barfleur needed to be taught a lesson. "I believe we shall." Gavin half expected to find the other gentleman with his nose in a glass of brandy and was surprised to find him drinking tea with Lady Turner and Mrs. Fitzwalter. He bowed. "Good day, ladies."

"We have come to collect Mr. Barfleur," Georgie said. "He promised he would accompany us on an errand."

His eyes widened and for a moment Gavin thought he'd bolt. "Er. Yes." Barfleur's hands came up toward his collar then dropped. "That was fast. I thought the information we needed would take longer to find."

"If you need to gather any items"—Georgie gave him a stern look—"you should do so now."

He immediately rose, bowed to the ladies, and hurried out of the morning room.

"That is odd," Lady Turner observed. A line formed between her eyes as she stared at the doorway. Then she glanced at Georgie. "Are you going far? Do you wish to use our curricle? Mr. Barfleur will have to sit in the groom's seat, but it will not be uncomfortable for such a short trip."

"Yes, thank you," Georgie said. "We were going to walk, but this will be faster."

Gavin had for a briefest moment considered taking the landau they'd ridden over in, but Georgie would need a chaperone if they took the vehicle. "I thank you as well."

More tea arrived, and they were pressed into joining their hostesses. The butler arrived to tell them that the curricle was ready at about the same time Barfleur reappeared, a grim look on his face. Had Georgie frightened him that much?

Less than twenty minutes later they entered The Running Dog, and Gavin had to duck to avoid hitting his head on a beam. The place was filled with local men who immediately turned and stared at them. For a moment he regretted that he'd brought her. Still, she had the right to see how this all came out.

She squeezed his arm. "Let us find a table and discuss our strategy before asking to speak with Jem."

"Good idea." At least then they wouldn't be standing around looking out of place. They'd be sitting with tankards of ale to drink as they attempted not to appear out of place.

Georgie indicated a vacant table just a few feet away. He'd rather have found one closer to the door, but needs must and the bar was already pretty full. To call it an actual table was a misnomer. There were three chairs at the end of one long table. She took a chair where she could view the common room as did he. If there was going to be trouble, at least they'd know it was coming and from which direction. Barfleur sat in the chair facing them, and Gavin hailed the barmaid.

The young woman was pretty in a very English way with blond hair and a milk-white complexion that she clearly kept out of the sun. Instead of bringing attention to herself by swinging her hips or lowering her bodice, she walked sedately to them. "Good afternoon. What can I get you?"

Georgie smiled. "I would like a glass of cider if you have it."

"We do, miss." The barmaid glanced at him. "And the gentlemen?"

"I'd like a pint of ale—" He raised his brows in a question to Barfleur, who nodded then hung his head. "Make that two pints of ale."

Georgie placed her hands on the table, clasping them together. "Mr. Barfleur, his lordship and I heard you mention a wager. What exactly did you wager and how much?"

The younger man flushed a deep red as he met her gaze. "I—we—well we said we'd supply enough fish for a meal." When Georgie raised her brows, Barfleur continued, "We wagered a pony."

She sucked in a breath. "And when you made the wager you thought you could win?"

"No." He hung his head again. "I've never learned to fish. But I couldn't let the others know." Gavin thought a man couldn't get any redder, yet Barfleur did. "My—my father tried to teach me, but he gave up. I've never even had a nibble."

"I see." Georgie reached across the table and patted the young man's fisted hands.

How in the hell could any boy in England not learn how to fish? Even ladies fished.

Good God, Barfleur looked like he wanted to weep. "I didn't dare tell them I didn't know how. That would be worse than losing."

"Yes, I am quite sure it would be. But this is your opportunity to do the right thing and learn to fish. I shall own myself surprised if Jem can't teach you."

A glimmer of hope entered Barfleur's eyes. "Do you think he would? After I tried to steal his catch?"

"There is only one way to find out." The barmaid brought

their drinks, and Georgie said, "Will you please ask Jem to join us? We have a question for him."

The woman met Georgie's eyes with a steady gaze. "Does this have anything to do with someone trying to take his fish?"

From what Gavin could tell, she returned the look. "In a manner of speaking. Amends must be made to him."

"I'll get him."

"Thank you." Once the barmaid left, she spoke to Barfleur. "I suggest you offer him a crown for each fishing lesson."

"I say, that's a great deal of money," Barfleur protested.

"It is a great deal less than being arrested and paying for a solicitor and barrister."

The man dropped his head in his hands. "I can't believe how stupid I was."

Gavin took a long draw of the excellent local ale. "I'd say I can't believe how you discount anyone below you."

Barfleur's jaw tightened, and Gavin made a promise to himself that his children would never behave in a like manner. "This is more than me paying the boy, isn't it? It's to teach me a lesson."

Before Gavin could answer Jem was standing next to them. "I heerd ye got a question for me."

"Indeed we do." Georgie raised her chin at Barfleur. "Sir?"

He closed his eyes and gave an imperceptible nod. "I'd like you to teach me how to fish. I've never learned." He took a breath. "I'll pay you a crown for each lesson."

Jem rubbed his chin as he'd obviously seen an older man do. "A crown for as long as I'm normally out. Any time after that'll be a half-crown extra."

Gavin was pleased to see Barfleur wasn't going to argue. "Very well. When do we start?"

"Tomorrow mornin' at six. Meet me where I was today."

"I'll see you then." Barfleur held out his hand and Jem took it.

"Wear somethin' you can fish in."

Gavin almost went into whoops watching Jem saunter back to his seat at the bar. "That went well." He finished his ale. "Are you ready to return to the Turners'?"

"Yes." Barfleur stood and glanced at Georgie. "Thank you."

"I look forward to eating the fish you will catch." Gavin would have had a hard time not gloating, but she was sincere.

They made their way outside and asked for the curricle to be brought around.

"If you don't mind," Barfleur said. "I think I'll walk."

"Not at all." That would give Gavin an opportunity to tell Georgie how brilliant her idea had been. It astonished him once again how much he was still learning about her.

A little voice in his head nagged at him telling him to give her what she wanted, but he could not. Although, he'd yet to even mention friendship and passion to her. He thought today would be the perfect time to press his suit, but the Fates had other plans. He had to do it soon.

Chapter Twenty-Four

Georgie watched as Mr. Barfleur strolled down the street. His step seemed lighter than before, and she was glad. She had no idea how old he was, but he really wasn't up to snuff. Someone should take him under their wing. Once she returned to Town, she'd ask her father if he could do it.

The curricle was brought out, and she held her breath as Turley lifted her into the carriage. Thank God for long stays. Yet, even with them, the heat of his hands caused her senses to scramble. Without a word, he climbed into the other side of the carriage and gave the horses their office.

They passed Mr. Barfleur and she waved. "That went well."

"It did." Turley slid her a smile. "Your idea was much better than anything I could have thought of."

"Thank you." A sense of pride filled her. It had been an excellent plan. "I just hope it works."

"As do I," he agreed. "I cannot imagine not knowing how to fish."

"It is so consummately an English activity. We all learned to fish." She did not think she had ever met anyone who did not know how to fish unless it was a servant raised in London, but even then . . . "I wonder if his father is one of those men who had little patience with children."

"I suppose he could be." Turley's voice sounded thoughtful. "But if he couldn't teach Barfleur, he could have got a groom or someone to do it."

"I agree." She recalled the terms of the wager and another thought came to mind. "Well, it doesn't matter now. He will learn from one of the best. I do wonder though if anyone thought to tell Cook they were supplying the fish. I cannot imagine she is one who takes surprises in her kitchen well."

"No." He frowned for a moment. "I can't either. Aren't those menus planned well in advance?"

That was a good point. "They are. So many items must be ordered." She could not imagine either Amanda or Mary taking the changing of the menus well. "Perhaps we should tell Lady Turner and Mrs. Fitzwalter about the wager. I have a feeling that Mr. Barfleur will be successful even if no one else is."

Turley's eyes widened in something like fear when he glanced at Georgie. "I shall leave that to you. Even though you and Adeline have assured me that marriage has improved the ladies, I do not wish to be there when they discover that their meal plans might be upset."

Georgie had to laugh. She never supposed that he would be wary of a woman's anger. But that spoke well for him. If it meant he cared what a lady thought. "Very well, I will do it. You may go hide with the other gentlemen."

"I will." They turned into the drive. "Do you remember if there is something planned for the house party this evening?"

Mentally, she reviewed the list. "Whatever it is we did

not plan to be there for it. There is a dinner and an informal dance tomorrow evening that we will attend."

He winged out his arm again and she took it. "May I have two waltzes?"

Goodness. That was the first time he had asked for two dances. "If there are two waltzes, I would be delighted."

"Thank you." He pulled out his pocket watch. "Shall we go around to some of the tables? You did wish to take one of the lemon biscuits home."

Georgie could not believe he had actually remembered that. "Thank you. I would. But first I must find either Lady Turner or Mrs. Fitzwalter." If she did not do it now, it might not get done. "And tell them about the fish."

"Very well. Lead on."

He and Georgie went first to the morning room where the ladies had been earlier, but they were not there. "They must be outside."

"There is no reason we cannot taste the offerings while we look for them."

"I suppose not." Was he hungry already? He found a table with various cakes, and they began sampling them. She took a bite of the most fabulous seed cake she'd ever had. "This must be the famous seed cake."

"The one Adeline couldn't get her recipe for?" Georgie nodded, and Turley took out his handkerchief and picked up two slices. "We shall see what Littleton's cook makes of these."

"I hope that the ingredients aren't too difficult to discover. I would like the recipe as well."

"I agree." Gavin led her to another table that held fruit and custard tartlets, and found one made with pears. "I won't be able to eat dinner at all after this. And I don't normally like sweets."

Georgie selected a custard tartlet and bit into it. "Mmm. This is good. I do not think I care if I can eat dinner. There are so few opportunities to truly indulge. I wonder if Adeline has even planned dinner this evening."

He popped a brambleberry tartlet into his mouth. "I think what I like about these is that they are not overly sweet."

"Indeed. The fruit is allowed to shine, I suppose one could say." Georgie scanned the area. "They must be here somewhere."

He thought the advantage of his height might help, but they were not in this area of the garden. "We'll find them eventually."

When they entered another area of the garden they came across Littleton and Adeline. Small plates of ice were lined up on the table at which they were sitting, and her countenance held a beatific expression. "I had no idea ices could be so good."

Georgie gave a light laugh. "Frits introduced ices to her, and she loves them."

"That is easy to see." Gavin wondered if Georgie liked anything half as much. "Do you have any favorites?"

"Ices?" Her eyes were wide.

"Any food."

Her head tilted in one direction then the other. "I used to love lobster patties, but that was because we rarely had them. Now, since they are so prevalent at suppers, I still like them, but I cannot say that I love them anymore." She shrugged. "I suppose once the Season is over, and they are no longer so available, I shall return to adoring them."

As she spoke he'd maneuvered them to the table set with ices. "Which ones would you like?"

"The lemon. That is my favorite."

He selected lemon for her and chocolate for himself,

and instead of sitting with their friends, he found a bench under an ornamental tree. "What about other foods?"

She had a contemplative look as she ate her ice. "Roasted lamb. My father does not like it, therefore we rarely have it." Fortunately, he liked lamb as well. "What about you?"

"Me?"

"Yes." She set the ice cup down. "What is your favorite food?"

"I don't have one, yet." Although, his favorite taste might very well be her lips, her neck, her—God! He had to stop this. "I shall tell you when I do."

"Hmm." She stared at him for a few moments, then rose. "Let us look around a bit more. We still must find our hostesses."

"Ah, yes. The fish." Even though he was more than happy to have her hand on his arm as they ambled through the gardens, he tried to think of a way he could get her back into the woods in order to kiss her. The Fates, however, were not on his side. By the time they managed to hunt down either Lady Turner or Mrs. Fitzwalter, Littleton and Adeline joined them. "I take it that you wish to go home?"

"The fish," Georgie said.

"What is wrong with the fish?" Adeline asked, clearly confused.

"Some of the gentlemen made a wager that they could provide enough fish for one of the meals without inform- ing either Mary or Amanda," Georgie explained. "We must tell one of them."

"I believe they already know," Frits said. "At least I know that Turner is aware of the wager."

"Well, then." Georgie shrugged. "That relieves us of any responsibility."

"Would you like to remain here?" Adeline asked. "We can send the curricle for you."

Gavin said a brief prayer that she would agree.

"No. I am ready to leave." She gave a wicked grin. "Aside from that, we took samples of the seed cake and some of the other sweets. I am hoping that your cook will be able to figure out what is in them."

"The seed cake?" Adeline's eyes widened. "I would dearly love to have that recipe."

All Gavin's hopes of getting Georgie alone again sank. "We still must find one of the ladies and tell them we are departing."

"We already did," Adeline said. "And Frits called for the carriage. It should be in the drive by the time we gain the front door."

Hell and damnation!

So much for that. Once they arrived at Littlewood, he'd have no reason to remain. Unless . . . "Do you plan to dine this evening?"

Littleton shook his head. "We will only have a cold collation. If you want more, you'll have to dine at m'mother's."

That was exactly what Gavin would have to do. Despite all he had eaten, he knew he'd be hungry in a few hours. "I suppose I will." He glanced at Georgie in the hope that he would see some sort of reaction, but her countenance didn't reflect her feelings. If he wasn't going to be able to be alone with her, there was no point in staying. "Shall we go?"

The others nodded their assent. As they strolled around the side of the house to the front, his frustration grew. First

Barfleur and now his friends. Georgie wasn't helping either. She had wanted, expected him to kiss her under the tree, but since then, she acted like nothing had happened or almost happened, and he didn't know what to do about it.

On the journey back, the ladies discussed the recipes they trusted Cook would discover, and Littleton's arm lay across his wife's shoulders as he regarded his wife with a besottedness that was becoming damned irritating. Especially when Gavin had to mind his p's and q's with Georgie. There had to be a way to get her alone again where no one would interrupt them. The problem was where? If he even asked to take her for a walk a maid or, more likely, a footman would accompany them. This whole thing would have been much easier if they were actually staying at the Turners' house. But there was no point in wishing for something that would not occur.

"That would be wonderful. Do you not agree, my lord?" Georgie said.

For a moment he thought she was speaking to Littleton, but he was Frits. Gavin was the only one she called "my lord." Another thing he wanted to change. "I'm sorry. I wasn't listening. What would be wonderful?"

"If Cook could discover the ingredients for the seed cake by tomorrow."

"Yes, yes, of course." He smiled at her. At least he'd done something right today.

They'd drawn up in front of Littlewood, and he helped her down from the coach. "I shall say a prayer that the secret ingredient is found."

She gave him what he thought of as her beatific smile. "I do not believe I thanked you for allowing me to handle the matter with Mr. Barfleur. Most gentlemen would not have permitted a lady to take the lead."

He held her lapis gaze and took her other hand in his. "In that case, most gentlemen are idiots."

"You might be right." The corners of her lush deep-pink lips rose. "But not you."

"No," he agreed. "I do not consider myself so." Except that he had yet to work out how to kiss her. "Have a good evening. Would you like to ride tomorrow?"

"I would. Thank you for asking."

He brought her gloved fingers to his lips. "Until tomorrow."

"Until then." As he stepped back, he saw the butler waiting at the door. No. They would definitely not be allowed to be alone together here. It was time to ask the ladies for ideas again.

Chapter Twenty-Five

Georgie entered the hall to find Adeline waiting for her. "Shall we take the cake and biscuits to Cook?"

"We shall," Adeline said slowly as she searched Georgie's face. "But first I want to know if Turley finally kissed you."

"No." Georgie heaved a sigh. Her one goal for the day, and she had been unable to bring it about. "Although, it was not for lack of trying. I found a grand old weeping willow by the river and insisted on seeing the inside. He was about to kiss me. I know he was when Mr. Barfleur had an altercation with a local boy. Suffice it to say we felt compelled to intervene."

"Well, drat." Adeline opened the green baize door and held it for Georgie. "There are only two more days of the house party left. I had so hoped that you and he would be settled by then."

"As you say, there are still two days." And two nights. "If only we could ride the horses by ourselves."

"Hmm." Adeline stopped at the bottom of the stairs. "When are you riding next?"

"In the morning." Georgie wondered what her friend had in mind.

"I cannot arrange it that quickly, but the day after I can come up with an errand for Johnson to do at the last minute."

"Before he knows we are riding." None of the other grooms had gone out with them, and they would probably not think of offering to go with them. "That might work."

"I will not be able to tell Frits until much later." Adeline grimaced. "He will not be pleased."

Turley had become much more attentive than he had in Town. Georgie prayed it was because despite his fears he was coming to love her. "If it all goes as I hope it will, he will be pleased."

"You are right about that." They walked down the flagstone corridor to the kitchen. "For now, let's see what Cook makes of the cake and biscuits."

Georgie touched Adeline's arm. "You do realize that you will never be able to serve the seed cake to either Mary or Amanda."

"I hadn't thought of that, but, of course, I could not." She reached the entrance to the kitchen, and flashed Georgie a grin. "The good thing is that we do not have regular visiting hours here." She stepped inside the kitchen, which was much more orderly than the one at the Turners' house. Then again, there were not the number of guests. "Mrs. Fanner."

"My lady." The cook bobbed a curtsey. "What do you require of me?"

Georgie pulled the napkins from her reticule. "We would like to know if you can replicate the seed cake and biscuits."

"The lady who served them was unwilling to share her recipe. Of course your seed cake is excellent, but there is something about this one."

The older servant smiled. "My recipe is from his

lordship's great-great-grandmother. It will not hurt my feelings at all to try to discover the mystery of this one."

Adeline grinned. "I knew I could depend upon you."

"As you always may, my lady. Just leave it to me." The cook took the handkerchiefs from Georgie.

They turned to leave when she thought of something else with which the cook might be able to assist. "You have been at Littlewood for a long time, have you not?"

"Yes, miss, I have."

"Do you know if Lord Turley has a favorite dish or food?"

"Most of the time he and his lordship ate everything in sight. But let me give that some thought."

"Thank you." With any luck at all, Mrs. Fanner would remember something.

"What was that about?" Adeline asked as they went back to the hall.

"While we were sampling the different offerings, I had a lemon ice and told him that it was my favorite food." Georgie pulled a face. "Well, almost anything with lemon in it tastes good to me. In any event, I asked him what his favorite food was, and he could not think of a thing."

"Interesting." Adeline paused on the way to the morning room. "Frits and I both have favorite foods. Well, favorite ices."

"According to Turley, he does not even have a favorite ice."

"Now that I find odd." She linked her arm with Georgie's. "I am certain our cook will know. Or perhaps, my mother-in-law."

Georgie did not know why she had not thought of Lady Littleton. She glanced out the window of the morning room. "Do you mind if I take a short ride? There is something I wish to work on with Lilly."

"No, not at all." Adeline added a pillow to the one on the daybed. "In fact, I shall take a bit of a nap. I am not quite as tired as I have been, but it's been a busy day."

Georgie wondered if she would be so tired when she was with child. She turned and hurried to her rooms. There was only one way to find out. But first she had to get Turley to admit he loved her. In the meantime, she would practice starts with her mare. He and Lochinvar were not going to win the next race.

"My lady, Lord Turley has returned." Cristabel's butler poked his head into the parlor.

"Thank you, Crothers. Please bring him to us."

The butler bowed and left. "Perhaps we will have some good news."

"I certainly hope that is the case," Lucinda said. "If not, we must take a more direct hand in the matter."

Constance set her glass of claret on the small table next to her. "Who would have believed that this would take so long? It is obvious that they love each other."

"Is it enough?" Lucinda asked. "We know that Georgie loves him, but I will wager that he does not have a clue that he loves her."

The three of them had been going round and round about this mess all to no avail. "We shall ask how today went, then make alternative plans if need be."

The door opened and Gavin entered the room. "Good afternoon."

"Good day to you." Cristabel glanced at her friends.

Constance gave an almost imperceptible nod before saying, "Did you kiss her?"

"No." Fortunately, he appeared disgruntled.

"Were you not alone with her?" Cristobel asked.

"Oh, we were alone. And we were finally in a place where we would not be seen, but there was an altercation over fish."

"*Fish*?" Lucinda shook her head as if unable to understand what he'd said. "I believe you must explain yourself. I had no idea you were going fishing."

Gavin grimaced. "We were not. One of the guests made a wager about catching fish and when he did not do it, he attempted to steal a catch from a local lad. We decided that we should intervene. Thanks to your granddaughter, the matter is now resolved. Unfortunately, to resume our walk afterward would have caused talk as everyone was by then in the formal gardens near the house."

"What bad luck." Lucinda took a healthy drink of wine. "Are you dining with her this evening?"

"No. We had a substantial luncheon and there was a great deal of food at the garden party. Adeline and Frits decided to have a light meal this evening."

"Unfortunately, we are going out for dinner," Cristabel did not for a moment think her son would forgo a larger meal, but she did believe that Frits would like to spend time alone with his wife. "I shall tell my cook that you will dine in your rooms."

"And tomorrow?" Constance asked.

"We are going riding in the morning and we have been invited for dinner and an informal dance tomorrow evening." He appeared frustrated about what had occurred earlier. "I plan to try to get her alone then. I understand that the gardens will be lit with small lanterns."

"You will be riding with Georgie in the morning," Constance said. "Surely you could find a time to kiss her then."

"I could if Johnson wasn't with us all the time." He cut a look at Cristabel. "You know how diligent he is."

She could not help but to pull a face. If anyone knew what a good minder the groom was it was her. "Yes, I am aware."

"If there was any way I could get rid of Johnson I'd happily do it. But I fear it would be impossible."

"We shall attempt to think of something to help you."

"Thank you." He bowed to them. "I think I'll go through my correspondence. I have received a great many letters and other matters to which I need to attend. Have a good evening."

"We shall, my dear," Cristabel sipped her wine as he walked out the door. Once the sound of his steps had receded she glanced at her friends. "We must stop relying on chance when it comes to Georgie and Turley."

"I agree." Lucinda placed her elbow on the arm of the chair and rested her chin in her palm. "What do you propose to do?"

"I shall write to my son and explain to him that Turley and Georgie must be allowed to take their ride alone in the morning."

"An excellent idea." Constance gave an approving look.

"There is no time like the present." Cristabel moved to the desk, and took a piece of paper.

My dear son,

> *It has become imperative that Turley has sufficient time alone with Georgie to press his case. Her grandmother and I agree that tomorrow during their ride would be perfect. Please see to it that Johnson does not accompany them.*

> *I am as always your affectionate mother.*

After sanding and sealing the letter, she tugged the bell-pull. A brief second later one of her footmen entered the room. "My lady?"

"Please have this delivered to Littlewood. I want an immediate answer."

"Yes, my lady."

Once the door closed, she glanced at her friends. "We have done as much as we can for the moment."

Not an hour later her butler returned. "This is from his lordship in answer to your missive."

She popped the seal and read the hasty scrawl.

I hope you know what you are doing.

She hoped so as well.

The next day Cristabel awoke to the sound of rain. Not a light pitter-patter, but the sound of a waterfall. "Well, drat. Are the heavens against them as well?"

Having been informed by Adeline that Frits had received a letter from his mother demanding that Georgie and Turley be allowed to ride alone the next day, she had slept deeply. Soon she would know if she should marry Turley or not, but the sound of a heavy rain slipped through the air and her bed hangings. She did not even have to open her eyes to know that no one in the Littlewood household was going anywhere today. Yet she sat up and listened a bit longer, praying it was one of those quick showers. It was not. A half hour later the rain was as steady as it had been when she'd woken. It might not even be possible for Turley to visit without becoming totally soaked from the carriage to the door. The first ride that she'd have alone with him was not going to occur.

Drat! And everything had been working out perfectly. She fell back to her pillows. Why was this happening to her? She gave herself a shake. Perhaps it would not rain all day.

After dressing, she went to break her fast. "Good morning."

"Good morning." Adeline glanced out the window and Georgie noticed that on this side of the house the winds were blowing fiercely. "Frits has gone out to help one of the tenants move their animals. The roof of their barn was leaking badly."

"Did he not know of it before?" Georgie poured a cup of tea and pulled a fresh rack of toast to her.

"No. He hadn't been informed. This is bad luck for you."

"Yes, but these storms usually do not last long." Although, this one seemed as if it would last all day.

"That's true." Adeline's face brightened. "This will give me the opportunity to read one of the new books that arrived yesterday."

"Which one is that?" Reading was always a good way to pass the time on a rainy day.

"Louisa Stanhope's *The Nun of Santa Maria Di Tindaro*."

Georgie had read all of Miss Austen's books, but she had unfortunately died the year before. "I haven't read her."

"I think she is excellent. You might want to start with *The Bandit's Bride*."

"I'll do that. Thank you." Naturally, it was not as pleasurable as spending the day with Turley. Still, it would give her an opportunity to find a new author.

The rest of the day passed as she had expected it would,

but the next morning dawned sunny and crisp. The previous day had given her a great deal of time to think about her problem with Turley. And she had decided that it would be better if she finally addressed his fears about falling in love. If that went well, then she had every intension of experiencing her first kiss.

He arrived in time to break his fast with them and took his usual chair next to hers. "I am grateful that we have sun for at least a little while today."

Georgie stared at him. "What do you mean for a little while? Why should it change?"

"The wind is light but blowing steadily from the west. On the horizon there are dark clouds. We should have time to get in a few races before it reaches us."

"In that case, let's not waste any time."

As she expected, no groom accompanied them. When they reached the path they used for racing, she was surprised to find it not nearly as muddy as she thought it might be. Thus far, they had won an equal number of races, but Georgie was determined to win the next one. In furtherance of that goal and unbeknownst to Turley, she and Lilly had spent a few hours practicing starting faster.

As Georgie brought Lilly to a stop she could not keep her smile to herself. "Are you ready to race?"

"Of course. We'll have to call our own start." He brought his horse beside her.

"You can do it."

"Would you like a head start?"

"No, thank you." He was going to have a surprise. "We shall win without taking advantage of you."

He said something else, but Georgie wasn't paying attention. Instead she listened for the number to be called. On the count of three, Lilly burst forth just as they had practiced. They reached the curve in the road and almost ran into a coach that had no reason to be there at all.

Quickly reining her horse in, Georgie turned to tell the coachman he was on private land when a pair of meaty hands grabbed her and dragged her off Lilly. "Let me go!"

Drat, of all the times not to carry a riding crop.

"Not likely. His lordship'll pay us good if we get you before tomorrow," the blackguard called out. "Open the door."

Another man went to grab her mare's reins. She couldn't let them take Lilly. "Kick!"

The scoundrel didn't even have time to shout before he was on the ground bleeding from his head.

"Bloody bitch," the man holding her spat. "If Lord Lytton didn't want you so bad I'd make you pay for what you done." He opened the carriage door and shoved her in.

Lytton? Why would he want me? And where is Turley?

He couldn't be that far behind her.

"We'll have ta leave 'im here." The coach dipped as the bounder climbed onto the coachman's seat. Thank God he didn't get in with her. "Let's get out o' here."

The carriage started off and Georgie scrambled up and tested the door handle. It was unlocked. Turley would be here soon. Lilly would lead him to her. But the blackguards probably had a gun of some sort, and she didn't want either him or, more likely, her horse to be shot. The only thing to do was jump.

A crack of thunder sounded as she opened the door. So much for the rain holding off. The ground rushed past. There was nothing for it. She had to get away from them. With any luck they wouldn't know she was gone until they were a long ways away. Georgie took a breath and jumped, tucking her arms and legs in as Hawksworth had told her. She hit the ground and rolled.

Her horse nudged her. "Thank the Lord you're here."

Taking a scant second she moved her legs and arms. Good, nothing was broken. Lilly knelt and Georgie scrambled into her saddle. A cold wind gusted and the rain started to come down in buckets.

Chapter Twenty-Six

When Gavin had asked if Georgie was ready to race she'd given him such a sly look he was sure she had a secret of some sort. What had she been up to?

Lilly had looked as if she was ready to go as well. Granted the mare was fast, but Lochinvar had already proven himself well matched. She wouldn't win by more than she had before. If she won at all. He'd wager on it.

"Would you like me to give you a head start?" He'd never made the offer before but couldn't think of anything else to say that might encourage her to give away her plan.

"No, thank you," Georgie scoffed, giving him an arched look. "We shall win without taking advantage of you."

"You seem very sure of yourself."

She patted the mare's neck, but didn't respond.

The only thing he wanted to win was her hand in marriage and her person in his bed. That however was not going well. Well, there was only one way to find out what the two of them were planning. "Very well. On the count of three."

"One, two, three."

She took off like the hounds of hell were on her heels.

He'd never seen a faster start at Newmarket. Fortunately, as he was stupidly staring at her, Gavin didn't even have to dig into his horse's sides before they were off chasing the ladies. Unless Lochinvar could make up the time, she would indeed win and by a good length.

A strange sense of foreboding pricked his neck, and Gavin urged his gelding faster. He'd be able to see her until the curve in the road, but that would be too soon. Just then Georgie rounded the bend, and he didn't like that he no longer had her in sight.

An angry scream rent the air, and shouts followed. When he reached the curve he could see her horse but not her. Had she fallen? No. Lilly pranced and pawed the ground. The horse wouldn't be so agitated if it was only that. He approached Lilly but the second she saw them she raced away. That was when he saw the coach swipping down the lane faster than was safe.

Bloody hell-hounds!

For less than a second his mind stopped. Then a rage Gavin had never known coursed through his veins. "Go as fast as you can, boy. We need to rescue Georgie."

The lane narrowed, but the carriage was still rushing away. Thunder cracked as if the storm was upon them, and suddenly the coach door swung open and Georgie stood in it, looked down, and jumped.

Gavin's heart plummeted to his stomach as she hit the ground. Lilly rushed to her mistress and knelt. He sent a quick prayer that Georgie wasn't injured. But he couldn't breathe again until the horse rose with his beloved on her back . . . *Beloved*?

She galloped past and shouted, "The tower."

That was the closest place, but if the coach came back,

it was the first place they'd see. And they were too far from the main house to reach it before the storm struck. But the numerous Littleton follies were all in good condition and partially stocked. "No, we need to be farther away. The German farmhouse."

Without stopping, she nodded.

Then the temperature dropped and the heavens opened up.

He caught up to her as she led her horse into the small barn attached to the side of the folly. The best thing about this structure was that the barn was attached to the house. He'd always thought that odd, but he was glad for it now. Slipping off her horse, Georgie began to rub the mare down with hay and found a blanket to throw over the beast. Gavin did the same for Lochinvar. Oats were stored in a barrel, and the water pump was, thankfully, inside.

When they finished, he enveloped her small hand in his, finding it much too cold. And she was trembling. "We must get dry."

Teeth chattering, she nodded and allowed him to tow her into the house. "There will be tea and biscuits at least."

"There should be more than that." Georgie wrapped her arms around herself. "I'm so cold."

"Well, it's not the warmest day." He was astonished she wasn't having hysterics. Then again, no lady who could jump from a moving coach would have hysterics. "I'll make a fire and fetch some blankets. You'll have to get out of those clothes."

"Y-y-es." She turned her back to him.

It had been years since he'd been in this particular folly. The fireplace was massive compared to the rest of the oak-planked room, which was furnished with a table and chairs as well as the bench in front of the fireplace. He was glad the windows were already shuttered. A flint was in a cubbyhole next to the fireplace, and logs were already laid. Once the fire was started, he filled a kettle with water and searched for blankets. He finally found them in the wardrobe in the bedroom. By the time he returned, she was down to her shift. The thin linen clung to her narrow waist and nicely curved bottom. She reminded him of a goddess, and that was just from behind.

Her fingers shook as she hung her clothes over chairs.

"I'll take care of those. You need to get warm." He draped the wool blanket around her shoulders. He wanted to ask her if she knew who had abducted her, but that could wait until she was warm. "This should help."

"Th-thank you." She turned to him, and Gavin sucked in a breath. Her hair was half down and dripping water between her breasts. She was the most beautiful woman he had ever seen. Slowly he removed the remaining pins from her hair and put them on a small table. The mass of rich chestnut curls tumbled down past her waist.

Beloved.

The word clamored in his head. Before he could stop himself he wrapped his arms around her, and vowed to himself never to let her go. "When you jumped my heart . . . my heart dropped to my feet. I don't know what I would have done if anything had . . . if you had died." He buried his face in her hair. The fear of losing her still stuck in his gut. "My God, Georgie, I love you. I tried not to. I tried to be strong, but I love you, and I want you in my life for as long as we walk this earth."

She cupped his cheeks with her still cold hands and searched his face. "I love you too. But it's not a weakness. Loving someone can bring strength."

"It didn't for my father." And now that he'd failed, it might not for him.

She wrapped her arms around him, and they stayed like that until she stopped shivering. "I think the water is hot. I'll make tea, and you get out of your wet clothing."

"I hope it's not stale."

Georgie glanced over her shoulder and grinned. "If this one is stocked like the others, there is fresh tea, milk, sugar, bread, and cheese."

"That's right." He'd completely forgotten the new protocol. "The servants that are being trained."

"Precisely." She rummaged through the cabinets and found everything she needed as he stripped off his clothing and added it to the rest of hers spread over the four chairs, drying in front of the fireplace, before wrapping a blanket around himself. The room was warming nicely, but there was still a chill.

A few minutes later, Gavin and Georgie sat next to each other wrapped in blankets and holding cups of tea on an old German bench carved on the arms and back with images of animals.

She leaned against him as if they had been together for years. "I know most of the story, but tell me what happened when your mother died."

He took a sip, then told her what he had not mentioned before. "So you see. I vowed I would never do what he did. I would never fall in love."

Reaching out, Georgie caressed his cheek and turned his head to face her. "You won't because you have seen what happens. And you have already shown yourself to be stronger than your father ever was. You lost your mother. Your mother"—tears shimmered in her eyes—"the most important woman in your life, but you did not allow that loss to destroy you."

"I didn't have a choice." Gavin couldn't keep the grim tone out of his voice.

Smiling, she kissed him lightly on his lips. "Of course you did. You could have copied you father's behavior, but you did not. You held everyone up and carried on."

He stared at her for a moment, unable to believe the love and trust in her eyes, and faith she had for him. "I never thought of it that way. I mean I know I carried on, but I never thought that I was stronger than him. Everyone always said how much I was like him. I needed to ensure that I—"

She placed a finger on his mouth silencing him. "I love you. And I know you are strong. Even if something was to happen to me—and I do not think it will. I come from a family of long-lived ladies—I know you will take care of our children and our holdings."

"Our children?" Gavin felt a smile tug at the corners of his mouth.

"Yes." Georgie nodded. "Our children."

"I should get down on one knee and propose properly."

She rolled her eyes to the ceiling. "You tried that the first time. I liked your second proposal much better."

What would have happened if he'd followed his instincts the first time and taken her into his arms? Would he have discovered, or be able to admit to himself that he loved her? "When and where do you want to marry? And please say that it will be soon."

"Not as quickly as our friends have wed, but at St. George's in two weeks. That will give my parents time to return to Town."

"St. George's?" Gavin wanted to groan. In fact, he probably had groaned.

"Yes." She flashed him a quick smile. "My mother has always wanted one of us to have a wedding there. Meg got married at our family's estate. Kit wed in Scotland. Who knows if or when my other two brothers will marry. They are both too young to think of taking a wife. And I can't place the burden on my younger sister. Therefore, we shall say our vows at St. George's to make my mother happy." Her eyes acquired a wicked look. "But that does not mean we cannot anticipate our vows."

Gavin's jaw dropped, and he snapped it shut. "What do you know about"—he swallowed—"about that?"

"My sister, having a feeling the information would be helpful, became a font of useful information. I might be innocent, but I'm not ignorant." Georgie frowned. "At least not entirely."

"Let's put that notion to a test, shall we?" Finally he'd make her his. Something he'd been dreaming of doing for months.

Leaning back, Georgie held up one hand. "First you must make me a promise. I have no desire to get with child and there not be a wedding."

That gave him second thoughts. However, at this point there was little he wouldn't swear to. "Anything."

Her raised brow reminded him forcefully of her grandmother. "You may not do anything to put your life in danger before we are married."

He drew her into his arms again. "You have my word."

Softly, he pressed his lips to hers, teasing and tasting. At first she seemed unsure of what to do, but soon her mouth softened, and she returned his kiss. He reached under her blanket and thumbed her nipple over her now dry shift. When Georgie opened her lips on a moan, he swept his tongue into her warm mouth. She tasted of tea and the ginger biscuits they'd found, something fresh. He reveled in the taste of her, of her soft body pressing against him, but wasn't at all prepared for the feel of her fingers tangling the hair on his chest.

Georgie knew she was playing with fire by inviting Gavin to make love to her. She also knew that she could never regret the way he touched her. Despite what her sister had said, she had not truly understood how good a kiss could be until now. Or how Gavin kneading her breasts could light fires over her body and create an ache between her legs. She shifted and he pulled her onto his lap, her thighs hugging his hips, and that's when she felt his member standing straight up between them.

This time when he groaned it wasn't because of St. George's. She felt wicked and wanton and didn't care at all. If he'd realized before that he loved her, they would already be married.

"God, Georgie. You're going to be the death of me."

"I certainly hope not." She nibbled his chin. "That would make for a very short marriage."

Holding her against him, he rose and the blankets fell away. "There are clean sheets on the bed."

"Are there?" she teased. She knew that all the follies stood ready to be used. Although, not all of them had the beds made.

"Um-hmm, and I started the fire in there. I'm going to show you how much I love you."

The rain still pelted the windows as he pulled down the covers and crawled onto the large bed. He took her lips again as if he was worshiping her mouth. It was all she could do to keep up and try to copy what he did. His large and surprisingly calloused hands stroked her body and where his hands went his lips followed. When he took one nipple into his mouth, she arched, wanting him, wanting more.

He grinned and stroked the apex of her thighs. "You're almost ready for me."

She was not quite sure what that meant, but it had to be a good thing.

Then he captured her lips again as he rubbed and entered her with a finger. Her body took over as she moved against him until she couldn't stand the tension any longer, then she shattered into a thousand pieces of light, and he entered her slowly, stretching her until she couldn't feel anything but him.

His body tensed and he stopped. "Are you all right?"

She hoped that wasn't the end of it. Surely there was more. "It didn't hurt as much as I thought it would."

"That's good." Gavin started moving again, and her body felt like a tightly wound clock. Then her body quaked, and he called out her name as his release took him. "Georgie, I love you."

"I love you too."

He kissed her forehead and rolled off her snugging her into his side as he did, making her feel as if she finally had a place she belonged. He stared at the ceiling for a few moments frowning before saying, "Who in God's name would have wanted to abduct you?"

She knew what the blackguard had said, and it was Lord Lytton's coach, but that it was Lord Lytton didn't make any sense. He seemed to be interested in Lady Aurelia. And he had to know that he could not get away with it. Still, Gavin had to be told. "It was Lord Lytton's coach. And one of the men said he'd pay them for taking me."

The arm around her tightened, and she could feel the anger in her betrothed. "I'm going to kill him."

"You are not." Turning over, she pressed her hands against Gavin's chest and rose above him. "You are not going to challenge him to a duel, or kill him, or anything else. You promised me you'd not do anything that could cause you to be injured."

Their eyes locked for several moments. When he finally inclined his head she breathed a sigh of relief. She might not know a lot about gentlemen, but she knew enough to know that once he'd discovered who might be the kidnapper, he would demand to go after him. This whole situation must be handled with a great deal of care.

Chapter Twenty-Seven

Gavin wasn't positive he'd said "injured," but he suddenly realized and appreciated the subtle intelligence she'd used when she had made him promise not to put his life in danger before they wed. "Very well. I shall encourage him to leave the country."

"Only if you can do it without putting your life in danger." She'd lain back down and cuddled next to him.

He listened to the storm rage outside as the storm within him ceased to exist. He'd take care of Lytton, but Gavin couldn't do it now. He glanced at Georgie. He never imagined he'd be happy to be in love, but he was. Her breathing slowed, and he knew Georgie, his future wife and mother of their children, was asleep. He almost wished they did not have to attend this evening's ball. Pulling the blanket over them, he closed his eyes. When he opened them again the rain had stopped.

"Sweetheart. Georgie."

"Hmm." She mumbled delightfully in her sleep, and he couldn't resist a smile.

"We must get dressed and go back to the house. We have to get ready for the ball." And he had to speak with Littleton about Lytton. If Gavin was to keep his promise to Georgie, he'd do well to have someone else there so that he didn't put his hands on the earl, or a ball in the man's chest.

"Ball?" Her muttered question made him want to laugh.

"Yes." He pushed back her dusky curls. "Are you always this hard to wake up?"

Her lapis-blue eyes glared at him. "I suppose that depends on my exertions before going to sleep." She sat up, causing the covers to drop to her waist. "I'm hungry. What time is it?"

He did his best not to look at her breasts. If he did, they might not make it back at all. "I have no idea. The storm has ended. To be honest, that is probably what woke me." Gavin glanced around, but there was no clock. "I'll look at my watch." She started to stand, glanced down, and frowned. "If you would like, I can turn my head." Her eyes widened. "Although, that would be a shame. I've always believed you are the most beautiful woman in the world, but now I know it for a fact."

A blush rose from the top of her breasts up her neck and infused her face. "I am not sure I know what to say to that."

"Say thank you." When Gavin rose her gaze roamed his body making him more acutely aware of his nakedness than he had ever been. And the fact of his cock hardening again.

"I think I shall return the compliment." Georgie suddenly shook her head. "We should get dressed."

"If we don't want to be caught naked we'll have to." He had no doubt that once the rain had stopped and they hadn't returned, Littleton had sent out search parties. "Do you need help?"

"No. My habit is easy enough to don." She went behind

a screen and poured water into a basin while he went to the other room, pulled on his clothing, and gathered hers. Fortunately everything was almost dry. "There is blood."

Striding back into the bedroom, he stared down at the sheet. As he suspected, evidence of her maidenhood was plain to see. "What do you want to do about it?"

Georgie took the shift he held out. "If we gather the bedding into a pile, perhaps no one will notice."

"We can give it a try." He'd have to make sure they announced their engagement as soon as they returned. He wrapped the remaining cheese in the rest of the bread she'd cut as she entered the room. "Here. This will tide us over until we can get something more substantial."

"Thank you." After gobbling the sandwich down, she grinned. "That was perfect. I do not feel as grumpy now."

"There is something I must remember." Gavin drew her into his arms. "Will feeding you always improve your mood?"

"Almost always." Georgie rose on her toes and kissed him. "I wish we could remain here for a while longer."

The sound of Lochinvar whinnying and moving around made Gavin tilt his head toward the window and listen. "We've been found."

"I'm glad we have clothes on," she said in a rueful voice.

"As am I." He took her hand. "Let's meet them outside."

Sitting on his horse, Johnson shook his head slowly back and forth. "Thought you had more sense than to let the storm catch you."

"There was a little more to it than that." Gavin pulled out his pocket watch. It was after five o'clock. "We need to return. However, I am fairly certain that there is a man lying dead near the curve in the lane." He'd go with the groom, but he didn't want to leave Georgie alone nor did he want her to see a dead man, again.

Johnson rubbed his chin. "I'll go back and get help. We stopped at the tower first, now I know why you weren't there."

"As I said. There's more to this story. We need to saddle our horses. I'll see you back at the house."

The groom nodded and rode off toward the lane. Less than thirty minutes later, Gavin and Georgie strode into the hall to find a servant reporting to Adeline.

"We were caught by the storm," Georgie announced as she went straight to her friend and embraced her. "Is Frits here?"

"No, he's out looking for the two of you." Adeline turned toward the servant. "Sound the signal, please."

"Right away, my lady." The servant bowed.

"Now then." She glanced first at Georgie then at Gavin with an intensely curious look on her face. "Was it just the rain?"

Georgie gave a small shake of her head. "No. There is more." She grinned and wrapped her fingers around his arm. "You may wish us happy. We are going to marry."

Suddenly writhed in smiles, Adeline managed to embrace both of them so hard, he could feel the baby kicking. "I do wish you happy. But you appeared so grim when you walked into the house."

He exchanged a look with Georgie. "Let us bathe and change first. Littleton should be here when we tell you what occurred." Suddenly a loud, low horn sounded. "I haven't heard that in years."

Georgie's eyes had widened. "What is it?"

"It's called an *alpenhorn*. This one is from the French

Alps. One of the earlier Lord Littletons brought it back from his Grand Tour."

"It saves a good deal of time when Frits or someone we need to speak to is out," Adeline explained. She linked her arm with Georgie's. "Come along and tell me how your betrothal came about."

Gavin followed the ladies up to the landing where the stairs parted, wondering how much she would actually tell her friend. "I'll see you in the drawing room."

Smiling, Georgie blew him a kiss. That was unexpected. Still it put a spring in his step that he'd never had before. He couldn't wait until this evening when he could tell the world and all the gentlemen at the house party she was his. But he still had to deal with Lytton.

"Gavin." Adeline's voice was filled with laughter. "You are staying at The Lilacs."

"Oh." She was right. "Thank you. I'd forgotten." Light laughter followed him as he made his way back down the stairs and out the door. Ah well. This would give him a chance to tell Lady Littleton, Georgie's grandmother, and the duchess what had occurred. They might have some ideas about how to handle his lordship and enable him to marry Georgie in less than two weeks.

Adeline covered her mouth in an attempt to hold back her laughter.

Georgie gave up the attempt as a lost cause and dissolved into whoops. "I take it the chamber he usually uses is in the other wing."

"It is." Adeline fanned her face with her hand. "I have never seen him so distracted. I must not be thinking either.

It would have been easy to send a message to his valet and have his kit sent over."

"You are not the only one not thinking. It did not even occur to me and apparently not to Gavin either." Other than the problem with Lytton, Georgie was happier than she ever had been in her life. She felt like dancing to her apartment. "I cannot believe we are finally engaged."

"I want the whole story about it." Her friend led her into her rooms where she saw a bathtub already set up in the dressing room. "The water will be here shortly." Adeline sat on one of two chairs near the bank of windows. "Tell me everything that happened."

Georgie felt as if she were floating on air. "Well, perhaps not *everything*."

"Oh, my." Her friend's eyes rounded. "I suppose it is a very good thing that you are betrothed."

"You know nothing would have occurred if I had not agreed to marry him." Her maid entered with a tea tray and left immediately after setting it on a small table. "But I need to start at the beginning." While she poured tea, she told Adeline about the abduction attempt, the possibly dead man, and how the thought of her being harmed made Gavin realize that he loved her. "We talked about his fear of falling in love, and he now realizes that he is much stronger than his father was. I must tell you that in an attempt to hide the . . . er . . . well what we did after he proposed again, we bundled the sheets together." Georgie pulled a face. "We did not know what else to do."

"Do not worry," Adeline said briskly. "I shall send my maid to deal with them." She took a long sip of tea. "You showed great forethought in making Gavin promise not to place himself in harm, but what is he going to do about Lytton?"

"I have no idea." Georgie finished her cup and poured another. "Whatever he does I shall be there with him."

Leaning back in her chair, Adeline rubbed her stomach. "Frits and I will come with you. If Gavin attempts to harm Lytton, or vice versa, my husband will put an end to it."

Or finish what Gavin started. "That is a good idea. I suppose we could find something to hit one or the other over the head with if need be."

"As long as it is not breakable." Adeline glanced at the fireplace. "A poker would work well, and they are readily available."

Georgie chuckled. "As long as we did not aim for the head." She thought back over the past few events at the house party. "It was a shock to recognize his coach. I had no idea Lytton was so interested in me. I quite believed he had turned his attention to Lady Aurelia."

Adeline tilted her head to one side as a line formed across her forehead. "Do you know, now that I think about it, I had as well. We definitely need to get to the bottom of his behavior."

"I almost forgot. I must write to my parents immediately." Georgie sat at the small burl writing table and drew out a sheet of pressed paper. "They have to return to Town immediately. Someone has to arrange for a time at St. George's and for the wedding breakfast, and I need new clothing." Finally, she would be able to wear stronger colors.

"If you would like," Adeline said slowly, "I will accompany you to Town and help you until your mother returns."

"Would you?" Georgie was surprised at the offer. Her friend did not like leaving the country. "I cannot thank you enough for the offer, and I shall take you up on it. The very soonest my mother could arrive is over a week."

"Well, then." Adeline bit down on her lip. This truly was a sacrifice for her. "I shall inform Frits. He will most likely wish to come as well."

Georgie rushed over and hugged Adeline. "Thank you. You are the best of friends."

After embracing Georgie in return, Adeline smiled. "I could not miss your wedding."

A wedding. Finally, Georgie was going to be married to the gentleman she loved. She supposed she would pinch herself every few days until she was wed.

Gavin made haste to The Lilacs. He had to bathe and change, speak with the ladies, then rush back to Littlewood. He hoped in that order. However, as he strode into the hall and headed for the stairs, Lady Littleton rounded the corner of the corridor into the hall followed by Lady Featherton and the duchess.

Lady Littleton's sharp gaze took in his appearance. "Good. I see you were found. I take it Georgie was with you. Did you get caught in the rain?"

He stilled for a moment, then it dawned on him that of course the people searching would have sent word or stopped by here. "Yes. Both of us." Thank God he was betrothed. "I have some excellent news to tell you, but first may I change?"

"Very well." Her tone indicated she would much rather have the story now.

"I shall not be long." Gavin put one foot on the lower tread of the staircase. "I promise."

"Are you dining at Littlewood?"

He had not discussed it with Adeline, but he generally dined with them. He added the second foot to the first. "Yes."

"Very well." Her ladyship nodded. "I shall send a note telling my daughter-in-law to expect us as well." He climbed one more step, waiting to be dismissed. "You may go. Be back down here in an hour."

"Thank you." Taking the remaining stairs two at a time he dashed to his bedchamber. He consumed a cup of tea and a sandwich while his bath was being prepared.

The bathing chamber was a room covered in colorful tiles with a tiled stove in one corner. At his main estate, Gavin already had water piped up to the floor the bedchambers were on. If Georgie agreed, they could make the room next to the pump into a bathing chamber.

He sank down, letting the water cover him as much as it could. The warmth made him want to dally. He wondered what Georgie would look like in a bathtub. Would the steam from the water make her hair curl even more? The image he had of her made his body tighten. Lord, every time he thought of her he got an erection. He had to make sure they set an actual wedding date and pray she'd agree to less than two weeks. But, damn, her parents had to travel back from somewhere in the north.

His valet poked his head into the bathing room. "My lord, your clothing is laid out."

"I'll be right there." Gavin dried himself, wrapped the towel around his waist, and chuckled when he recalled the look on his beloved's face when he'd risen from the bed this afternoon.

Why had it taken him until today to admit he loved her?

He had laughed at Harrington, his sister's husband, for being so blind about love, and now he'd done the same thing. Then again, Gavin's brother-in-law had had no reason not to fall in love. At least he'd had the forethought to bring the betrothal ring he intended to give Georgie. His family had several of them that had been passed down through the generations.

He grinned to himself. "Ardley, please get the ruby ring I brought."

The valet, who had been straightening up, turned to face Gavin. "Am I to wish you happy, my lord?"

"You are." He couldn't hold in his smile any longer. "Miss Featherton has done me the honor of agreeing to be my wife."

"Sir . . . my lord—" Gavin thought the man was going to burst with joy. He'd never seen his valet smile before. "I wish you nothing but happiness. Miss Featherton will be an excellent viscountess. It will be nice to have a lady's touch again."

"It will." With the exception of some structural renovations, nothing had been done since before his mother had died. "She shall have free rein to do as she pleases."

Ardley ducked back into the dressing room and came back out holding a rectangular wooden box. "When will we return to London?"

"Probably within the next couple of days. What is that?"

"When you asked me to pack the ring, I discovered a parure that matched it." His valet opened the box. "I thought you might want the necklace to go along with it."

"Well done." Gavin cast his mind back to the list of jewelry that belonged to the estate and could not remember it being on the list. It looked familiar, but he did not remember ever seeing it before. At least not . . . "Where was it?"

"It was in a section that belonged to your great-grandmother Turley. I do not think anyone has looked there for years, and I do not believe she ever wore them. When you asked about the ruby ring, I remembered that the necklace existed and searched the entire room."

"No. They wouldn't have suited her." A painting of a dark-haired lady came to mind. "She was wearing it in the portrait hanging in the gallery." And the entire set, in fact, everything in that section was unentailed. "No one since has been interested because they all had fair coloring." He took the box, removed the necklace, the velvet sack it had been in, and placed it and the ring in the sack. "Thank you."

"It was my pleasure, my lord." Ardley bowed. "I hope Miss Featherton likes it."

"I'm sure she will." Now to go tell her grandmother and the other ladies that they were betrothed before they could interrogate him about this afternoon.

When Gavin entered the drawing room the ladies were already there. "I have what I hope you will think is good news. Georgie has agreed to marry me."

"Excellent, my boy." The duchess nodded approvingly.

"I agree." Lady Featherton's bright blue eyes sparkled with delight.

"I could not be happier for the two of you." Lady Little-ton embraced him and patted his cheek. "Have you set a date yet?"

"Not an exact one. She is thinking in about two weeks. I plan to speak to her about it this evening. Naturally, her parents must have time to return to Town."

"Come have a glass of claret." Lady Littleton went to a sideboard and poured a glass.

"You may sit next to me and tell me how it all came about." Lady Featherton patted the seat next to hers on the sofa.

He debated how much to tell them, and decided that he could omit everything after her acceptance. When he finished he said, "I shall have a word with Lytton and inform him he must leave the country."

Brows furrowed, the ladies exchanged glances.

"We shall attend the festivities this evening," the duchess said cryptically. He knew from bits of conversation he'd overheard that they had visited the dowager Lady Turner, but the ladies had never attended one of the entertainments.

"An excellent idea," Lady Featherton chimed in.

"Naturally, we must change. However, we shall see you there." The clock struck six and the butler knocked on the open door. "Lord Littleton's coach has arrived for you, my lord."

Gavin tossed off his wine. "If you ladies will excuse me, I must away."

"Of course. We all wish you happy." Lady Littleton bussed his cheek.

Chapter Twenty-Eight

As Gavin climbed into the carriage, he wondered why the devil the ladies had decided to attend the ball when he could be spending more time alone with Georgie. Before he could work out a reasonable answer, he'd arrived at Littlewood. When he strolled into the drawing room Georgie turned from the window, and he caught his breath. God she was divine. The neckline of the snowy white ball gown was cut low enough to show the soft swells of her breasts. Yet now that he knew how they looked and tasted he wished she'd covered them up a bit more.

The bodice of the gown sparkled as she moved toward him, and he could see the pale-pink embroidery had small glass beads scattered throughout. "You take my breath away." Upon reaching him, she began to curtsey, but he captured her hand and stopped her. "I love you."

Her smile lit her eyes, and he wished he had sapphires instead of rubies. "I love you too."

If only he could drag her to one of the follies. When Gavin drew Georgie to him he remembered he was holding the sack. "I brought something for you."

She gazed into his eyes showing him how much she loved him. "I think I already have everything I want."

A light chuckle came from the direction of the door, causing him to release her and hold out the pouch. "These are for you."

Georgie's brow puckered in confusion as she took the satchel. "Thank you."

"Drat. I'm doing this all wrong." He took the bag back, and drew out the ring. "This has not been worn for many years. I hope it fits you, if not, we'll have it changed." As he took her right hand, her lips formed a perfect "O." "I hope you like it."

"I love it. Put it on me."

Gavin couldn't believe his fingers were shaking as he slid the ring on her finger. It was a little tight going over her knuckle. "Do you wish to have it enlarged?"

"Not at all." Georgie wrapped her hand around his. "It is not uncomfortable, and it will not fall off." The ring had one large square-cut ruby in the center flanked by diamonds. "It is perfect."

"There is something else." She released his fingers. He stuck his hand into the pouch again and a delicate necklace of rubies and diamonds appeared. "Will you wear it this evening?"

"It is perfect. Yes, I will wear it." She smiled and turned her back to him. "Unclasp my pearls first."

"Here," Adeline said. "I'll take them."

"Thank you." In place of the pearls, cool metal touched her skin as the rubies were placed around her neck. As soon as he dropped his hands, she turned around. "How does it look?"

"I think they suit you." Adeline pointed to a small gilded mirror hanging on the wall. "Look for yourself."

"Oh, my, yes." Georgie couldn't believe the change the necklace made. She actually looked more mature. "I must buy some earrings to go with the set."

Gavin came up behind her and kissed her cheek. "It's part of a parure. I remembered the ring. My valet added the necklace. But neither of us thought about earrings."

"It doesn't matter." She took his arm as they walked back to their friends. "I can wear the ones I have on. Thank you. I have never been given such a lovely present before."

Frits gazed at her for a moment. "I've seen them before in a portrait at Rivercrest." He glanced at her. "It's one of the only paintings with a dark-haired lady in it."

"I daresay, they have not been worn since that time," Gavin added. "I had forgotten about all of her jewels but the ring. You may have them all if you wish. They are not entailed."

Georgie was stunned. Naturally, she knew she would have use of the estate jewelry, but to receive a whole jewel box of gems was beyond generous. "I do not know what to say. How am I going to thank you?"

A slow smile dawned on his face. "We can talk about that later."

Heat rose in her neck as she understood his meaning. "But that is not just for you."

"Lord, I hope not." The words came out as a low growl.

"Come along you two." Adeline placed her fingers on her husband's arm. "We must dine before we depart, and poor Creswell has been standing in the door trying not to interrupt."

The butler bowed. "I and the staff wish you and his lordship happy."

"Thank you, Creswell," Gavin and Georgie said at the same time.

Then he looked at her and they both laughed. This was what she had wished for in a spouse. Someone to laugh with. To share laughter and a family.

He brought her fingers to his lips. "May we start telling everyone this evening?"

"We may." She was more than ready to tell the whole world. "I wrote to my parents and had the letter sent off. It will surely arrive before any gossip can reach them."

"I've written to my sister and my aunt as well." He tucked her hand firmly in the crook of his arm.

As they made their way to the dining room, she thought about the one dark-haired lady. "By the way, who is the lady to whom the jewels belonged?"

"I am not exactly sure." He glanced down at her. "It might take a bit of research to find her name. The only thing that is of aid to us is that the portraits are all in order from oldest to newest. That will give us some idea of when the marriage took place. On the newer paintings someone had the forethought to label them with their names and dates. I don't know if she is one of those or not."

"If she is not, we will find her and add her name to her portrait." Georgie was determined to do what she could for her benefactress even if she had been dead for centuries.

Gavin's mien took on a thoughtful expression. "Do you remember when Adeline and I were so sure that we were strictly descended from the Saxons?"

"I do." Georgie smiled to herself knowing what was coming next.

"It might not be the case in my family." He pulled out her chair at the dining table.

"We will not know until we discover who she is. Are all the portraits of Ladies Turley? Or are there ones of the wives of younger sons?"

"That is an excellent question. One to which I do not have an answer." He took his own seat. "In fact, I don't even remember what she was wearing."

Georgie waited until Frits was seated. "Do you remember anything else about the dark-haired lady?"

"No." He shook his head. "I only remember thinking that she stood out amid all the fair hair."

"I can ask my steward to search for the information and send it to us," Gavin offered.

"No. Thank you. I would much rather find it myself." She placed her serviette on her lap. "A mystery to solve."

"Other than becoming engaged"—Frits held up a glass of champagne that she suddenly realized was being served to the rest of them—"what else happened today? Adeline said you wished to speak to me about it." He raised a brow. "I have already been informed about the possibility of a dead man."

Georgie exchanged a glance with her friend. They had agreed that Gavin should tell Frits.

"Three men, including the one who might be dead, attempted to abduct Georgie. They were driving Lytton's coach, and acted on his orders."

"Adeline and I do not understand it." Georgie took a sip of champagne. "We are both positive that he is interested in Lady Aurelia."

Frits shrugged. "Let's see how he reacts this evening. For now, I want to wish the both of you happy. I can't tell you how pleased I am that you are finally together." He gave Gavin a smug grin. "I understand you finally realized what the rest of us have known for a while."

"You were right. One can't tell one's heart what to do." Gavin raised her hand and kissed her knuckles. "I have learned a great deal about myself today, and about my betrothed. She is a lady of forethought."

Many gentlemen might have been upset about her stipulation or ignored her. She knew they existed and was happy that Gavin wasn't one of them. "I intend to be married to you for a very long time."

He raised his glass to her. "And I plan not to do anything to disappoint you in that regard."

She held his light-blue eyes. "I am glad we are in agreement. I'm certain there will be other things about which we will disagree."

"But not that." His voice was firm, and she heard how far he was willing to go to keep his first promise to her. It boded well for their future.

That evening when Georgie, Gavin, and their friends entered the Turners' house for the ball, Lord Lytton was speaking to Lady Aurelia. Gavin was certain that the man would be worried or, at the very least surprised to see Georgie, but all he did was smile and wish them a good evening.

Once past the couple, Georgie's fine dark brows drew together. "That is very strange."

"I have to agree." Surely Lytton had not expected to see her. "He's either an excellent actor or something is going on about which he is not aware." Gavin took Georgie to where her grandmother and the duchess were sitting with Lady Turner. Everyone had turned out for the ball, even the mothers who had not been seen all week. "Can you remember exactly what the blackguards said about Lytton?"

Georgie's lips pressed together, and she slowly shook her head. "Only that this would make his lordship happy."

"A strange way to put it." Gavin drew her a bit closer to him. No one was going to touch her tonight with the sole exception of himself.

"Now that I think about it, I agree." She gazed up at him, and he wanted to kiss her and declare their betrothal so that there would be no doubt that she belonged to him. "I believe we should have our little conversation with him sooner rather than later."

"We'll wait until Littleton and Adeline join us, then we'll decide how best to go about it."

Georgie glanced around. "Where have they got to?"

"Speaking with his mother." Well, it made sense her ladyship would be present when her friends were here. "When Lady Turner and Mrs. Fitzwalter said everyone was attending this evening, I have to admit I thought it was an exaggeration."

Georgie cast her eyes to the ceiling. "They would not be ladies worth their salt if they had a good chance of getting the Duchess of Bridgewater to attend their ball and did not make a push."

"I've never thought of it in quite that way." Although Gavin should have. "It will raise their credit with the *ton*."

"Indeed it will. In fact, it would not surprise me if the next time they were in Town they are invited to more select entertainments."

He didn't need to ask how word would get around. Polite Society was a hotbed of gossip. It wouldn't take a day for the news to be all around Town. "I take it that we will invite them to our entertainments."

"Naturally." Georgie smiled at one of the other guests ambling by. "Despite what occurred last Season, I have come to know both ladies and there is really no harm in them."

He was about to object that there would have been a

great deal of harm done if the ladies' former plan to entrap his friend had come to fruition. At this point, he supposed all was well that ended well. Littleton was not holding a grudge.

Georgie tightened her hand on his arm. "Here they come."

Littleton and his wife were slowly making their way along the side of the surprisingly crowded room and had just reached them. "It took you long enough."

"Unlike other people"—he gave Gavin a pointed look—"we have been married long enough that we can take a modicum of time to greet other guests."

Next to her husband, Adeline closed her eyes and shook her head. "We asked Lord Lytton and Lady Aurelia to join us. When they do one of you will ask to have a private word with his lordship, and the rest of us will follow."

"That is a very good idea." Georgie gave their friends an approving look. "We had expected a reaction from the gentleman when he saw me, but there was nothing."

"Yes. We thought it was odd." Adeline glanced to the side. "They will be here shortly. Hmm. Did you notice the way he is looking at Lady Aurelia?"

Gavin looked at the pair, but they had been stopped by the lady's brother. "Not particularly."

"One thing at a time," Georgie said in a voice tinged with humor. "We can play at matchmaking after we resolve the current issue."

"Lady Littleton, Miss Featherton." Lytton bowed. "This ball appears to be quite well attended."

"Indeed it does." Georgie dropped a slight curtsey. "Lady Aurelia, are you enjoying yourself?"

"I am." The lady curtsied as well. "I have been looking forward to this evening."

"Before the dancing starts"—Gavin focused on Lytton—

"there was a matter I wished to discuss with you. Do you mind if we repair to the library?"

Lytton looked at Lady Aurelia. "If you do not mind, my lady?"

"Not at all." She raised one brow. "In my experience gentlemen always have a need to repair to one room or the other for a *brief* conversation."

"I assure you, my lady, this will be indeed short." Gavin gathered Littleton with his gaze and the three men headed toward the other side of the room.

Now Georgie and Adeline just needed to get rid of Lady Aurelia.

"Lady Aurelia," the duchess said from the chairs behind them. "Please attend me. I have something about which I wish to speak with you."

She glanced at Adeline, who nodded. "Certainly, your grace."

Adeline took Georgie's arm. "That was good timing."

"That was the duchess being helpful." Georgie led her friend in the direction of the library. Fortunately, she had been there before.

"Your grace, ladies." Young Lady Aurelia—well not that most people would call her young, but Lucinda and Constance did—curtsied. "I have not seen you for a long time, Aunt Bridgewater."

"That, my girl," Constance said, "is because you no longer come to Town."

A light pink stained Lady Aurelia's cheeks. "Aunt, you know that I was not very successful during my Seasons."

"The *ton* is full of numbskulls." Constance's voice was firm and reassuring.

"Yes, it is." Lucinda was pleased to see how self-assured the girl had become.

"Well then, what do you think of Lytton?" When she had agreed to let Constance do the talking, Lucinda had not expected her to shoot a broadside.

This time the lady did not blush at all. "I think he will do nicely."

"We've been receiving reports, and Lady Featherton and I agree."

Lady Aurelia narrowed her eyes the tiniest bit at Constance. "Aunt Bridgewater, do you know why Lord Littleton and Lord Turley took Lord Lytton to the library?"

"Of course we do." Constance rose from her chair. "And it's about time we joined them."

"Only if you are certain you wish to marry Lord Lytton." Lucinda watched the girl's countenance for any sign of distress.

Lady Aurelia was silent for several seconds. "I would like to wed him. We have found many mutual areas of interest this week. I think it would be a good match."

"Excellent." Lucinda took the young lady's arm. "We should not waste any more time."

Chapter Twenty-Nine

Georgie and Adeline arrived on the heels of the gentlemen. Gavin opened the door and ushered everyone into the room. A fire burned in the marble-trimmed fireplace and, although the curtains were drawn, wall sconces and candelabras had been lit. Clearly the room had been made ready for their use.

He poured the wine and brandy that was on a long table. Georgie made a note to ask him when he had notified Lord Turner that they needed to use the room.

Everyone but Gavin had taken seats at the table, but he stood behind her with his hands resting lightly on her shoulders. But despite his apparent calm, she could feel the tension radiating from him.

"Lytton, there was an incident that occurred today that you might wish to know about."

His lordship inclined his head, but he was clearly at a loss as to why they had called him here.

"Three men in your coach attempted to abduct Miss Featherton."

His lordship's face drained of color, and Frits quickly pressed a glass of brandy into Lytton's hand. "Drink."

He drank almost half the glass, and his voice was still not steady. "How?"

"We were racing." Gavin squeezed one of her shoulders. "It's something we do a lot. Miss Featherton got to the end first." She was impressed that the fact did not even embarrass him. "The coach was there, and two men grabbed her. Fortunately, her horse kicked one of the men. We do not know his condition. They shoved her into the coach and took off. What they did not know is that Miss Featherton's brother-in-law had taught her how to fall. She took it upon herself to jump out of the coach."

Lord Lytton covered his face with his hands. "Dear God."

"We got away, and she, as you can see, did not suffer. I sent servants back for the man who had been kicked, but he was no longer there."

Lord Lytton leaned his head back over the chair as if he could no longer hold it up. A few seconds later, he glanced at her, and she could see his distress in the lines that deepened around his mouth. "I thank God you were not injured, Miss Featherton."

She reached up and covered Gavin's hand with hers. "When we arrived this evening we quickly realized that you had no knowledge of what had happened. One of the men said that you would be happy now. Do you have any idea why he would say or think that?"

Lord Lytton dragged a hand over his face. "I came to this house party with the intention of courting you. But, it soon became crystal clear when I came upon you riding that day that Turley here had the advantage. I had mentioned the possibility of making you my wife to my coachman and groom, and probably said something about wishing that you were interested in me. The day I returned from the ride, I told them that I had been mistaken. At the time I'd already met Lady Aurelia and decided to see where that would lead. Please forgive me. I had absolutely no idea that those sapskulls would do anything so ill-advised and—"

"Dastardly?" Gavin supplied.

"Yes, dastardly and whatever other description I can think of." Lord Lytton took another drink of the brandy. "I cannot apologize to you enough." He looked at her with abject regret in his eyes. "What do you want me to do to them? How can I make it up to you?"

She curled her fingers around Gavin's hand. He was not going to be happy with what she had to say. "If you must know, the whole situation worked out to our advantage. We are now betrothed."

Behind her, he growled. "Only due to Miss Featherton's skill and bravery. If she had been any other lady, the situation would have been disastrous."

"Turley." She kept her tone soft, but it was still a rebuke.

"No, no, Miss Featherton. Lord Turley is absolutely correct. My servants must be punished. If you wish to call the magistrate, I will not make excuses for them."

He did have a point. Things could have turned out very badly indeed. "I suggest you talk to them when you return. If you wish me to give information, I shall." Still, she could not understand why servants would go to such lengths. "I have noticed"—Georgie wanted to ask this question carefully—"you have proposed marriage to a number of ladies since last Season. Is there a particular reason?"

"There is." A flush rose into his face. "My aunt has complete control over all the property that is not entailed, including most of the convertible assets."

What a horrible situation. "In effect, you have the title and land but little money."

"Yes." He nodded and started to pick up his glass of brandy then stopped. "She has given me notice that she will pick a lady for me if I do not select one for myself. The problem is that she is quite particular about the qualifications the lady in question must have." He drummed his fingers on the table as if trying to make a decision. "My servants are concerned about the type of lady she would demand I marry." He grimaced slightly. "My aunt is not well liked in my household."

The door opened and Lady Aurelia followed by Georgie's grandmother and the duchess strode into the room.

"I believe that is where I come in," Lady Aurelia inclined her head at the group before addressing Lord Lytton. "You are not aware of the negotiations, for I can call them nothing else, between my mother and your aunt."

While she was speaking, the gentlemen had jumped up and brought sufficient chairs to the table. Georgie poured three more glasses of wine. This should prove interesting.

Once the ladies were seated, Lord Lytton said, "You are correct. I know nothing of any such schemes."

Before Lady Aurelia could respond, the duchess said, "You should know that my niece has had many offers for her hand, but by no one she wished to marry. Naturally, I stood by her when she rejected them."

Lord Lytton's hand tightened on his glass, but he had the sense not to comment.

"Thank you, Aunt." Lady Aurelia turned to his lordship. "I was convinced to come here to meet you and ascertain if you would suit me."

"And do I?" The poor man sounded as if he had swallowed a frog.

Gavin, who was still standing behind Georgie, coughed.

"You do." For a moment, she thought the lady would propose. Then a slight blush painted Lady Aurelia's neck and cheeks.

"In that case"—he glanced around the table—"and in the presence of witnesses, I am asking you to be my wife. I will be the best husband I can be to you. That I promise."

The color in her face deepened. "And I shall be the best wife I can be to you. I accept."

"Very prettily done," the duchess said.

"I agree." Grandmamma rose. "Just think how thrilled Lady Turner and Mrs. Fitzwalter will be to have two betrothals announced at their very first ball. They will set a fashion."

Gavin groaned again and the duchess slid him a look. "What do you have to worry about? You will be married."

Georgie twisted around and tried to see his face, but couldn't.

"Your grace, you are absolutely correct. In fact, I shall be so happy wed to Georgie that I will wish the same happiness on my fellow man."

She had never heard such fustian from him. "That is doing it a bit too brown."

"Not at all, my love." He bent down and kissed her cheek. "Look at how Littleton worked to get us together."

"Come along." The duchess headed toward the door. "We need to find at least one of our hostesses."

They dutifully followed the duchess and Grandmamma out the door.

"I do not have to ask if she is really going to do this," Lady Aurelia commented. "My aunt is equal to anything."

Georgie wondered if the lady knew about how the two grand dames got Kit and Mary together or helped Meg and Hawksworth. "Truer words were never spoken."

One footman was sent running to find Lady Turner and Mrs. Fitzwalter, another was sent to bring up more champagne, and a third was to find Lord Montagu, Lady Aurelia's brother.

Gavin held Georgie's hand. "If I had had any idea how formidable your grandmother and the duchess were I would have been more terrified of them than I was."

As she had barely seen either lady the whole time they were here she had to ask, "What did they say to you?"

He gave her a sheepish look. "I asked for their help, along with Lady Littleton's, in convincing you to marry me. Naturally, they questioned me in order to make sure I was serious about you."

"Naturally." The image of him being subjected to an inquisition made her want to laugh. "What did you tell them?"

"That I liked you a great deal as a friend and that we had a good many things in common. I also explained why I could not fall in love." He grimaced. "I was an idiot not to realize that I was already in love with you and had been for months." Gavin raised her hand to his lips. "Then the duchess asked if I had passion for you."

Georgie held her breath. "And you said?"

"I told her I did." He grinned down at her, his love shining in his eyes. "That I had a great deal of passion for you, and they said they would help me."

"I am very glad that they did." The others had walked

ahead when they'd stopped to talk. It was the first time they had been alone since this afternoon. Georgie was astounded how quickly her world had changed in the space of a day. Less than a day. "I do wonder how much longer it would have taken you had I not been abducted."

A shudder ran down his arm. "I don't even want to think about it." He glanced up and down the corridor before drawing her into his arms and pressing his lips to hers. "I might have lost you forever."

"My lord, Miss Featherton." A footman came running to them. "Her grace wants you at once."

"Of course she does," Gavin grumbled.

Georgie held back a chuckle. "We are coming straightaway."

"Why do I have the feeling that I will not be able to be alone with you again until our wedding night?" She had never heard him sound more morose.

She tucked her hand in the crook of his arm. "Never fear. I am positive that we will find a way. After all, we are now betrothed and will not be closely chaperoned."

"Thank God for that." Gavin had never been so happy. It was amazing how good being in love felt as opposed to being determined that he wasn't in love. If only it hadn't taken almost losing her. "That means that I can have all your dances now."

Her lilting laughter cheered him even more. "Yes, it does."

By the time they returned to the ballroom, the duchess, Lady Featherton, and Lady Littleton were in close conversation with Lady Turner and Mrs. Fitzwalter. Next to the ladies, Littleton hailed Gavin and Georgie and they strolled toward the group.

"They're going to have it all arranged by the time we reach them." Not that he expected anything less.

"They are indeed," Georgie agreed. "I will be lucky if I am allowed to have anything to do with the arranging of our wedding breakfast."

He recalled that his sister was happy to let his aunt and her future mother-in-law take care of the details. But if Georgie wanted to have the responsibility, he'd do everything in his power to make it happen. "Do you want to be in charge of it?"

She glanced at him, her bottom lip pulled between small white teeth. "Not really. But I must do something other than shop for clothing. After all, I already know exactly what I want in the way of gowns."

He knew one way he could get her alone before the wedding. "You could redecorate my—our town house."

"Hmm." She gave him a considering look. "Now that is an excellent idea. Would I have free rein?"

"Absolutely." He could already see her in his bed in the middle of the afternoon. "I will even accompany you anywhere you wish to go to look at furniture or fabrics, or anything else you might require. Naturally, you will have all the accounts sent to me."

She gave him a wide grin. "You either trust me a great deal or you like to live dangerously."

They had just about reached her grandmother and the others, but he stopped. "I trust you with my life. What are a few rugs and wall coverings compared to that?"

"Nothing at all." Their eyes met, and Georgie reached up and placed her hand on his cheek. It was all he could do not to drag her into his arms and kiss her. "We had better join my grandmother and the duchess."

"I suppose you are right." While the ladies were talking, he'd try to convince Littleton to allow him to stay at Littlewood tonight.

Their two hostesses nodded at whatever Lady Featherton and the duchess were saying. A table covered with bottles of champagne was next to them. Then the two older ladies inclined their heads and stepped back. Just a few feet away, Montagu stood next to his sister and Lytton smiling like a cat who'd got into the cream. Gavin had been just as happy for his sister when she'd wed, but only because she had wanted Harrington so much, and the marriage kept his father from making a horrible choice of husband for her.

"I wonder why Montagu is so pleased," Gavin said more to himself than Georgie.

"From what I have seen, Lady Aurelia has nothing better to do than try to guide her brother's life." Georgie's eyes sparkled with mirth. "She is the elder by thirty minutes and never lets him forget it."

That brought out a chuckle. "I would have thought that being twins they'd be close."

She raised one shoulder, shrugging lightly. "Oh, I think they are, but there is always some family rivalry, especially as he was born the male and the heir."

"I used to like to tease my sister." Although, she had not found it as much fun as he had. He'd always wished they'd had a larger family. "I would like to have more than two children."

"I shall do my best, but I draw the limit at five." Georgie's voice was so low that only he could hear her. He'd have to remember to ask her the reason.

"Ladies." He bowed. "Thank you for allowing us to announce our betrothal at your ball."

"My lord." Lady Turner was smiling so widely he was surprised she could speak. "You could not have chosen a better place. We are absolutely delighted!"

"It is our pleasure." Mrs. Fitzwalter's smile matched her friend's.

The dance had stopped and Lord Turner clapped his hands. "Ladies and gentlemen, we have two announcements to make."

"This really is going to be an exhibition," Lytton mumbled.

Lady Aurelia grinned. "How could you think it would be anything else?"

Gavin laughed. "It won't last long."

Lady Turner nodded to the footman on her side and Mrs. Fitzgerald did the same to the footman next to her. The servants, bottles of champagne in hand, began to fill everyone's glasses.

Once that had been completed, the ladies motioned for Lytton and his betrothed to come forward.

Lady Turner handed the couple glasses of champagne, then turned to face the ballroom. "We are pleased to announce the betrothal of Lady Aurelia Tapton and the Earl of Lytton."

Before people came forward to congratulate them, Turner held up his hand and Mrs. Fitzwalter handed Georgie and Gavin glasses of champagne, and copied what her friend had done. "And the betrothal of Miss Featherton to Viscount Turley."

By the time they had received everyone's good wishes, his face hurt from smiling. Over Georgie's head, he and Lytton exchanged glances. It was the first time Gavin had felt an ounce of compassion for the man.

Littleton and Adeline came up to Gavin and Georgie. "I think we can depart now. My mother, your grandmother, and the duchess are accompanying us. They wish to discuss the preparations for the wedding breakfast."

Fortunately, "with us" did not mean in the same carriage. Even though Littleton's coach was spacious, the older ladies decided to take the carriage in which they had arrived.

Chapter Thirty

Some twenty minutes later, as Gavin, Georgie, Littleton, and Adeline passed the town of Littleton, Adeline yawned. "No one is going to make me go to bed. I intend to remain awake until we have worked out all the details."

"Well, perhaps not all the details," Georgie said. "My mother will wish to be involved."

"That is true." Adeline yawned again and Gavin didn't know how she'd manage to meet her goal. Apparently carrying a child was tiring stuff. "But we have already discussed going back to Town immediately, and I do not want our plans changed."

"Sweetheart," Littleton said, "you do not particularly like being in Town."

"That is also true, but Georgie is my closest friend, and I am determined to be there when she goes shopping."

"Perhaps you would like to do a bit of shopping as well?"

"That too." Adeline slumped against him, and a soft snore came from her part of the coach.

Gavin had been holding Georgie's hand and squeezed it. "Do you think the ladies will wait until tomorrow?"

"I have no idea." She leaned against his arm, making

him recall the first night they'd come back from the Turners' when he had so wanted her to feel comfortable enough to do so.

"She might just need a nap," Frits offered.

"You might be right," Georgie agreed. "She frequently takes a short one during the day, and it restores her."

Gavin hoped that was the case. Otherwise, they would be forced to wait until tomorrow for the ladies to work out all that they must. "When do you plan to return to Town?"

"Adeline and I agreed we would do so immediately." He didn't need to see Georgie's face to know that she had scrunched it up. "If not tomorrow, then the next day."

"That's what she told me," Littleton said. "Fortunately, it's not that far. I already sent word to open the house."

"If Grandmamma and the duchess plan to return as well," Georgie mused, "they will want me to stay with them."

Gavin was about to tell her not to borrow trouble, but that is exactly what would happen. "We can only wait and see what they have to say."

They fell silent and the only noise was Adeline's soft snores and the horses' hooves on the road and the coach behind them. Sooner than he expected they reached the front door of Littlewood.

He helped Georgie out of the carriage, and, fortunately, Adeline woke with a start and more energy than he'd seen from her all week. She led them to a small parlor where a fire was being hurriedly lit, then sent for tea, wine, and brandy. They had all had enough champagne for the night.

The moment everyone had what they wanted to drink, she took charge in a way that he'd never seen before. "I wish to start by saying that Georgie and I have already agreed that she will stay with me until her mother returns to Town." Adeline waited until the other ladies assented. "We shall begin shopping." Again the ladies nodded. "Georgie, do you have any particular desires regarding the ceremony or the wedding breakfast?"

"None at all except to ask that you choose colors that look well on me."

Her grandmother grinned, and Gavin wished he knew what that was all about. As far as he was concerned she looked beautiful in everything.

"Well then," Adeline continued, "what else do you wish to discuss?"

Georgie covered a smile with her cup, and the ladies glanced at each other.

"Nothing at all, my dear." Lady Littleton rose. "When do you plan to depart?"

Adeline rose as well. "Tomorrow by midmorning or early afternoon."

"Very good." Lady Featherton moved to Georgie and bussed her cheek. "Have a pleasant journey. Send me a note if you need me for anything. I have no doubt your father will be pleased to stand the nonsense."

They accompanied the ladies to the door, and before Gavin could ask what her father was expected to stand the nonsense for, the duchess called out, "Turley, you will accompany us."

"That's what I was afraid of," Georgie muttered.

"Look at it this way, it saves Littleton and Adeline from having to chaperone us."

Georgie sighed. "I suppose you are right."

Even though their friends and family were all around them, he drew her into his arms and kissed her. "I'll be back in the morning to accompany you." A thought made him pull a face. "Unless, that is, they decide I should provide an escort for them."

"I love you." Her arms tightened around him.

"And I love you. Sleep well. I'd try to sneak out, but I doubt they'd let me."

"We'll be together soon." Georgie stepped back. "Until tomorrow."

The door closed behind him and Adeline yawned. "Thank the Lord. Now I can go to bed."

"That was a masterful performance, my love." Frits did not even get the sentence out before he began to laugh.

"I agree." Georgie chuckled. "I do wonder how long they will try to keep Gavin and me apart."

"Until you set a date," Adeline threw over her shoulder as she strode toward the stairs. "Depend upon it. They will not care about an early baby. God knows there are enough of them. They will want to make sure he doesn't die before the lines are signed."

"Drat." Georgie had thought of the obvious way he could be killed but not all the other dangers of life. "Well, it's a bit late for that."

Frits stopped and his eyes widened. "Despite what Turley said, I knew something had gone on."

"I do not know why you are surprised," Georgie retorted. "It will be your job to keep him safe until we are married."

"Of course it will," Frits grumbled as he followed his wife up the stairs. "Now that the horse is out of the barn, I don't suppose I need to worry about you and him in Town."

She was not quite sure she liked being compared to a horse, but she did agree with the sentiment. "Exactly."

Georgie stayed awake as long as she could hoping that Gavin would come, but eventually Morpheus took her in his arms, and the next thing she knew the sun was shining in her eyes. "What time is it?"

"Not that late, miss." Smith stepped out of the room and spoke to someone in the corridor. "Your tea will be here shortly. I would have had it ready, but you looked so tired last night I knew you'd sleep later this morning."

Georgie wondered exactly how long she had remained awake last night. But it didn't matter. Her grandmother and the duchess would have kept poor Gavin up until he dropped from exhaustion. "Do we have a more exact time of our departure?"

"Yes, miss. Shortly after breakfast. Your trunks are already packed, and have been sent down to the baggage coach."

That was fast. "How late is it?"

Her maid answered the scratching at the door and brought tea and a piece of toast to her. "We knew last night we'd be leaving this morning after everyone was up and had broken their fast."

She thought of all the shopping she had done at the fair. "Did everything fit?"

"Oh my, yes. You did not buy that much." Smith waited until Georgie had finished her repast. "I left out your yellow carriage gown."

"Thank you." That was one of the few gowns she had that was brighter than pale. "I cannot wait to have richer colors."

"That will be much easier." Her maid took the tea and plate.

"Do you know if Lady Littleton is awake and about?"

"Like you, she slept later. You'll be down in good time."

The room was already warm for which Georgie was glad. She shoved her feet in her slippers and padded behind the screen to wash in the basin. A bath would come later today. In short order, her maid had her dressed and was packing the remaining items in a satchel when she made her way to the breakfast room.

Adeline had just taken a bit of toast when Georgie joined her. "Where is Frits?"

"Up and supervising the packing. I believe he has also sent a carriage to The Lilacs."

She said a short prayer that Gavin would be allowed to accompany them to Town. "I hope that is successful."

"For your sake, so do I." Adeline grinned. "You'd better eat. Frits does not like going to Town, but when he does, he's like a horse going to the barn. He wants to do it as soon as possible."

Georgie selected baked eggs and ham. When she took her place she pulled over a rack of toast that had just been set on the table. "I shall be as quick as possible."

She had almost finished eating when the sound of voices came from the direction of the hall, and her heart skipped a beat. But the only person entering the room was Frits. "Turley will not be accompanying us."

"I cannot say that I am surprised." Although she had prayed and hoped he would be with them. And her heart ached that she would not see him today.

"I wouldn't worry too much. My mother and the ladies will depart before noon." He gave her a sympathetic smile. "He'll be with you as soon as he can manage it."

"I know." Still it ruined the rest of her breakfast.

Frits glanced at Adeline. "I have decided I was very wise to keep you here until we were married."

"Yes, you were." Adeline gave him an arch look. "But your mother wasn't a week away."

"You have me there." He grabbed a piece of toast from the rack in front of her. "When will you be ready to leave?"

Adeline's head swiveled to Georgie. "Less than a half hour."

"There you are, my love. We will be with you soon."

"I'll see you outside." Frits strode out of the room.

Georgie placed her serviette on the table. "If you will excuse me, I'll see you in the hall or out in front."

"I'll come with you." Adeline caught up and linked her arm with Georgie's. "I know you are disappointed, but the news was not unexpected. Think about it like this, soon no one will be able to keep you apart."

That did make her feel better. "I know you're right. I just wanted to spend time with him today." They reached Georgie's rooms, and she thought about Gavin's offer to redecorate his—their town house. "Gavin has given me the freedom to renovate Turley House. Would you object if I start while I am visiting you?"

"Not at all." Adeline laughed. "Please tell me if I can be of help."

"I will. He said that he would be happy to visit furniture houses and other places with me, but Parliament is still in session, and I would expect him to attend meetings and votes."

"Well, if he was like Frits, he'd be with you. But I know how much he loves politics."

And that was one of the many things Georgie loved about Gavin. "He does, indeed. I know you do not share my passion, but I am looking forward to holding political dinners and other entertainments."

"I do not," Adeline agreed. "Yet, both Frits and I are very happy that our friends enjoy those types of things."

Georgie linked her arm with her friend's, ready to join the carriages, when Frits and Gavin dashed into the room, both trying to get their broad shoulders through the doorway at the same time. She glanced at Adeline and doubled over in laughter.

Adeline's hands went to her hips. "What do you think you are doing?"

"Lytton's here." Gavin turned sideways and entered the dining room first. He looked at Georgie. "We all forgot that we need to discuss how we're going to deal with the men who tried to abduct you."

Drat. So much had happened since then the event had completely gone out of her mind. And she did not want to "deal" with it. She wanted to return to Town and immerse herself in all the things she must accomplish to wed the love of her life. Staring at said love, she rubbed her forehead. "As far as I am concerned, Lytton has my permission, nay, my blessings to settle the matter without my assistance."

The gentleman entered the room followed by her grandmother, the duchess, and Lady Littleton.

Grandmamma came straight to Georgie and wrapped fragrant arms around her. "If that is what you wish, that is what will be done."

"No." Gavin's whole body was rigid with anger. "They must be punished. I'll send for the magistrate."

"And have the event be all around Town by tomorrow?" The duchess's icy gaze focused on him. "I understand your anger. Indeed, I share it. But to prosecute a case would involve all the sordid details to be made public."

He opened his mouth and closed it. Then took a deep

breath. "She was never alone with any of them. I can attest to that."

"My dear boy." Lady Littleton gave him a compassionate look. "Of course you would say that. You are marrying her."

He stared at her for several seconds then dropped his head foreward and clutched his hair. "And no one will believe me."

"I am afraid that will be the case." Her tone held a wealth of concern.

"I hadn't thought about that." He had never sounded so defeated, and Georgie felt sorry for him.

She wrapped her arm around his waist. "It will be all right." She glanced at Lord Lytton. "It is in your hands. What do you propose?"

His lips flattened as he surveyed the rest of them. "I spoke with my coachman last night. His brother was the man who was injured. They and their family have served my family for generations." His jaw moved as if it hurt from being clenched. "They know what they did was beyond the pale. In addition to that, my groom has still not regained consciousness. My coachman swore to me, and I believe him, that the original idea came from the man I hired in London to act as an outrider. That in no way excuses his actions. However, it did make sense. I cannot conceive of anything that would have made him or his brother come up with such a felonious scheme. He agreed that his pay should be docked for the next six months." Lytton wiped his hand down over his mouth and jaw. "I will have the magistrate jail the other man until the next assize. When no other evidence is given, he will be released."

"That will be in about two months." Frits nodded. "The question is what will he do after that."

"If only we knew someone with a ship," Gavin mused quietly.

Frits started to open his mouth when Grandmamma and the duchess exchanged a glance, and Georgie knew exactly what they were thinking. "Hawksworth."

"Well, you must admit that your sister's husband can be extremely useful," the duchess said.

Georgie had not wanted to be involved in this. She attributed Gavin's revelations that he loved her to the abduction, and for that she could not be upset. However, the action could not go unpunished. On the other hand, she did think the punishments were uneven. Then again, they were his lordship's responsibility, and he knew them better than she did. "I assume Grandmamma will write to him. Who will remain to tell the magistrate to release the man, or shall we all remain here until the matter has been resolved?"

"I shall stay." Lytton appeared grim. "He is currently in one of Bottomley's cellars. He may remain there until he is collected."

"No, no." The duchess gave her head a shake. "Give the butler instructions. I am quite frankly surprised that you managed to keep Bottomley here for so long. And you have a wedding to attend."

Good Lord! Georgie had completely forgotten about Lytton and Lady Aurelia, and that the lady was the duchess's niece. "Do we have an agreement?"

The gentlemen exchanged glances and nodded.

"We do," Gavin said.

"Splendid." A broad smile appeared on Adeline's face. "Your grace, please feel free to use the desk in the morning room for your missive. I shall instruct a footman to take the message to Lord Hawksworth." She glanced at the rest of them. "Is there any reason we cannot depart?" When no one answered, not even the duchess, Adeline walked to the door. "Then we shall be on our way. Creswell, please show the duchess to the morning room."

He bowed and Georgie thought his lips twitched the slightest bit. "With pleasure, my lady."

Once she and Adeline were settled in the traveling coach—With Lord Turley there, the older ladies decided Gavin could accompany Georgie. He and Frits had decided to ride—she finally breathed a sigh of relief. "Thank you for extracting us so expertly."

"I must say, that confidence seems to come from being in charge. I would never have thought to do such a thing before I married."

Georgie thought back to what her friend had been like when they had first come out. Shy and retiring, except when her sense of justice got pricked, had described Adeline. "I think you are correct." Georgie wondered what she would be like after a few months of marriage and the thought almost scared her. She was not and had never been shy and retiring. Then she recalled her sister and knew that whatever she did, it would be for the benefit of others. "I believe I am looking forward to married life."

Chapter Thirty-One

Gavin was glad Frits had arranged that their party stop for a leisurely luncheon before arriving in Town. The sole purpose of the respite was to allow the senior servants to arrive before them. The inn was known to Frits and even though it was busy, the landlord found them a private parlor. The parlor was well appointed with lace curtains, a large table for dining, and three sofas.

The duchess and Lady Featherton had managed to bring Lady Aurelia with them. "Lord Lytton is following. I expect him here shortly."

Gavin and Frits exchanged a glance. They had both promised to at least attempt to like Lytton. Still, the story Exeter had told Gavin held them back. "Perhaps we should ask him about it."

"But not here." Littleton glanced at the ladies. "Once we're back in Town."

"Of course." Gavin looked at Georgie, who glanced up at the same moment with a resigned expression on her lovely face. "It's a plot to keep us apart."

His friend raised his mug of ale. "I have absolutely no

doubt you are correct. You will still be allowed free access to Littleton House."

"I'd rather she had free access to Turley House." He knew he was grumbling. In the grand scheme of things, two weeks was not that long. Still . . . "What am I going to do for two weeks?"

"Depending on when the banns are called, you might have to procure a license."

"There is that. I can only hope that she decides my house needs a great deal of redecoration."

Littleton snickered. "I have a feeling gowns and the like will come first."

Gavin remembered the orgy of shopping that had been done before his sister's wedding. "That's true. But"—and the thought made him happier—"once the initial selections have been made, the gowns must be sewn and that does not require Georgie to be present."

"There is that. And you have the Lords. Something must be going on there. Exeter can bring you up-to-date."

"That too." Although, Gavin would be happier if he could just take his betrothed to his estate and marry there. "It will go by quickly." It wouldn't but he'd keep telling himself that.

He and Littleton were sitting on a window seat at the front of the building and the sounds of carriages filtered in from the yard below. "I wonder when Lytton will arrive."

"Not soon enough. I wish to depart within the hour. We've given our servants more than enough time to arrive in Town."

Carrying a glass of wine, Lady Littleton strolled over to them. "You look as if you wish to leave."

"We were just discussing it," Littleton said. "That and Lytton."

"Ah."

Suddenly, Gavin got the impression that her ladyship knew much more about his lordship than they did. "I have to assume that if the duchess supports that match, he cannot be as bad as we think him."

"You are correct. She is aware of a great deal, including the reason he jilted a young lady." She took a sip of wine then glanced at both of them. "His aunt demanded it."

Littleton's jaw clenched and Gavin did the same. "Or she'd cut off any funds."

"Yes. She also made him feel as if he was never as good as others. You see, his mother's grandfather was in trade."

"That explains a lot."

Littleton nodded. "It does indeed."

"I do not believe he is a bad man, simply one who has never been in control of his life or felt that he deserves his station." She took another sip of wine before ambling back to the other ladies.

"Drat it all." Gavin took a pull of the excellent local ale. "I suppose we'll have to try to like him."

"I rather think that was the purpose of her coming over here."

Footsteps could be heard coming from the corridor, the door opened, and the landlord said, "Here they are, my lord."

"Thank you." Lytton stood in front of the now closed door as if he didn't know what to do.

Lady Aurelia pushed back her chair, but Gavin poured beer into a mug. "You should try the ale. It's quite good."

The man gave him a grateful look. "Thank you. I shall."

"The ladies are discussing weddings. Or rather clothing for weddings," Littleton added.

"Has your groom awakened yet?" Gavin asked. After giving it much thought, he decided Georgie was right. Who knew how long it would have taken him to come to the point if it hadn't been for the abduction? He was still glad the ringleader was going far away, but, strangely, no longer held a grudge against the other two.

"That is the reason I am late. He is very lucky. He confirmed his brother's story and expressed his regret for his part in the situation." Lytton took a pull of the ale. "He has a wicked headache that will probably last for the next few days. The mark of the horseshoe will take longer to go away."

Gavin finally asked the one question that had been nagging at him. "What would you have done if they had succeeded in abducting her?"

Lytton's eyes widened. "Sent her straight back to Littlewood. I knew it was only a matter of time before you and she were betrothed. And I was attempting to work out if Lady Aurelia would accept a proposal from me."

In one way, that would have worked out, but Gavin wasn't certain he would have been able to express his love for Georgie. No, it all happened the way Fate had planned it. "Let's gather our ladies and go." Then he remembered Lytton. "Unless you require sustenance?"

"No. I'm as anxious to reach Town as you are." He smiled. "I too have a wedding for which to prepare, and an aunt to visit."

And, Gavin thought, life with a lady who would never allow anyone to denigrate him. Even his aunt. It wouldn't take long for Lytton to finally become comfortable with who he was and his station in life.

Gavin set his mug down "Ladies, are you ready to resume our journey?"

Georgie was beginning to think they'd never leave the inn and was pleased that Gavin had taken matters to hand. They stood next to the Littleton coach as everyone else got themselves sorted. "I wish you were riding in the coach instead of on your horse."

"It won't be for much longer." He placed one arm on the carriage, leaning in closer to her. "I think it would kill me to be so close to you and not even be able to kiss you."

His gaze dropped to her mouth. She had not thought of that, but it was true. Despite their schemes, she still had a feeling that they'd have a difficult time finding time to be alone. "I mentioned starting to redecorate Turley House, and my grandmother told me flatly that even betrothed ladies did not visit bachelor residences."

"We'll think of something." His mobile lips flattened. "If my sister comes over, perhaps she can spend—no, that won't work. Lady Exeter spent a good deal of time at Exeter House before they wed. I'll ask Exeter how she managed it."

"That's a good idea. I'll speak to her." Georgie wanted to put her arms around Gavin. "I hope my letter gets to my parents in good time."

"As do I." They fell silent until a coach door closed. "Let me help you into the coach, and we'll be on our way."

His gloved hand, warm and strong, fell to her waist as he opened the door. "We'll manage it somehow."

"I know we will." Even if she had to disguise herself and sneak over. Her grandmother had told her stories about doing that to go to village fetes when she was young. Hopefully, Dorie would have some ideas.

Adeline entered the carriage and gave the coachman the signal to go. "Frits told me that he and Turley had a short conversation with Lytton. It seems that the incident with the lady was due to his aunt."

The gentlemen had seemed to get on a bit better. "That does not surprise me at all. She sounds like a thoroughly unpleasant woman."

Adeline nodded. "I believe that is the general impression."

"Did you hear what my grandmother said about going to Turley House?" Georgie had been at the other end of the table when her grandmother had voiced her opinion.

"No, but I can guess. As my sister-in-law always says, where there is a will, there is a way." She glanced out the window. "I did not think I would be going to Town at all this autumn. What do you want to do first?"

"I suppose we should visit Dorie and Henrietta and tell them about my betrothal." That would give Georgie an opportunity to speak with Dorie. "Then I must visit my modiste."

"I wonder if we will slip back into the schedule we had before Dorie and I married," Adeline mused.

"Only if you intend to add three gentlemen to our usual route." Georgie had no doubt that Gavin would want to spend as much time with her as possible. But the thought of him and the other men joining them at the shops and the Pantheon Bazaar made her smile.

"I had not considered that, but I daresay you're right. Frits and I have never been in Town as a married couple." Adeline's lips curved up. "This ought to be interesting."

Especially considering that he did not attend the Lords,

and did not have estate matters with which to busy himself. "Do you think he will be bored?"

"That is an excellent question." Adeline tilted her head first to one side then to the other. "I have no idea. I do think he will expect to spend much of his time with me."

Oh, dear. Neither of them had thought of that when they conceived the idea of Georgie staying at Littleton House. "Well, we will simply have to make do with what we have."

Adeline wrinkled her nose. "I suppose you're right. Although, I imagine Turley will haunt the house. Especially if we cannot think of a way for you to get in and out of Turley House unseen."

This was becoming much more complicated than Georgie had expected. There was definitely something to be said for marrying outside of Town. "I'm beginning to wish I was having the ceremony at Rivercrest."

They had passed over Kew Bridge and were now going through Hammersmith. It would not be long before they reached Mayfair. It was not until they turned into Grosvenor Square that it occurred to her that she had no idea where Turley House was located. The coach came to a stop.

Adeline peered out the window. "Do you know I have never been here?"

At first that surprised Georgie, but it was true. "Shall we refurbish your house as well?"

Her friend laughed, but then a rare sly expression dawned on Adeline's face. "We may well be able to use that to our advantage."

"I do not understand how." Wherever Turley House was it was not in Grosvenor Square.

"If there are constantly workers and others going in and

out of my house and the same going in and out of Turley House, it will be easier to slip in and out undetected."

"I would simply have to use a town coach to go between the two residences." But only if the carriage was unmarked. She could easily use the one her father owned. "You're brilliant!"

Adeline grinned. "I do have my moments."

The coach door opened, and Frits was there to assist her down. "We must discuss it with Frits and Turley."

"Discuss what with us?" Gavin said, taking Frits's place in front of the door.

"Adeline had an idea that might enable us to skirt my grandmother's mandate." Georgie placed her hand in Gavin's.

"Let's discuss it after you get settled." He escorted her into the hall. "I'll be back after I've bathed."

Reaching up, she kissed his cheek. "I look forward to it."

"Miss." Crothers bowed. "The housekeeper has taken the liberty of putting you in the blue bedroom at the back of the house. If you would follow me?"

She glanced around for Adeline, but saw the back of her skirt disappearing into the corridor. They would have to speak later. "Lead on, Crothers. I am certain the bed-chamber will be suitable."

"The last person to occupy the rooms was the older dowager Lady Littleton," he said as he led Georgie up the main staircase, heading left when he came to the split in the stairs. "She especially enjoyed the view over the back garden."

As at Littlewood, the rooms consisted of a dressing room, bedchamber, and parlor. "Where is Smith?"

"She took two footmen and went to Featherton House

in order to gather some things you will require now that you are back in Town."

That made sense. They had dressed much more simply in the country. "Thank you."

"I have ordered a tray to be sent up."

"Thank you, Crothers. I could use a cup of tea."

A footman she hadn't seen before brought in a tea tray as the butler left and put the tray on an old-fashioned tea table. After she had poured a cup, she ambled around the rooms. From the parlor, there was not only an excellent view of the garden, but a small balcony as well. Georgie grabbed a shawl and opened the door. This would be a lovely place to sit if the weather was warmer. But ever since the day she became betrothed, it had become colder.

"Georgie?" Adeline called.

"I'm out here. Have you seen your rooms yet? Do they have a balcony as well?"

"I have not had time." She walked out and shivered. "Brrr. Let's go back in. I expect we will have company soon. I had completely forgotten that Dorie and Henrietta live on Grosvenor Square as well."

"That's right. I hadn't thought about it either." Georgie went to the teapot. "Would you like a cup of tea?"

"No, thank you. I am going to look at my chamber. I will meet you in the morning room. There is a footman positioned in the corridor if you need help finding it."

"Thank you." Getting to her rooms had been simple enough. She could ask for directions to the morning room once she was in the hall.

Georgie finished her tea and was on her way to the hall when the front door opened and Crothers said, "I shall tell Miss Featherton you are here."

She quickened her step to the stairs and down to the landing. "Gavin."

"Georgie." He stared up at her as if they had not seen each other in months.

And he did not even wait for her to descend, but took the steps two at a time, and took both her hands when he reached her. "I can't bear to be without you."

"I missed you too." If only there was a way to marry sooner, but there was not. This was going to be a very long two weeks.

Chapter Thirty-Two

Gavin wanted to carry Georgie down the stairs and back to his house. He could do it without being seen if he went through the mews. He could probably even borrow one of the town coaches and have it back before anyone knew what he'd done. The only thing keeping him from acting on his impulse was knowing that she would be harmed by it.

He took her hand and walked down the steps with her. "Where is everyone else?"

"Adeline is looking at her chamber. I do not know where Frits or his mother are." She frowned for a moment. "I am not even sure Lady Littleton is here. We are to meet in the morning room."

Gavin had been in and out of this house for years and knew most of it. "Where did they put you?"

"I have a lovely set of rooms in the back on the left. There is a small balcony."

He knew exactly where she was. The balcony might be useful if the master's rooms were not a few feet away. "The ones old Lady Littleton used to use?"

"So I was told." He led her to the other side of the hall

and down the corridor. "I saw a similar balcony several feet away."

"The master's rooms." If no one else heard him trying to get to the room, Max would sound the alarm.

"Oh." Georgie sounded disappointed. Had she been thinking he could sneak in to her? "I must tell you about Adeline's thoughts. She thinks that if she begins redecorating here, and I start redecorating at your house—"

"Our house."

Georgie gave him a rare shy smile. "Our house. That there would be enough going on that no one would notice if I slipped back and forth. I could use one of my father's unmarked coaches."

"Or you could use my unmarked coach."

They entered the morning room, which was decorated in pink and cream colors. "Do you think her scheme would work?"

"It might." He found a footman setting out a large tea service. "Are you expecting anyone?"

"We thought Dorie and Henrietta might come over." She followed his gaze. "Hmm. Perhaps Exeter, my grandmother, and the duchess as well."

"In other words, everyone." There was no way he'd be able to get her away from here now.

"Well"—she grinned at him—"Perhaps not *everyone*. I doubt if Lady Aurelia and Lytton will be here."

"Speaking of them, I went straight from here to St. George's and reserved a date. I ran into Lytton as I was leaving. They are having the ceremony as soon as he can arrange it. Apparently, Lady Aurelia sees no reason to delay."

"Good for her. I have no doubt that the duchess was extremely direct in telling her about his aunt." Georgie looked at the biscuits now on the sideboard. "I wonder if they are ginger."

"I wonder if Cook was able to work out those recipes."

Littleton and Adeline could be heard coming down the hall speaking with someone else. But it didn't sound like Lady Littleton.

"It sounds like Dorie and Exeter."

A second later Georgie was proven right.

"Georgie." Dorie Exeter rushed to Georgie and wrapped her arms around her. "I am so happy for you." Dorie glanced at him. "And you as well. I am so glad everything worked out." She glanced behind her. "Henrietta will be here soon." After their last meeting, he wondered what kind of reception he'd receive from her. "All is forgiven. You must accept that we will always protect our friends."

"So I have seen." He tugged Georgie closer to him. "You have no need to be concerned about her now. The only thing I want to do is get married."

"That is what you wanted before," Miss Stern said as she strolled through the door. "I assume that it is now for the right reason."

"It is for the right reason." Georgie turned her cheek for a kiss from her friend. "You are the only one of us who has not found the gentleman you wish to wed."

"I am in no hurry." Miss Stern gave a light shrug. "I will meet him when I meet him."

Lady Littleton joined them with Lady Featherton and the duchess, and Adeline began serving tea.

The ladies soon took Adeline to a table at the other end of the room, and Littleton and Exeter joined Gavin.

"Congratulations." Exeter slapped him on the back.

"Thank you. The ceremony is in two weeks." And not

a day longer. Gavin hadn't been able to make it first thing in the morning, but ten o'clock was close enough.

"We'll look forward to celebrating with you."

"Thank you. I think I'll look forward to having it done. I have gathered that there will not be much for me to do." And that would be the worst of it. He'd come to realize that no one was going to allow him to accompany his betrothed everywhere she went, and he'd be left with little to do but watch the clock.

"Except plan your wedding trip."

"That's a good point." Although Gavin wouldn't plan it without asking Georgie what she wanted.

"We didn't have to wait for long either, but it's hell." Exeter put his cup down. "The ladies are kept occupied, and we are not. You don't even have the Lords to take up time. In fact, we're going to return to the country after your wedding. There's really nothing to do here at the moment."

Two weeks of nothing but waiting. He'd have to find something to do when he couldn't be with Georgie. Unless, of course, she could spend time at her new home.

The object of his thoughts came up and slipped her hand in his arm. "We are going to the modiste. The sooner I get started on my wardrobe the better."

They hadn't been back more than two hours, but it was already beginning. "Will you join us at dinner?"

"Of course." She gave his arm a squeeze. "I'll see you then."

After Georgie and her friends left, Littleton came over. "You look like you need an occupation."

"What do you have in mind?"

"Carriages and horses. I'm told that your betrothed does not have her own carriage."

"You'll also need a landau," Exeter said.

"And horses to pull both." Gavin finished his tea. "That is an inspired suggestion." He'd never actually designed a carriage for a lady. "Where shall we go to discuss the details?"

"My study," Frits said. "I have large sheets of paper left from when I designed the curricle with Max's box."

They spent the rest of the day going over designs of sporting carriages for ladies and the necessary landau. The following morning a letter from his sister was delivered from the Foreign Office informing him that she and her family would arrive within the week and would stay with her in-laws. Perhaps keeping busy would not be as difficult as he'd thought.

Georgie reveled in finding the colors that suited her best and ordering new gowns. Adeline and Frits accompanied her to Turley House where she met the servants and was able to tour the house. It had not been redecorated since Gavin's mother became Lady Turley, and that had been many years ago.

"I refurbished my rooms," he said as he accompanied her and the housekeeper. "But that was all."

"I'm not surprised. You were not using them." She took notes of colors and fabrics that would be needed. Fortunately, the linens were all in good order. "We could start, but it would not be completed before our marriage."

He did not want to be here all autumn while the house was finished. "Let's plan to do most of it before we come for the Season next year."

"That sounds like a better idea. When will your aunt and cousins arrive?"

He'd received a letter that morning from his aunt informing him they would stay with him as it was easier than opening their house. "In a few days. She is not good at informing one exactly when she plans to arrive."

"Interesting." And not at all convenient. "I heard from my mother. They are already traveling to Town and should be here at about the same time. Not knowing their plans, Grandmamma sent messengers out to find them."

"For all that she appears to be a sweet older lady, she is frighteningly efficient."

Georgie chuckled. He was not the first person to have misunderstood her grandmother. "She is a sweet older lady. She is also ruthless in achieving her ends."

The housekeeper had left them alone, and he pulled her into his arms. "Do you know what I'd give to be able to take you back to my bedchamber?"

"About as much as I would give." She rose up on her toes and pressed her lips to his. His hands slid down and over her derrière, drawing her closer. "We are not going to be left alone long enough."

"Reluctantly, I have realized that." He took her hand and they walked down the stairs. "Where do you wish to go for a wedding trip?"

"Paris." She had always wanted to go to the city. Then she remembered that Gavin's sister lived there. "But, if you do not mind, I do not want to stay with your sister. At least not at first."

"Agreed. We would be much more comfortable alone. I know of an excellent hotel that would be perfect."

* * *

London was thin of company, but, between the two of them, they had so many family members come to Town that it seemed there was always something planned. Even Mary, Kit, and their new baby came for the wedding.

Her wedding day was finally here. Georgie gazed into the mirror and marveled at the way the royal blue gown made her skin glow and brightened the rubies around her neck and hanging from her ears. "It is perfect."

"I'd say so, miss." Smith packed up the last of the items on the toilet table and put them in a bag. "You've been saying all along that the brighter colors would look better."

Gowns of red, emerald blue, bright deep pinks, and other strong colors had been arriving for the past few days, but this was the first time Georgie was allowed to wear one of them. Her mother had very definite ideas as to what was proper for an unmarried lady as opposed to a married lady, or one minutes away from being married, should wear.

A knock came on the door. Smith answered it, and Adeline, Dorie, and Henrietta strode in.

"I have never seen you look better." Adeline hugged her lightly. "We come bearing wedding traditions." She put her hand in her bag. "This is something blue. Although it seems a bit redundant when you are wearing blue." She handed Georgie a ring with a single sapphire.

"It's perfect." Tears of joy pricked the back of her eyes.

"There is to be no crying," Henrietta said sternly. "If you start the rest of us will follow. I have something borrowed for you." She handed Georgie the same gold combs that she had loaned to Adeline and Dorie.

Smith took them and fitted them into Georgie's hair.

"And I have something old." Dorie clasped a ruby bracelet on Georgie's arm then stood back with a pleased smile. "The minute I saw it I knew it would be perfect."

Mama, Grandmamma, and the duchess strolled one after the other through the door.

"We have wedding presents that we have been keeping for today." Mama embraced Georgie lightly. "We almost waited until after the ceremony but decided that there would be too much excitement. This is from my side of the family." She handed Georgie a large, deep rectangular box.

She opened it and found a long strand of matched pearls, earrings, and a bracelet. "These are beautiful." Georgie almost felt bad that she was wearing her new rubies. "If you wish me to wear them . . ."

"No. Save them for another time."

Grandmamma stepped forward with another box. "This is from the Featherton side of the family. The moment I saw your dark hair and blue eyes, I knew they belonged to you."

Inside this box was a heavy necklace set with emeralds and diamonds. "Thank you. They are magnificent."

The duchess bussed Georgie on the cheek. "You'll have to go to the stable to meet my gift. When I found out that Turley was having a phaeton made for you, I bought you a pair of matched bays to go with it."

Adeline quickly handed Georgie a handkerchief. "No crying."

She blinked rapidly to stave off the tears. "Thank you so much. That was something I never expected."

The duchess had a smug look on her face. "I know."

"Come along." Mama started shooing them out of the room. "Your father is waiting. You do not wish to be late to your own wedding."

"She cannot be late if I am attending her," Henrietta said. "Because I am never—"

"Late," the rest of them finished for her.

She grinned, then her brows drew together. "When I finally wed, I shan't know any single ladies to attend me."

"Perhaps we'll meet someone new," Dorie said as she linked arms with Henrietta. "If not, I will attend you and bother tradition."

Georgie would miss them, but it wouldn't be long before they were all back together again. "Let us go. Turley is probably already at the church."

"And if I know him"—Adeline raised a brow—"he is waiting anxiously for you to arrive."

Chapter Thirty-Three

"Do you have it?" Gavin, Littleton, and Exeter had arrived at the church hours ago. Or perhaps it was only a few minutes and just seemed like hours.

"Shall I give you the same answer I gave you a few seconds ago, or would you like a new one?" Littleton drawled.

The "it" was the betrothal ring that would magically turn into a wedding ring during the ceremony. Henrietta had handed it to him last evening as they all left the dinner party that included both his and Georgie's families. "No. I just want this over."

"That's normal," Exeter commented. "Be thankful that you decided to travel today. You'll be able to have your bride alone much sooner."

Gavin and Georgie had decided to start the trip to Dover. It was a good eight hours or more, and they wouldn't finish the trip today. As he usually traveled straight through and didn't know any of the inns along the way, his brother-in-law recommended an excellent one around Maidstone where they would spend the night.

He pulled out his pocket watch. "Damn, still five minutes to go."

"If you hadn't insisted on being so early, you wouldn't be so wrought," Littleton retorted.

Gavin almost snapped at him, but that wouldn't do any good. They'd spent most of the time waiting in the back of the church as two other ceremonies took place. He'd had no idea St. George's was this busy.

"It will all be over soon." He was surprised at how fatherly Exeter sounded.

Gavin's sister and her husband entered the church, and finally, the side door opened, and Georgie's friends walked in followed by her mother, her father, and Georgie. "She is exquisite."

"She is," Littleton agreed, but Gavin had the feeling he was looking at his wife. "She wore the rubies."

"So she did." He'd assumed that her family would have jewelry for her to wear. Perhaps she had chosen what he'd given her instead. He stepped forward and held out his hand for her.

"Not yet." Lord Featherton grinned, holding Gavin back. "You'll have her soon enough."

The clergyman joined them. "I take it everyone is here?" They nodded. "Then we shall begin."

Soon he had Georgie's hand in his and they said their vows gazing into each other's eyes as they did. When the cleric got to the part about promising to love her he was relieved that he truly did love her. He slipped the ring on her left hand and a few seconds later they were finally pronounced man and wife.

"Wife." He knew he had a silly grin on his face.

"Husband." She reflected his grin back.

"You must sign the register," the cleric said. "I don't know why so many couples don't think of that."

"I would not have let them leave without signing it,"

Miss Stern said, and Gavin knew she would have dragged them both back to accomplish the task. Whoever she married would have to be willing to let her lead at least some of the time.

The Eighteenth Day of February in the Year of Our Lord Eighteen Hundred and Nineteen. Littlewood, England.

My dearest Georgie,

 I hope this short letter finds you both happy and in good health.
 Yesterday I gave birth, and I am pleased to report that both Frits and I were right about the sex. I had twins! A boy and a girl. We have named them Guy Randolph Charles and Amelia Georgiana Cristabel. Frits still maintains that my sweet little Amelia was the one kicking me the hardest. However, since Guy is larger I believe it was him. Not that it matters. They are perfect in every way.
 Frits and I would be honored if you and Turley would agree to stand as their godparents.

    Your loyal friend,
    A.L.

"Well, that answers why she seemed so much larger than normal," Georgie muttered to herself.

"What did you say?"

She glanced up to find her husband standing in the doorway of her parlor with a disgusted look on his face and a letter dangling from his fingers. "I received a letter from Adeline. She has had twins. A boy and a girl. They have asked us to be godparents."

"I am glad she was more informative than Littleton. All he did was say the babies had been born, and he was never going through that again."

Georgie tried to stifle her laugh and lost the battle. After several moments she was finally able to speak. "He is probably a bit overwhelmed."

Gavin sauntered to the sofa and sat next to her. "I suppose I shall find out how bad it is in a few months."

She took his hand and placed it on her stomach. "I do not know if you will be able to feel the babe move. It's a light, fluttering sort of feeling." The baby moved again. "Can you feel it?"

"No." He shook his head. "Not yet."

Well, that was disappointing. "Perhaps in another week or so the movement will be stronger."

He slipped his arm around her shoulders and drew her closer to him. "All that matters to me is that you are both healthy."

Rivercrest, July 1819

As her maid stuck another pillow behind her Georgie waited impatiently to hold her new son.

"You did an excellent job of it, my lord." The midwife kept shaking her head as she finished looking the now clean baby over. "Don't know many men that would step in like you did."

Gavin's emotions ranging from relief to smugness to disbelief that anyone could doubt his competence flickered across his face. "I've helped birth cows and horses. . . ."

"I want my son," Georgie whispered to her maid. "Immediately."

Without even interrupting the conversation, although, Gavin did glance at her as if to ask for help releasing him from the midwife while her maid liberated the baby and brought him to her. Gavin would have to suffer a bit longer. She had her new son, Benedict Edward Turley, in her arms and just wanted to enjoy the soft, warm bundle who was showing definite signs that he wished to be fed. She ran her palm over his small head covered lightly in dark brown hair. They had wondered if he would take after her and his great-great-great-great French grandmother, or have the typical blond hair of the Turleys. They had their answer.

Gavin's old nurse helped Georgie situate that baby. "There you go, my lady."

"If I'd had any thought that her ladyship's travail would be so quick, I would have insisted on leaving the Mustoes as soon as their babe was born." The midwife handed him the ointment she had for the place where little Benedict's umbilical cord had been severed. "Use this for the next week or so." The woman shook her head as she glanced at Georgie. "At least a week early and so fast. I would never have believed it. I know you're glad your husband took matters in hand."

"Extremely glad." Her mother and Lady Littleton were due to arrive tomorrow. They were going to be surprised that the baby was already here. It had been an unwelcome shock to discover that, other than Nurse, who had assisted two or three times years ago, the rest of the females in the house had very little experience with birthing a baby. "He did not even flinch."

"You have a good man. There's no denying that." The midwife closed her bag. "I'll be by to look in on you in two days." She inclined her head and left the room.

Gavin shut the door. "I never knew what a rattler she was." He stepped over to the bed and sank into the chair next to Georgie, searching her face. "You are well?"

"Yes." She glanced at their son before smiling at him. "She was right, you know. I am extremely fortunate that you knew what to do."

"I'm only happy that the birth was not complicated or long." A shadow passed through his eyes. "Good Lord, Georgie. It's a deuced good thing that you started your pains early this morning. I'd hate to think I might have been out and about."

He had a point. Once he'd left the house he could have been anywhere on the estate, and they would have had to have found him. "Perhaps we should buy an *alpenhorn*."

"That is an excellent idea." He sprawled in the chair and watched the baby nurse, a soft smile on his face. "What a story we'll have to tell little Ben when he gets older."

They would have many stories to tell their son, but none would be better than the one when his father delivered him.

AUTHOR NOTES

Parliamentary elections were held in August 1818, and the subsequent autumn schedule was light, which gave me the idea of being able to have a house party in the middle of what would have been a Season.

As longtime readers will know, I look up the words and phrases I use to ensure that they were used at the time of the book and in the correct context. That leads me to the word "swipping." I originally wanted to use "barreling," but that word wasn't used until later in the century.

The story about the Great Dane playing at eating grass to get the attention of a herd of cows is a true one. My second Great Dane, Abby, did that and succeeded in enticing the head cow first, then the entire herd over to meet her.

Although Georgie's older sister and brother are mentioned, they were very busy with their own doings during the time her book was set. However, you can find out more about Kit in *A Kiss for Lady Mary*, and about Meg in *Miss Featherton's Christmas Prince*. Both books are in my The Marriage Game series. Just stop by my website www.ellaquinnauthor.com and they are easy to find. You will also find all my social media links there as well as the links below.

I love to connect with readers and I can be found on Facebook at www.facebook.com/EllaQuinnAuthor; on Instagram and Twitter @EllaQuinnAuthor; and on Pinterest at EllaQuinnAuthor. I'd love it if you join me and fellow readers on my Facebook group The Worthingtons.